THE PIPERS

and the First Phase

KUIR ë GARANG

The Nile Press
Calgary, Alberta

THE PIPERS AND FIRST PHASE

PUBLISHED BY THE NILE PRESS
thenilepress.com

Printed in Canada

Copyright © 2012 by KUIR ë GARANG

All rights reserved. No part of this book may be reproduced or transmitted in any form or by any means without written permission of the author.

ISBN 978-0-9916789-0-7

For Garang Isaac Kot and Elijah Aguer Deng Bior
You'll always be in my memory for you showed me that no matter our religious, political and social views, true humanity transcends everything

For Monica,

Hard work is seen in how neat and organised you make Kingsland look. You are organised diligent and fashionable. And your Sensous Heart, and YOGA!!
September, 2012

Calgary, AB

Kuir

1

Africa was just another backward, heathen and natural place when Little was a child. A claque of evangelizing enthusiasts was feeding the world with nefarious haughtiness so poor Little fed reluctantly on their availed agitprop. Africa? Yes. It was simply a place where people went to understand how things were when the world was created, when it evolved. As a child, he tried to distance himself from a place too superannuated to be desirable. Dark, not innovative, torpid and enlightenment proof, Africa was a place too easy to disown.

However, after getting to junior high school, Little started to realize he was a Pandian who actually wasn't one. He was at the periphery of the society; at the mercy of poverty and marginalization. Without Little knowing, the monstrousness and strangeness of Africa therefore started to diminish, to lose effect. The lethargic Africa started to whisper bewitching voices, echoes.

You're mine, Little!
You're doomed like me!
Don't disown me!
I'm naked but cloth me!
I'm slow, so energize me!

Africa's humble snivels didn't bother Little much then. They were gigantic realities there about to remain for the world's scholarship. What made Little embarrassed the most was that his friend, Christopher Fox, knew more about Africa and Africans than he did. Even if Little's reading of literature related to Africa was superficial, his connection with Africa became a desire to know and want more. Fascination with (and the love of) the Dark Continent soon after surged inside Little. Still, there was no driving force, no credible impetus, and no anchoring reality.

Sitting in his backroom office, Little comically looked at the tired Chris and laughed. He studied the poor fellow's face. The imploring pink face, hooked nose and blue, feline eyes unnerved Little. The eyes were between authority and destitution. Little wasn't used to that.

"I always admired you, Chris. Look at what became of you."

Still with a grin on his face, Little patted Chris on the back. That gesture seemed sincere but it had a bit of concealed disdain for the whole of the Pandian law enforcement system. Little's dark, shiny face antagonized police work. Sincerity on such a face was painful to believe, remote to comfort and too emotive for any law. The face beckoned smiles, but showered in cynicism.

"One time you were an envied detective, then a promising and sought-after accountant. Then *boom* and all was gone. I don't understand."

Blackman's words uttered with a smile invite suspicion and fear, disguised as scorn. They act as good subjects for a postprandial gossip.

Chris knew Little well enough not to fear him though.

"Neither do I, Little," Chris said, flattered but controlled. He twitched his downward-hooked nose; his feline eyes too lovely to ignore.

Little sat comfortably like a contented pre-Islamic Arab man in the Arabian Peninsula. Like *many* poor black kids in Panda, Little had his understandable brushes with the law. But nothing beats a determined single mum's resolves. With his mother's help, Little came clean. Pure. Responsible.

But you might wonder. Indeed. Little had great, almost flatter-ing respect for Chris though, his childhood buddy. He wanted Chris to manage his bar after Chris's job search led nowhere. Was it a friendly offer or a *gotcha* payback? It'd be stupid of Little if he thought so; if he wanted to mock his friend. Chris was down to a point where even bartending would have worked to pay his bills.

As a matter of fact, Chris had his reputation to protect though. Perhaps Little wanted to protect Chris's reputation too. But just think about what people say!

A job is a job. Everyone matters, they say. Shoot! Not everyone matters in the same sordid vein. Think about it my friends. If you'd achieved a senior position, in a corporate world, say; getting edged into a lower position would hurt like pulling out a tooth without anesthesia. Now flip it. Say you started at the bottom and remained there for a while. Then you left the company having not earned any promotion. Now, you went somewhere and started at the bottom. You'd have no complaints. Why? Why? People are not always the same that is why. Philosophical mambo-jumbo would reduce this to a ruin though. But no, not everyone is the same.

"I can't afford to pay you, Chris. I'm sorry!"

Surprised, Chris scanned Little's dark, haughty face and momentarily contemplated Little's words. Little arched his eyebrows upwards and placed his left leg on a tea-table in front of them. Without uttering another word, he fixed his bloodshot eyes on Chris.

"Dude... you aren't joking, are you?"

A smile lit Little's dark face as he crooked his lower lip upward.

"If Jesus was African then yes, I am!"

Chris didn't like mixing life-changing situations with comic slight. "But why...if the White Jesus could answer?"

Chris's voice was a little coarse and disappointed. *Perhaps god is using me as an experiment.* Little wasn't moved any bit.

"Man, I just told you. I can't afford to pay you!"

"Dude, you can pay me anything. Day-Town Commercial told me this afternoon that my contract will not be renewed."

Little shook his huge head slowly.

"No, I can't make fun of your status," Little said with a confusing, nearly irresponsible smile.

"It's something else, right? It isn't about the pay."

Little fixed Chris with one frightening stare.

That was it. Doom follows the doomed.

2

Back in his heydays, Chris was an excellent police officer; and a skilled accountant too. His contractual assignments professed his skills. With his high profile detective work, Chris wasn't new to camera, but the peak of his career excitement came as an assignment to retrieve a stolen African tribal artifact. UK's MI6 had located the artifact and he was chosen as one of the able-minded detectives to bring it back to Day-Town.

Chris didn't quite understand the essence of the assignment then. Being at the peak of his detective career, he took everything for granted. The fact that he was part of the assignment empirically satisfied the proof requirement that he was both excellent and ethical. But Chris knew his weaknesses though.

He knew that all humans are fools of varying degrees. Yes. All of us! But we're not all fools all the time and at the same time. We may not know when our idiosyncratic, spatiotemporal stupidity might call, but we always perceive it consciously when it does. It's always customary to hide, deny or dismiss it. But the ultimate fool is that one, the one who has no spatiotemporal break to his foolishness yet denies his having ever been a fool.

Chris was a good fool though. Searching to know his limits was personally imperative. A good fool knows how hot his tea needs to be; how sweet his coffee has to be.

Little knew too that Chris was a good fool. In all fairness, Chris didn't just know how to calibrate goodness meter. He acted out of Aristotelian virtue.

However, for Chris, coming back to their Ice-Corner after the mission was more exhilarating than the actual journey and the royal pleasantries. He understood the beauty of going to Europe, and England for that matter. During the visit, they were exceptionally treated to sumptuous royal receptions. Chris, for some reasons, expected his coming back from England to usher in a new beginning. Fame and Fortune! Mind you, it was confusing. It was perhaps a beginning of an end, or a sudden end to *a* beginning.

Unlike the quibbles and dangers of police work, the mission was simply a journey. It was also a typical collection of an artifact.

Chris remembered vividly going back to Ice-Corner–his neighborhood. Yeah, he was coming back to see the capital of the most powerful nation on the planet, Panda, and the most elegant city, Day-Town. Why was his coming back such a fuss?

Chris had smelt novel European airs. He was feeling significant.

It was mid-summer in Panda; really hot... simmering. You could see people's faces shiny with sweat, atmosphere thick and humid, the sky clear but heat heavily hanging over the city like dark clouds of ominous, uninvited summer rain. But it wasn't so much about the weather as it was about his coming back to Day-Town with fresh air of newness, of veracity and proud beginning. Chris still didn't know exactly why he was chosen to be part of the team. Not until years later.

The artifact was a controversial piece. It was given to former Pandian president by an African chief *somewhere* in Africa. It was a personal gift for having built clean water taps and a school in his village. But some of the politicians in that country needed the artifact. It was a cultural embodiment of pride and connection to their past, they'd argued.

When the president left office, he'd instructed his aides to take the artifact to his new residence, south of Day-Town. On that fateful day, six Pandian presidential guards were killed and the artifact stolen. There went the story!

There had been no trace of the artifact for a number of years until United Kingdom's MI6 recovered it somewhere near Liverpool.

The African tribal chief was from *somewhere* in South Sudan.

The mission was of course to Liverpool then to London where they stayed for three weeks. For a North American, it was a palpable rejoinder. The sumptuous receptions became more purifying than the job the officers were sent to do. They attended many state and royal functions. You can guess those elegant traditions of the finely mannered English people; their smooth and intellectual accent, their unassuming civility.

Of those memorable events, one was, obviously, striking to Chris. It was some Duke's or lord's function, he didn't remember. Good old Chris only saw the content of the parties rather than the flattering, inane titles.

It was in that royal function that Chris saw a haunting figure of an African woman. She was traditionally dressed in brown, yellow and orange dress. Her hair was covered in the same piece of clothing material; just like Ngozi okonjo-iweala, only leaner. She was stunning, naturally charismatic and enamoring. After the official welcome, the fiesta air wasn't very regally suffocating etiquette wise.

Chris hated the intellectual mist though. With so much pain he tried so hard to convince his shaking nerves that he could talk to her. Her coming to such a function told Chris she was enormously privileged. However, some dense intellectual mist scaled him off; weakened his thoughts and he stood straight, guard-like and frozen. What if she came to know he was a cop, just a low-grade detective? His beautiful pink face and superb manners wouldn't save his wounded ego. Chris tried but his stomach was papery; stuffed with a noisy army of butterflies. She was the type of girl one would mold if one were told to make one. Just perfect!

When Chris's desires became too strong for his ego to reason back the urge, he tried to leg forward. Stupid! He found himself closing his eyes as beads of sweat pimpled up his face. He felt a strange sensation: warmth actually. It rode down his trunk in one quick flick. Chris was determined though. Then the intellectual mist became a wall.

A tall, bearded African man tapped the girl's right shoulder from behind. Chris shied away. She charmingly smiled and turned. They walked forward, away from Chris. Disappointed, Chris stood still, saddened but relieved. *What was I to tell her? What was I feeling toward her? Please never guess!* Then a female caterer woke him up from his trance. The world around Chris was bustling and jostling, excitement perfuming the air! The drink server gave him a drink. *That was all I got. Poor me, wouldn't you say?*

Chris later learned that the disappointing, bearded man was a professor of mathematics and African studies at Oxford. The girl, he was later told, was his research assistant; a doctoral student. With debilitating admiration and infatuation, Chris had tried all night to just, just say 'hi' to her; to only see her smile. The intellectual wall was so thick that Chris had to give up. However, he kept the girl's picture on his head, for years.

At the time, Chris was a part-time accountant working for various companies on contractual bases. That mix of detective and accounting work won Chris followers. Good citizen! He was a man who could make money if he'd established his own accounting firm. Simplicity guided him to protect Pandian citizens. What fool can't admire that simplicity?

Soon after his coming back from the U.K, Chris received a call from one of the Burns Investment Inc. branches to be their chief accountant. Chris was asked to work part-time on a full-time salary. That meant he could continue with his detective work if he wanted to. For all it seemed, it was an offer too good to refuse; an offer even the *godfather* can't offer.

Having been humbled by such an offer, Chris left his detective job to work for Burns Investment Inc. Those were the good times.

3

Uncle D sat under his favorite mango tree as he smoked from his pipe. Unless he was going to the capital city, he wore only a traditionally custom-made red and white sheet that was wrapped around his shoulders. When going to the capital, he put on his *blue* suit. For reasons not known to anyone, Uncle D hated black suits or any other color for that matter. Many people knew Uncle D in the village of Werpionkor because he arrived with seasons. Between June and August, Uncle D's compound was full of life. He brought kids biscuits, candies, clothing and toys. A few days in June were always boisterous with laughter.

However, the kids and the villagers knew very well when Uncle D didn't want visitors. With his pipe, a three-legged chair, a newspaper and a small gadget the villagers didn't know what it was for, they knew he had to be left alone.

He had no kids, no wife and they didn't know where he usually came from. For twenty years, Uncle D dropped in and out of Werpionkor. There were rumors around the village that he was the village's guardian. There were also rumors that he was the president of the country; that he changed his body to run away from the problems of his presidency. In any case, little to nothing was known about Uncle D.

The village kids passed by Uncle D as he read his newspaper under the mango tree. The breeze and the wind blew his grey hair back and forth. He waved at them and they waved back. Every kid in Werpionkor knew when Uncle D needed a handshake and when waving was enough.

He received occasional visitors but no one knew who they actually were. They came on bicycles and motor bikes. While Uncle D always came to Werpionkor by truck, none of his visitors drove to the village by car. They all rode on bicycles.

There were no prominent people from Werpionkor in the government. Apart from the occasional mobile clinic run by a local NGO, Uncle D's truck was one of the few auto-visitors to the village. The villagers did justice to the fact. They mobbed the truck with admiration anytime Uncle D arrived.

Besides the occasional dust-storm, the environment was hot but breezy. Uncle D savored the postprandial reading under the smiling shade. Barrenness mocked the landscape. The sprinkles of trees gave meaning to the nearness of the equator. Searing, smiting heat built visual apparitions over the stretching vista. Available dots of trees paled in the face of angry barrenness. Mirage elongated kids' trunks as they played at a distance. Their dark bodies appeared watery, elongated and ghostly. Uncle D loved it, admired it, savored it and smiled it in. The calming and humbling vista was incomparable, sweetly heavenly.

What could be better than this?

Uncle D had heard of a local NGO worker who was beaten by local ruling party vigilantes. The neighboring village, unlike Werpionkor, was politically active and volatile. The polio vaccination truck was a political agitprop, they'd argued. The Poor fellow suffered broken facial bones, shattered cranial bone and severed spinal cord. He vomited blood and hardly moved the right side of his body. The truck was left on the roadside, rammed onto a tree. It was an accident, they'd argued. He died from his injuries three days later. The rival Member of Parliament argued against claims that it was political intimidation. It was an accident. Sure. Proofs. No monstrous proofs. No proofs means take it as I say it.

One of the culprits was saved or failed by his conscience though. Just judge it. The brown-faced, chubby lad confessed. A lie loaded onto a good or a jittery conscience always falls off. It doesn't find room. The poor fellow struggled to keep it in. No. It was fighting for room. It couldn't get it. It felt off. The poor guy confessed. It was ruinous. He had to die, to go, to disappear. Six days before the trial the poor fellow was found hanging from the ceiling of his witness protection house. You wonder. Good old house heard him. It gave him a rope. What a house? What a wish-fulfilling house?

Werpionkor's elders took a sinister stance after the death of the mobile clinic worker. No more killing of our visitors, they'd roared. Young people threatened to fight, to level the neighboring village. Counsel, good counsel prevailed. The elders wished strongly against any ruinous rush to feud. Wisdom prevailed. A stern warning was sent and it was heeded. No more killing of Werpionkor visitors. Werpionkor was known as a village of ferocious warriors and wise counsel. Dared them and you were doomed. Mock them and you had the first laugh. Their words were accepted in an instant.

Uncle D couldn't be any prouder. He enjoyed the aftermath, the sacrifices of others. Human, altruistic sacrifices unite cultures.

4

"You'll love this, I promise," Judy whispered as she walked past Chris. Chris wasn't in shape financially, socially and even physically so he remained silent.

"Oh honey, forget about Little. You'll get another contract. Besides, you have me. Better still, you can part with your helpless ego and get any entry level job."

"I can't believe you're even considering that!" Chris said and looked out through the window.

Outside, through the curtain leaves, Chris could see the sun hanging low; humidity thinning. It was that self-reflection atmosphere. Chris was sitting in the living room as Judy cooked. The TV in front of him sounded like a distant sound of useless music. Sweet, he was always at it; comparing his life and her culinary expertise. Her cookery was always garnished with parsley and cilantro, giving it that fine, European-cuisine appeal.

Judy was a strange girl. She showed you things she didn't even like if you liked them. However, she wasn't pretentious. Her motives were geared toward making others feel significant. Her living room walls were plain yellow, naked; decorated only by a lonely, framed picture of her father. There was nothing else, literally.

For some strange reasons, Chris and Judy always discussed *Chris's* life. Their conversations would start with something about her, but it would stealthily drift away and end with Chris being the central topic. Judy's life was obscure, it seemed. However, Chris knew her: her charms, her riches, and her simple and enamoring humility.

"It might have been the beer. You drink too much these days, Chris," Judy said putting dinner on the table. He didn't like talking about how they met because they met in a bar.

Chris hated Cilantro smell, but it made him feel important. Of the Spaniards, Judy always said.

"No, I don't drink a lot, I think," he said and walked to the table. Judy handed Chris the dishes and he slowly, one by one, placed them on the dining table.

"Yes, you do Chris," she said walking back to the kitchen. This time, she was dashing to the kitchen backwards, facing Chris. He clumsily walked back to the couch and continued watching TV.

When cooking, Judy always wore a brown apron she said her mum gave her. The writings at the back, on the apron's helm, joked: 'good things are not touched but felt.' Such writings always reminded Chris of inspiration from Siddha's Moksha, or Buddhism: those serene oriental pretensions, the power of the mind as argued.

In college Chris had a Tibetan friend, who always reminded him about meditation time and the power of concentration. At first, he was a nuisance to Chris. Time changed things though and the Tibetan's reminders became a normal part of Chris's residence life. Chris could use such a concentration now.

Judy lived alone in a high-end suburban neighborhood.

Chris didn't hate her type. He didn't envy them either. However, Chris remained uneasy about the nature of their relationship. When Judy's dad died, he left her a fortune, a really spoiling fortune. However, Judy behaved herself really well with her fortune. Judy Grant wasn't *a* loose cannon. Some people positively spoil their fortunes while others have their fortunes spoil them.

Judy was stable personality wise. She didn't have a Paris, a Lindsay or a Kardashian in her. These tawdry-attitude girls bask in boundless riches; trying contemptible simplicity that's dry, arrogant and childish. That wasn't Judy though. Ms. Grant lived modestly.

Chris loved her and she loved him. Isn't that what fools always want to hear in a relationship? Oh, respect was another stupid ingredient. Well, honesty and...you know what? Relationship ingredients are infinite and personal tastes are variable.

The dinner was now ready but the normal topics continued: Chris's drinking problem and his job search...

"I'm picking myself up, okay? Did I tell you that? That's what I think."

She shook her head and frowned. "What's that...picking yourself up?"

"There's this kid who passes by my place every Sunday. And every time he passes by, he looks at me and says: 'Africa! Africa! Africa!' He says that three times, smiles wickedly and leaves."

Judy grimaced, smiled and sat down. With her fingers, she beckoned him to the dining table.

"Honey, why can't you talk to the kid?"

Chris staggered to the table. She served him one look and dashed to the kitchen. With a bottle of wine and two glasses, she came back with a distinct clink.

Judy loved the idea of wine at dinner. The thought that she was a perfectionist scared her, but she was nothing but just that: the real purist.

Is rejection of the character the very essence of its very possession?

"He runs away," he said about the mysterious boy and took the food to serve himself. Chris served Judy and served himself as she poured herself a glass of red wine. She then said: "Why're we even talking about it?"

"You think I'm losing it, don't you?"

"Honey, I think you've started to see yourself as either incapable of anything or capable of everything."

"That's not fair, I think!"

"Believe me, anyone telling you something else wishes you down."

Chris intensely fixed his gaze on her. She started eating, fast.

"What exactly do you mean by that?"

She took another sip of wine and sighed, deeply. A small pigeon hovered outside then perched by the window. With a nostalgic gaze, she lovingly stared at it for a while. The bird then fluttered away. After a brief reflective pause, she looked at Chris and said: "Honey, you don't want to move in here because of your big ego; too proud to get a small entry level job; and you're here telling me a *black* boy who keeps telling you something you *think* you don't understand. It's something you can easily find out."

"Why do you talk as if you're not in North America? And why'd you think the kid is black?"

"C'mon, Chris! What do I look like? 'A cocooned socialite'?"

"Please, that's certainly not what I think of you."

Honestly, Chris didn't know what she loved in him. What was it exactly? Beauty, simplicity or what? Her gaze was genuine and she had no discernible pretensions. What was more perplexing was the fact that her company of friends was mixed: Asian, African, Arabic and European. That defied any suspicious, begrudging curiosity.

With food still in her mouth, she stretched, got up and dashed to the kitchen. Then her phone rang with the usual annoying shrill.

"I'm glad you used the word please," she said as she reached for the phone receiver.

Chris was becoming irritated, really irritated. However, she knew what she wanted, what she always said in his presence, and what she could say to pacify him. With an affronting glance, she looked at him and picked up the phone.

"Are you punishing me? That's what I think," he sorrowfully said. She looked at him again, placed her right index finger on her lips to shush him but found it unsatisfying. Bending toward him, she covered the receiver with her left palm and said: "I'm advising you as a friend."

Still with the phone in hand, she grinned childishly and spoke into the receiver. The look on her face was confusing, however, she was smiling. With one long, intense gaze, she extended her right hand to give Chris the receiver.

5

Little Mike knew he wasn't pretentious, but life had cornered
him. He was a huge black man with a deep, basal voice. To
say the truth, he was neither unlucky nor was he lucky. His
life was between being a black man and being just *a* man. That's a
stupid cliché, don't you think?

"You can be who you wanna be," his teacher in high school used
to say. "The society doesn't define who you become. It only exploits
whatever vulnerability you have or expose."

But everything Little came to understand in his life was different
though. Societal conditions, perceptions and expectations defined
who he'd become. He looked at his watch. It was approaching 1.00
p.m. The lady hadn't shown up though — thirty minutes late. To
keep his mind engaged, and to prevent his emotions from getting
stirred up, Little switched his mind back to the past.

"They were all idealistic bullshits of societal cheerleaders.
They're impracticable. Get into the real world and tell me if those
nightmarish bullshits stick out as beautified by some of our early
educators: parents and teachers," one of Little's classmates, who'd
dropped out of school, once told him. He met Little a few months
after dropping out. With cunning wordiness, he tried to convince
Little about the 'lucrativeness' of what he called *a* business. You can
guess what business that was. Little had adamantly refused. Naïve
was Little? Smart would you say?

Little suddenly jostled back to the present and looked up. Another thirty minutes had gone by. Across the street, below, Little
spotted Chris with a group he assumed was African. Their tradition-

al attires made Little assume they were Africans. Their cars hinted to a special class. They were one black Cadillac, a grey BMW and a white Porsche. The group, together with Chris, crossed the street, entered the cars parked on the street and drove away

"That's weird. Chris?" Little said to himself as he absentmindedly stared at the trail of their cars.

As he watched the cars thin out to the right after the second light, Little went back to his dreamy state and started punching his past recollection buttons.

To many people, the past means nothing; to Little though, it was everything. But Little was just uninformed that is. He was a self-righteous, ambitious young man who was unfortunately oblivious of the realities of the life around his place of birth.

"It'll be a matter of days before you follow me," the same 'lucrative business' dropout fellow had said laughing and left. That was a tip of a huge iceberg. However, Little wasn't so much of a dork even in high school. He was sociable and also knew what was impractical and impracticable.

After high school, however, his life became fraught with inspiring turn-rounds. From being an A-student and mummy's boy, to selling silly drugs, to being sent to the *juvy*, all had something to teach Little. He was lost but found, mentally impoverished but redeemed. Life was a bumpy road. The bumpers in his life's road were closely spaced when he was young. As he grew older and wiser, the spaces between the bumpers increased. That was something Little couldn't forget. Life was precious. While death may be precious, he knew little to nothing about that preciousness. Preciousness of life and certainty of life challenges make the thought that death may be good nonsensical.

All these thoughts flashed through Little's head as he waited for his would-be new supplier. He was sitting outside the mall in an out-door sitting area on the second floor.

"What's wrong with the lady?" he asked himself.

Little wanted a new deal with a new beer supplying store. He'd delegated his lawyer with a group of able employees to do the negotiation, but the supplier said she wanted to meet him first.

"We're a personable company and we love seeing happiness in our customers' eyes first, before he delegates someone else."

Little needed no more words for a reason. The supplier's words were both humanely articulated and professional.

6

Judy was avid, passionate and focused. She was one of the Ivy League types who treated people with humility and flattering respect... yet people still doubted their humility and genuineness. The mystery being, you, the one that's dazzled by their goodness, don't doubt them. They intoxicate you with outwardly benevolence. You bask in their shiny goodness, dazzled and dazed to near stupidity. Any doubting part of you is neatly, artistically catered for. Now you sit down and sing: "Heaven, how great is the person. Multiply *her*."

You remember the phone call, don't you? Yes, that phone call turned out to be a mysterious call from someone named Isaac Burns. The call was mysterious not because Chris didn't know Isaac, but he never expected the call; not in a million years. Chris's demise started in one of Burns' companies: Burns Investment Inc. Chris knew Mr. Burns. He'd never met him in person though. The call was consoling to Chris to say the truth.

"Someone named Isaac Burns. He said you guys went to the same high school," Judy had told him as she gave him the phone. She too knew who Isaac was for he was a prominent, always-talked-about Pandian tycoon and philanthropist. Like always, Judy's input was just but another heart-warming humor.

Chris had to go. The phone call though unexpected, was worth answering. Of all the calls he was expecting, Mr. Burns' call wasn't one of them. Chris took Judy's car with uncertainty wind. It was hot outside and all over the city that day. The crisp wind from the open window dazed but calmed his nerves. Daydreaming had to be severed. Not that it was possible. In essence, Chris didn't expect much from the call; however, the call was from someone he couldn't associate negativity with. So his good manners, simple formality and professionalism guided him.

§

The likes of Mr. Burns were what, in the early twentieth century, you'd call capitalists. Now we call them Philanthropists. They used to employ the weak and pay them little just to get them by. They were the Marx's and Marxists' targets. Now they built schools for the down-trodden, contribute *unselfishly* to numerous foundation funds especially those that carry *their* names... to fight diseases, poverty....in far worlds.

In their then small worlds, in their shots at success, they were 'nobodies'. They struggled just to get what they wanted. Their germinal phases started with no one giving a damn who they were and what they were after. In their struggles to create a sense of presence and significance, they became nerds, selfish dorks and what have you. There was no reason for them to sleep. Day and night they labored; sleeping on their dream chase. They cared little about the world. Then gradually they grew and suddenly they hit the jackpot: *success*. Everyone now gave a damn who they'd become. They became sought after as exemplary carers. Shoot! With their success they became the face of those who give a damn about what the world is. See? They became informed, brilliant, and scholarly. With no doubt they became world citizens, truly. In the bountiful-ness of their riches they became our eyes, the trusted ones. So much for that!

But that day reminded Chris of whom he'd become: Chris the pauper, the uninformed, the weak-hearted.

The struggling Chris was told to meet Isaac at his mansion out-side the city. It was a nice, high-end suburban neighborhood. For some strange reasons, no one was at the house except the guard. Had it not been for Judy, it'd have been assumed that Chris was hallucinating; his usual being, the constant attention to tick tocks of the clock.

Luckily, it wasn't a daydream. The call and the request were as true as human being end in death.

"I'm sorry sir. I wasn't told of anyone coming," the guard said without any expression on his face and slowly closed the door. Chris buzzed again, furious and belittled. The guard jumped to the gate, fixed Chris with a soldiery face and barked: "Sir, Isaac left with his girlfriend an hour ago. They have a reservation in Grecian Alfa Hotel. He didn't tell me *nothing* about *nobody*."

The guard was a young African-Pandian; between 20 and 25. He wore a moustache that made him appear Middle Eastern or North African: Afro-Asiatic, as Chris heard years ago in his history lessons. The young man's voice was feminine and his gait gay. Chris stared at him as he strode back to his cabin. There was something about his look that was more than what a typical guard could dispense. He had a typical guard's uniform. On his cellular phone casing were two words that made Chris bewildered. However, Chris's head spun with the typical thought: heck, the meaninglessness of some brand names, logos and impressionists' writings. But then his intense, Hip Hop look and attitude struck Chris hard. With no doubt in Chris's mind, he was very rude for a responsible security guy. The typical friendliness of the urban security guards was wanting, gravely wanting. As he was about to take his seat, the words stared straight at Chris: *The P Brothers.*

7

After Isaac's call disappointed Chris and added to the sorry state of his issues, Judy meaningfully introduced Chris to some of her friends. They were to meet at Chris's house to discuss what they'd talked about days earlier. Chris had arrived at his house a few minutes earlier after walking the city for opportunities.

"They could be some assets to you," Judy had said.

Chris faced a huge incubus. *Am I a human being?* One could say yes, however, Chris had little to think of as making him worthy. His ingenuity and enthusiasm were all draped neatly and sadly tossed into unfairness furnace.

"Beat yourself that hard, but your pride will beat you harder and ruder than you'll ever endure...then life will continue with the monstrous rest," Judy had added having seen his blank and hesitant face regarding her friends. He knew what he felt and how he was beating himself: anything worse than that was fatal.

Chris was waiting for Judy at his apartment: *202C-98 Freedom Street Southeast.* In essence, Chris's house fitted for *Prison Street.* Well, *Freedom* and *Prison* rhyme. They're just two different ends of the same thing: existence. No! They're the same ends of life. This sounds snobbish. They're the rewards of how you lead your life. Bullshit! They're conditions engendered by one's choices in life. That's naïve. They're conditions of existence based on one's life's conditions. That sounds about fair.

For some reasons, Judy didn't come so Chris scuttled to the living room and lazily picked up the phone. He felt like everything in the room was looking at him with amused contempt. It was as if *damned* was written all over him.

"C'mon Jude, pick up the phone," Chris said speaking into the receiver.

Chris was really dazed by heat, loneliness and penilessness. He put the phone down and as he approached the balcony, a hot current of air blew onto his face. Surprised, he frowned, turned and threw himself onto the coach. Then the phone rang. Instead of getting up to pick up the phone, he lay on his belly and reached for the phone. He stupidly pushed it and pulled the connection off the jack. Feeling slightly silly, he tried to put the connection back in but he'd already lost the call.

Chris came to know a day later that the caller was Judy. She'd called to apologize on behalf of her friends and herself.

Judy wasn't the smartest person among all the people Chris knew, but she kept very detailed records of everything concerning her. Chris hated that; however, he loved her dearly and that love masked any negative thoughts about her.

"I called you yesterday but you hanged up on me. My friends told me they'd something urgent to attend to and sent their regrets. Mum also called and wanted me to meet her. Yesterday, you seemed to have picked up the phone, but then I heard a loud bang and everything was quiet. I never called back because I thought I'd be disturbing you," she'd said with a begrudging calm and annoying self-righteousness.

Chris curiously looked at her, empty-headed and embarrassed, but he knew what she'd conjectured.

"You didn't think I'd do anything stupid to hurt you, do you?" he said trying to test waters.

"Honey, if a girl tells you that she has complete confidence in you and that you can never do anything bad, or swears as knowing you in completeness, call her a liar."

"Why'd you say that?"

"Honey, men do a lot of bad things, but girls pray that men don't do them when girls know they're doing them."

"That's uncharitably sexist...and a horrible conceptual conjecture, Jude. That's what I think."

"It'd be humbling and consoling if it was only a concept. It isn't. It's a fact."

Fact! Fact! Fact! What's a fact? Different minds have different facts. Same situations have different facts. Same witnesses confess different facts. *What in the end can you tell me about facts?* Chris called such a situation a vain certitude, a creepy verity.

"No!" he said as if subconscious.

"Honey, as long as I don't know it, you're fine."

Chris stood there neither believing what she said nor dismissing her claims. Well, he didn't know what to say to her in connection with women's businesses and their take on men's mentalities and daft tricks.

Judy and Chris were talking as she was getting ready to go to work. She'd spent the night at his humbling apartment.

Chris gave Judy's assertions a very political interpretation. The thought that Judy was right scared him, but he wasn't scared because Judy would get a point out of his miserable mental porousness. To believe that Judy was right would be insulting to Judy and, indeed, any woman the world over. In addition, such assertions never ever remain in the simplest way they are said. They have connections that are always the intended targets.

Chris knew they were meant to tap into men's susceptibility to erring. Sure, men are weak if smartly taunted with their brains multifariously engaged. Don't even guess what happens when they're having sex with women. In the act, they're temporarily deprived of their brains' functions and meaningful consciousness. Even worse, they become ten times dumber than a herd of pigs. They snout away their pleasures as everything else in the world withers away. It's the real purification by stupefaction: the ultimate enlightenment and salvation!

Judy meant so much to Chris, but there was that politics about Judy's talks that always made Chris solemn and humbled. Panda was a politically charged environment. Think of race relations and affirmative actions!

Little Michael had told him once that *the third world* is very much cynical and skeptical when it comes to all the dealings of the developed nations. Panda, the richest nation on earth, couldn't be taken seriously however much it tried to evangelize the essence of goodness and decency. Chris believed that some race relations enthusiasts, infatuated with race relations complexities, had the same mind-set Judy had against men. As long as what they, the Wide White World (WWW), say is not heard in the way they say it – and this is assumed in badness – then all is fine. But such claims are hard to ascertain because everyone assumes the righteousness realm.

"We talk Chris, but this nation cannot allow us to be who we are. To act decent, we lose ourselves, whether knowingly or unknowingly and what is sung is: 'they want to be like us'. And if we let things flow the way they're required by the majority, then vilification microphone is turned to our ancestral soft spots. Do I have to deny it, no; do I have to take it as said, well, you'll help me."

Little had said once with his usually slow, hesitant and cynical tone. Chris, then, perceived the words as cynical and rhetorically empty? *Who's not restricted by this country?* It was not so much about targeting the *ancestral soft spots* for the search of the soft spots blackened the path toward Little's intended culprit – the country – that unfortunately, the likes of Little made but were now trying to destroy. Again, unfortunately, the same souls, the likes of Little, were the ones bent on putting it to shreds. Though Little's assertions could curve a spot on truth sculpture, they were more of self-praise than objective, substantive claim.

Little experienced the same experiences Chris experienced, but he whined more than he needed to. Though at times rational and sensible, Little frowned with triviality and that masked his words' vibrancy. He was persistent and inflexible. However, Little Michael learned a lot from what the system instilled in him. He duly became conscientious and law-abiding. Unfortunately, Little's disposition, physique and his small fortune made him vulnerable to crash with jealousy.

Little, as you might have guessed by now, wasn't a third world citizen. He was an African-Pandian who spoke as if he was African.

Mentally exhausted, Chris left the past. He got up, tried to walk to the balcony when the phone rang. Still mentally occupied, he grabbed the phone, almost losing the line again.

"Jude?!"

"Hold up big boy!"

"Isaac?"

"I need you in my home office tomorrow. I'm sorry about the other day. My secretary told me about your coming as relayed to her by the security guy. I'd sincerely forgotten. Jane also told me you called home later that day. I had a meeting with a friend, Christine, from Sivals. After that meeting I went to a dinner party in honor of an African chief."

"So..."

"Well, I mean...I'll be waiting for you tomorrow at 11.00 sharp."

He hanged up as Chris stared at the phone. *Maybe heaven is visiting me!* Contented with the call, Chris paced to the balcony and a group of six boys, black boys that is, whisked by on three bikes. They were both wearing long, black t-shirts with the words: BEST, BRIGHT, SLICK AND PATIENT.

One of the boys threw something at Chris. Chris quickly ducked to protect his head. A piece of rock hit the wall and fell onto the metal floor of the balcony. He recovered from the scare, but as he stared at the stone, he realized there was a piece of paper attached to it. Still shaken, Chris feverishly opened it: *They're back, they're smack, and they're the best.*

"What the...?"

Chris couldn't finish the statement. The boys pedaled back so he ran for cover. This time they didn't throw anything at him.

Christopher Fox was a lean, 6.1 feet, brown-haired, loose-tongued Caucasian man who loved bothering his friends. He was thirty-eight and unemployed. The girl, Judy Morning Grant, was his girlfriend.

8

U ncle D knew Werpionkor was his sanctuary. However, he didn't want the villagers to see him as some sort of a hermit. He brought goodies for the kids and invited the village elders for a feast. The feast was a mix of traditional and modern goodies.

What many villagers didn't like at first was the idea of Uncle D insisting that both men and women be sitting on the same feast table without subordination. There was furor at first on the mention of such an idea. The suggestion went begrudgingly against a tradition set thousands of years back. It was an insult to the ancestors, some had argued. However, Uncle D was likeable in deeds; and most of all, he talked with admirable wisdom. The old men of the village didn't know how to shun a sage with so deep a wisdom; so inviting an orator.

The oldest among all the elders in the village was an old lady called Nyanbenypieth. She was dark-skinned, tall and slender. Her hair was long but she had it always braided in a traditionally gaudy manner. At times she had it painted with a brick-red substance. Her refusal to use a walking stick for support was a sign of healthy arrogance.

Nyanbenypieth had the last word during Uncle D's feasts. While it was untraditional to the villagers for Nyanbenypieth to have the last word, her charm, wisdom and dry humor won the entire village over.

The consensus the male elders reached to allow Nyanbenypieth to have the last word spoke volume of the high regard in which the elders held Uncle D. Nyanbenypieth was about eighty or so.

"We don't know you, but we have gone through life long enough to learn a lot. A man of good conscience is known by both his words and his deeds. We'll grant you your wish," One of the elders said after the meeting.

"You're very right. I didn't know what to expect, however, I trust the wisdom of the African ways. I chose an African village and trusted that my desire and wish for a quiet place could be granted by any African elder-man and elder-woman. Little did I know I was right! My happiness will not be in words, it'll be seen. I thank you all my brothers, sisters, mothers and fathers."

As he looked around, his words sounded idealistic and lacking of substance. They even sounded distant, insincere and vacuous. He knew they weren't. However, his conscience defied him. It was telling him off, it was mocking him with a dry African humility. The wrinkled faces around him oozed historical and timeless humility and wisdom. What came out of their mouths was as it was. They weren't pretentious. He knew his heart was as clean as theirs, his intentions noble. But his conscience fidgeted under guilt-ridden heaviness.

It was the unfairness of the world on this old, poor wisdom that he felt he could shoulder. He learnt from them, he felt good when with them; yet the world outside looked down on them with igno-rant sympathy and contempt. The world only comes to them for exploits; exploits that put the poor wisdom down and elevate the supposed men of knowledge. He sneered at his own self and stared at the pure happiness blanketing the village.

Young boys and girls ran around with unblemished, untainted joy through clean primordial foot-paths. Young women and young men loved each other with noble, rudimentary purity. Dispute cases were presided over with wise counsel.

Uncle D shook his head and looked at the horizon.

It was red with looming smoky dust storm; the sky clear and blue though. The interspersed trees smiled at him. This is paradise; he said and looked at the elders with respectful orbs.

9

You could imagine how Little felt after waiting for an hour and a half. No one showed up to apologize to him either. He was furious; feeling more belittled than he could stomach. However, unexpected mishaps are part of every business undertaking. Risks and begrudging disappointments are ubiquitous when it comes to unprofessional business people. As Little immersed himself in his bitter thoughts, his cell phone rang, disturbing his bittering composure.

"Little!" he said with hidden fury.

"I'm truly sorry, Mr. Michael. We had an emergency. That's why we couldn't inform you in time. We apologize for that inconvenience," a lady said in a very polite but specious voice over the phone.

To call the incident an inconvenience would be an irresponsible understatement. It was a rude disappointment, that is.

"A thirty-second phone call prior to the meeting or immediately you experienced the emergency could have saved me the agony of nearly two hours of fruitless wait," Little said as calmly and as slowly as he could.

"Like I said sir, we sincerely apologize for that. There's nothing beyond that that I can tell you. We're truly sorry!"

The lady sounded distant, impatient and contemptuous. Her tone carried disappointing emptiness. Little hated her more than he loathed the idea of the time meaninglessly wasted.

"When's the next meeting then?" he asked, irritation suffocating him.

"We'll let you know sir."

"What?"

"We'll let you know."

"You gotta be kidding me. Hello...hello...!"

She hanged up on me? Bad business move!

Little didn't know what that meant; only that fiasco was pending. Indeed, something was wrong, terribly wrong. *She didn't just hang up on me!*

He sprang up, looked around; sweat dotting up his dark face. Nothing around him could calm his disappointed nerves. A group of lovely, elderly white women were laughing their time away at a nearby table. To Little, they sounded like squirrels on a hot summer day: cute but of little help to him. He sat down with his palms on his head, deeply thinking. After a period of deliberation he looked at the squirrels next to him and walked down stairs; toward the parking lot.

Little sat inside his car; numerous thoughts rushing through his supposedly discriminated mind. Without much power and wealth, fighting such discriminatory business practices alone is most of the time a folly of the weak. But Little knew that the lurking iceberg was substantial. It was a potential danger he didn't want to strike his head against if he could completely reign on his stirred up emotions. There was no doubt getting control of his emotions was paramount; however, his emotions were not on his fingers. He could have easily closed his palms, open a sealed container and throw them in. But no, the emotions were getting out of control and their consequence would not be in Little's favor or anyone for that matter. Having thought for a while with no clear resolves, he turned on the engine but then turned it off.

Little was starting to question the value of being noble, being good, being civil. The weird European-styled yellow building nearby rudely mocked him. Birds fluttering overhead frowned at this dark, sweat-filled face. He immersed himself in his thoughts so much so that the loud murmur about his car window had disappeared. Nothing but anger roamed about on his mind. The violent interlocution between bad and good thoughts smote and raced each other through his head. He sat there as various thoughts went ferociously at one another. They slashed at one another as they fought for dominance, for the first one to act, to show complete potency.

Little was a big but simple man with simple resources after simple dreams. He'd tried to run away from trouble. The speed of trouble was wickedly divine though. It was also unfairly selective.

He rudely turned his engine on and carelessly swerved off.

10

Aguard in an orange uniform opened the gate. Chris was a little surprised for the guard was a young beautiful black lady. She was friendlier than the gay-looking guy on his first disappointing day. Impressed, Chris looked around with a little but elevated ego and exhilaration. The gate was painted brown, the writings in black. Chris drove silently before bursting into lazy but soft country tune. His voice sounded like a dirge-singing voice.

Life, maybe, is a long dream just as some philosopher once said of existence. A dream is only a dream when you've woken up not when you're still dreaming. Chris was, perhaps, still in a dream, a very long one. Or maybe his life in this world is his third or fourth form of existence. He may have died in some other worlds in order to come and live here. Believe what you believe, but Chris was having a good day.

Singing (or something like it) made Chris high, besides a few bottles of beer. It soothed him, romanticized his existence, raised his platform higher and gave him a sense of worthy existence.

Standing outside having parked the car in that scented, patronizingly decorated scenery, he stretched and played with his car keys like an amateur volleyball player. He then headed to the door. The door was dazzling in a warm sunny morning; diverting the reflected sunrays onto his sunglasses.

Built above the entrance was a deep brown strip of arcade-like attachment arching downward. Chris loathed the stupid architect who added that redundant and tawdry piece of architecture. That tawdriness made the front part of the house look like a mosque, a temple or a government structure in atavistic theocracies. Chris had seen such pictures in former Pandian president's collection of cultural artifacts and photographs.

Isaac was standing guardedly by the window. He'd been watching Chris since he drove into the compound. Jane, his girlfriend, was seated on the couch next to the back door.

Jane was a quiet lady, averagely beautiful, less talkative and reserved. For some strange reasons, Jane had a compulsive natural fear of African-Pandians. However, she admired African-Pandians in their absence. She defended them even when they were on the wrong, but she felt sick in their company. No one understood the scientific essence of her fear if at all it had any. Jane almost fainted the first time she sighted Isaac with a black man.

Though Isaac had termed it medical, Jane never talked about it; its origin and future consequences. Why she brooded it when she knew it had vivid, destructive and emotionally embarrassing consequences confused about everyone.

"As long as god knows I don't hate them," she'd told Chris days later.

Chris nervously pressed the white button by the door.

"It's open," Isaac said in a raw and harsh voice speaking into the intercom speaker. Chris respectfully opened the door and entered, uncertain yet happy.

"Good afternoon *big boy*," both Isaac and Jane said in unison.

Chris smiled disinterestedly not sure why they used his high school name. From his impression of the room, Chris remembered being in that house, but he couldn't remember when. It may have been after they brought back the *tribal artifact* from the United Kingdom. However, he couldn't remember meeting either Jane or Isaac. He'd seen them on T.V though.

So Chris knew the place to the minute details: affluently furnished with all exotic accessories. A big bright horn, which Isaac brought from South Sudan, hanged in the living room. Isaac bought it from one of his visits to South Sudan. Jieng (Dinka), a tribe in South Sudan, is known for its long-horned cattle.

The wall resembled some East African game park: lions, giraffes, cheetahs, elephants, buffaloes, all suffused the wall.

Still with the wonders of the room in mind, Chris begrudgingly surveyed the pictures. The reordering of the decorating items in the room made him fidgety. Chris didn't know what the African pictures meant to Jane and Isaac. He could only guess.

For one, James Thialcegam was embarrassingly if not condescendingly idolized by the West. This mortified Chris. He considered such romanticized glorification banal; almost an apotheosis. Though James was most of the time at odd with Panda's foreign policies, he still commanded significant support in regard to how he viewed race issues not only in Africa but also in Panda. Chris had no reason to despise him. However, he believed James's fame sold the soul and dignity of his people. Like many freedom fighters, he paid his due, but he was, Chris believed, being irrationally nice.

11

We hardly know who you are, Isaac.
Your success is immutable, given the time frame of your surging.

Those were some of the statements Isaac faced. But they meant little to him though. Isaac Burns became an entrepreneur after his grandfather left him a spoiling fortune. His drive for success was unmistakably authentic. The expansion of his businesses to all corners of the earth was remarkably appreciable. Anytime he was faced with the demand of *who* he was, Isaac evaded the questions by narrating the origin of his great-great-grandfather's road to reliable and worthy life style. This beginning-of-the-world story always frustrated his interviewers. Anytime the thought came to his mind, he'd smile and look out of the window in readiness to narrate his frustrating story. In essence, not many people understood the ins and outs of the start-up of his business. Even Jane Baker, his girlfriend, didn't understand everything about his business empire. And for good reasons, Isaac loved that fact.

Isaac lived with Jane Baker, his high school sweetheart, in that description-defying mansion. Despite years together and the bond of trust they'd built over the years, the pair didn't see stepping up the altar as a necessity. Age and marriage weren't anybody's favorite topics in Jane's and Isaac's house. As a matter of fact, Isaac was three years younger than Jane. At 39, Jane wasn't bothered by her age. Jane was, too, a little taller than Isaac. Both Jane and Isaac were okay with whatever differences they had.

With the success of his business, Isaac, with strong backing from Jane, decided to reach out and give back to the community and the world. His philanthropic work with the homeless and low-income families in Day-Town was remarkable. This encouraged him to establish two orphanages in Day-Town. With his developing and expanding philanthropic heart, Isaac was considering building two more orphanages and schools in Africa: in Kibera (Kenya), Sivals, and Yei, South Sudan.

However, Isaac wanted to both exhale and breathe in moral breeze. He therefore needed sons of the land; insiders who could give him scholarship and insightful first-hand information of the nature of both the governments and the grassroots. It was with this understanding that he sought the help of the brightest and not-so-naïve African intellectuals. No doubt, he got some. Groping in the African savannah and tropical rain forest for sound-minded, mentally objective but realistic Africans wasn't easy. Isaac had to therefore forage through the load of African intellectuals in North America.

"They're some of the finest, analytical African minds. You'll love them."

A professor friend at Columbia University in New York told Isaac what he wanted to hear: someone who could help him understand Africa and its people. Isaac neither regarded himself as pretentious nor did he think he was assumptive. He knew humbling little if not nothing about the *Dark Continent* and he therefore wanted to be true to both the continent and his own very conscience: the thought that the dusty-foot cattle-keeper on the plain of *Pan ë Jiëng* needed to be respected; the creativity of the Luo fisherwoman rowing the Nile needed a humble eye; the tradition of the Zulu dancer needed a non-condescending place in the Euro-dominated cosmos. For Isaac, respecting Africa was of great personal importance; something he regarded as being enlightened first then patted on the back later for exuding humaneness and kind-heartedness.

"But don't you know the perception educated Africans have toward the west?" Isaac had asked his friend out of respectable, normative realism.

"Life my friend... life is a master."

Isaac didn't quite understand what the professor meant. The friend sounded so complacently capitalist that Isaac felt embarrassed. All the tiny hairs at the back of his neck felt like needed breeze in a hot summer room. Yet, Mr. Burns was confused. *Damn them profs*!

"Well, I mean...mmm...what's that supposed to mean, my friend?" Isaac finally blurted.

He'd sighed, looked Isaac straight in the eye and said: "There're those who think they have 'themselves' or those who say they know who they are, and that what others say of them doesn't define them. I say bullshit!"

Isaac was still hanging, confused and intellectually bullied. The wordings and the context were becoming even more perplexing. The professor was sounding more Confucius than helpful. Isaac clearly didn't understand what the professor meant. With hidden embarrassment, Isaac stared at him and smiled his ignorance away. The prof continued: "Let's not talk of their perception of the west, but their perception of *you*. That's what we're talking about and that's what we want. Give them what they want and you get yours. The rest is history if not capitalist."

Isaac didn't like what the professor said but he found himself smiling. That was exactly what life was. *But fuck life, I said, fuck life.*

Isaac wanted to be a pure helper. Yes, a stupidly pure helper. He didn't want some stupid friend's rationalization of what could be, what should be, but what's morally required. Isaac knew he himself sounded like some nerd philosopher writing papers in a lonely cubicle of his office.

"P.D Michael teaches here at Columbia and Osmani Osmani is a lawyer and consul at the Silavsian consulate in Heritage."

All Isaac could do was nod.

12

Osmani Osmani had only heard about Professor P.D as he was known in the US. He'd never met P.D, but he'd read many of his academic papers and books, his stance on brain drain, Euro-Africa relations and Afro-American relations. Osmani admired him, but he didn't agree with many of P.D's strong positions. But many of P.D's colleagues hated his guts; his work. Withal that, P.D's work was widely cited and read.

Michael had made life an *idealistic dream.* At 6.4 feet, P.D was an imposing figure with stocky build and strange basal voice. His bushy face added an authentic pretense to his professional air. He didn't talk much about himself in respect of Nietzsche.

As much as P.D wanted to embrace American conservative ideology of libertarianism and realism because of their practicality, his idealistic stance on them mocked him with a simplistic resilience. Well, there was something funny about the ideal dream as P.D always joked. A dream is a fantasy. An ideal life is a fantasy. What was with that combination? It was like *Sahara Desert* kind of a situation! An emphasis of the highest order if not a redundant one.

Osmani continued to strangely stare at the letter long after his secretary handed it to him. He wondered what could be in the letter. It was toward late afternoon and the west coast climate was dazing. He placed the letter on the table and walked to the window. Michael's name crossed his mind.

P.D Michael, Columbia University

To Osmani, nothing stirred curious or interesting thought in P.D's name. Everything P.D wrote was perhaps some unrealistic idea typical of academic minds. Political pundits thought less of many academics. These books addicts always have no much money, no power whatsoever. They live in their own ideal world, the platonic world.

Osmani thought of one of Kant's claims. Kant was a cunning, arrogant, but brilliant philosopher whose influence to the likes of Neil Bhor, Einstein and others was apparent after they read Kant's *Critique of Pure Reason*. With mind boggling irony, Kant wondered why scholars are at times dismissed as irrelevant in practical life withal at times, politicians get scared and confused when scholars write strong and impacting opinions in politically or religiously charged ambiences.

The world is full of contradictions: created or evolved from contradictions, lived in by the contradictions, guided by contradictions and would probably be destroyed by contradictions. What was the fuss about again? Oh yeah! Michael, the professor!

Whatever the letter contained, Osmani was smart enough to know how to deal with Michael. He could just live with available contractions and dismiss whatever vanity the letter contained. But it wasn't any professor writing. The man was real. P.D was a man who wrote the most pressing issues in the most pressing way in the most convenient of times. His writings were known; his thoughts were read from Tokyo to Sao Paulo, from Vienna to Cape Town, from Sydney to New York. Well, P.D wasn't Patrick Healy but he'd amassed a wealth of creditable respect. He set his goals and followed them to the last letter of his pronouncements.

Who am I kidding?

Outside, Osmani could see young and moneyed hearts speeding toward the beach in their convertible sports cars and huge-rimmed sport utility vehicles. Wind blew their long blonde, brown and black hairs beautifully backward. Echoes of their excitement carried their laughers farther and louder; the heavens respecting their endowment with great amazement. Their tanned faces glistened with sunscreen. Young and rich African-Pandians showed off their significance in equally surpassing terms. Big brown muscles flexed every girl toward them; round bottom and satisfying breasts coupled with naturally brown and chocolate faces and short hairs broke many necks. The sight was intoxicating and Osmani's neck started to ache. Those young hearts lived life as if they only had twenty-four hours to enjoy it. Sadly enough, Osmani wasn't one of them. He'd have loved such a life with all its costly aftermath.

Osmani stopped thinking for a while and looked at the paper on his desk. He was a dirty-faced Sivalsian diplomatic. His forehead was brown; his cheeks dark in a chocolate manner, his lips darkened by cigar smoke. Unlike P.D, Osmani's hair was dark and straight, his face looking more Indian than African. He was about 5.5 in height with a very annoying, repulsive Dr-Philly moustache. In Sivals, he was an Arab, but in Panda, Osmani was 'Black.' However much he didn't like that step downward on *the* ladder, Osmani had to come to terms with the rest of the damned African descendants. However, Osmani had distinguished himself in his profession well enough to be bothered by whatever his identity was.

What does P.D want from me?

But Osmani knew his own controversial speeches, his fame just as a consul. He was famous in the world that some people had thought he was the Sivalsian Ambassador to Panda. He remembered that bitter-sweet day.

Three days after Osmani delivered a speech on immigration and brain-drain to Panda in University of Juba, South Sudan; he got a congratulatory call from the Ambassador. There was no fuss about it. Osmani had just delivered a similar speech a month before in Tokyo. He was good at it, the ambassador had thought.

But things got complicated a day after when the Sivalsian ambassador to Panda stormed into his office with a newspaper demanding an explanation. The sight of the angry ambassador sent chill through Osmani's spine. Imagine the ambassador flying 1000 kilometers from Day-Town to Heritage simply to complain about an editorial error that wasn't Osmani's fault. Osmani had looked at the ambassador once and slowly but heartily read the headline. The ambassador then read the headline after Osmani.

"'Sivalsian ambassador to Panda, Osmani Osmani, gives a ground-breaking speech in Juba, South Sudan'. When did I do that?"

The ambassador fumed as Osmani stared, lost for words. He could only stare, confused. Osmani soon after became conscious of his speeches and the press. The incident was an honest editorial mistake, but Osmani wasn't so sure the mistake wasn't deliberate. The newspaper, *Heritage Precedent Daily,* was one of the giants in the media world. Their editorial policy and staff were reputably unquestionable. Well, if New York Times can confuse *Obama* and *Osama,* then anything can happen.

After the ambassador's surprising anger, Osmani called the paper to inform the editorial officials of the gross, unfortunate mistake. The usual happened as it always happens in the west: official apology. Osmani had to live through it. In the following issue the paper issued a correction and an official apology.

13

Sister J, Sister K and The Minister laughed their time away in the comfort of caffé Java on Adelaide Tambo drive in the suburb of North Durban. They were sitting outside. The place was a little crowded, but fitting. Faint musical murmurs engendered a soothing and comforting clime. A few gags from souls nearby annoyed the refined atmosphere. However, the trio was sipping in the delight of the Africa's orange orb overhead. She hid behind smoky clouds, smiling her way into another passing smokiness.

The message to Uncle D was that of heartfelt achievement. The trio had visited Johannesburg's Soweto slums. They were pleased with what they witnessed. Their drive was tourist-like and sophisticated. Needed delight punctuated their exit. Children played with real soccer balls. Real soccer fields sprouted throughout the neighborhood. The sound of their voices was jovial, beckoning and heartwarming. At a distance, a row of orange roofs greeted one from afar. Rows and rows of newly built houses spread smiles throughout the township.

"When I first met Uncle D, I thought he was a mindless opportunist," Sister K said.

Her yellow face suppressed the beauty of her dyed hair. The hair was annoyingly yellow. Or say, blonde. The hair was short, trimmed and typically nappy. She was slim but athletic. Her nearly oval face stressed her Africanness. Dresses were her delight. Pants? Not so much. It was hard to adduce her speech style. It was between serious and silly. However, she was at time precocious and stern.

"You couldn't beat me to that if you tried. I hated the man," The Minister said. He was a lanky, brown fellow with professional humor.

"Do you think we'll get the info from Hayiroh in time?"

"You heard what Mama said: 'It's bread and butter.'"

"Yes, she's always on top of things. What a woman?" Sister J said.

Sister J was a refined white woman with a very meticulous approach to issues. She was neither plumb nor slender. Strangely, her brown hair was always dyed deep black. Perfect described her. She was swift and majestic in gait. Sitting with folded legs on a chair calmed her. Her steps were quick and short. Failure was one of the things she hated. She talked much only if she had something to explain.

The Minister was not only enjoying his time with those beautiful ladies, he was doing what his conscience craved. He'd juggled his odds and he'd be sent through hade's gates should he come to the open. However, his heart smiled at night when he slept, his conscience draped in white, heavenly and hiemal crystal cleanness. His political brawniness was unquestionable. The Minister had one stone for two birds.

"Do you guys have any messages for Mama? I'm flying this evening," The Minister said.

"No, honey, I don't have any. I'm meeting The Maid after tomorrow in Day-Town. She's actually a good actress. I'm impressed by her work," Sister J said.

"Dear, Uncle D laughed at me when I showed him The Maid a few years ago. He laughed at me for about two minutes. She was blonde, funky and Paris-Hilton like. No one could take her seriously," Sister K said laughing.

"You guys were looking at the color of the cover I guess. I have to go to my hotel ladies. I've already talked to the government officials concerned and your work will be just fine," The Minister said, grabbed his jacket and smiled.

"Say hi to your wife, dear" Sister K said laughing.

"You're such a naughty girl, Sister K. I'm not ready for divorce yet. Let me continue to enjoy the smell of fried eggs and the beautiful aroma of Panda's coffee in bed. You couldn't do that, could you?"

"Bye sir!" both Sister J and Sister K chorused.

"Let me hear good news ladies," The Minister said and walked toward the taxicab parked on Adelaide Tambo drive near the café. He waved as the taxi gunned off.

14

"He's such an altruistic gentleman, visionary and reconciliatory, but he betrayed the soul of his people. Take it as that. He's great, I give you that, but calling him the greatest African is an insult to the essence of Africanness in Panda, Africa and the whole world," Little had complained once about the revered James Thialcegam. Little's lower lip arced upwards as usual when serious and dismissive.

Even if Chris didn't regard James in the same dismissive light as Little did, he understood Little's grievances. James was a palpably famed ideology of the west: be good for us and be famous, compromised for the good we believe in and be of famous and enduring legacy. Sincerity is always sacrificed in this case. But how many authentically altruistic men do really exist in reality? None! Yes, absolutely none!

"Good afternoon Chris, want some beer?" Jane asked, waking him up from his brief none-of-your-business trance. He smiled, now sincerely.

"No, I'm fine, thank you," he said and continued to survey the perplexing load on the wall.

Isaac clumsily got up and slowly dragged his feet to the washroom. He seemed to have been driven into demeaning indifference by Chris's presence.

Chris stared at him slightly flabbergasted. He soon brushed Isaac's action off. *He's just being rich.*

"Isn't this unfair?" Chris asked revealing his contemptuous recollection about the arrangement of the pictures on the wall.

"What?" Jane asked feigning a surprised complexion.

"Why put these two figures together? You can't be serious?" Chris said the statement and doubted it himself as soon as the words left his mouth.

"Yes, they're all Africans, oh, also, well...Africans."

"Anyone who doesn't know you guys and what you believe in would have a hard time convincing himself or herself that you like these guys at all. That's what I think."

Jane chuckled as Chris was starting to get uneasy, withal mesmerized.

"And what exactly do you mean by that, Chris?"

She was relaxed, comfortably seated and confident. Chris was about to speak, but soon found the words drying out of his lower lips.

She sat up, still relaxed and calm.

"What's wrong with the photos, Chris?" she asked again.

"I'm sorry if I'm unnecessarily reading too much into this. They pride in branding us the problem, that we're the problem. This arrangement would be like ridiculing some of their best political brains? That is what I truly think to say the least."

"What do you mean *we* and what *problems* are you referring to, Chris?"

"You're not teasing me, are you?" he said with a surprising and irritating grimace.

Jane laughed like a wicked demon satisfied with her contrivance.

"Was what I said that funny? I don't think it was," he said again, a little unsettled.

"Indeed it was, Chris!"

Jane said, tossed a gum into her mouth and started chewing it like some innocent child.

Isaac clumsily came back from the washroom. He sat down, his face wrinkled as if in pain.

"Well, we can go to my office, Chris," Isaac said and Chris got up.

Rattled, Chris took one quick, curious look at Jane as he readied himself to follow Isaac. She was staring at him. In her hand was a dark-blue book she seemed to be surveying. After staring at Chris with rude intensity, she started to curiously lift the book with her left hand and waved the book at him. Without looking up she said with a smile: "We'll finish our conversation some other time, Chris."

Isaac looked back at Chris and said hesitantly: "Well... I mean... you guys seem to have bonded already. That'll be of great help to me."

Confused, Chris didn't know what to think of Isaac's comment nor did he know what to make of Jane's comical indifference toward the African pictures on their wall.

Having failed to ground any of his curiosities and concerns, Chris followed Isaac to the office. Just like his future, everything about meeting Isaac was covered in a cloud of uncertainty like a Blackman's future, as Little always said.

Isaac's home office was a fairly spacious room with two brown, wooden chairs facing each other and one ugly yellow table mediating between them. Chris hated that hypocritical simplicity. Well, it was humbling. Both the table and the chairs seemed custom-painted by an amateur painter. There was only one cabinet behind one of the chairs. On top of the cupboard was Nelson Mandela's portrait. There were no computers, no large files of papers.

"Welcome to my little paradise, at home. You can have a seat...please!"

Chris hesitated then slowly sat down.

"Nice place!" he absentmindedly said, not knowing exactly what he meant.

"Well, not many people appreciate this. They think I'm being hypocritical."

Chris smiled. *Count me among them.*

"It's not what they say, but what you feel and mean. It might not be of any value to others but to you it might mean a lot. That's what I think."

Chris felt a little apprehensive after saying that statement. *Of course I'm lying, sir.*

Isaac curiously looked at Chris, opened the cabinet behind him and removed a file of papers. He still didn't know why he was there and what Isaac thought of him. Given the situation he was in, Chris wanted to face his demons against all odds.

"You sound like smart guy."

There he'd started it, Chris thought. *Nice kick in my butt.* Sarcasm and civilized mockery are the best ungrudging trimmers of egos.

"I don't think so. I sound like someone with opinion, I think."

"I'm sorry if I..."

"No, no, I understand. So, how long have you been...?"

"In business?"

Isaac finished the sentence and added: "It's been Eighteen years now. Look, I don't..."

A phone suddenly rang, interrupting him. He quickly scanned the phone number on the screen and then looked at Chris.

"I'll call her later. Look, this is why I meet people here. I always think that being home would be less stressful. I'll cut to the chase. I've a very good mission in Africa. It's a mission that'll be very close to my heart."

He got up, paused and looked out of the window.

"I was looking for a retired police officer. I couldn't get the one I wanted. Then a friend of mine told me about you."

"I was..."

"Convicted... I know."

"Then...."

"Well, I went over your case with my lawyers and they have good reasons to believe you were set up."

Chris was swimming in a tumultuous sea of perplexity. Even with a possible silver lining, he still didn't know what Isaac was trying to arrive at. However, Chris was a mixture of different emotions. With all the adversities he faced, he'd trained his mind to believe in nothing until whatever that thing was, the thing in question, materialized. However, his heart drove him into optimism most of the time. That brought him some functional hope and, in the face of all the monstrous conditions he was in, propelled him ahead however vacuous that functional hope was.

Rationalizing problems was why he loved his friend, Little. Little rationalized things in the most bizarre way you could think of. He told Chris once that some run-way slaves and Indians in the US tried to fight the US government. It was at the time a stupid and suicidal decision. Their chance of getting heard or successful was impossible if not remote. In the 1830s there was an allied group formed by African slaves and Seminole Indians fighting relocation. This group called itself Seminole after the Florida Indian tribe. They fought the government knowing they could not succeed. Little argued that to be prompted into action doesn't always stem from the motivation to succeed. It is the importance of the action and the reason behind one's acting in the first place. Their group leader, Osceola (Billy Powel), was arrested when the group was duped into a fake peace meeting in October 1837. Osceola later died in prison and was buried without his head. The Seminoles used their hearts for everything.

As he stared at Isaac, Chris used his heart, *reason* aside.

Being in the company of someone of Isaac's caliber was enough a reason to keep Chris's hope alive. Isaac started the meeting in a manner Chris wanted. It wasn't about the results; it was about personal value and deserved respect.

It was about time someone realized that.

"I still don't understand," Chris told Isaac after his alluding to his incarceration confused him.

"This..."

Jane burst into the office with a phone in hand, never bothering to knock.

"Not now honey. I'm..."

"It's Christine..."

"I know Jane..."

"You should take the call!"

Jane's facial contortion wasn't scary yet it wasn't promising. To make matters worse, Isaac wasn't looking at Jane. Chris thought Jane's face carried some sort of painful reflection. She continued to mutely stare at Isaac with the phone still extended toward Isaac.

"You might wanna take the call...I th-ink," Chris said as Isaac looked at him then at Jane.

Looking at Jane attentively, Isaac realized at once something was amiss, remarkably amiss. Without any further delay, he slowly took the phone from Jane. As if with affronted spirit, Jane continued to stare at Isaac as he readied himself to speak.

15

Dengiya knew the world around them wasn't promising. The lost hard drive was giving away more than they'd thought before the end of the First Phase. It was a beleaguered clime for the weak. You wonder.

The top conspiratorial first percent always celebrated. Their sumptuous classic English balls sheltered them from the destitution by their luxurious windows. The drought sounded mythical to them. They laughed at the thought of villages being mercilessly swept away by angry waters. Opportunistic, the red, roaring waters seemed. The angry force nudged the weakling banks with monstrous ease. The furious nature knew the disowning masters. Those fat, polygamous douche bags! No. They were the intellectuals, the wise voices.

Wide mouths and plugged ears they were.

The reports Sister K received from Hayiroh weren't good. But why would it surprise them? Greed. Lies. Big bellies were laughing out their nocturnal rapacity. Their thundering growls were always self-righteously ghostly. Who would dare the black masters? The weak smiled their fears away. Sorrow-induced tears at the corners of their eyes were winked away stealthily. Or they quickly wiped them away lest the black masters saw the weak cry. Punishment, devilish punishment would follow. How dare they humiliate the black master?

Dengiya knew things had to move fast if their mission was to be successful. Yes, monstrously fast. As Uncle D wasn't reachable, the group had to meet to plan the course of action to take. However,

The Minister, Mama and John had been very instrumental in providing crucial intelligence.

Efficiency wasn't so much an African darling, an inconvenience that is. This helped John and Mama to squeeze out intelligence through sloppy intelligence institutions.

Dengiya stared absentmindedly as Sister J talked over the phone. The rest, crammed into that tiny room, were laughing softly next to him.

"Don't stress yourself too much Sister J. We have your back," Mama had said.

Mama was a humble and highly educated African woman; simply a rarity. Her nature defied the group's curious and suspicious concerns.

"I can never doubt what comes out of your mouth Mama!" Sister J had said. "Since Uncle D isn't available now, we'll be sending you all reports of our parts of the plan. We'll have to work with the available intelligence."

"I see. Burns Investment is feeling the pinch of the operation in South Africa. We're ahead of them. An insider has actually suggested to Isaac our person."

"Thanks, Mama! We love you honey."

Sister J turned, looked at Dengiya with a puzzling smile and said: "I think we should start."

Dengiya looked at The Maid and said with his croaky voice. "Do you think your man can take it for a few more months?"

The Maid frowned, smiled then winked childishly. "I think he'll take it. He'll feel useless at first but he'll be fine. What's the purpose of doing this?"

"Making what, honey?" Sister J asked in a vexed voice.

The Maid looked down, glanced at Sister J and said.

"Why take an indirect route?"

Dengiya shook his head and aimlessly ran his right-hand fingers through his hair. "Do you know what it feels like to live your life blindly?" Dengiya asked with assumed, hidden claim of wisdom.

The Maid begrudgingly frowned.

"No!"

"Unless you know what a given situation feels like, you can only empathize, not compare yourself with someone who's actually experienced a given situation," Sister J said.

"I understand that but this guy has actually had his fair share of society's implicitly oppressive fingers."

Sister J smiled. "And we're making this worth his while."

"I know the end result but I'm worried about the poor guy's emotional and mental state, that's all."

"Point taken!" Dengiya said turning his chair toward the group. "We could have chosen another poor black person but hey, he's good for other things, you know."

"We keep coming up with ideas that are puzzling even to our own selves. We want to let those kids in the ghettos and slums understand that their future isn't entirely in the hands of others. We need them to be innovative, creative and courageous. We don't need minorities to live at the mercy of the oppressors materially and emotionally. We don't need them to be perpetual consumers of everything prejudicial: racist attitude and societal filth," Dengiya said with his croaky voice.

"We don't need people to always feel emotionally paralyzed when they're compared with monkeys or chimpanzees or gorillas, or called bitches. Every single person in the world has his or her own monkeyness. If people are shown their own monkeyness, they'd think twice before they call others monkeys or insinuate that others are monkeys," Sister J said.

"And of course, we don't need people to use our ideas against others."

"That'd be counter-productive."

"They have to be applied only in self-defence."

"And how are we supposed to achieve that without raising suspicion?" The Maid asked.

"Girl, a book is in preparation," BG1 said.

BG1 was a tall, sturdy, charcoal black, brawny fellow. He always responded as if with a grudge.

"What's sad is people of good-will are always many but indifferent," Sister J remarked with resignation.

"Breaking the status quo is difficult, however, a good cause, once accepted by a powerful few, gains ground. We have the capacity to make things work," BG2 said. He was a brown-faced fellow with brawniness of a body builder.

"Exploiting people's emotions has been used since the dawn of mankind. What's sad is people are beginning to be negatively wary of emotionally charged situations," The Maid said.

"As long as we understand..."

"We know what to do?" The Maid said interrupting Sister J.

"We're done with that," Dengiya said.

"We've not used SNSIS for a while," BG1 said in his begrudging manner.

"Does The Minister know about the *flaws* within SNSIS?" The Maid asked.

"We can't let him in on everything."

"The flaws don't know who they're giving the intel to and for what. All they care about is their pay," Dengiya said.

"We have to reduce digital storage and transmission of information," Sister J said.

"First, we'll hire a homeless fellow with a few bucks and tell him to take a small embroidered handkerchief to a public toilet. A toilet cleaner will pick it up and drop it into a marked garbage bag. A garbage man will pick it up and pocket it. The paper will be picked up as he washes his overall. Whoever has the handkerchief will go for a coffee with a message code holder," The Maid said.

"I like the homeless part and the code holder modification," Dengiya said.

"Or we could put a message in a coffee cup; a custom made cup that looks exactly..."

"Like the ones in the café," The Maid said looking at BG2 who she'd interrupted delightfully.

"As usual, we're *phased*. Once we get a word from Uncle D, we'll set up a meeting," Dengiya said.

As sister J stared at her colleagues, a chill of humbling exhilaration ran through her entire body. She smiled. Who could have guessed? A young white girl confusing the world most sophisticated intelligence all in the name of justice. Yes, Justice. Naïve, simple justice delivered to the weak, the poor. Insanity, mere insanity, she thought.

Dengiya's croaky voice always honed their resolves. The felonious world is always the most vocal. The good breathes silently to a point of indifference. A vocal greed brandishing its hungry resolves and a silently apologetic but passive good all engender a wicked world. Sister J shook her head. *Why should people be like that?*

Everybody trickled out one by one. Outside, the monks milled about, murmuring and prayerful. Their unreadable faces fascinated sister J: calm, indescribable, inscrutable faces dignified by shiny baldness were comical. They were serious nonetheless. They murmured away their desires, never bothering anyone. They lived meagrely never begrudging anyone. What a beautiful life? *Why wasn't the whole world like that?*

She trod through the murmuring baldness and walked to her car. Still admiring the monks, she waved at Dengiya, who was getting into a taxi, and stared at the ominously cloudy night. It was symbolic.

16

It wasn't clear what happened to that beautiful, out-of-this-world assurance. The supplier's administration promised to get back to Little after the no-show at the rendezvous. No one got back to Little unfortunately. As you'd expect, Little's patience was wearing away, really thin. To make sure any misunderstanding between the two parties was solved amicably, Little called twice. He was told that 'we're working on it, Mr. Michael.'

Little realized then that something was amiss. The whole situation was becoming dangerously tormenting and disaster beckoning. He managed to control the monsters of anger inside him though.

"It's been three days since the day I waited for nearly two hours," he said really fired up, furious but pretentiously controlled. It was no brainer Little expected a proper response given the length he'd gone to suppress the volcanic lava inside him.

"We pride in our service, Mr. Michael. You'll be proud of the service you'll get."

Little resolved that he'd had enough of sugar-coated treatment. Philosophy and business have never and will never couple. He screamed at the receptionist only to find out that the lady was some smart ass. He vomited a deviant squeal to make up for his anger but the lady only let him yell his heart out without hanging up; just listening. The receptionist had probably cringed away for a fleeting second. When she made sure Little wasn't going to scream again, she calmly and confidently said: "That probably helped."

That was it. Little hanged up and picked up his Jacket from a hanger behind him. With a swift, furious turn he reached for his keys on his office desk and dashed out.

It was toward evening and the traffic was at a tortoise pace. With the sequence of events, Little was becoming too infuriated to notice the traffic. The developing belittlement wasn't about the supply anymore. It'd turned into self-esteem fortification. They were infringing on self-esteem he'd spent a good fraction of his tumultuous young adulthood trying to protect.

"You have to take some time out if you're angry baby. It helps. It can protect you from stupid and dangerous impulses," his mother always said.

It isn't the time, mother...it really isn't.

Little wanted one thing. Really! One thing! To just put his hand from one orifice to the other... of whoever was on his way.

What they did to me and continue to do to me is the cruelest of all insults.

As the thoughts of such debasement started to weigh heavily on him, Little decided to take a fast route. With a rude, swift and reckless swerve, he turned onto Central Street heading north. The traffic was all the same: conspiratorially jammed. *Not you too, traffic.* Well, traffic is like Mother Nature. When she's decided, there's nothing a motorist can do but wait for her to decide it's time for you to go your way.

After thirty minutes of annoying press-and-break pace, Little again swerved left, turning onto Ninth Avenue heading west. Ninth Avenue was comparatively relaxing.

"Better start to treat me well," he said to himself again as the lights turned green.

Little drove on for a while on the same course until a black Mercedes joined him on that lonely street. It was Mercedes-Benz GLK. Having driven past three lights on that straight route, Little decided to take the route he should have taken in the first place. However, to bring Little back to his senses, the black Mercedes turned his way, right after him.

Coincidence! Mere coincidence!

"Don't try me now. I'm angry and dangerous as hell."

Little was trying to convince himself he was not disturbed by the black Mercedes behind him. Still, he decided to take a right turn, just to be sure. The Mercedes was still behind him. Now wary of the Mercedes, Little decided to slow down. The Mercedes than changed lanes and moved to Little's right. The guy rolled down the window as the light turned green. Little drove ahead and the Benz was like a jet fighter. It whisked past him and came to a stop at red light.

In the Mercedes Benz, there were two guys; one wearing what they called African dress, the other was draped in a hooded sweater; his rude glasses staring at the furious Little. They were either African-Pandians, from the Caribbean or Africans. Little rudely stared at them; the usual stare of kids in the hood. The hooded guy stretched his neck toward Little and smiled as the other guy pressed down on the accelerator. Little accelerated, overtaking them and yelled: "What do you guys want?" the guy driving just smiled at Little.

"I'm gonna kick your ass," Little yelled.

"You have a soul and that's what we want," the one with the hoodie said.

"Fuck you," Little lost his cool.

The one wearing the African dress thrust his head out of the window while still holding the steering wheel and yelled: "You're too nice to say that, Mr. Michael."

He knows my name!

As Little looked in front of him, he realized he'd passed his exit. "Losers! How did you guys know my name?"

As little was about to arrive at a light ahead of them, it turned yellow. There was a sign warning: *camera in red light!*

As Little had had enough of the bullies, he went through yellow light assuming they'd stop at red.

They know my name?

But guess what? they were just but outlaws. Little looked back and they were behind him. They'd run through red light.

"Shoot!"

Little knew the controlled soft-spoken-ness and civility was masking the real nature of the guys. He'd got company. His mind rolled back the tape to his stint in jail.

"Little, no one likes to be a criminal. Everyone loves to be a good citizen; however, we all don't get the opportunities to be good citizens. We try as much as possible to be law-abiding citizens, but then trouble comes to us. It just comes to us at the door-steps of our own houses. Talk of determining factors. I remember one time when a drug vendor ran away from the police and disappeared behind our house. When the police chasing after him found us on the door-steps of our house, they believed we knew who that run-way vendor was. Having failed to catch the vendor, the police rounded us up. Now, could we blame the police or ourselves? We couldn't blame the police because the kid looked like us. We couldn't blame the police because we had records and we had some drugs in our jackets. But we couldn't blame ourselves for the record because we wanted to live life. We sometimes pledge to ourselves that we wouldn't do drugs, but then we go back to our apartments where we find our mum's boy-friends shouting at our mothers and our little sisters crying on the floor asking our mothers for *a* glass of milk, just a glass of milk. What do you do? Of course we deserve to be here because we were vendors. But we have few if not nothing to choose from...or don't we? If the conditions of our social surrounding force us to be who we are, then why blame us? If the police are only doing what they are supposed to do, then why should we hate them?"

That was Little's *big brother* in jail. He was a very articulate and philosophical con man.

Little mentally came back to the present and saw a turn to the left. He immediately changed lanes and turned left. The Mercedes guys did the same. Now the situation was becoming dreadful as

Little started to sweat: fear dawned. The angry Little was becoming frightened. But as a gentleman, he tried to rationalize his fear. But no, it didn't work. He drove for a while then took a swift illegal U-turn. They did the same. With the rude guys tail-gating him closely, Little started to get scared. *Little, calm down, you're in charge.*

Having been mentally worked-up by the threat of the guys after him and the last few days events, Little wanted to remove his cell phone to call the police. His ego advised him to wait. He fearfully turned right and drove straight, then turned left toward his destination. With understandable hesitation, Little looked back only to realize the guys had gone straight. He breathed a sigh of relief for the first time in almost thirty minutes.

There was no question Little's manhood, for a moment, had gone. With profound anger swallowing him he realized he was sweating and panting heavily. After a moment, he pulled up by the street next to a huge warehouse complex. Taking time to compose himself and gather his thoughts for the next course of action, a car whisked by and he jumped up in fright. "What's happening to you, Little?" Little said to himself and braced for *whatever it was.*

As he sat staring at the warehouse, Little's manhood streamed back slowly as his anger neurons started to work. He came out of the car with a straight poise and a composed, pretentious face. A lean, blond man approached him. The man quickened his steps and said, almost yelling.

"I'm sorry you had to come here, Mr. Michael!"

Little scornfully fixed the man with a rude gaze. The man was ideally a dead-man walking. Little wasn't in any mood to take any patronization with civility. He wanted to devour someone alive; someone who'd embarrassed him and continued to cause agony in his life. As he stared at the man walking toward him, Little realized the man was very tiny for the type he craved for a punch. The short fellow extended his hand to greet Little. Little disdainfully looked at him, not wanting to shake his hand but he quickly changed his mind. After a brief hesitation, he shook the short-man's hand.

"I was about to personally drive to your place. I'm the supply manager."

Little blankly stared at him. *Yeah, tell me something!*

"What I want is a contract agreement, sir. There're many suppliers I could go to. Why're you guys wasting my time? I have a business to run and I thought you guys understood that!"

The man looked sympathetically at Little but only smiled. His tiny head and pink face innocently fanned Little's lit fury. Little's face was about to go ablaze.

Again, the man grinned. "Getting another supplier would be a good idea."

Little cringed with a begrudging frown.

The tiny, pink head was getting bigger and prouder as Little's anger surged. *What did you say?*

"What?"

He smiled showing his orange gum and curved, yellow teeth. "I'd advise you to seek the service of another supplier."

Little sorrowfully smiled. Anytime he looked at the man, the man's height increased; the head inflating. The whole matter was turning into a comedy; a serious, ridiculing comedy.

Little subdued himself into a subservient calm and said, slowly and quietly like always with his curled-up lips: "Was that what you wanted to drive to my place to tell me?"

The tiny, pink face shook his head and shifted his feet timidly. "I actually wanted to personally deliver a letter to you."

"A what?"

17

Osmani edged close to the table. He hesitated as he stared at the brown envelope proudly staring at him. Stupid academics, he thought. Idle theorists, words players: that's who they are.

P. D Michael, Columbia University, New York City

He looked out through the window. It was the same: people having lives to live, money to spend, cars to destroy, and dreams to gamble with: the Whitneys, the Britneys, the Parises, the Lindsays....

"What am I doing?" Osmani told himself, pulled the chair and ruinously sat down with a thud. Then he thought of one of Michael's papers. He'd read that paper and felt touched yet undermined. Behind him was a small, two-rowed shelf with books, journals and magazines. With a calm sway, he looked at his bookshelf, fingered through the titles then removed a worn out journal.

Michael, P. D, *Brain drain and Socio-political beneficiaries*, Journal of African Studies, Vol. XXIII (2002), pp. 345-385

...We are entitled to our opinions. That is why a host of defunct, outrageous and self-incriminating opining of dismal knowing is tolerated. Brain-drain is spicy to many, and painful to a few. Let's not claim to know how we can better deal with it when what we say about it only benefits us....

Osmani looked at the letter and thought about the part he'd quoted.

"He lives in a cocoon."

He probably should see Dr. Phil or Dr. Drew.

Osmani lived by the words of his mum. Born to a family of three, Osmani Osmani was the youngest of the three. He was spoilt so to speak. The siblings were a brother and a sister. The brother died in tribal clashes in Piondu, Sivals, and the sister practiced medicine in Hayiroh. She was more reserved than he was.

"I'll literally do it: spoil you," Osmani's mum used to say when he was just a young boy and she lived by her words. She did spoil him.

"We don't live by the terms of what we want to live by, but by the terms of what makes us comfortable," she'd always said.

Osmani would just stare at her, intrigued yet confused. But being the youngest, he lived by the terms of what he wanted. He got things he wanted when he wanted them. He cried when he wanted to. He laughed when he wanted to.

"What was mum saying?" he asked himself and looked at the letter again. Perhaps his mum had the likes of P.D in mind. He couldn't know. This academic was perhaps a confused soul of dichotomized heart.

"This man needs help."

Yes indeed! P.D needed help.

Osmani savored the thought but he was priding with emptiness. Having satisfied his mind with all he wanted to think about, Osmani grabbed the envelope. With Christmas passion, he admired it for the last time after which he frantically tore it open, tearing off the right side of the paper containing the letter. Feeling a little guilty, he pieced it back and spread the content on the table. With a seemingly comfortable sigh, he started to read:

Confidential!

To:
Dr. P.D Michael
Professor of African Studies,

Columbia University,
New York City.
Osmani Osmani
Senior consul,
Sivalsian consulate,
Heritage, Panda.

From:
Isaac Burns
CEO and Chairman, Burn Investment Inc.,
Burns Industries and Burns Construction Inc.
Day-Town, Panda.
August 27, 2002

Sub: A Request for a Friendly Favor

You might have heard about me, but I would rather introduce myself. I am Isaac Burns of Day-Town. I am an entrepreneur/philanthropist who would want to reach out to the needy.

I started a few years ago with two orphanages in Day-Town, but I believe I can reach far beyond the borders of Panda.

I am writing to you, having been informed of how valuable you could be to me. I need to understand the peoples of Africa. I need any little I can understand to help launch two more projects in Africa.

I would be honored if you could accept my invitation to meet me in Day-Town this weekend. Everything from accommodation to transportation will be arranged.

Sincerely,

Isaac Burns

Confused and doubtful, Osmani read the letter again but his mind remained blank.

"Isaac Burns? You gotta be kidding me!"

Osmani smiled to himself and walked to the window. As he walked back to the desk, a phone rang. He stared at the phone for a moment then picked it up.

"Yes, Betty!"

"I have a Mr. Michael on line 3."

"Pass him through, please."

Osmani sat down, picked up the receiver and pressed the 3 button.

"Yes, Mr. Osmani speaking," he said with hesitation in his voice.

A voice from the other end of the line confidently said: "I'm Mr. Michael of Columbia University. I sent you a letter two days ago, did you receive it?"

Osmani looked at the envelope.

"Yes, yes, I just finished reading it."

There was a slight pause then the caller said: "He expects the feedback by tomorrow evening."

Osmani's dark face puckered up, feeling a tinge of mortification. Whether he savored the idea or not was a moot thought.

"Do you know the specifics?"

There was a deep sigh on the other side of the line. It was characteristic of honorable-man's disappointment.

"I'm afraid not...but that's why he wants to meet us."

That made a lot of sense. Osmani was savvy in etiquette.

"Ok-ay...I..."

"I'll call you back, Mr. Osmani. You can also call me on the number that appears on the small piece of paper. I hope it came with the envelope. Talk to you soon."

He hanged up.

"That's too good to be true."

Osmani didn't know why P.D sounded pressured. Then he looked at the letter and it was only three days old. He started to resent P.D. *Money don't make personalities.*

18

T he arrangements were in order. P.D was to board Werda Air, WA297, first class to Heritage from New York City. The two gentlemen would then finally fly to Day-Town in Isaac's private jet.

When everything proceeded as planned and the two African gentlemen kept their words about the arrangement, Isaac had nothing but respect for the African gentlemen. They were men of their words.

These men were honorable and intellectually accommodating. They'd called to express their appreciation and acceptance of the invitation. They were of course delighted to come and meet Isaac in Day-Town. Coming to the Pandian capital, the heart of world economy and politics was heart-warming; not to mention meeting someone of Isaac's caliber.

But was Isaac flattered, undermining himself or excited? It didn't matter. The good Isaac got what he wanted. Throughout his life, Isaac always wanted to be perceived as someone who cared about the plight of the needy. There he was, warming the hearts of able-minded Africans.

"It'll be a great honor to have both of you at my service," he'd said as both men listened to him on a three way conference call.

As time turned 3.00 pm, Saturday, Eastern Time in the US, Isaac instructed the jet pilot to fly to Heritage. Time was starting to make Isaac feel humbled as he was inflating with excitement. Altruism sang self-praise songs at the back of his mind. There was nothing he wanted more than to see their faces lit with enthusiasm, their lips with smiles, and their hearts with gratitude.

To fire up Isaac's confidence, the pilot told Isaac she was on her way to the airport. Sweet beauty! For all the five years she'd worked for Isaac, Nyanjieng ë Piath had never been late. She was a tall, skinny and dark-skinned twenty-nine-year old South Sudanese. Her deep, dark face amplified the delight you felt when she smiled. Good enough, her obedience was unquestionable but she stood her ground with begrudging fervor when ordered to do something she didn't like. It was not surprising some dignitaries refused to be flown by her, fearing her ability as a full-pledged pilot. She'd humbly smile their concerns away with that wickedly charming smile: "I swear by my life, you'll be fine. I work for Isaac Burns for god's sake!"

That humbling assurance embarrassed any concerned dignitaries even if they flew in the jet with grave uneasiness for fear of a possible crash.

But don't guess what happened with Isaac's arrangement. Thirty minutes after Isaac finished talking to Nyanjieng, he received a call on his private cell phone. Calls going to his private phone weren't always good news. He too didn't recognize the caller's number. With premonitory hesitation, he let the phone ring for a few more seconds then picked it up. After the call Isaac became disappointed, almost furious. He couldn't remember having ever been more disappointed than he was that day.

"I regret to inform you that I'll not be able to make it to Day-Town as planned. We've had an emergency back home and the ambassador has requested my service in this," Osmani humbly told Isaac.

"Well, I can talk to the ambassador to have someone else do it."

Isaac said and realized he'd overstepped his calls. *But what the heck?*

"That's ok-ay sir, but no. I don't mean to sound negative but this is one of the reasons for which I was brought to Heritage."

"What's the nature of the emergency," Isaac asked knowing he was into forbidden territory.

"I'm sorry I can't say that, Mr. Burns."

"Well, when..."

"I'll make sure I come to Day-Town even if it's at my own expense to make up for this upset. Thank you, sir!" Osmani said and hanged up.

Isaac stared at the phone for a while before putting it down. Osmani's offer didn't go far enough to pacify Isaac. He was understandably angry, really furious.

Good things. When will they ever last long? Good thoughts beckon frustrating filth with begrudging ease. He shook his flecked face and stared at the phone. The unsettling office silence rudely settled upon his angry soul. *Africans, can anything ever go smoothly with them?*

Isaac suddenly dismissed the thought. He shook his head. *That's unbecoming of me.* Kill the thought, he urged himself. Prejudicial thought, ra—. No. Isaac suddenly stopped his thoughts. It wasn't racist. He suddenly shot up and adorned a smile. It was a self-congratulatory resolve. It wasn't racist, he assured himself with a potent finality.

19

The small man found himself painfully writhing on the ground. Was Little back at it? Was he destined to be a jail asset? He didn't know.

Little couldn't even remember ever hitting the man on the face. He could only remember the man approaching him, happy and confident. The next thing he knew was the man was twisting with pain on the ground in front of him.

Little got out of his brief trance only to see two uniformed police officers approach him cautiously, guns out and ready. As the world stood still and angry in front of him, Little realized his childhood nightmares had started all over again. His childhood legitimate anger was violence; his humility and altruism were translated as humiliating subservience. Either way, he was a loser. From the look on the officers' faces, Little knew he was back where he'd started: jail. Doom followed the doomed. However, this time his anger was violence in every sense. *I deserve anything after this.*

Little left jail years ago with a sworn testimony that he'd not go back again. There he was behind huge, ugly and rude bars. Behind those restraining metals, Little was regretful and uncertain as he sat with other gloomy faces. An officer walked to the cell entrance and threw a letter at him. Without any interest, Little tore it open and read it slowly, his mind on what his mum was going to say about his unfortunate and childish conduct.

Dear Mr. Michael,

We apologize for we will not be able to enter into any business agreement with you. We have more clients than we can provide adequate and satisfying service to.

We will be delighted if you could find another supplier. However, we will be more than happy to service you in the future should our conditions change; and you are still interested in our service.

Sincerely,

Sean Suppliers,
Customer Service Department

Little read the letter over and over again and realized he was being taunted. There was no doubt on his mind that he was being *patronized*, but he was in custody. What could he do? As he finished reading the letter for the fourth time, his mum walked to the cell's entrance with an officer.

"Mr. Little Michael," the officer said with a mocking, girlie smile.

Little sprang up as the officer threw his items at him. Grace, his mum, disdainfully looked at Little and said: "Who between me and you do you wanna kill?"

Knowing where the conversation would lead to, little kept quiet. Grace Michael was a strong woman who never wasted her words. She was short, reserved but tenacious. Her hair was always kept short. Everything in, into or out of your head should always be kept short, Grace always told Little.

Little, for good reasons, feared her. But he didn't fear her because of the ferocity of her commands or the wickedness of her parenting style, but for the mere fact that she was very Afrocentric.

Grace once threw Little's cousin out of the house when he called Nelson Mandela a *sell-out*. The expression on her face then told Little that criticizing Africans was a touchy topic.

As Little left with Grace, all he could think of was his first stint in jail. His spell in jail was more informing and eye opening than he could ever explain. It made him the man he'd become. But Grace was the best part of his life. He knew he'd be undermining her importance in his life if he pretended to know good words to describe how he appreciated her. Little grew up as a bad kid, but Grace knew the son she carried in her womb for months, the son she raised, and the son that was influenced. Like most black kids in North America: *"mama is all we've got."*

The store and the bar couldn't have been a success were it not for her. She was his whole life. Every vista ended with her; every scenery had Grace at the end. She was his spiritualizing statue, a reassuring figure and voice when he saw phantoms in dreams and frustrations. But there were other unlikely inspirers that managed to shape his thinking, his general reflection and who he'd become. While Little didn't take Afro-centrism with Grace's fervor, he realized that it was something to explore; something good for one's intellectual development. Thanks to those bad kids in jail. They acted like his prototypes, his cautioners; his counselors. Those losers, for the society wanted Little to call them so, were normal people with normal dreams and aspirations.

Ever wondered about justice, how it's rendered? Ever seen how it reflects human weaknesses? Ever realized the pointlessness of some penalties? You could go on and on and on.

Justice, justice, justice! What's it? Well, it's to give the offending soul a lesson not to offend again. Wait, is that it? No, try this: It's to pacify the offended by making sure the offender suffers. No, it's a reassurance to the offended that someone cares — that the society is there for them — that the society is organized and civilized. Now, in the name of justice, who's stupid, the one who criticizes killing murderers as a form of Justice called retribution, or is it the person who thinks killing murderers is Justice? Who cares anyways? You? Maybe Little!

Justice is a search for truth and the correct methods of straightening a path deviating from justice. Law is an *assumed proof* based on evidence. Law is attainable with ease; justice *is* with difficulty if it's attainable at all. Capital punishment is not justice but law delivered. Maybe!

Little didn't know. Sometimes he saw law (called justice) as simply...revenge.

What was it again, oh, Justice, and the point of killing someone and calling it justice? Spare us the thought, irrationality.

Paradoxically, Little did appreciate all the guys in prison for they taught him that the shortest way is not always the correct and safest way. Behind every mysterious happening, there exists a hiding wall; an excuse, escapists' paradise. Many people love the shortest way: *my big brothers' way* as Little called it.

Little tried his big brother's ways only to end up with big black men staring at him in a not-so-funny a way, in a not-so-good a place, and in not-so-convenient a time. However, some brothers in jail made him realize that people are not what we see. Yeah, it sounds like a tired cliché but this was different. Believe it! They were big black men, in big black places who'd done big black deeds.

Little vividly remembered one of them. He was playful, slightly childish, but unforgettable. When the man first saw Little in the jail dining hall, he said aimlessly: "Man, I had this dude in my hood who, after finishing high school, told us he was gonna go to college. I told him, 'good luck'!"

Little remembered the fellow as a short, dark-skinned brother whose white smile, patronizing and playful utterances kept Little going. He made Little laugh in a good way. In jail, most of the things inmates laughed about were abhorrent. They were always laughs about others' misfortunes. But this brother would come to Little and yell: 'college boy' let's play, college boy what're you thinking....college boy...college boy...?' The nagging transformed into admiration and then friendship as time went by.

"What happened to the guy you said," Little would eagerly ask.

However, the man's actions mystified with time to Little's dismay. He'd at times leave without answering Little's questions. At times he'd sit and talk about other things and intentionally ignored Little's innocent queries.

He instead talked about seemingly irrelevant issues. There was the papal selection—the 'conclave'—the holy occasion that was supposed to be open and transparent but was serially turned secretive. He said he wanted to believe in god but that people made it so hard for him to do so. God is not the people. Focusing on your relationship with god exclusively was the solution, Little had said. Upon hearing Little's comments about god, the man laughed hysterically. His hysterical laugher startled Little, however, his answer surprised Little even more. What he said was brilliant, sincerely outside the man's league. Perhaps the man read it from some nerdy philosophical writings and used it to dazzle Little. Dazzling people with ideas not well understood is typical of people with limited knowledge and inflated egos.

He said Little was oxymoronic. The same people he was told not to trust were the same people who exposed him intellectually and emotionally to the idea of god in the first place. 'Use a time machine to go back for some 2500 thousand years not to see these Christian god's men and you have no idea of god as we know it now.' The answer was poetic and vague but Little understood what the man meant. While the answer about god was brilliant, it wasn't the main instrument that fascinated Little about this guy.

It was the college boy story. Not Little though!

"What do you think happened to the college boy?" he asked Little one day having come back to himself.

"He dropped out," Little blurted.

He looked at Little, smiled and tapped him on the head.

"What? Why did you do that?" Little said with a frown, lips curled upward.

He smiled condescendingly and said: "I had a very wrong impression of you. You looked stupid kid, really stupid. I thought you were here because some smart friend of *years* tricked you and threatened to kill you if you said he was the mastermind of whatever you guys did."

The man's statement stupefied Little, however, the man was smiling, an occasionally sincere smile.

"I don't know what you mean," Little said. Perplexity was written all over his face.

"My boy! My boy! That's how smart people think. They don't always judge prematurely. And when you see them rushing to judgment, be careful, they want to trick you," he said, smiled again condescendingly and left shaking his head.

Little stopped his journey back to the past and looked at his mother. Grace was driving reflectively. They arrived at their house but as he got down, Little saw Chris getting into his car. He yelled.

"Chris!"

Chris got out of the car and came toward Little.

20

O n the day of that mysterious call, Isaac told Chris to leave. After Isaac took the call, Chris knew whatever that situation was, it was grave. Isaac said 'hello' and his face immediately puckered up. The stress was apparent. But Chris had little if not nothing to worry about regarding the disaster that'd befallen the big man. Isaac was moneyed. Anything that needed credible lawyers or money was on his fingertips.

"I'll give you a call, Chris. We'll finish this some other times," he'd said after taking the phone from Jane and said 'hello.'

Chris had looked at him and knew the man was in pain. Luckily, Chris and Isaac had no agreement or friendship whatsoever for Chris to brood over Isaac's pain. He let things pass the way they'd come. Whatever Isaac's situation was, things would still remain the same. Tomorrow the sun would shine and the moon would appear. All the beggars would flood the streets and big shots would be suited up for their comfortable chairs and brown, smiling desks. Chris would too, wake up.

However, two days later Jane gave Chris a pressing call.

"Isaac would like to see you at his home office tomorrow," she said with a mellow voice that made him nervous. Conveying messages was one of the things Jane didn't do well. Her messages were conveyed without any formality or compunction. Words flew out of her mouth with unrestrained ease; her voice firm but uncertain. In any case, she did her duty: conveyed the message as per Isaac's request.

When Chris arrived at Isaac's residence, the same writings taunted him.

FALCON RESIDENCE, WE ALL MATTER!

The rude guy opened the gate. He looked at Chris and the man's cell phone casing stared.

P BROTHERS

Curious, Chris intensely gazed at the guard as the guard frowned.

"What?" the guard grumpily asked.

"I'm sorry. Please excuse my ignorance."

"Sorry about what?"

"Out of curiosity, what does that one mean?"

"What?"

The guy was so rude that Chris felt like yelling 'whatever dude'. Chris remained civil and calm though.

"The 'P BROTHERS'."

"Are you asking me because it carries the word 'brothers' and I'm black, or have you never worn any clothing with writings that don't make any sense...and you just don't give a rat's ass what the writings mean?"

"Jeez dude! I'm sorry!" Chris told him and turned to go.

"You've nothing to be sorry for," he said as Chris walked away.

Annoyed, Chris looked back once and smiled pretentiously with bitterness inside him. That's what we always do in North America, isn't it? We smile away our resentment, internalize our dissatisfaction and give an impression we like the world around us. Our internalized resentments mixed with our social surrounding and parental indoctrinations transform our *inner us* into hate-filled reservoirs. All in all, Chris wasn't yet transformed into a political, hate-filled reservoir. He didn't like that rude man still. What he didn't like the most from the man was the fact that he continued to rudely stare at Chris as Chris walked away.

Jane opened the door as Chris was about to knock.

"Hi Chris," she said as she opened the door.

"Hi Jane!"

Jane looked radiant and professionally impressive. Chris didn't sense the vocal ambience she showed when he talked to her over the phone. She slowly and quietly led him into the living room.

"How's Isaac doing?" he asked as he moved his eyes around, staring at the African pictures on the wall. Remarkably enough, Jane sighed, looked at Chris but quietly walked to the fridge before answering his question.

"He's got some glitches with his partners in Africa," she said looking confusedly at the items in the fridge.

"What'd you like to drink, Chris?"

"Any beer would be okay, I think."

After a period of hesitation looking into the fridge, she grabbed a bottle of Heineken, gave it to Chris and left. It took about five minutes for Isaac to come to the living room as Chris sat alone. He was smiling for some strange reasons as he stared at Chris.

"Hello big boy," he said extending his small, pink right hand to Chris. Whatever they meant by 'big boy' and wherever they got the inspiration to call Chris so didn't bother him at all. He just brushed it off like a really dear visitor's fart. Isaac's confusing show of unreserved enthusiasm was drawing Chris's attention. His gloomy face of two days earlier was gone. Must be money at work! Despite all the hypes in his voice and action, Isaac still looked wearied and overworked.

"Let's go to the office," he said and walked to the washroom.

The office looked the same, except that a fax machine was placed on the desk. There were files of papers on the left side of the desk. As Chris sat down, Isaac walked in.

"Well, I must apologize for last time," he said reaching for his seat behind the desk.

"It's all in the name of business. That's what I think."

He sighed deeply, foraged through the papers and said: "Well, I mean, it'd be comforting if all that happened was in the name of business."

Chris kept quiet for whatever would come after the remarks would be negative.

"Well, let's not get caught up by another urgent phone call," Isaac said.

With dreadful calm and slowness, Isaac got up, walked to the shelf and came back with what seemed like a faxed message. Still standing with that paper, he momentarily looked at Chris and sat down.

"Like I told you the other time, my lawyers strongly believe you were set up. You could be compensated for that, but that's not why I called you here. I have businesses in Africa and I need a strong heart that can stand up to the *African test*."

Chris didn't know why Isaac thought he knew him well enough to think he could stand the test of Africa's adversity insuperability. Understandably, Chris didn't care though. The man speaking to him was Isaac Burns and that was all that mattered to Chris. In the capitalists' world, money moves mountains, and money not only talks, it divinely whispers.

After a thoughtful pause, Isaac sighed with discernible pain in his voice then continued.

"I called you the first time because I wanted you to go and be a manager in training in South Africa. With a year of hand-on experience, I wanted to transfer you to Hayiroh to take care of issues there. Your accounting background can be very valuable."

He slowly looked at Chris while squirming on his seat. Chris was firmly fixed on his seat. The information was suddenly dropped on him so he didn't know what to say. Chris's response was confused.

"What...."

"Then that phone call came. It was from Christine. I'm not at liberty to discuss that now, but you'll soon know what it was about.

All I need to know is whether I can trust you enough to be my right-hand man in Africa?"

Chris squinted. "I don't think I can answer that to anybody's satisfaction, I think. All I know is I trust myself. But the events that led to my arrest and conviction have put that to the test. To trust me or not to trust me isn't up to me."

With a humane expression on his face, Isaac looked at Chris with reassuring confidence and said: "Good people make honest mistakes, but I doubt you made any mistakes prior to your conviction. I know what climbing a ladder in corporate world is. To get promotions you have to have no one better than you. You were obviously better than many around Day-Town."

"But why exactly did you choose me?"

Seemingly challenged by the question, Isaac looked down for a while then said: "Well, I was advised by a friend who knows you well. Clean police service and strong accounting credentials sound like things Africa need."

What good friend? Chris didn't ask him though.

"How do we go about it?"

"I'm sorry to say this but I need you to go to Hayiroh a day after tomorrow. I'll not be able to tell you anything about why you're going, but Christine will fill you in on arrival."

Upon hearing what Isaac had said about the departure time, Chris felt like a heavy load had landed on his head. A couple of minutes passed before he could utter a word.

Hayiroh? A day after tomorrow? That was a sick joke. Isaac's request (or command) sounded too soon; too nice to be a genuine offer. But remember, Chris was using his heart and emotive impulses. Reasons and rationality were denied entry into any would-be time consuming alliance.

"That'd be too soon, don't you think?"

"I know, but it's really important, very imperative that you go."

"Was that the glitch Jane mentioned to me?"

"Yes, well, in part. I plan to open orphanages in Sivals, Kenya and South Sudan. I needed African advisors on this project. I got two very important and able African professionals. They were supposed to meet me today, but one of them had to cancel the flight because of call of duty. P.D. Michael, a professor at Columbia University in New York City, has made it to Day-Town. I've sent someone to pick him up at the airport. Osmani Osmani, the second advisor, had to attend to an emergency."

"I don't think I can make it a day after tomorrow."

"Think about it tonight and give me a response first thing in the morning."

"Mr. Burns, that's too soon!"

"Call me Isaac. It's important. I chose you because I trust my informants."

Chris knew what Isaac's last statement meant. Going to Africa was Chris's start-over chance and he had to use it. Nothing made sense whatsoever.

21

The elders received Uncle D's letter. They were sitting under Uncle D's mango tree with two mysterious visitors. They were two women: strange but beautiful, fast-talking but sensible. Having changed their thoughts about the woman's role in their society given Uncle D's influence, they let Nyanbenypieth officiate over what the visitors had come to convey. One of the visitors was a middle-age lady with a class appearance. Her appearance, dressing and gait, looked regal. Her companion was a lady the villagers thought had lost her skin color. She looked like a ghost, a real ghost.

However, everyone was excited to hear that the funny looking lady with feline eyes was Uncle D's friend. Kids wanted to touch her hair, her skin; to closely check her eyes. To them, her hair looked like a fine horse's tail; very beautiful.

"He sure is a man of wonder," one elder said.

"And he can make friends with anyone. What a special man?" another elder added.

Nyanbenypieth rose majestically and waved everyone to be silent. She moved her lips hesitantly and looked around. As if with contempt, she smiled.

"Uncle D never ceased to surprise us. And he always does it in a manner that warms our hearts. In the name of our elders, our village and our ancestors, we welcome you. You may tell us what you have come here for."

It was searing hot but still. The dusty wind had blessed their meeting with an absence. The dust-storm had listened to the needy.

At last! After a brief hesitation, the middle-age lady rose and smiled shyly. She appeared less strange: her face, her nose, her hair, were all familiar. Her skin was slightly ghostly, almost yellow.

"It's a great honor to be here today with you. Werpionkor means a lot to Uncle D and his friends. My name is Mama. My friend here is called Sister J. Uncle D will not be able to make it to Werpionkor this year because of other engagements. Instead of sending you a letter to let you know, he sent us here as a sign of respect for the hospitality you've shown him for all these years. He sent us as a sign of respect to you," Mama said and sat down.

"As it has become a norm with his arrival, we've brought all the things he always brings with him. Remember, if his other engagement finishes in time, he'll join you for the rest of his time here. His apologies are abundant," Sister J added.

Nyanbenypieth smiled and shot up.

"The elders of this village have never disappointed this village in wisdom. They know a good and wise man. He doesn't have to apologize. He's not an idle man," she said and walked toward Sister J.

Nyanbenypieth nodded and ten young men walked toward two pick-up trucks parked next to the hut. Mama and Sister J walked around greeting elders one by one as everyone rejoiced in the exploits of Uncle D.

As the night fell, Sister J and Mama sat together with the elders as the young and the brave danced their night away around the bonfire. It was a heart-warming back to basics. Dark, oiled faces sweated the night away. Genuine strength, real excitement, unblemished beauty and innocent purity of heart filled the welcoming, starry African night. Girls swayed their stocky African hips teasingly at men flexing their dark, shiny muscles. Their white eyes and white teeth shone and twinkled brightly behind their black complexions. The dance was rhythmic as they circled round and round. At times they jumped up and down in perfect ease. What a sight to behold? Their singing was a little discordant but enjoyable.

Sister J was having the best day of her life. Mama had dozed off through the lullabying sounds of the village songs and rhythmic dances. It was time for Sister J to shake the meagre stock making her hips. She knew the smiles on their faces exemplified the whiteness of their hearts. She suddenly stopped as her heart and mind flooded with alienating ideas. They were poor, dusty, ragged and clueless. Yet, their lives were fulfilling and innocently admirable. They hated no one, wished no one down, and cared for themselves. Their organized and respectful ways made them humble and courteous to respectful visitors. Their wealth was acquired through strict honesty; societal status was earned not demanded with force. It was a society too rudimentary and humbling not to envy. She stared at Mama as she peacefully slept on the front row among the elders.

22

Isaac met P.D in Grecian Alfa on Sunday morning. He was a fine man with refined intelligence. His cautious approach to issues impressed Isaac more than his knowledge of the world. Isaac was seated at the far corner of the restaurant when P.D walked in. You couldn't miss him. Tall, stocky, dark-skinned and bearded, P.D walked confidently and lankily after talking to a waitress.

"P.D Michael, right? My pleasure," Isaac said

"Mr. Isaac Burns, I must say."

P.D had a refined African accent. Not too deep to be African but not really lost to be North American.

"Please have a seat."

P.D looked around then said: "Thank you."

"My pleasure...my pleasure indeed!"

Isaac said and glanced at the waitress in what appeared like a coded signal. With an impressive athleticism, she legged toward them in quick lovely strides and looked at P.D.

"Mr. Michael, the young lady would want to talk to you," Isaac said with a smile as the young beautiful lady looked at P.D.

"What would you like to drink, sir?" she said with a heart-warming smile.

"I'll have Fanta in a brown glass with no ice in it."

"You gotta be kidding me! I mean...this is..." Isaac marveled.

"That's true, Mr. Burns."

"And I love that choice...and you Mr. Burns?" the waitress remarked.

"Well, I'll have two SMIRNOFFS."

The waitress tilted her head to the left and swayed away slowly. Isaac looked at P.D and said: "I'm glad you came. You have no idea what this means to me."

"I'm here in North America making a good living. This is the least I can do for Africa."

"It's sad that one has to give back only when well off."

"You're right, but that's the reality of today's world...of our world I should say."

"Exactly!"

"*They're exactly exploiting them in a way they don't know*," a man at a nearby table said.

Isaac and P.D turned their heads to the near-by table. The guests at that table seemed to be engaged in their own heated debate.

P.D looked at Isaac and said: "I went to Nairobi, Kenya, last summer to give a lecture on African Indigenous religions. After the lecture a small South Sudanese boy walked up to me and said: 'Mr. Michael, that boy over there said you've sold your soul.' The boy said pointing at another boy and ran away."

"What was that supposed to mean?"

"The world has gone to the point where one can't assume anything or undermine anyone."

Isaac tried to connect what P.D had said to the realities of the world. He couldn't get the connection.

"Which means?"

"*It means your help is not welcome and we'll teach you that you don't belong here.*"

The same man at the nearby table said again. The answers were so specific to Isaac's questions that Isaac thought the man was answering him. Isaac grew nervous; a little annoyed.

The annoying guests on the nearby table were four: a Caucasian man and a Caucasian woman and two African-Pandians. Isaac didn't know who was exactly answering his questions among them. From the answers, the guys seemed to have paid close attention to what Isaac and P.D were discussing. The specificity of the answers was so exact that Isaac was tempted to ask them. Civility straddled Isaac's path to negativity though. He safely and smartly severed the thought. Asking people he didn't know was not such a good idea. The guests sitting next to them looked intellectual and engaged in their own debate. After a period of dialectic with his own self, Isaac settled for a coincidence. However, Isaac was becoming nervous and confused. *They were so specific.* Concentration was becoming tricky, the feel-good sentiment P.D's arrival had engendered was ebbing away. Real world!

As the waitress came back with their drinks, Isaac saw someone at the door. Still nervous and agitated, he looked back to check the annoying guests at the neighboring table. They were gone. He couldn't understand how. Their presence was as real as the threat of death when life is sweet and full of promise. And as he knew, anything that can't be proved, never happened. Simple empiricism! *Was I hallucinating? No, I wasn't.*

"Were there people next to us a moment ago? I'm getting confused," Isaac asked P.D.

P.D tried to hide his surprised face. Isaac didn't notice it anyway.

"Yes, there was a fine young lady and three men at that table."

Isaac didn't want to think too much about the annoying guests. To salvage his deteriorating mood, he turned his attention to the man at the door. By intuition, Isaac assumed the man at the door had something to do with them.

"That's Mr. Osmani," P.D said matter-of-factly.

"Osmani?"

"Indeed."

Isaac was lost for words. After Osmani's call, Isaac had no hope Osmani would be coming. However, Isaac, with good pretensions, didn't show his disappointment after Osmani's failure to join them. He remained a stately gentleman. All he maintained was nothing but praise for these African intellectuals. Looking at the stocky figure approaching them, Isaac stared indifferently. There he was: not short but not tall either. Osmani had talked briefly to a young man at the front desk and walked confidently toward P.D's and Isaac's table.

"Osmani Osmani," he said, his huge palm engulfing Isaac's.

"Isaac Burns."

"P.D Michael."

"I thought you'd gone to Sivals," Isaac asked hastily and precociously, more confused than surprised.

"The ambassador commissioned someone to take care of the mission so I could come here."

"That's very gentlemanly of him," P.D remarked.

"What did you tell him? I feel hugely gratified," Isaac asked, still confused.

"I didn't tell him anything. I'd guess the ambassador received your message very well. He has great respect for you. A few hours after we talked, the ambassador called and told me you called for a favor. He's very supportive of development initiatives in Africa, especially Sivals."

A stream of hot blood quickly rushed to Isaac's head. He felt dizzy. Confused and stupefied, Isaac kept quiet. P.D and Osmani had probably noticed his reaction. Biological reactions on a Caucasian person's face can't be missed.

Isaac obviously didn't call the ambassador. That fact alone sent crippling jitters down Mr. Burns' spine.

I sure didn't. Why's Osmani lying to me? What's Osmani plotting?

Isaac stared at Osmani with a begrudging intensity. He couldn't place his suspicion anywhere on the man. Osmani was freely and confidently chatting away with P.D. Dazed by Osmani's possible plot and potential consequences, Isaac sat there lost in thought as P.D and Osmani hit it off.

Something was terribly wrong. Isaac could sense it but he couldn't see it. Business atmosphere, modicum and experience in multicultural environments helped him stay composed not to betray his thoughts through any stupid words or actions. He was becoming nervous yet maturely self-controlled.

Is this a dream? Please tell me it is.

23

Isaac remained cautious with Osmani. However, he immediately became dazzled and enamored by Osmani's eloquence. After his surprise show at Grecian Alfa, Osmani became more accessible than P.D. These guys became his advisors about Africa: its land, people, weather, economy and all that he needed to know. With time and humbling study, Isaac became conversant with many African tribal rituals; their emergence, significance and the appropriate ways they are officiated. This filled Isaac with enormous pride and earned him respect from home and abroad. He would soon be invited by business giants in Day-Town to speak to them about the uniqueness of the tall, smooth and dark-skinned Nilotes of South Sudan called the Jieng (Dinka). He felt both honored and flattered.

Osmani's diplomatic voice and status became a great help to Isaac.

On the other hand, however, Isaac came to realize that P.D dreaded rationalizing things; especially things he feared or things that pricked deep into the heart of Africa as a continent and his people as *black*. He avoided making high profile speeches and his stance on many African issues was not known well outside his profession and interested parties. But Michael was an accomplished academic and scholar whose objectivity was Humean and ethical outlook marred in Kantanism.

P.D's exacerbating and knotty nature made Osmani an instrumental lean-on tool; a man who could make sense out of anything even nonsense. As Isaac came to realize, Osmani liked rationalizing African issues and he liked public addresses. Without exaggerating,

Osmani was Isaac's man. With a little of garrulousness, Osmani still backed up his peppery methods with hard facts. His piety was unwaveringly authentic and grounded in flattering science.

Wind doesn't blow because god told it to. Lightening, Thunder, Hurricane, Earthquake and Tsunami don't occur because god is angry. Disease and human tragedies are not god's retributive rendition for immorality and impiety. Simply put, Osmani wasn't a face-value man. A breeze on his face on a hot summer afternoon was his natural delight; snow-blanched backyard wasn't, to him, a divine rendition but a simple sight to be breathed in.

However, Isaac was very crafty and smart when it came to what he talked about with the two men. Business ventures in Africa are always dogged by controversies. He wasn't aware of his ventures being controversial; however, a smart man always leaves room for *what ifs*! Among other things, Isaac always remembered one advice from one of his friends. The advice was a seemingly objective and realistic view on helping Africans. It's a view that invokes what philosophers have come to call Singer's Principle: doing something moral if the cost of doing it isn't detrimental to the well-being of the moral agent acting.

"How'd you feel when you help six of them live well? Well, you'd have helped them go to school, find good foods, go for further studies in Great Britain, or here in Panda or US or Canada. They'd then settle as decent human beings leading decent lives in the most decent human sophistication. How'd you feel about yourself? Fine I guess; great or philanthropically a superhuman. But tell me one thing, Isaac: If you go back to Africa and see all other hungry, malnourished, chronically diseased children and women; will you stop helping them because you did your job, or will you go on and take another six? At times you'd convince your soul that you did what you did and if you didn't help the misery before you, god would not blame you. Would you feel any better? But suppose you became too humane and a nonpareil soul. You went ahead and took another six! Your taking them, surely, wouldn't help your soul, because your second help, unlike the first one, would be something out of guilt. You'd be praised, but you'd be nothing short of stupid inside.

"You can't do it. You've been given your life, live it. Helping them is vast and unattainable, but helping yourself out of that is something you have control over—attainable to the highest peak. If you can help them live well without losing anything, then well and good. But I can't stop you from being a good man, a moral man; a superhuman. If it doesn't cost you much then do it, otherwise, you're doing yourself a disservice."

That was his friend Arnold. Arnold died five yours earlier in Congo where he was working with Catholic Relief Service (CRS). He was shot dead by an HIV positive African Catholic catechist who believed CRS was intentionally refusing to give condoms to local people to exterminate them. The ardent catechist alleged without argument that HIV was designed to kill his people with pious brutality and self-righteousness.

"However pious we are, our human nature is god's fault. How should we be punished for having the feelings he gave us. I didn't ask anyone to make me feel the way I feel. However, like any conventionally responsible human being, I've tried with all my powers to control my feelings. God knows I tried. Now, I'm being punished because of how I feel with this end-of-the-world idea of self-control. This will be the end of this nonsense."

The catechist had said before shooting Arnold.

Arnold's advice almost became a great daily temptation to Isaac. Day and night, he reflectively resisted it to a large extent. Any random full moon made Arnold's brutal honesty flicker in Isaac's intuition. A drive through the slums of Nairobi, Soweto, Juba and Hayiroh elevated the enormity of Africa's problem and further authenticated Arnold's advice. Our dear Isaac struggled with a heart-breaking dilemma. *Can I do the impossible or make profit?*

However, Isaac's capitalist mind didn't dismiss Arnold's words outright. He refined them for the purpose he wanted to accomplish. At a small cost: Sweet Capitalism!

As things moved on well between the African gentlemen and Isaac, P.D's wife became a bit of uneasiness for Isaac. She showed up in the mix without Isaac realizing. He'd at first dismissed her as simply an African woman who'd no much to say in a gentlemen's circle. Good enough, Isaac was deep into African traditionalism so much so that his perception of the African woman was poisoned. She was a charcoal black, slender woman with snow-white teeth. Her dark face exaggerated the whiteness of her smile. The annoyingly humbling part was the fact that her face was graced by beautifully, hilly and beckoning dimples. However, behind the dimples and the white smile lurked a poisonous Afro-centrism. And for good reasons, Isaac was always consciously nervous in the company of P.D and his wife. P.D had a wife who was smarter than any smarter person Isaac had ever seen. She had a thing with words.

But his fear of Mrs. Michael didn't deter him. He wanted to, and he did indeed try to, understand some perplexing occurrences. The mental recurrence of the problem of the guys at the Grecian Alfa and why Osmani blatantly lied to him were on top of his list.

"Well...I mean...I believe if the West really wanted to honestly help poor countries, it could," Isaac said to the Michaels on one of their uncomfortable days in New York City. He'd dropped by the Michaels' place after which they went out to have dinner at a Japanese restaurant together with Angela, P.D's wife. *Kadoma Sushi* on 301 W 45th ST was P.D's favorite place in Manhattan. A good meal with good friends in a familiar place is an unbeatable delight. With the calm engendered by the feel of the place, they ate sushi in a serene, traditional, oriental atmosphere.

"You're right, but there are many implications of what you've just said. The *will* might be there with the west, let us say, but we have to understand what that means. What I'm saying is that, we have to understand the political and social state of minds of African politicians. Are they really incapable of maximizing their resources or is it the case that there are no resources at all. What I see is that the west might be interested in helping or is even helping as we speak, but is the *will* there with our leaders to maximize whatever little help the west provides? I mean ugh..."

P.D was trying to respond with a lengthy and twisted entice-ment. He was trying to make a point but he found himself hand-waving. Blaming African leaders bluntly in his wife's presence was a thorn under his feet. The end of that kind of talk was apparent to him: fortuitous self-gratification, as Angela always said.

P.D always searched for words to spice up the blame if he had to blame.

Angela never believed in the supposed corruption of African leaders as the sole or the overriding cause of poverty and political turmoil in Africa. Iceberg always has a bottom, she always said.

"You mean corruption?" Isaac asked; a little intrigued.

"Right, we might simplify it like that but it goes far beyond that," P.D said and looked at Angela.

She looked away, trying to hide her amused face. Her frivolous address to P.D's take on the topic never changed. Even in the presence of others, she duly maintained her stance.

"Well, I believe there is a part I can blame on the African lead-ers, but we also have to remember that they're subjected to many conditions by western leaders, western businesses and historical ties. There're many selfish western entrepreneurs who're after making money and don't care any bit about the people. Some recruit the help of corrupt senior government officials."

Isaac proudly said and looked at P.D then glanced momentarily at Angela, feeling confident.

"We also have to remember that these men are business people whether they're government related agents or private individuals. Even humanitarian workers have something in their lives that propels them; that inner, small inaudible voice that says: 'they'll look at you differently after this.' If these people are not propelled by material needs, then the mere fact that they feel great after having helped someone is a prize. You can't help someone and don't feel anything. That'd be extraordinary or outwardly. Just as there's no such a thing as a free lunch, there's no such a thing as 'I'm doing this altruistically or pro bono.' There's always a prize; whether material or spiritual.

"This is their sole purpose of going to Africa, I mean, the business related and government agents. They don't decide to go to Africa as a good-will decision to go and help these poor Africans. If you have one or two clean, unselfish, non-hypocritical business leaders who don't misuse those chances then we might thank the gods for them. But those monsters just don't care and it's the duty of the ministers in question to know that the ordinary persons are their people. It's not the businessmen who should give any kick about them."

Angela said, sat back on her seat and sipped her Nestea with a young girl's girlie air.

Isaac felt a little uneasy, his digestive system working faster than he could eat.

Angela talked as if she knew something about Isaac. However much Angela's words sounded intentionally sarcastic, he wasn't going to bluff though. There was something about Angela, even when she wasn't speaking, that unnerved Isaac. The way she looked at him was not normal and the diffused target of her opinion was patronizing. However, Isaac was a real gentleman.

"You know, I mean...look, Angela, just because they're ministers doesn't mean they're angels or they're rich. There're few good ministers but there're greedy and unscrupulous ones who're out there to grab any simple catch at the expense of the people and the economy. If we in the west sing clear conscience: being leaders of the world, moralists...then why can't we lead by example. That's why I don't blame the poor ministers. I know we have our interests: economic, diplomatic or whatever..."

Even with the words coming out beautifully and intentionally soundly, Isaac still found the words, the food and the drink hard to handle. Anytime he uttered them, the words were increasingly becoming bigger and hotter than the spicy and multi-colored food in front of him. Having borne the weight of Angela's words with gentlemanly exactness, Isaac looked at P.D but he was looking down; eating his food with pronounced and remarkable calm. P.D perhaps looked down to avoid commenting on the predicament. His action might have been pure innocence. No doubt, there was great effort required for Isaac to look at Angela. When Isaac ogled at her direction, she was staring unflinchingly at him.

She smiled; deceptively perhaps and said: "At least one good person has to lead the way. If you think of the suffering African-Americans people went through here in America, you'll realize that it wasn't only the voice of the oppressed Blacks that did the work. It was some section of the oppressors that helped ease the struggle. We're lucky..."

"All those who helped in the civil rights movement were oppressed. There was not a single soul that was not oppressed among the civil rights people," P.D said after a long period of silence; interrupting Angela with a very good intention.

"I know what you mean, but they only became oppressed after they joined the struggle."

Angela riposted defensively.

"No!" P.D said lightly and went back to his seafood. Both Isaac and Angela curiously stared at him like they were waiting for him to save them from an impending doom.

"Can you explain that my dear?" Angela said with a comic frown on her face; a kind of Mr. Bean's surprised frown. P.D remained unbelievably calm as if he'd heard nothing. Isaac, in all essence, didn't know what P.D meant.

"You know why a section of the oppressors joined the civil rights movement in the first place, right?" P.D melodramatically asked but then continued to seriously savor his food.

"Well, they were oppressed in their spirits and conscience, I guess?" Isaac found himself saying to the delight of both Angela and P.D. From the look on Angela's face, Isaac felt gratified. Putting a non-sarcastic smile on Mrs. Michael's face was like performing a miracle. However, something still displeased Isaac after correctly hitting on what P.D meant. Mrs. and Mr. Michael were looking at Isaac with surprise. It was as if a douchebag had just had a flash of intelligence. *I know I've been misunderstood all along.*

"There's nothing more you can say P.D. I know that's what you meant. Sometimes some words don't need to be explained. They just sink into the soul. I don't know why that slipped out of my conscience. Their souls where oppressed for a long time and they couldn't take it anymore. And..."

"They wanted to release their souls from oppression and dispense with any guilt in their conscience," P.D said interrupting his wife after a period of eating and silence.

"Right there dear," she said then turned to Isaac and said: "Isaac, you're the man!"

Angela's face was blank so Isaac didn't know what judgment to pass. Was her compliment truthful or sarcastic?

"Perhaps!" Isaac said rather withdrawn and started drinking his glass of red French wine.

Everyone remained silent as the words already uttered started to sink in. In a pretentious battle of brains, what's true and what's falsely asserted aren't always easy to differentiate. After a period of eating and sipping with reflective calm, Angela looked at Isaac and smiled.

"Oh dear, I didn't finish what I was saying. We're lucky to have you, Isaac. Good people like you, who know the world well enough and who're moral in every sense, should take the lead."

Angela said and smiled demonically at Isaac, and broadly for the first time.

Isaac didn't take the words very well. He choked on his food and had to excuse himself to go to the washroom. After coming back from the washroom, Isaac requested that P.D took him to his hotel. Knowing that Isaac cared a lot about his health, the Michaels knew he wasn't feeling okay.

24

P.D drove Isaac to his hotel room. Manhattan's night is always alive and lively. The streets were crowded with people going to god-knows-where. Streets and street lights flickered by as P.D drove on. Rowdy yellow taxis honked their way past as pedestrian dangerously and carelessly squeezed their way through; some even jaywalking. The country music FM radio station in P.D's car sounded distant, soft and drowsily beckoning, the night outside enticingly smiling.

Isaac sat reflectively as he enjoyed New York's night sailing beautifully by. Angela's words raced dangerously through his head. He failed to understand why her words sounded honest and intentionally promotional of his work yet his conscience dismissed them. *Am I getting paranoid?*

"How're you feeling now, Isaac?" P.D asked after driving silently for a while. He was a man of few words and he hoped Isaac knew that.

"Yes! It was such a good night and we talked about things that made me think a lot about my work as a philanthropist."

"What's there to think about? You should see yourself as exemplary...or better still, evangelize the nature of your work so others, who are well-off, can emulate you."

"I guess so. However, I feel I'm not doing much."

"You're right. That's the nature of good people; never satisfied with doing good work. I have to warn you though. If this becomes an obsession, it might lead to your demise."

Isaac didn't say any other word. He jumped down from the car, waved at Isaac and walked to the door as one of his body guards grabbed the jacket from him.

§

P.D drove back to the restaurant with a clear air of appreciation for Isaac. He found Angela listening to a soothing Japanese music she'd requested. They left the restaurant with smiles on their faces, albeit for different reasons.

"I've always taken this for granted but how did you know Isaac exactly?" Angela asked P.D when they'd gone back home. She was putting on her night gown as Isaac groped for his pajamas in the closet. With a rude smile on her face, she slowly sat down on their bed anticipating P.D's response. P.D slowly turned and stared curiously at her. However, he decided not to dwell on why she was asking that night of all the nights.

"His friend, who's also my colleague at the university, told me that a friend of his was looking for someone who can reliably help him know more about Africans, Africa and its complex problems. That's how we became friends. Why?"

She smiled and said: "When I talked about non-hypocritical businessmen in the west, he became uneasy. He didn't even look me in the eye."

"What're you insinuating?"

"I'm not suggesting anything my dear. I'm just curious. When I continued the topic he'd started, he choked on the food."

Angela said and smiled again.

"Don't be ridiculous!"

"I'm sorry, okay? I'm not suggesting anything take it that way."

Angela said and laughed with her usual 'I'm serious but don't take me seriously' kind of laughter.

P.D found some truth in what Angela was saying but he dismissed it on the ground that he'd be tempted to contemplatively dwell on it and possibly be tempted to ask Isaac. For all P.D knew, Isaac was a powerful man. If he crossed Isaac's way, he'd have no life in the U.S. Being a rich Pandian with vivid, powerful and enviable business interests and connections in the US, Isaac's influence was ubiquitous. Getting unwisely and conspiratorially in Isaac's way was an unthinkable offense to contemplate.

Isaac was one of the capitalists' voices who determined where politicians' suns rose and set every day. They initiated and supported political policies and modalities that determined whether democratic moons would appear at night or not. Wind blew from where they sat and smelled of them. They are a few belief systems shy of godly reverence.

There was no reason to believe Angela's words, but there was no reason not to believe them either. But either way, he chose to assume nothing happened and nothing was ever uttered. However, P.D was rattled by the thought that Angela could do secret inquires about Isaac. Not only was what Isaac could do to them dangerous to think about, the mere thought of anyone doing clandestine inquiries about Isaac was dreadful.

What P.D feared the most was the fact that Isaac could arrange anything against his wife. He grew both apprehensive and confused. The only reason why P.D came to the west was to make an honest living while airing his opinion. No one was going to make him throw it away. Not Angela of all people. He was happy with his resolution though consciously cautious.

No one could ever fault Isaac if Isaac framed him. No one would want to bother about him, an African, who was neck to neck with Americans in a way everyone felt uncomfortable with. He had to fight his conscience and implore Angela to assume nothing was wrong with Isaac; that nothing ever happened.

Angela understood P.D's position. They resolved not to talk about Isaac's suspicious action that night. Of course, Angela was a smart woman so she knew what it meant to go against a man such as Isaac. The Michaels agreed to keep quiet about it. However, Angela swore secretly not to forget the incident. For their safety, Angela promised not to talk about it further; however, she maintained that she'd continue to give her opinion in case the topic came up. With that understanding, P.D decided that leaving her out of their meetings would make things a little easier to handle. That didn't work. The decision was hard to effect considering how close they were. A person of Angela's caliber wasn't like a little girl whose attention could be dispensed with by giving her simple douchebag trickery. Both Mr. Burns and P.D admitted, however, that Angela was intellectually stimulating despite her unorthodox take on current issues.

25

Chris talked to Judy with heart-warming delight and hope the same day he talked to Isaac. Looking into the mirror, he realized he'd internalized his satisfaction with Isaac's request. His face was glowingly healthy and his eyes shining with novel flair. Smiles characterized his face and agility stamped his enthused spirit. The air in his apartment smelled fresh and relaxing. His jolly spirit was elevated by Judy's receptive understanding. That girl never ceased to amaze him. She did it in a manner that made him want to cling to her for all entity.

After he explained to her what Isaac had said, she received it with humble and calm 'I'm happy for you' kind of a way. She was with no doubt, positive about it. Chris was however a little curious about why she accepted it that quick. He'd anticipated a staunch opposition in the name of love. Having explained everything to her, Chris stared but she wasn't sarcastic or mocking him in any way. She was indeed supportive.

"I'd be concerned considering the fact that you don't know the content of the mission. However, I believe you're strong, smart and focused. You could make a fortune out of this. This is your big chance honey. I feel funny saying this about Africa considering the fact that you're leaving Panda," she'd said.

Chris thought for a moment. She had the same thought he had. *Can it be love? Our thoughts matched.* After a brief reflective pause, Chris dismissed the superstitious thought.

"I didn't expect this," Chris confusedly said.

"Didn't expect what honey?"

"I thought you'd object to my going to Africa."

"Are you kidding me? This is your life. I don't have to be that selfish. I love you and that's why I need you to be happy."

Chris was on cloud infinity. It was of course a folly for him to be very excited as he knew nothing of why he was going to Hayiroh, Sivals. But it was possibly a start of a new life; whatever that life was. He knew many people who went to Africa on vacation only to turn it into their homes. They created a passion for the land and its people. You wonder why? Considering going to Africa as a god-given opportunity, Chris did what Isaac had told him to do.

"If you have African friends, talk to them. It'd give you a sense of the people and what the land would be like to you. I know a fairly good deal about Africa, however, I'd like you to experience the feeling first hand from real Africans."

Isaac was pretentiously right.

Chris had to see Little to tell him about his going to Africa. Though not African himself, Little was well connected with a number of Africans who could be of some assistance to Chris. Judy's friends could also be helpful, Chris thought.

As everyone knew, Little stood against anyone who talked ill of Africans. His position was unintelligibly maintained though. He'd just dismiss any argument against Africans even when the argument was valid and sound.

In high school, Little's personality was hidden in a blank stare and short responsive sentences in class. At break time, he'd sit alone reading lifestyle magazines. What was impressive about Little was his love of calm conversations when anyone sat next to him. Not at any time did he initiate any conversation, however, when started, Little would respond with interest coupled with intelligible anecdotes. This is what drew Chris closer to Little. They'd sit and talk about fear in racists, the divisiveness of multiculturalism, the ridiculousness of god, nonexistence of truth in politics and the impossibility of bumping into *pure* altruism. Chris still fondly remembered those days.

Chris happily arrived at Little's house. No one was at home. It was late morning, about ten or eleven. The weather was remarkably welcoming... a nice winter day. He was glad it didn't snow that day. As Chris was about to enter his car to head back home, he heard someone calling him: *Chris!* He slowly looked back and the sturdy Little Michael was staring at him. Grace was walking toward the house.

"Hey!" Chris said hesitantly.

"What brings you here at this time of the day...in the morning?"

Chris sighed, looked at Little and said: "I came to see you."

"I had some stupid glitches with my suppliers and the police. I spent the night in custody, can you believe that? Can't you wait till evening? I'll make a note about it. My guys will not scare you this time," he said smiling.

Uncertain of what to say, Chris kept quiet for a while then said: "I'll be there at six ...sharp."

"Great! See you then."

Little said and walked to the door as Chris turned and paced back to his car.

In high school, Little struggled with weight issues. His weight gave him insecurities, which he expressed in either anger or self-imposed isolation. However, that wasn't what bothered Chris about Little and his existential complexities. Chris didn't have to worry about being stopped by the police because he was driving a nice car. People around him always assumed he was the smarter of the two. Honestly, he hated that.

There was always fear in people's eyes, on the street, in the presence of Little, unless someone saw Chris walking along side Little. That uneasiness with Little existential prominence made Chris uneasy and questioning of his own existence. *What did I do to deserve my privilege?* With all his heart, Chris prayed for a situation in which he'd be on the defense against his existential essence and instrumentality to the society. That was a North American natural impossibility. In high school, that never happened. He prayed for a day on which he'd have the opportunity to painfully say 'you don't know what it's like to be like me.'

As much as he wanted to believe he was privileged, he still felt lost and emotionally guilty. He wanted to feel what's like to be Little.

Little had to prove he was intelligent. Chris didn't have to. It was natural. Little had to prove he was friendly with everything about him exuding exceptional innocuousness. No one saw the innocuous essence of Little without proof except Chris.

Chris went to countless workshops aimed at combating the effects of racism; however, he became even more disappointed with both their contents and methods of delivery. What disappointed Chris the most was the facilitators' attitude and innocent verbalization of their beliefs. While intending to claim that all races are equal, they innocently and unknowingly promoted themselves over and above the people they were trying to help. Saying that one is privileged in a society, while true in every sense, mocks the essence of all campaigns against racism. Chris avoided any situation that'd reflect him as privileged. Hard as that was, Chris devised situations that fostered his equality with others not situations that emphasized how privileged he was.

Now, with his economic troubles, he could perhaps say the magical words he'd always wanted to say: 'You don't know what it's like to be me.' And there was no way the brown-haired, hook-nosed, pink-faced and talkative Chris liked the sound and the content of the words.

26

Little made himself comfortable in the living room as Grace brought him a cup of hot coffee just like he liked it.

"I'm sorry mum. I didn't mean to do that again," Little said remorsefully looking at Grace after handing him the cup.

Still not saying a word, she gave Little a look of a disappointed mother and left for the kitchen. She slowly walked back into the living room holding a cup of tea. With the same blank and reproachful stare, she sipped her tea once and sat down on the couch.

"I'm old. I don't need many words to be convinced as to whether you were right or wrong. I know what happened and why you did what you did. But this is what this society wants from you. If you'd gone in for life on this petty offense, would you say you're innocent? You're a societal hypothesis; a societal experimental procedure, not a societal paradigmatic man. "

She paused, took another sip and said: "You struck a man in the face. That's all they need to know. Do they need to know the circumstances that led to the man being knocked in the face? No! Or maybe you should read *Black Like Me*."

Little didn't know what to say. They sat in silence for a while as Grace gracefully sipped her tea. Little's coffee was still sitting on a coffee-table next to him. It was untouched as he sat thoughtfully.

"I just lost it ma. I can't even remember when I did it exactly."

"Does it matter to anyone?"

"No, but..."

A phone rang loudly interrupting Little and disturbing the uncertain but quiet ambience of the house. He stared curiously at

Grace, who stared back at him, still sipping her tea. After a few more rings, Grace got up, walked wobblingly to the phone and picked it up.

"Grace."

For some strange reasons, Grace didn't like hellos. She preferred saying her name instead. There was a very short pause after she answered the phone then she looked at little.

"It's for you," she said.

Little awkwardly looked at her, walked clumsily to the phone and grabbed the receiver.

"Mr. Michael speaking...who am I speaking to?"

"Dengdit," the voice on the other line blurted.

"Dengdit? Dengdit who?"

There was a short pause as Little tried to think. The name sounded familiar.

He laughed. "I'd rather you stuck with Dengdit."

The man sounded confident yet impolite.

Little crooked his lips upwards: "Don't you think that's somehow rude?"

"I understand. I'm sorry about that, but I've no choice in talking the way I'm talking."

"Wha—, what're you talking about?"

"Mr. Michael, let's not argue about my name."

"What do you want?"

"Nothing!"

Little's lips angrily curved upwards. "Then leave me alone."

The man laughed. "I can't."

"Why? Are you drunk or something?"

He laughed. "Is Chris meeting you tonight?"

Little was hesitant. *How did he know that?*

"He's meeting me, yes. Why?"

"I'd like to meet you too."

"Noooo!"

The man laughed with a whizzing sound. "You've already agreed to my meeting you."

Little found the talk silly and pointedly annoying.

"This is ridiculous."

He whizzed laughingly again. "Indeed it is. Anything we do is ridiculous, don't you just hate that. Anyway, I don't want to waste your time. The number that appears there is my number. Don't hesitate to call me if you change your mind about meeting me."

The man whizzed his laugh and hanged up. Little turned to look at Grace but she was gone. He sat for a while and a thought struck him.

"That can't be!"

He sprang up and literally ran to his room. In his drawer, there were letters and parcels. He frantically schemed through them.

His lower lip was up and out. "No way!" he said as he stared at the letter.

§

Dengdit's influence on Little had strangely strayed onto his mind after Grace bailed him out. He was the man who changed his view of himself and of the world. But the man was dead. Little knew that with concrete certainty. It's been more than twenty years since the man died.

He's alive? That can't be! Little fondly remembered one of their informative and transformative talks.

"You haven't explained to me what happened to the guy who went to college," Little had asked.

As was always the case, Dengdit acted irresponsibly before he answered any questions. Little stared as Dengdit first wolfed down his food. Dengdit then started licking the plate disgustingly and hungrily. He then rotated his neck. The muscles on his neck rattled as he belched, looking at Little. Feeling nauseous, Little frowned and stopped eating.

"Why? You want to go to college?"

Little didn't know what to say.

Dengdit looked at Little but Little only nodded. With occasionally sincere smile, he gave Little a funny stare, started laughing and left. Little then assumed the man despised him. On the third day from their first encounter, Dengdit sat next to Little in the dining hall.

"You wanted to know what happened to the guy."

Little shook his head.

"C'mon kid!"

Before Dengdit could tell Little anything, two gigantic guys walked to their table. Little tried to leave, but one of the giants grabbed his left shoulder and said: "Where're you going, college bug?"

"Did you just guess or did you hear me talk to him?" Dengdit asked the offending giant.

"What does he look like to you, a convict?" the giant said with a smile. Without saying anything else, the giant stared contemptuously at Little and frowned. After the interruption, Dengdit smiled and said: "He wants to go to college."

With demonic intentions, all the offending mouths around the table burst into a monstrous laughter.

"You can go now, college boy!" the offending guy said, still laughing hysterically.

Little there and then started to hate them; really bad. Dengdit, who he thought was becoming his friend, didn't help him at all. Looking contemptuously at them one by one, Little felt like his eyes were being rubbed against the world's hottest pepper.

Two months later Little was, to his delight and relief, released from jail. With his developing contempt for the bullying gigantic guys, Little never bothered to ask Dengdit about the fate of the 'college guy'.

However, in a strange turn of events just a year after Little started the bar, he received a letter from Dengdit. Dengdit explained to him what happened to the college guy. He did it in small bits.

July 21, 1985

Little Michael,

We all have hearts and minds to be what this society wants us to be. But does the society really want us to be what it wants us to be? No, Little, No, a thousand NOS. All there is is a realists' factory of intentions. This society wants us to be where I'm writing from; where my thoughts can be ridiculed however sound they are.

We're forced into singing, we're forced into sports, and we're forced into quick-money making. All in the name of one thing: 'they've natural talent for it'.

Bullshit! If you thought someone else wrote this letter, Mr. Michael, then just know that brains are rotting in jails, just the way they want them.

Dengdit, a Piper Brother

After receiving that letter, Little first didn't figure out who 'Dengdit, a Piper Brother' was. The letter had no return address. It had no stamp either. Nothing. He couldn't write back. A good guess was that the letter was hand delivered, but why and how, he'd no idea. But then something flickered in Little; something beautiful, a yearning for knowledge and information. Obviously, he started to frequent the local university library. With insatiable appetite, he read Jeremy Bentham, Kant, Hume, Sartre, Fanon, Diop, Du bois...you name it. Soon after he registered for his high school equivalency examination, passed it and enrolled in a local university part-time to study political theory.

With appreciable knowledge of himself, the world and the people around him, Little felt like he'd became a man for the first time... alive; an African-Pandian. But that wasn't enough though. Dengdit's second letter made him wild. He'd go to the bathroom and cry after reading his words. All he kept on asking himself was *why.*

July 28, 1985

Little Michael,

My friend's name was Albert. After attending Central State University to study Political science to prepare him for Law School, Albert didn't know there'd be something else to come between him and law school.

But one week into his program, he called me and said: 'Dengdit, brother, this dude asked me how much my parents make a year. I told him I came here on a scholarship.

He said: "I don't know why I even asked the obvious!"' But Albert was experienced enough so he was a patient man. He ignored the engendered sentiment. Then second year saw Albert top of his class, becoming teachers' favorite. You're not too young to know what that means, Little Michael.

Dengdit, a Piper Brother

Now Little knew who was writing, but still, Little had no idea if it was Dengdit's letters or what he read in the liberal philosophical thoughts that made him informed and kept him reading on and on. Night and day, in his bar's office, he consumed writings about radical groups, about Pan-Africanists' movements, about Fanon, about Che Guevara, about Steve Biko and about Malcolm X. The world was crammed onto his palm, onto his fingertips. Informed and happy, Little felt like a man sitting on top of the tallest building in the world, having the most amazing, revealing and satisfying view of all corners of the earth's significant entitlements: in other words, the Augustinian god's vintage point.

Understandably, Little's views on punishment changed. Punishment was becoming revenge in his view. A man subjected to conditions beyond his control should be reformed not punished. A man whose biological determinants force him to do conventionally unspeakable crimes need prescriptive rehabilitation for societal benefits. Capital punishment underlined the closeness of humans to our animal nature; our true natural being. Calling Capital Punishment justice is to demean what could be rightfully called justice. Justice is to *try* to do the right thing to correct the misdeed. Appeasing the wronged by ascribing to our revengeful animaliness such as Capital Punishment is primordial and scathingly unprogressive.

But Little wanted to be alive. With the success of his business, he wanted to enjoy life; to bite hungrily at that sweet cake called good life. He decided that it was wise to therefore keep things to himself. But that was the beginning of the Afrocentric adventure which, he didn't know, would be long and arduous.

Seeing Little's increased obsession with books, Grace became increasingly concerned and suspicious of his love of reading.

"Don't read too much. I don't wanna lose you," Grace would gracefully put it.

His lips would delightfully curve up. "What reading does to the mind is like what swimming and gymnastics you go to everyday do to your body."

"And you know what gymnastics does to those who take it too far."

Little would smile at her and leave, so happy and innocent.

Little's office was inside the bar, at the back. It was no surprise he'd turned half of it into a library. Reading made Little embrace humility and simplicity; a strange phenomenon for a chubby, tall and basal-voiced Blackman. His mum was surprised that he didn't live an ordinary life of a well-off African-Pandian. No fancy cars, no fancy parties, and no hate of books. No one knew who he was in the mind and in the heart, except his mother and Chris.

What everyone assumed about him was what was conjectured to be the known phenomenon about black people: love of money and glamour without class, continuity and innovation.

After receiving the second letter from Dengdit, a year went by without any letter. Little felt both empty and curious. He decided to write.

November 19, 1986

Dengdit,

I wasn't a man until I met you. I wasn't a human being until I read your letters. But let me tell you one thing: all forces of evil start with myopia of evil-love.

One thing is certain though: they all lose at the end. I did nothing, you did nothing, and we'll stay that way.

There might be no gods or God, but there is one sure thing: TRUTH! We might all be incapable of attaining it, but it exists, independently of us. A few attain it. These are the just; the ones who don't live long enough for us to see the fruits of their minds and hearts.

Best regards,

Little Michael

Another six months dryly went by and there was no word from Dengdit. Little started to get concerned and unsettled. Then his worry turned into crippling emptiness. He felt hallow. However, his love of reading gave him solutions for any situation. It was amazing he stayed faithful to all the literary and philosophical idealism he read. Those ideal prescriptions worked for him like lock and key though. He stayed put for another two months. However, Little felt like a prisoner in his own skin, in his own head. There were no brotherly, spicy words. He couldn't concentrate.

Grace realized his melancholic state and politely and comically inquired.

"You aren't exercising your brain too much, Little, are you?"

He shook his head pretentiously, but she knew him more than he knew himself.

"I was just asking you. You know what to do: I'm always here for you," Grace said and left.

Little realized something strange about Grace.

She was always concerned about him, worrying about him. But Grace seemed to be less worried of his state of mind. In her usual motherly care, she'd have sat by him and made a huge deal of it. But Grace looked radiant, happy, and less worried. She left it to his discretion. That wasn't Grace, indeed it wasn't. But he was happy she was enjoying her life.

Little stopped thinking about Dengdit for a while.

Grace came back from her room looking different, radiant. Little was surprised that Grace didn't even ask him about the caller as the caller had talked strangely to Little.

Is Dengdit a live? No!

Little remembered visiting the prison after years without any word from Dengdit. It was a hot summer day, his dark face glistening in the sun, his shirt sweaty and dusty. Scanty trees whisked by him, but he found no consolation in them. The breezy air from the open window didn't allay the effect of his heated body. It was time he became someone else. Little was driving to *Southern End Prison Center* (commonly called SEPC or Sepsee). You wouldn't guess the specialty he became at SEPC.

The guards treated him like dirty, repulsive and stinky linen. He'd have taken refuge in what black people liked singing the best: *They're racists*. But no, no! The guards allowed many black people to visit. Little was the only one fenced off by being told that no one of such a name was ever taken to SEPC. With all the explanations and proofs he presented, Little left, tired and unsuccessful. A few weeks later Little received a letter claiming Dengdit's death.

June 22, 1987

Dear Friend,

The forces of evil have won. Dengdit is dead, but we'll not stop there. We'll eradicate poverty in Africa, we'll eliminate ghettoes in the US, Panda, Brazil, everywhere and we'll prevail.

Your friend,

Sister J, a Piper Sister

Little stopped thinking and sprang up. Grace stared at him with a nearly frigid smile. Surprisingly enough for Little, she didn't ask a single question. Little thought their relational ambience was getting inscrutable because Grace was acting in a manner that wasn't characteristic of her. He stared at her completely rattled, and said: "I'll be back ma."

With that, he ran out, to his car and he was on the road.

At the prison gate, Little frantically and breathlessly told the guard the name only to realize the guard was looking at him as if he (Little) was demented. The guard was a fat white man with a chirpy, girlie voice. To say the obvious, the man's belly oppressed the dark blue uniform holding it down.

"Are you sure of the name sir?" the guard cryptically said.

Little realized that SEPC had changed into a sophisticated prison. It was so changed that the guards used computers at the gate. The guard, again, entered the name in the Mac desktop computer. He frowned, looked intensely at Little and said: "There's no one with that name in this facility, sir."

Little's lips scornfully curled upwards. "Are you sure?"

The guard frowned and looked at Little with I'm-not-stupid-am-I face. With no any other workable alternative, Little left with so much hesitation hoping his recalcitrant old self would return. But heaven was perhaps following him with her other disciples. Nature had laid down a buffet of incomprehensible and unwanted events.

Little arrived at the house only to see two cops waiting for him, handcuffs hanging patronizingly, pointed toward him. Grace stared at him, helpless and seemingly indifferent.

"Mr. Michael, you're under arrest for inciting violence in our society."

Little smiled disdainfully, crooked his mouth proudly, looked at the officers with an arrogant show of pity and then looked at Grace. She wasn't laughing, unfortunately. Her oblique stare instantly changed Little's perception of the whole situation.

"Mum...?"

Grace sorrowfully and mutely entered the house; never even looking back.

He sneered. "I hope I'm not being punk'd. This might be a sick prank."

However, the grave look on the officers' faces petrified Little. He remained wordless as they artistically handcuffed him.

27

C hris innocently came to Little's place of residence just as he was told. For all the atrocious reasons, Little wasn't home. Grace stood at the door with no particular, suggestive ambience as she begrudgingly stared at Chris like always. She frowned then told Chris light-heartedly that Little was taken in for questioning by some, unnamed officers.

Chris was an ex-officer and he knew he could easily find out where Little was being questioned. But looking at Grace's face, Chris found nothing suggestive of the typical motherly concerns. A mother whose only son has been arrested always shows conspicuous emotional dispensation. Her face looked relaxed, her voice crispy; words streaming out uninterruptedly. Chris thought her behavior was conspiratorial, estranging and unbecoming. It was the police officer in Chris at work; discerning as always and judging even when judgment wasn't required.

Chris didn't meet Little for a long time after Little dropped out of High School until a few years later. Little dropped out a few months before graduation. The dropout caused mistrust between the two of them. Little saw Chris's skin color as the very manifestation and procurement of his personal plight. He didn't see it necessary to accept that a color can be shared by people who don't share the same values, and the same values shared by people who don't share the same color. The mistrust started immediately after Little dropped out of high school and aggravated by Chris's work as a police officer.

One incident was the catalyst. Chris had gone, with his partner, to interrogate Little after he was arrested on drug possession charges. Chris remembered being easy on him as a young rookie; twenty-one, two or three. However, Chris's partner had no sympathy for anyone caught on drug dealing charges. Taken in deeply by his self-righteous, dogmatic realism, Chris's partner had this to say: "I sound and appear like am being unfair to him, but you have to remember that my being unfair to him, if at all I am, is not only helping him but his community at large," Chris's partner had said.

The words struck Chris hard despite the speaker's pretentiousness and self-righteousness. They were true in no absolutist sense. Being another child schooled in his own hard-knock school of self-righteousness and cynicism, Little had looked Chris in the eye and said: "Mr. Officer, we enter a way only to find out that it's been blocked at the end. We enter another one and it's all the same. Tell me Mr. Officer; tell me what we have to do to survive."

"There're many ways, Little," Chris said just to sound responsible and respectful of the uniform.

"What ways? Do you see frowns on people's faces in any office before they even hear what we have to say? Yes, what we're doing is wrong. But it's a wrong done to survive."

Chris's partner found no sense in Little's argument. It was self-righteousness against self-righteousness presented in different colors, understood under different normative spectacles and presented under different circumstantial indoctrinations. Looking at Little with sympathetic grin, he said: "You dropped out of school having not known what school could have done for you and you tell me there are no ways?"

Little sneered with crooked lips. "How in hell do you stay in school if you don't have food on the table?"

"I can't verify that to make it sound convincing to you that you made it up; but look here pal, if our ways are blocked by people who know a language we speak, we can talk to them civilly for them to open those doors."

Little scornfully smiled with a twisted mouth. "I wished you were the one who closes the doors. You'd be kind enough to open them."

Chris's partner was getting irritated.

"I'm trying to be civil to you and you..."

"Easy!" Chris said and looked at Little.

"You know that what he's saying is true, Mr. Michael, don't you?"

Little scoffed. "I want him to understand the pressures we face. I admit our deeds are wrong in every sense. But tell me sir. What'd you say if you don't see your mum at all at home because she works three jobs to get enough to feed you? You try to be civil and conscientious enough to look for a legitimate job only to be frustrated by frowns and strange gazes that tell you one thing: 'I think you opened the wrong door son!' You love to go to school but you can't stand the sight of your mum's agony and the struggle she goes through for you. Frustrations know no counsel!"

Chris left the room having failed to gather his thoughts for a more credible counter example.

When Little was released, having served his time, he came to look for Chris at the station. He wanted to meet Chris despite the fact that he'd pretended not to know him during the interrogation; only calling him Mr. Officer.

Having dwelled on a little of his past, Chris left the past train of thoughts and stared once more at Little's home and drove straight back to his apartment.

Chris really wanted to meet Little. Having failed to either meet Little or get any credible information from the rude Grace, he made some phone calls to gather where Little had been taken by the police. No one knew where Little was, unfortunately. Having phoned all the guys he knew in the surrounding precincts, he went to Little's bar for some answers. He was told confusedly that Little was resting at his house.

"Little isn't feeling well so he's resting at home," a lady named Paris had said.

Something was fishy.

Where the hell is Little?

28

The incident was silly, yet funny. The officers who arrested Little were all black; four in total. In no terms were they rough with him or something. It at first appeared like he was being arrested but, at the end, they didn't arrest him so to speak. They said they had something sensitive they wanted to discuss with him at the police station. Funny still! They were the ideal police officers, the ones you'd always want to see on the streets, the real law enforcers.

Little, at first, saw the handcuffs and the look on their faces and knew the past was back. The kind of faces that'd tell him: 'you're damned, Little!' Then some sign language changed everything. He knew something awaited him, something strange, something dreadful. He'd been arrested several times before, but this one was different. What made the arrest different was the fact that he wasn't accused of anything substantial. As they approached the spot where the cars were parked, he saw three other cars and frowned. The whole situation was becoming different if not silly. Standing, leaning on one car bumper, was a sturdy white lady officer. She was blonde, green-eyed with a strange look of disinterest. Serious and cowgirl-looking, she was standing alone. The officers who'd come with Little nodded at the lady, looked at Little mutely and left, entered their cars and drove off. The strange lady looked at Little, hesitated as she smoked her cigar calmly then said: "Let's go!"

Little was hesitant. *Go...go where?*

The lady officer didn't remind or rebuke Little as he confusedly stood in the same place. She just stood leaning in the same place, in the same manner looking at what Little couldn't tell. When Little realized the lady wasn't bothering him, he entered the car. Having seen Little seated and relaxed, she made a quick phone call and jumped onto the driver's seat. Little was surprised to see that inside the car, there were no police paraphernalia. It looked nothing like a police car. He didn't mind though. The way they conducted themselves impressed him.

He respected that impeccable cleanliness, that ideal law enforcement. Black officers always went over the top to show they were equal. They in the process acted with heavy-handedness toward their fellow blacks. That day changed Little's perception of the police; at least temporarily. The uniform meant respect, law enforcement meant civility, and femininity meant justice. The car hummed away as Little sat like a helpless fly trapped in a sealed container. In front, the strange lady officer busied herself with her assortment of CDs. Her actions were somewhere between Beyoncé Knowles and Paris Hilton or Kim Kadarshian. However, there was some calm dignity that Little loved about her.

29

Isaac started to sense a bit of reservation in Christine's voice. This, he didn't tell Jane. Jane wasn't always in the loop when it came to all Isaac's business ventures, at least, at the beginnings. Jane only knew some of Isaac's businesses in Africa, it was claimed. He didn't tell her of the orphanage until it was up. Philanthropic ventures were always intended as surprises to Jane. Whether with good reasons or lies, it was the capitalist's mind at work. Indeed as a sweet surprise to Jane, and sweet indeed it became to her innocent mind.

It was surprising that Isaac valued Jane's advice. He kept her in the dark on some crucial things. This made one wonder about the nature of their personal and business relationship. It was no doubt, he trusted her given her role in his business empire. Jane too trusted Isaac; something which came as no surprise to many.

Isaac didn't need many words to convince Jane to quit her job long before the business thrived to its current state. Her decision to quit her job impressed on Isaac positively, however, it invited scorn from friends and relatives. Quitting a well-paying accounting job to jump under uncertainty waters seemed unintelligible to Jane's friends. However, she was in love despite others' laughs. Even with her devotion and prominence in the business, Isaac still, for some reason, didn't think he had a reason good enough to trust her completely.

Jane Lincoln had a clean conscience that Isaac at times dreaded. She had soft and mouldable emotions Africa didn't want. *There're times one needs such passions but it's not all the times such goodness works.*

Isaac held dearly to that sentiment. Such sentiments walled Jane away at times. However, her effect on Isaac's conscience shortened the longevity and strength of that wall. Without any vivid and assumed complete understanding of the person of Jane however, Isaac didn't want to take risks when nascent ideas cropped up on his mind, or when suggested by trusted friends. Everything would remain a romantic surprise unless things went bad.

Christine was brainier than Isaac had thought she was. Though Isaac had his doubts about Chris, he hoped indoctrination could bring him to shape. The man needed a meaningful life. Chris's gaits, his steps, his choice of words and his body language suggested the man needed serious help. Isaac was happy Chris still looked up to him as the giver of that very life. But for Isaac to steer through his required compass, he had to let Chris be in the loop without giving him what he needed—at least, not when the mission was not retired.

Isaac was watering his potted plants when Jane came from her appointment with the dentist. Jane and Isaac weren't married. While Isaac had no reason to believe Jane questioned why they weren't married given the fact that much of the business was in her hand, Isaac didn't know she had her worries.

She was patient and discreet so that helped him. However, sometimes the other mind might not be predictable to the required comfort level. Perhaps she thought of a possible misuse of her kindness. Nothing held as truly as Jane's state of mind he didn't know. Isaac had heard rumors of her complaints but he had no reason to believe they were true. What he fancied from the rumors was that she wanted to be with him. Jane denied everything when Isaac asked her. Enticing her, imploring her and pleasing her, all came to nothing. She said nothing to admit being unhappy with the way they were. In this, Isaac was acting a fool.

"How was the appointment," Isaac asked still watering his plants.

"It was great only that I'm getting old—the dentist told me."

"Well—I mean—that sounds good."

Jane gave Isaac a disapproving, scornful look. Isaac quickly, but ignorantly, realized what his statement had wrongly implied.

"What? You want me to get old, Isaac? I can't believe you'd say that!"

Isaac put down the watering can and opened the door to the balcony. Jane just stared at him in utter disbelief. Her eyes were popping out, her hands on her hips. She was astounded more than she was worried at what Isaac had said. With confusion on his face, Isaac walked to the kitchen to wash his hands. Moments later, he came back drying his hands with a white towel.

"Well, I didn't say I wanted you to get old."

"To leave then, Isaac?"

"Getting old to me is a blessing."

"So you get rid of me and get a younger one."

"You see...I mean...every man needs a good looking wife. If you weren't you won't be talking to me right now."

"I'm not your wife, Isaac."

"It makes no difference what you're to me—I mean—I need you. Well, this is what I meant. Many people in some parts of the world, even here in the west, dream and pray to get old. Many don't reach the age you're in. Those who reach it, instead of praising whoever gave them the chance or at least becoming happy for having reached that age, complain."

"We're saying different things, Isaac."

"We're not."

He folded the towel and threw it onto the couch.

"Then what, Isaac?"

"What women mean, and indeed some men, by getting old is what they think other people think of them. You might not be sure of inner feelings of your boyfriend or husband and therefore, cannot know whether they pretend to love you or not. But why can't one just believe in the fact that nothing bad is hinted to?"

"You're confusing me, Isaac."

She put her hands in her jeans pockets and leaned against the wall.

"You should be confused because you ladies confuse us all the time. Why's it that one likes to be admired by those she has no business with? Is it in the spirit of a woman to see a million eyes on her hips, lips and chest?" Isaac said, removed the towel from where he'd thrown it and sat down.

"Let's not pretend it's only women's business to be admired. What betrays women is honesty. We say what we feel and don't pretend we're okay when we aren't. Why should I think what others think of me is a nonissue? If people say something good about us, it's only about respect and not the liking of it *per se*. The way women are addressed is negatively interpreted to give wrong premises and that's why you take this issue to your literal conclusion."

Isaac put on a condescending smile.

"You're getting into a different business if you talk about honesty. That's far-fetched. When it comes to women's image, their words are as literal and as deep as their lips' depth."

Jane walked away from the wall, stared at the pictures on the wall, turned and said looking at Isaac: "And so are men."

"If men's dishonesty or pretense, if I may, can design a spoon, women's can design a crane."

Jane dispensed a puzzling look and stared at Isaac with an expressionless face. "What?"

She crouched and grabbed the towel from Isaac. Instead of answering Isaac, she started laughing hysterically. The metaphorical implication overwhelmed her. Even though Isaac didn't intend it that way, the statement came out funny. The shift in the weight was apparent. Bemused, he curiously stared at her. "I'll let my goddess answer it," Jane said recovering from the prolonged laughter.

"Why don't I find that funny?" Isaac said, shot up and stood by the window.

"That's why I love you, Isaac Burns," Jane said wiping off tears from her eyes.

30

Christine assured Isaac that it'd be okay to give Chris time. They therefore had one week to finalize Chris's arrangements before he went to Hayiroh. State of art arrangement was requisite for any African adventure.

"I've men who're more than able. If your man requested a week, let him knock himself out before he braves Africa."

Christine sounded cheerful and confident. That was what Isaac always liked about her. She made the dreadful comical and hope engendering. Isaac therefore decided to meet Osmani and P.D before Chris left.

Confidence and jubilation were in the air. A boost wouldn't be bad. Isaac came to realize that Osmani was helping in bringing some of the items he wanted brought to Panda. Osmani had helpful diplomatic immunity. As long as business was thriving, Isaac didn't ask the ins and outs of the use of Osmani's diplomatic immunity. There was nothing else to do but to thank Osmani.

Isaac wanted a sense of geographical fairness and therefore met the guys in the city of Heritage. The meeting was lively. Isaac's concerns with Osmani were getting worn off as he came to understand Osmani. His concerns about Osmani were getting into the background and turning inconsequential by the day. As time passed by, Isaac realized he asked questions and they answered him the way he wanted.

Heritage was of course multicultural. Despite the stains of slavery and segregation, the city had developed into something of exemplary cultural inclusiveness. The old European style architecture had been left to the old part of the city on the ocean shore. The city center with skyscrapers was moved inland. The old city has remained a tourist attraction though.

After the meeting Isaac tried to call Hayiroh to talk with Christine about Chris. Reports about the second quarter were impressive. A week earlier they had a discussion and Isaac was impressed by the numbers from Durban, his Africa's headquarters. But this time, Isaac never got hold of her. His messages to the secretary seemed to have fallen onto a Saharan fertility. Angst was developing. He was getting a little worried. However, Isaac knew Christine's performances were impeccable. She'd done so many transactions and consultancy for him that he trusted her more than anyone else. That trust was unquestionable.

Isaac was smart. He knew the risks and possibility of some of his business associates bending into corrupt practices. He was comfortable with Christine's incorruptible heart though. With time, he comfortably realized that he'd unconsciously trusted Christine with some elements of the life of his businesses in Africa. That was unusual, but not to a businessman. Christine knew all Isaac's business connections in Africa. While Jane was in charge of all Panda's businesses, she didn't know every detail of Isaac's investments when first initiated; especially in Africa.

Jane was the backbone of Isaac's business empire. No question. But Isaac didn't assume he knew Jane's conscience well enough to be comfortable with her first reactions in matters of intricate nature. Jane's clean and soft heart could harden such perplexing ideas, haunting her as illegal. They could make her stumble over words to undeserving ears. But Christine was a recondite element; a plastic bag you could prick even with the sharpest of all pins and still not leaking. She was a bag you could use to store water and not be worried about any damage that could cause your water to spill.

But Jane was unbeatable. With Isaac's consent, she expanded the boutiques to include fashion outlets and schools in different cities across North America. Isaac also tried to buy a good portion of steel business in the US. He clinched his teeth and hoped for the best. However, steel business in the US, while not as popular and lucrative as it used to be in the 1940s, was in Isaac's heart for some reasons. Harry Truman got his embarrassment in 1950s. But Isaac was a businessman. *Good luck was the word though.* He was aiming for a distant monopoly. There were, too, credible rumors that Isaac had a large part ownership in a Malaysian oil giant. With the Chinese, Isaac had a presence in Sudan and South Sudan. He was able to tap into the developing market in Sudan and South Sudan besides his Malaysian connection.

Human right voices were China's problem and so they were his too.

Though a western and a developed country, Panda had more liking for some Eastern socio-political ideals. This instilled some fear in Isaac not to be completely and closely tied to either the west or the east.

If the naïve and liberal-minded hearts in Canada and United states—those who think they can change the world—decried what they called atrocities in Sudan and South Sudan, Isaac knew he had safe passages. He was capable of showing that he was on the moral side.

However, the whole idea of Africa's investment wasn't Isaac's idea. It was Christine's. With all the noise of 'you could make a fortune here', he'd ignored her advice for years. However, Isaac had good ears for profits. With hearty rationalizations and back-up data, Isaac didn't see any reason otherwise. It was Christine at her best: *African outside, asset inside.*

Like all pretentious capitalists, Isaac started with an orphanage to warm the locals' hearts. The year was November 30, 1986. *What's the best way to sway the locals anyway?*

BURNS' OPHANAGE

Good life, proper education and prosperous future

Again, the orphanage idea was still, so to speak, Christine's. Isaac at first didn't like the name for it had too much of connotation branding to the children. He didn't want the children to feel they were without parents. While he didn't want to pretentiously think the children's reality away, he wanted the orphanage to be their home. This prompted the name change.

BURNS CHILDREN'S HOME

Good life, proper education and prosperous future

Christine had at first played down Isaac's concern as a comic input on practicality. "They'd soon know the truth about themselves anyways," Christine had said.

While the idea of the orphanage became too endearing for Isaac to ignore, it is good to remember that it took Christine two good years to prevail on Isaac that investment in Africa was lucrative. From 1984 to 1985 Christine talked to Isaac about investing in Africa. She knew the war in South Sudan would engender a lucrative opportunity especially for businesses established in neighboring Sivals, Kenya and Uganda. But Isaac wasn't a fool. He had his own plans for Africa's investment. Truth be told! Africa isn't the foremost investment ground. It was a short-term investment as Isaac believed vehemently. Unfortunately, he didn't tell Christine that his decision to invest in Africa was only exploratory and short-term; a public relation stunt. Knowing that such investment trials were only PR initiatives to change people's view of capitalists, he decided that the orphanage shouldn't carry his name. With the likes of well-known figures establishing foundations that carry their names, Isaac wanted to be different. He wasn't Oprah Winfrey or Bill Gates or Bill Clinton or anyone else. He was Isaac Burns; a don't-thank-me-for-it kind of a person.

The orphanage name had to be changed to reflect what Isaac presented as his philanthropic belief: *philanthropy without self-praise, PR connection and self-interest.*

Isaac couldn't come to term with how deluxe he felt with the *name change* and the *press reviews* about his personality and philanthropic intentions. He'd aced himself into the highest point on the moral scale.

HAYIROH'S CHILDREN'S HOME

Good life, proper education and prosperous future

Isaac makes Panda meaningfully and selflessly proud –**Heritage Chronicle**

Mr. Burns brings out the real meaning of philanthropy and altruism – **New York Times**

At least he's not after promoting his name –**Washington Post**

Isaac is the true embodiment of western values –**Globe and Mail**

Now, we can say, that's true help.–**Day-Town Governor**

Someone can now talk of philanthropy without talking about himself. –**Montreal Gazette**

Un vrai philanthrope a emerge – **La Presse**

All these thoughts whisked through Isaac's head as he wondered about what could have possibly happened to Christine. *Has Africa finally got the best of me?*

When Christine finally called two days later, Isaac found his finicky breath back. Those two days were long, arduous and dreadful. The concern was aggravated by his Sivalsian government connection: honorable Vincent Miochariya. Getting hold of Vincent was, too, becoming an endeavor.

"I'm sorry I had to finalize the details before I could call you," Christine said with pronounced humility.

"Well...I mean...I know you know your work. There's nothing to worry about with someone who knows her work."

Isaac wanted to sound sincere. It was no use. Christine was discerning to a very uncomfortable degree. "I hope you're not patronizing me, Isaac."

"If only I've been before."

Christine laughed loudly but Isaac could tell she was forcing the laughter. He feigned his side.

"You're something Isaac, you know that?"

"I wished I could join you for an afternoon swim in Malindi and then prepare for Dave to kill me."

Dave was Christine's boyfriend: a sturdy white guy with a feminine voice. He lived with her in Hayiroh. Dave worked in Panda's embassy and Christine was the business consultant for the embassy and all Panda's trade and investment relations.

Isaac laughed his worries away, satisfied at the arrangement. When it came to what Christine said, Isaac needed few words for comfort. She was a puzzling mistress of words and problem solving.

"Call me when you finalize the arrangement. I hope you don't send me some hopeless and ready-to-grab-anything Pandian."

"You'll be pleased with him; an ex-cop and accountant."

"Bye Isaac!"

As he put down the receiver, a cold wind of fear coiled up through Isaac's body. He felt something he never felt before. *Making arrangements can't prevent her from calling me.* Concerns about Christine started to surge. But Isaac had nothing to support his concerns. He started to use an untraceable phone any time he talked to Christine. That was a cheap thought, however, it gave Isaac the comfort he needed.

But why would a man be so wired up in intricate business connections, be divided, twisted by moral inner voices, and still be with a clear conscience? Isaac had it all: the money, friends, fame, but comfort seemed to be light years away from him. It never flickered as misery, because his conscience was too hard to corrupt. Could that pluck off the comfort feathers of the care he was giving to the weak even though it was so much doctored to please?

On any account, he was not religious, but when one's soul is hapless and forlorn, one can't help but steal away some supplication; shielding oneself from word-mongers. The divine becomes valuable in times of needs.

§

That night Isaac couldn't sleep. He thought about Christine's suspicious actions and Vincent's problems with Khartoum government officials.

Vincent was Isaac's help inside Sivalsian government. With all the unconnected dots, Isaac was becoming increasingly jittery.

"Some of the wares destined to your branch in Khartoum have been seized by the government. Don't worry we're working on the issue with Vincent," Christine said.

"Seized...what for?" Isaac said with withheld agitation toward someone he respected enormously.

"It could be political."

"I..."

Isaac suddenly woke up. Jane was staring at him, saying nothing. He couldn't sleep.

Angela whisked through his mind, and then everything else followed. There was Osmani's lie, the guys in Grecian Alfa and the possibility that Christine and Vincent could be using him. But what could Isaac do? Nothing, absolutely nothing! He had to wait. *Stupid me! Who's ever trusted the Africans!*

The following morning Isaac went to the office and called Christine, first thing. He explained his concerns about Angela. But he shied away from divulging Osmani's lie. *That should wait.* Christine didn't know P.D that well, but she'd read something about Angela years back. It was a newspaper article in which Angela had lashed out at some corrupt government officials in Sivals, Kenya and Sudan. She'd said a little about multinational corporations but the gist of her article was for Africans to straighten up.

Poverty neither sleeps nor does it go on holidays, she'd claimed. She'd also claimed that twenty percent of African children die before the age of five. It was grim.

Every three seconds a child dies of poverty: the snapping of fingers by celebrities. There are about 200, 000 child slaves, 120, 000 child soldiers. Now who gives a kick? Angela has asked.

However, Christine assured Isaac that his narrative wasn't worrisome.

When he told her how he choked on his food, Christine laughed. It could have been a co-incidence, she'd said.

"If they understand you, and also understand that that's Panda, and indeed if they knew anything, they'd do their best for themselves," Christine said.

Isaac cringed. He was a principled man. Threats made him jittery too.

P.D helped him enormously, professionally and personally. He'd not lay any rude hands on P.D. Isaac would prefer jail than wishing or calling harms on others. He believed he was a man of integrity. Any fabrication could finish him. His good moral status would come crushing down.

"Michael is a good friend of mine. He respects me and I respect him and through him and Mr. Osmani, I've come to know a great deal about Africa. Like any other westerner, I knew little to absolutely nothing about Africa. The truth and the lies about it are never told in the way they really are. In books, all that's written is mockery; whether subjectively or objectively. I'd held our western view abbey for a good amount of time, but because that was the only information I had about Africa, I had to believe it. I saw no reason to ask Africans for I assumed they didn't know any better than our western anthropologists. But when I was informed by a friend in New York about P.D, a South-Sudanese-American, I immediately flew him to Day-Town to talk to him. His words and the way he put them made me feel like I was in a fantasy land. It was hard to believe him at first for he sounded too promotional of Africa—exaggerating history—I'd thought. But being the businessman I wanted to be, I took his words. You can see me now."

Isaac had talked at length that Christine changed her stance on the issue.

"You make it sound bigger than I'd thought. Is there something else to it or is it the very same thing you said at the beginning? If that same thing is your only worry, then I see no reason why you're making a big deal out of it. Make sure your guy, Chris, is coached well enough and ready for us to finish the business so that such worries are dealt with once and for all."

Christine advised and consoled him. Isaac took it with graciousness and avoided the topic whenever he met Osmani and P.D.

31

Little sat calm and confused inside ravelment paradise. The lady drove the car gently out of town; singing in mignon voice.

"Hey, where're we going? There's no police station there!"

She remained unresponsive; not even concerned Little could break the glass and run away. Little could even overpower her. *What's this?*

"I'll break the glass, young lady!"

She put on some country song and started singing as if Little didn't even exist. Her head moved from side to side like an excited teenager.

"Hey, miss, where're you taking me?"

She looked back and said: "Why can't you just shut up and enjoy the ride!"

Completely rattled, Little looked back. There were no cars; only residential buildings. He wondered what the lady hoped would help her. A gun maybe, Little thought. *I'm from the ghetto woman.*

Being black in Panda was not as grave as being *black* or *African* in America, Canada and some parts of the *third world*, like South Africa, India and the greater Mohammedan cosmos. It was different in substance and imagination but not bad in imaginable and unimaginable imagination. This used to be Chris's and Little's humorous connection back in high school: *bad in imaginable and unimaginable imagination.* Something bad in such a manner was something that was woefully bad beyond anybody's comprehension.

The long held heritage mantra attaches a strong string to the statement: heritage is heritage, especially the superior one.

In high school, this thought removed the veil on Little's face. With it he started to discern mockery and condescension within loaded implications. Past aside, Little came back to the present.

He sat sombrely as the lady drove to god-knows-where.

They arrived at a seemingly rundown motel 30 kilometers outside the city. She parked the car and called out loudly: "Let's get in!"

She left Little standing and entered.

Little was getting utterly baffled. There was no question he could break into an athletic sprint. He didn't. With confusion written all over his face, Little followed the lady in out of curiosity.

Inside the motel, red window curtains stared at him. Little hated that color. There were three brown couches opposite the reception. Next to the reception desk was a long-legged stool and a weird funky blond guy was sitting on it.

The lady was standing by the reception. She wasn't talking to anyone. An African-Pandian receptionist smiled at the lady and handed her a key. The receptionist, a slim and friendly-faced figure, wore long, Jamaican dreadlocks.

"Let's go!" the lady said.

With her confusing indifference, the lady walked toward the rooms. Little was like her tail. They momentarily stood outside room 214 as the lady keyed the door open. They entered. Interestingly enough, there was no one inside the room.

"I'll be back," she said and left.

Having made sure the lady was gone first, Little stealthily tiptoed to the door. For all the confusing reasons, the door was open. *What the hell is happening?*

Dazed, Little started to become more curious than afraid. Before he could engage his brain, three officers walked into the room. There was one yellow table and two black chairs in the room.

"Sit there!" one of them said pointing at one of the chairs. He was a tiny, coal black man with huge dread-locks. The second one, a white man, removed a black and white photo as Little sat down on one of the chairs. The third officer, a pigmy-looking African, sat down opposite Little. He was beige, almost half-black half-white. Their badges looked genuine.

"Do you know this guy?" the black pigmy asked. Little stared at him straight in the face.

"Chris?" Little said surprised.

"That answers it."

"How about this?" he asked, showing Little another black and white photo.

Little frowned.

"What's exactly going on here? Why am I being grilled like this?"

They looked at Little as one of them reached for a grey mini-cassette player next to Little and played it.

We can do it, Little, we can blow this country up. We need money, and you have it. I have secret meeting places.

Little stared both petrified and baffled. He remembered Chris to have said something of the sort. But where, when and why Chris said that, he had no idea.

"Was that Chris, and you?"

"I don't know... I don't remember!"

"Well, the jury and the judge will not find that hard to *know and remember*. You know what sucks in law? Evidence!"

Little's lips curled up angrily. "That doesn't prove anything, man. There's nothing specific in that recording."

"Now you're talking," the white officer said.

Little realized he was on the path of self-incriminating. He kept quiet.

"Tell us what you're trying to do, Mr. Michael."

Little remained quiet, his mouth crooked. The white officer looked at him and removed an envelope from a file of papers.

"We better let the evidence do the talking," he said and gave Little an already opened envelope. Little frowned, grabbed the envelope and stared at their faces one at a time. As he was about to open the letter, the coal black officer said: "Save it for dinner."

He looked at Little and nodded at the white officer.

"What type of relationship do you think you have with Chris?" the coal-black officer asked.

Little was getting confused and angrier by the minute.

The white officer, a brown-haired, lean and well-dressed fellow lankily got up, paced to the door, changed his mind then came back. He absurdly nodded at the other officers and fished out another mini-cassette player. After a period of hesitation surveying the recorder, he pushed it toward the black pygmy officer. The black officer silently stared at Little as the white officer pushed the player in front of Little. Little stared like a bull being led to the butcher's knife.

Little is not as simple as you think he is. He's connected, you know, but we can use him. He thinks highly of me as his friend. Dengdit can't be serious.

He stopped the player then said: "That's your friend, mmmm?"

Little felt anger surging inside him, but he knew what they wanted. Any outburst would sling him through dirty corridors. He took a deep, painful sigh then sneered scornfully, his mouth crook-ed. "It'd be a great justice to me if you guys told me what you're really up to," he said so pretentiously calm having numbed himself to a critically civil composure.

"Don't insult us please, Mr. Michael," the white officer said.

"It's not about what you think of what I said; it's how I meant it."

They laughed simultaneously.

"We're not stupid, Mr. Michael."

"What do you know about *The Pipers*?" the black pygmy asked.

Little shook his head and sighed very much irritated.

"They're a good fictional creation by Pan-Africanists to make sure that black people have something of a hope still existing."

"You seem to know their deep existential philosophy."

"So you think I'm part of them, eh? I'd be a happy man."

"You've seen all the recordings we've obtained. We have one that proves you're part of The Pipers."

Little scoffed, crooked his lower lips upward and smiled: "You guys are so naïve. Go ahead and bring it and stop wasting my time."

The officers looked at themselves and smiled.

"Right, we'll drive you home. But you'll do us a favour. You'll receive a letter in three days. Read that letter, do whatever it tells you, and shut up with it."

Little's nose twitched. "I can't promise to do something I don't even know. Can you guys stop this nonsense and talk like real officers?"

The black officer frowned as the white officer stared back at his partner and walked to the door. Little leaned back and sighed again.

"It's your call, Mr. Michael. Judge the situation the way you see fit. The recordings are beautiful and law-friendly," the black officer said.

Little remained seated as the two men walked to the door.

"Let's go. Someone is waiting for you outside."

The officers left through another door, at the back.

Little smiled sarcastically to himself and got up. He stared at the empty chair in front of him then walked to the door and out of the room. There was no one at the counter. He stood staring at the counter and a young Indian lady walked to the counter from the back room. The slim dreadlocked lady wasn't there. Little confusedly looked around.

"Can I help you sir?"

Little hesitated, shook his head then walked to the main entrance.

He mumbled 'I'm okay,' and got out.

The same lady driver was waiting for Little. She was puffing a cigar and dancing with one foot. Her appearance was different. She was dressed like a country music superstar: a short, blue skirt, a brown cowgirl hat, tall brown boots and a yellow leather jacket.

32

The strange lady drove in silence as smooth, mignon country tunes played on the radio.

"Can I ask you a question?" Little asked.

She kept quiet for a while as Little waited, tense and curious.

"No."

She said with a harsh, devilish voice.

Little then decided to remain quiet for a while.

Even with all the rudeness and indifference, the lady was a good driver; faithfully observing speed limits and traffic signs.

"Did you read Nineteen Eighty-four by George Orwell?" she asked and started singing to the country tune on the radio.

Little was lost in thoughts so he couldn't get the whole question.

"I'm sorry I didn't get the question."

"Did you read Nineteen Eighty-four by George Orwell?"

Not knowing the point of the question, Little frowned and started to squirm on the back seat.

"No."

"Go and read it."

"Why?"

"Do you know what's common with these groups of people?"

"What group of people?" he hastily asked.

Little looked at her face in the rear-view mirror. She was smiling.

"Women, blacks, Africans, native Americans, Australian natives, Jews, gays and lesbians."

"I don't know?" Little said and sat back.

"Stop being stubborn, Mr. Michael!"

Little laughed sarcastically and crooked his lips up. "Look who's saying that!"

"You're wondering why I keep asking you these questions when I don't give you answers or even care you exist."

She slowed down. Little looked back ahead, curious about the slowdown. A police car's siren was flashing behind. She looked back at Little and said: "The world is rough, Mr. Michael. Be a strong man and do what's right all the time and I mean all the time even if it kills you. Whatever happens, never mention me or what happened today to anyone. Not even your mum. Promise?"

"Hey, hey, what're you talking about?"

She smiled charmingly for the first time. Little stared at her, still looking confused. Nothing, in more than one hour, had made any sense to Little at all.

"What's going on? What's your name?"

She smiled again.

"Here're the keys."

Little only stared as pimples of sweat formed on his face.

She got out, her hands raised. The two officers got out of the police car. They walked toward her, grabbed her by the shoulder and led her to their car.

Little tried to get out but he was fixed down by fear. Then there was a gunshot and the place was dead silent.

Little jumped out of the car. As he tried to open the front door, one of the officers said loudly: "Sir, you can drive home! Leave the car by your house. Someone from the police will pick it up tomorrow."

Little hesitated, confused and scared. He managed to ask though.

"What did she... what have you done with her?"

"For your safety and records sir, I advise you to go."

"No, I need to see her. What have you done to her?"

The officer hanged up his head for a while then walked toward Little. Little was furious. Disdainfully smiling, the officer stopped in front of Little with belittling stare.

Little angrily sneered. "I need to see her."

"You need to see her? Oh, you're in love already?"

Amused, the officers stared at one another.

"What're you talking about? There was no *a her*, there was never *a her*, and there'll never be *a her*. You got that...brother?" the second officer said.

"No, I didn't get that...sister!"

The officer put his hand in his pocket and removed a 5 mm revolver. He pointed it at Little's head. Little didn't cringe.

"I hope you can go home now, or be *a never* like a *never her*."

Little stared at the officer. The man's face was freckled and his hair was long, blond and tied at the back as a pony-tail. He loaded the gun and Little knew the man meant business. Rattled by the loaded gun, Little turned, got into the car and gunned off.

§

That night Little couldn't sleep. *Who're the guys*? Who was the lady? Who were the officers that acted so unprofessionally? *Why's Chris spying on me*? However, Little was warned. That young lady driver and the unruly officers were clear in their warnings. He had to shut his all up.

The night was long and torturous. He heard every chirping of the insects, every song the birds sang, and the sound of all the humming machines in the house. Little of course had past criminal records and any fabrication, distortion of facts—seconded by his nature—would not serve his black soul. He knew he was cornered in a way he couldn't escape.

Obviously, he had to act protectively. No doubt, Little didn't think things over really well. The stupidity that was supposed to be cops' unlawfulness became his. His fear walled him away from making the right decision. Dazed and bedevilled by the events of the past twenty-four hours, Little didn't think straight.

The offending cops were free and about. The stupidity became his as he gave in to the world's desires. But he wasn't sure who the legitimate cops were. What was the favour they talked about? Could he afford to do it? What if it was illegal? Favours in such situations were always dreadful.

A small light started to edge out the darkness. The red sun rolled into the clear, blue sky as Little walked to the window to enjoy the only good thing he could perceive as pacifying.

33

The Khartoum's seizure was still in place. Isaac had no idea why things had become difficult for the big fish. Christine was persuasive and Vincent had great political might. Such political muscles would move mountains.

"We'd had a complication and misunderstanding, Isaac, but I assure you we'll take care of the situation," Vincent told Isaac over the phone weeks after the seizure. He'd called to assure Isaac everything was okay. From the look of things, they were far from comforting if okay.

Vincent didn't persuade Isaac well enough not to be skeptical. Isaac, however, couldn't tell the truth from the lie. He just had to hope. Hope isn't a doer but it keeps a yearning, hopeless soul going, working.

"Well, I've never at any time had any doubts about your work, honourable Miochariya," Isaac said rather uncertain of what he meant at that moment. The times were really uncertain. It was the prayer line that Isaac had to hope would do the magic. The toll of the anxiety showed in the depth of the lines on his forehead. He was helpless nonetheless. Solving the seizure wasn't on his hands. Neither were the lines on his fore-head. He looked up and saw Jane legging noisily toward him. She was dragging her feet.

Isaac think, think!

"Who's that?" Isaac thundered.

Jane smiled knowing exactly how Isaac felt about business phone calls at home. Her face puckered up and he knew who it was.

"Hello Christine!"

To exacerbate Isaac's feelings even more, Christine first sighed; a dreadful sigh. Her sighs either professed bad business prospects or something grave. This added to the already tensing situation and dangerous thoughts in Isaac's skull. Isaac was getting perturbed. Certainly, he didn't need any more stress, anxiety or trauma.

"That says a lot Christine."

"Indeed it does."

Now it was Isaac's turn to sigh. He sighed and rubbed his temple with his left middle finger as pimples of sweat formed on his face.

"I knew something was wrong, but I just finished talking to Vincent and he was upbeat about the whole operation."

"We'll probably take care of the situation..."

"*Probably*...Hello, you're breaking up, Christine...hello!!"

Isaac, at the worst of times, lost the line. The game had begun. He tried to call back but the line was dead: no tone. *Now this is Africa.*

He shot up for a moment only to lazily sit down.

Trying Vincent was the only alternative available to Isaac.

The Voodoos of Africa had begun their work as Vincent was not reachable. Vincent was out for a dinner with the president, Isaac was told. Too soon!

Isaac was being tormented, his stomach burnt, and his intestine crawled violently. It was torture beyond acceptable insuperability. His stress response mechanism was starting to instigate the adaptive mechanism. Maybe that was too soon to say.

34

Something else happened, but Chris had no any idea what it was though. He'd called the nearest police stations and all the ones he knew, but Little seemed to have dropped off our massive cosmic body. There was no sign Little was arrested either.

Chris had to do what he didn't want to do again: call Grace. What she said struck him hard. That short gracious intellect always made Chris mentally enamored even though he hated her guts. On that day her words didn't enamor him, however. She struck him as an arrogant, hard-to-please, irrational old lady.

"I've never lied in my entire life and you're accusing me of lying? What interest do I have in my son being arrested if you weren't calling me a selfish idiot?"

Chris was scared, literally. Grace was someone he perceived as unconventionally minded and he was always wary of her words, but this time her words were scathingly different. She charged like an angered lioness. That wasn't characteristic of her. Grace was always calm, civil and considerate yet assertive and uncompromising. This time she was completely out of character.

"I'm sorry, Mrs. Michael!" Chris said.

"You surely are," she said and hanged up.

Chris didn't know what to do. Such out-of-blue changes of attitudes were just but protective strategies. As a former detective, Chris knew from experience that good old Grace was hiding something.

Grace's protective behavior wasn't top of his problems though. Chief of all Chris's problems was the fact that he only had about four days to leave for Africa and he couldn't find Little. He desperately needed to talk to Little. Grace's escapist artifice couldn't scale him off his plan though. Determined, he picked up the phone again.

"I'd like to speak to Little please."

Chris humbled himself with the stupidest of all humilities; his voice sounding innocent and mellow. On the other side of the line, he could hear rude shuffling of papers.

"In a minute...thanks," a sweet, young voice chirped. *Never heard that voice before! But wait...in a minute...Little is there?* Chris waited for a couple of seconds and then Little's idiosyncratic voice manned the line.

"Whassup Chris? What's going on?"

Chris's consciousness momentarily vanished. *Where'd Little been? Why's he that enthusiastic and jovial?*

"I don't know dude. Your mum said you were arrested yesterday."

Little feloniously laughed, twitched his mouth and said: "Arrested, are you dreaming? I wasn't arrested."

This is stupid, Chris thought. He felt blood rushing away from his head as if he was going to faint. He gasped for air like an asthmatic person.

"Dude, you mean you..."

"I wasn't arrested. Would you like to speak with mum to..."

"No, I think that wouldn't be necessary. I just want to speak to you."

Already schooled in Grace's demeanor, Chris didn't want to further inflame her stirred up sentiment.

"Come on over."

Little's usual grumpiness was gone. Weird Indeed, Chris thought.

Chris hanged up and all his senses seemed to have left him. *What the heck is going on with Little and his mum?* Totally opposite, completely separate: there was some unfolding drama.

On that chilly afternoon, Chris entered Little's bar. He was dressed up like a sixteenth century Eskimo from the northern tip of Canada. He was wrapped up to almost circular composure in all-white attire: white cotton pants, white silk jacket, and a hoodie.

Wani and Wallace were some fellows Chris never quite understood. They were like officers trained never to laugh. Wani was five-seven with dark complexion, bulging muscles and a pronounced forehead. Wallace was six: light-skinned, fair-complexioned, adequately built but reasonably muscled. They never answered any questions directly nor did they converse with any visitors. They just nodded in the direction of the action needed any time Chris came in. They asked the same question every time: *who, what do you want?*

But on that winter day, Chris was used to them. Maybe!

"Little Michael please," he said and chuckled.

Wallace and Wani looked at themselves and at Chris. Wani nodded at Wallace and Wallace walked away.

Everywhere smelt of liquor, wine and beer. Barbecued chicken ribs, wings, lamb, pork, beef...filled the air.

Wallace stumbled on a bottle of beer lying on the ground and Chris ran back in reflex fright. The two men mockingly smiled. He bit his lower lip in bitter, resentful anger. Conspicuous show of anger wasn't wise there. What else could he do? He was *a* nothing. They could mould him into fine dough in seconds.

Chris just stared at the two post-looking giants and felt minute and insignificant; stupid and worthless.

"Guys, it's sometimes, I think, good to know what can torment someone else," Chris complained.

Wallace looked back.

Wani stared at Chris silently and disdainfully.

This is such a place, Chris said to himself.

"Get used to it...it's here not there," Wani said pointing at Chris and outside. Chris cringed.

Chris didn't understand Wani's reaction. Yes, he didn't want to understand anything from men who treated him arrogantly and unfairly. What Wani meant by *here* and *there* was a complete cynicism he wasn't prepared for.

§

Little was with Janet and Paris in his office when Wallace entered.

"What's it, Wallace?" Little said looking at Janet. Wallace kept quiet and folded his Herculean arms on his formidable chest.

"I know you have big muscles, damn it Wall..."

"There's a white dude outside. He says he wanna see ya."

"White dude? You don't know him?"

"I don't know anyone. I only know me."

Little grinned impressively. The girls jointly laughed. Then Janet took the laugher out of context. They all curiously stared at Janet as she continued to laugh; relaxed, contented yet puzzling.

"What's so...that funny sweetie," Little said as she continued with her hysterics.

"That's the sexiest statement I've ever heard: 'I only know me'."

She continued laughing.

Wallace joined the hysteria as he left the room.

Paris and Little stared absentmindedly like people dropped in the middle of a desert; lost and puzzled.

§

Wallace emerged laughing, looked at Wani, at Chris, bent his head toward Wani and then nodded. Not interested in their attitude, Chris walked off.

Sometimes it's good to be racist.

The tempting aroma of the barbecue was becoming intense. Beer, liquor and barbecued beef: you know what that means?

Chris followed Wallace sleepily with a twisted neck. Barbecue!

Little was chilling inside with the girls. Paris was a twenty-four-seven, twenty-seven year old slim brunette who knew nothing about anything and knew everything about nothing. The other was Janet, a quiet sister who neither braided nor straightened her hair.

"Get out dude; we're having fun here, okay?" Paris said and continued to massage Little.

"If you think I'm impotent," he said, pretending not to be looking at Paris.

Paris was bare to the toe; fairly built, with breasts of African virgin of seventeen. Unlike Janet, Paris was never shy.

As Paris massaged Little, Janet sat on the couch reading a book with an interesting title: *Season, the Grass' Problem*. But what got Chris hooked and thinking about the book was a quote from an African writer. It cried: *while considering someone weak and inferior, it would be oxymoronic to fear or hate them.*

"What's it Chris?" Little roared.

Chris mutely folded his minute arms and enjoyed the scenery, the room ambience.

35

"Let him come here!" Janet said, put the book down and moved toward Chris. Chris tried to moisten his throat with saliva but it was no use. It remained dry.

Little stared at Chris with angry cat's eyes. He tried to get up but Paris pressed him down.

Chris was getting confused as Janet walked slowly and teasingly toward him. *It could be a good day.*

Janet was the badge of men's desire. She was simple but smart. It was no surprise she frequently and boldly told Little his weaknesses without being afraid of Little's reaction. With surprising strength of will, Janet reproached Little about his drinking and treatment of Paris. But Paris was the most likeable although in a different context. She allowed Little to do what he wished. Janet on the other hand didn't and that made Little hesitant when it came to things concerning Janet.

On their first encounter, Paris's vibrancy and womanliness were in flattering abundance. Within a short time, she became his handbag, a backpack. He went with her everywhere. Little deadly trusted her and she gave it back in kind. She reflected in Little, both the ignorance and unconscious unfairness of men to women. However, it was hard to say exactly whether Little was actually being unfair to Paris.

Paris was happy, well accommodated and freer. Was that all the-required of a woman?

Janet on the other hand was a completely different breed. For that reason, Little didn't trust her the way he trusted Paris. His heart was stupidly fixed on Janet though.

As Janet touched Chris's shoulder and her eyes met his, Chris understood why Little loved her. She was exquisitely beautiful. Blood flow from Chris's heart increased; flow to the brain decreased and the flow to the loin doubled.

Janet had a lovely cinnamon face and skin.

Chris smiled and momentarily closed his eyes. If someone in love is always on cloud nine, Chris was on twenty.

She removed her top and gently rubbed his right shoulder.

Little tried to get up in protest, but Paris pinned him down. Chris was enjoying the drama.

Little's lower lips curled up wildly: "No, Janet, no, no...!" Little said in a rather clear voice, looking weak and helpless.

Janet frowned, looked at Little with a vivid tenacity and started unbuttoning Chris's shirt. That was too much for Little to take. He grew tempestuous, his eyes turning red. Little's reaction was some wildness Chris had never seen.

He jumped, inadvertently knocking Paris down. Paris felt on her buttock and lay still, motionless. Little angrily grabbed Janet by arm, leaving Chris thirsty, dried up and frozen.

"Dude, I'm sorry, terribly sorry. I couldn't resist and besides, I thought you told her."

"Told...what?" Little didn't know what to say. They sat in an incapacitating silence as Little stared at Chris, furious; anger-heated from the hair to his toe nail. His eyes were red, his gaze ferocious.

Chris stared as Little fumed, sweating profusely. Paris lay down seemingly unconscious. They were all mentally preoccupied that they'd forgotten about Paris. From the look on his face, one could tell that Little was holding back enormous anger toward someone he respected deeply. Having seen the ferocity on Little's face, Chris felt sorry for Little more than he did for Paris.

"Where's Paris?" Chris asked.

They all felt their hearts beat, then silence followed. A moment passed as they looked at one another and then jumped to look behind Little's seat.

"I'm fine," Paris said as she got up, bleeding from the temple. "I'm..."

"I know who you care deeply about now, Little!" she said, wiping tears off from her eyes.

They all stared remorsefully and helplessly. Janet stared scornfully at Little, then at Paris. Paris winked at Janet then hurriedly grabbed her clothes, slipped them on skillfully and left the doomed room. Surprised, Chris stared at Little, helpless yet angry.

Paris opened the door and said: "I don't know. Maybe I don't understand myself, Janet. You were right about me."

Deeply angered, Chris couldn't contain his anger. He'd, for a moment, forgotten Little's ferocious gaze. Still with that innocent gaze, he dashed after Paris.

Having sensed that Chris was behind her, Paris turned, looked mockingly at him and said: "If what I think is what you're thinking about then forget it."

Chris and Paris were at the entrance part of the bar. Still wary, Chris looked back only to see Wani with the same dark look. Paris opened the door, got out, removed her lighter and started to smoke, standing outside.

Chris stood still, not knowing which step to take. Seeing Chris still standing in the same place, Paris came back; rudely pulled his arm and said looking at Wani: "I don't know." She let go his arm and looked away. "You know what beautiful people like you don't know?"

Unsure of what to say, Chris shook his head slowly. She took a deep puff then looked at him again, deeply and boldly in the face.

"You never know you're important until you're useless, but I've no idea what you're doing here, nor do I know why you're following me. If you want to die young, then continue to follow me. That man in there didn't do anything to me. I did wrong him."

"What...I think...?

"Shhhhh!"

She hushed Chris like a child.

"If I were you, I'd go in there and say whatever I wanted to say. After that, I have a word for you: fuddle-duddle! Should you talk about me, or tell any of your friends that you saw a beautiful white girl being mistreated by a mean black man, then you'll have yourself to blame," Paris said with a begrudgingly sarcastic grin and left. You didn't, Chris thought. *What...has the world suddenly turned mysterious and philosophical?*

Strangely, not a word Paris said entered his ears. From what he knew, Paris knew everything Little owned: all finances and secrets. That incident made Chris wonder why Little trusted Paris more than anyone else. Chris stood stupidly looking at Paris as she got into a taxicab.

Little came out of his sanctuary and stood behind Chris. His lips curled up with a sarcastic grin.

"Don't believe what you see if you didn't understand it," Little said as Chris followed the trail of Paris's taxi.

"We're bright when happy but brighter when angry," Wallace said as Chris looked back.

He winked at Chris and left.

"See you tomorrow, Chris. I gotta go home," Little said casually and left.

As Little opened the door to enter, a mailwoman walked to the door. She looked at Little and walked through the door as Little held it open for her.

Wallace folded his arms across his chest and stared intensely at Chris. The mailwoman removed the letters and gave them to Wallace. Wallace walked backwards, turned, pocketed one and put the rest on the counter.

36

Three days of waiting were more than a torment for Isaac. His office felt like a tortuous dungeon and the house felt like a timeless, unlit box. Everything seemed to have stood still.

As a desperate last attempt, Isaac tried more than a dozen times to call the Sivalsian president. Unlike western leaders, African leaders have absolute powers of ancient kings and emperors. Isaac was put on hold only for the phone to tone off. Trying again, he was told the president had a meeting and wasn't taking any calls.

"Your world is not coming to an end you know," Jane said, trying to infuse some life into him. Isaac looked at her but said nothing.

"Well, what do you think happened?" Isaac asked after a pause.

She grinned, came toward him and blew him a hard kiss.

"I believe everything is alright. I'm going to the office."

Jane left and the intensity of the silence rattled Isaac in his tiny, pretentious home office. Then the *kkrrring* of the phone tore through the silent air. He reflexively jumped to his feet, stared at the phone then slowly picked it up as if it was some bomb that was about to explode.

"Isaac," he said and listened.

Then both Christine and Vincent said simultaneously: "Hello Isaac!"

First, there was silence then Isaac felt himself sigh, a sigh of relief.

"Are you there?" Christine asked.

"We're sorry about not getting back to you in time," Vincent said.

Isaac took a deep breath as silence invaded the line. This time, the silence didn't have much effect on him.

"Well...I was almost getting hospitalized."

They both laughed.

Even with the deluxe civility he wanted to maintain, Isaac didn't laugh.

"Even a quick phone call could have saved me the agony."

"Beat it Isaac. That's why Vincent apologized," Christine said. "We had to take care of the issues before we gave you some good news."

Isaac felt his heart rate starting to lower its pace upon the mention of *good news*. Those three torturous days had his mind occupied with premonitory drama. *Good news is godly now, at least.*

"You mean the confiscation is taken care of."

"Yes," Vincent said.

"It was quite complicated, Isaac. We also had some confiscations in Mombasa, which we took care of. Construction and mining equipment have reached Hayiroh as we speak. The textile imports are deep into the ocean," Christine said.

Isaac could feel her ego inflating.

"We also had the confiscation in Khartoum, Sudan dealt with," Vincent said.

"What's happening guys? What have I done?"

"We're fighting against some unseen forces, Isaac. We believe you're being watched by a group that knows the internal workings of some of your businesses."

"How's that possible?"

"That's the million dollar question, Isaac."

"And how do you guys deal with such situations?"

Vincent sighed. Christine laughed and said: "It's Africa, Isaac, beat it. What do you expect?"

"Don't tell me you did what I think you guys did."

"Don't patronize us, Isaac."

"What's that supposed to mean?"

"I'm even sorry I said Africa. I just wanted to be realistic. But things cannot be handled in some idealistic western liberalism."

Isaac felt beads of sweat forming on his forehead.

"Isaac, we had to argue our way out of this," Vincent said.

"That means my company is now involved in corrupt practices."

"Mm mm, watch your words, Mr. Burns!" Vincent sounded distant and offended.

"Businesses are built on risks. And...honorable Miochariya, bribery is not supposed to be part of business risks. It's not, should not be and cannot be!"

"Mm, what're you insinuating, Isaac? That we are corrupt African nincompoops trying to make big bucks out of your brainchild?"

Isaac felt his heart stabbed, his chest cavity tightened. He was out of breath. Vincent and Christine had to be pacified. He struggled to correct the misreading.

"Well...I mean... what I'm simply saying is, let's be as clean as possible."

Extreme pretense had to be exercised. Isaac spoke as calmly as he could.

"Isaac, giving someone resources to do something for you involves risks. A token given for a job done beyond one's imagination deserves appreciation whether financial or otherwise. If that qualifies as corruption in Pandian economic policies, then here is Sivals, it's not Panda."

Bewildered, Isaac remained silent, deeply thoughtful.

"Do you know what we had to do to secure the goods in Khartoum?" Christine asked.

"Tell me please!"

Christine cleared her throat.

"Don't get all wild out by this. In Sudan, we had to arm a Southern rebel unit to storm the store with a few elements in the Sudanese army. There'll be no record of our involvement. The rebels will say they thought the store was an ammunition store and then give us the products."

Isaac touched his forehead and stared at the ceiling. The humidity in the room thickened.

As Christine and Vincent talked, the flow of information was becoming too excessive and suffocating for Isaac. Isaac was losing his breath. It was one nightmarish act after another.

"You mean the death of civilians in Khartoum I heard on BBC has something to do with Isaac Burns."

"Careful. If you take media side then you'll be at loss and misery. It's a third world infrastructure."

"I..."

"Don't worry about anything."

Don't worry? Is that what I'm supposed to believe?

Isaac was indulged in corrupt business practices. Yes, he was. How was he supposed to get out of it? He'd sworn to stay clear of tempting lucrativeness. Now, he'd become engulfed in a wave of a well-designed political juggernaut.

Pandian tycoon behind Sudanese Civil War

That'd make a good front page headline.

Burns burning innocent civilians

They blame Africa, but they engineer behind the scene economic and political carcinogens

Burns built the orphanage to mask his real, rotten self

Whatever the case, the damage had already been done. He had to go with what Christine and Vincent had concocted until he thought things over.

§

A day after Christine and Vincent surprised Isaac with the bribery issue; Isaac called both Osmani and P.D. They had to talk for a session of political and social therapy. Over the phone, P.D was supportive.

"You have to understand people with whom you have business partnerships. Let them understand the principles you stand for," P.D had said.

Osmani on the other hand didn't sound as encouraging as P.D.

"That's the beauty of understanding people before you indulge with them," Osmani said.

Isaac looked offended. *As If I understand you!!*

While the phone call was helpful, Isaac suggested that they met for a more intimate and serious chat.

This time Isaac needed a change in venue. It was an unlikely venue. Ben Chili Bowl wasn't the typical place in which to find someone like Isaac even if it was frequented by famous names. These names adorned the wall. However, the place offered the privacy Isaac fancied. Whoever was after Burns' businesses was smart enough to cover all his tracks.

The front of the restaurant was red, white and yellow. Inside it was noisy but lively. Isaac loved the burgers and the chili dogs. The African gentlemen didn't mind the fat.

They found a comfortable place away from the bustle and hustle of the service desk.

"Okay. I keep wondering what someone might have against someone like you, Isaac," Osmani said as they placed their chilis and burgers on the table.

"It's not always good to assume self-righteousness but I think I'd be justified if I assume this position in this case," Isaac said with smugness.

"If you can sustain it, I'd have no problem with that position," Osmani said as he swooped down on his burger.

"You're right. Some people, sometimes uncritically, want objectivity," P.D said.

"Well, let's not get too philosophical," Isaac said and looked at P.D.

P.D was smiling while Osmani was busy with his red fellow. Isaac continued when no one responded.

"I mean...I hope you guys thought about what I told you about the increasing frequency of confiscation of my items in Africa."

"What I find frustrating is the essence of the issue holistically speaking," Osmani said and looked at Isaac and P.D.

"Well...I'm sorry...I didn't understand that?"

"You said Vincent told you you're up against some forces."

"Yes!"

"Is there any creditable merit to that?"

"I'm not following you."

Osmani looked at his burger.

"What he's saying Isaac is that there might be some other explanations," P.D said, cautiously explaining Osmani's remarks.

"Which are?"

"Do you trust your business associates?"

Isaac sat back.

"Absolutely! You guys aren't suggesting some blackmail here, are you?"

P.D looked at Osmani and said: "That maybe right, but what we're advising you to do is to look at the bigger picture before you accept what's not critically evaluated. Dissident groups are easy targets for scapegoat. We don't know exactly who's actually engineering these confiscations so be careful."

"As people who've been with you for some times now, we'd advise you to have a look first within your circle," Osmani said.

"He's right. But don't lose sight of what Vincent said," P.D added.

Isaac stared at the ceiling for a while then said: "What you're telling me is to be cautious of anyone."

"That'd be the best way to put it. We wouldn't want you to be unnecessarily suspicious though."

"Yes, yes. We'll of course keep our ears open for information," Osmani said.

"I first thought of political blackmail because I'd refused to dis-invest in South Sudan and Sudan oil sector. All the noisy human right activists bore me really bad! What Christine and Vincent told me is that purported information is sent to the governments concerned that we are importing items without proper documentations."

"Sometimes their cases depend on who they are and what their convictions are, however, most of them seem to win at the end," Osmani said.

"We have western activists who'd taken their activism to the very extreme; however, I've not seen such a thing in Africa. Unless you guys know something I don't know," Isaac said.

P.D smiled as Osmani laughed. Isaac stared at the African gentlemen and said: "Did I miss something?"

"Isaac, civil wars are other manifestations of extreme activism."

"No..."

"Your western understanding would perhaps rule them out. However, they're fervent activists; strongly believing in their value judgment."

37

Paris was the most naïve character Chris had ever seen in his life. Why that girl, with beauty surpassing anything he'd ever seen on T.V; with a mind he'd ever countered, could be so enmeshed in Little's recondite network, confused him.

She had a brain to think, had a body to attract, and had a mouth to convince, yet she was stuck with Little.

"You're my friend and I wish you no harm, but you have to understand that she means so much to me."

Little told Chris in a clear, convincing and believable voice. It was something Chris wanted to believe but he had no reason to. Paris deserved more than that humiliation.

Convinced of his resolves, he sealed his conscience, convinced his weak behavioral spots and cleaned off everything Little had said. Even with Little's pleading voice, Chris took Little for a slick fellow. *It's all a game.*

"But you...!"

"Chris, leave her alone. Don't see cards on the table, people around it and money in their pockets and conjure that they're gambling. It's easy to force people to gamble with your life when they don't need to."

"But I...," Little hanged up before Chris could even voice his worries.

Chris admired the girl yes, but all he wanted for her was for Little to respect her as just any other human being. *Where's Panda heading to?*

Chris's rescue mission failed so Paris was back with Little. He met her in the afternoon the same day he talked to Little. He was on his way to Isaac's office.

Paris's saga spoiled Chris's talk with Little. However, the mystery and stupidity about his going to Africa was continuing. He had to tell Isaac about a mysterious phone call that warned him against going to Africa. Blackmail or otherwise, he had to tell Isaac.

On that afternoon, Paris looked more beautiful than she'd ever been, but she had a young African-Pandian man by her side. The young man looked at Chris and Chris realized that all he had to do was to vanish; vanish just like spirit in a windy day.

Paris and the man crossed the street and entered a parked car. The look on the man's face spoke nothing but something like 'mind your biz pal.'

Paris acted as if Chris didn't exist at all. The man had also given Chris a look: awful, awkward and disdainful. If he was the boyfriend, then he was a dead man walking, Chris thought to himself. Having read their moods, Chris had to let them disappear before he could proceed.

When he reached Isaac's office, his world stood still.

"Sweet lord!" Paris said. "Can't you stop following me?"

Chris felt his throat running dry, his nerves numb; his head heavier and bigger than Everest and Kilimanjaro combined. His chest heaved. Chris was breathless. He was angry, betrayed and belittled. Speechless, Chris watched Paris and the young man walk past him without saying a word. She gave him one demonic grin as they walked away. Sanity was not in Chris though.

"She likes you," Isaac said holding the office door.

"What was she doing here?"

"She came to look for my financial support. She wants to contest the next general election," Isaac said trying to be humorous. Chris was not in the mood. Dejected and stupefied, he stood reflecting and composed.

"Come on in."

Chris got in and sat down uninvited, very much interested in what Paris wanted in Isaac's office.

Isaac pressed a phone button and spoke into the speaker.

"Can you give us some coffee please?" he said and looked at Chris. "What brings you here? Don't follow the girl. You know she can accuse you of stalking."

"I got a call today. Some African guy told me I'm signing my death warrant if I enter the plane tomorrow night."

Chris ignored what Isaac said about Paris intentionally out of anger. How could his attempt to help her turn into stalking? *What an ingrate?*

"I don't know what you're talking about. Well, if you don't want to go, Chris, then tell me."

Chris sighed as his chest was starting to get congested. *People are being stupid and irrational.*

"You're making me sound phony so let's drop it."

"No, Chris...I mean...look. This mission is very crucial and you have to know that if people get to know that you're associated with me in any way, they'll say a lot of things for your attention."

"It's okay, I think."

38

Dengdit stared at the monks as they milled around. The sight of them reminded him of his people back home in South Sudan. He was happy with what he'd discussed with uncle D and his previous conversation with Sister K. The information contained in the lost hard drive wasn't that revealing. They had to act fast however.

Sister J had gone back to Hayiroh to prepare the way for the team. She was to come back that day and go back again. A busy lady she was.

Sister K was still in Hayiroh.

After a period of purposeless staring, he entered the room.

"I'll blend in just fine. I'll probably get a job," Sister K said.

"Getting a job would probably give you the best blending in you'd need. How about the accent?" Dengdit said.

"I can fake it better than anyone."

"Don't overdo it though."

"Do you think they'd know?"

"You know better than many people when things come natural and when they're faked."

"Now you're making me feel guilty."

"That either means you're a good person or I have a way with words."

"If it makes me appear condescending then I'll kill myself."

"I hope no one else in Panda feels like that or the country would depopulate," Dengdit said with a smile.

"That's funny don't you think? Well, I just don't understand why powerful people aren't always humble."

"Give an example."

"Panda? USA? Britain?"

"Those are countries."

"Ruled and inhabited by people."

Dengdit smiled.

"What're driving at?"

"Remember North Korea and Iran?"

"Yes?"

"I just don't understand why someone would point artillery at someone and present the same person intimidated using the artillery as immoral."

"You've read 1984 by George Orwell, haven't you?"

"Five times."

"It's power you know."

"And they stand in front of the world audience and profess sublime morality. Pathetic don't you think? North Korea and Iran are weak compared to our powerful nations but we say we can't negotiate with them because it'd lower our status in the world as the most powerful nations. I don't know how?"

"That makes them human. Don't beat yourself, Sister K. All you can do in this world is what's within your capacity. You're already doing morally superior deeds. And besides, their immoral platform makes one thing clear: the average person in the village in Africa should be proud of herself. These supposedly socially advanced humans are still on their evolutionary journey, self-discovery. We haven't reached the destination yet."

"I wished the world knew that," she said getting out of the room.

"Bye Sister K. See you when you come back. Say hi to Mama and The Minister for me."

Sister K smiled, waved and walked out of the room.

Dengdit stared at the graffiti writings on the door.

Love showered me with spit.
Patience had the train leave me.
History has become too precious and brittle.
Humility had me a capitalist hand.
I was raped but they blame me.

He smiled as BG1 and BG2 noisily entered the room. BG2 Stared at him and said.

"You look like a child who'd seen a ghost, man."

"'History has become too precious and brittle'. What's that supposed to mean?" Dengdit asked.

"I've stared at those writings for a long time. They keep me thinking without coming to any real, appreciable meaning. I always think the line you've just read means that history is being protected by all means by those who wrote it," BG2 said.

"I think BG2 is right. When something becomes too dear to you, you keep it as if it's fragile. You caution anyone who'd want to temper with it. The mainstream society, which was favored by history, tends to protect the status quo. When you go against it, you're forced to face the music," BG1 said looking at Dengdit.

Dengdit smiled looking at the guys and thought of Uncle D's words.

"Giving a distinction between the color people have been given and who they are ontically speaking has either been lost or ignored in history. There're people who, when they say something bad, their words are rationalized to mean: 'I know he's a nice person and he can't possibly say that. I think this is what he means or we'll have to wait and let him explain what he means.' When a poor, unprivileged person says something presumably bad, their words are taken at face value," Uncle D had said.

Dengdit had laughed. "But in North America many minorities are allowed to say things whites are considered racists for. We have many minority pride events. When whites try to do the same, they're considered racists."

"That's on face value. Whites have dominance that doesn't need protection or reinforcement. Minorities have a position that needs to be heard not actually made prominent. And paradoxically speaking, most of the things we see as free reign for minorities are paternalistic concessions."

He smiled. "That's harsh, Uncle D!"

"What's harsh is to pretend you're empowering someone when you're actually disempowering them."

"How's that possible?" Dengdit said with a frown.

"When a white person, who campaigns against all forms of discrimination, puts him or herself in a privileged position then that person is actually disempowering those that are supposedly being helped."

"But in theory a white person in North America is privileged by the mere fact that he's white."

"And when you emphasize that in a group of underprivileged races, then what you're doing is basically elevating yourself further and that makes you feel even better than when you came. The privilege that isn't an issue when you're among your fellow whites becomes significant."

Dengdit nodded reluctantly.

"The audience feels that because this person is helping them, then he's valuing them; when in actual sense his position as a privileged person is being reinforced, being emphasized."

Dengdit looked at both BG1 and BG2 and smiled.

"You've heard from Uncle D and Grandma that we've got the documents from Durban and Khartoum," Dengdit said.

"Man, they're more detailed that I could have imagined," BG1 said.

"I'm still concerned about the lost hard drive. Western security dogs might exploit it."

"It'll perhaps give them a glimpse into who we are but it'll not give them any meaningful lead into who we actually are, how we operate and what our operations are. We'll talk more about this in our next meeting. We are doing extra screenings to ascertain whether Chris and Little actually don't know anything."

39

L ittle became wary of Chris. He studied Chris but there was no conspiracy in his eyes.

Chris was ready for Africa and had dropped by Little's office to talk about what Isaac had played down. They discussed the issue and Chris left.

Knowing the confusing events of the previous few days, Little knew there was some element of truth to the threat. He didn't want to alarm Chris, however. Chris needed a change of environment more than he needed anything else. But concealed, unknown, surprising solitaires exist. There was no doubt Chris deserved a restart window to make some fresh beginning in Africa. He couldn't set me up, Little told himself as he walked to his car. Chris had denied having ever spied on Little. While the recordings could not have been made up, Little believed Chris because of the manner in which he denied the police claims.

Grace stood staring at him from the window.

Things had relaxed a bit for Little: no more cops at the door, no more mysterious police officers, and no more stupid favors.

He put on the engine. As he was about to put the gear in reverse, he saw Grace in the rare-view mirror, waving.

What?

She had an envelope in hand. Little stopped and rolled down the glass.

"I found this letter in your room when I was cleaning. I'm sorry I opened it."

He stared at the envelope.

40

C hris headed to Judy's apartment as he had a spare key. She knew he'd be there. It was quiet and calm, the apartment tidied and cleaned, the air freshened and soothing.

He walked to the kitchen, opened the fridge and saw a note placed craftily on a plate; just like a birthday present. Three candies were placed neatly around it. Chris gave a mechanistic, childish and satisfied-lad smile and reached for the note. Excited, he playfully threw one candy onto his tongue and started to unfold the paper. As he opened the paper, he heard a creaking sound at the backyard. He hesitated then continued to open the paper. It was beautifully colored. The edges of the paper were decorated with light green and purple flowers, bordered by tiny heart-shaped drawings. At the bottom left of the paper stood, on one leg, a sketch of a green dove. The letter was soothing and romantic and Chris became humbly enamored. When he recovered from his trance, he started reading.

Sorry honey, I...

The creaking sound began again but he assumed it was Judy.

"Judy?"

Silence! He continued reading; now with one ear raised.

...am gone for three days with a friend. There...

Chris heard a bang then silence. The wind whistled outside; whirling dried snow up across the backyard. Stealthily, he walked slowly to the backyard, opened the door slowly. There was no one outside. He trod back defiantly; furious, but immediately sipped in the delight of his thoughts about Judy's letter.

There...

Now some ferocious footsteps sounded and he knew he had company.

"Judy, stop playing games, okay? I'm enjoying the letter," he said, engrossed in and enamored by the letter. With some precise skills he didn't know he had, Chris quietly, slowly and tactfully scuttled to the front door.

"You can't surprise me Judy. Come out!"

There was smile oiled all over his face. He then jumped to twist the door lever. Swiftly and confidently, he pulled the door knob. Ouch! He found himself on the floor. Seriously hurt, he groaned, writhed and started to pant.

She's so dead!

"Judy, what's this?"

Before he could look up, he sensed three bodies standing heavily over him.

"Don't even look up," a deep, raw, thunderous and accented voice warned. It sounded African. Chris tried to lift his eyebrows, but then came the warning.

"Nah, nah!" one voice warned him.

"Where's Jeng?"

"What?"

"I said where's fuckin' Jeng?"

"Maybe these white people call him Daniel or Dan," another rude voice said. The voice sounded something between masculine and feminine.

"You have the wrong house, I think. I know nothing of what you guys are saying."

"He's such a liar," a female voice sounded together with a kick to his right ribs. Chris groaned painfully then yelled.

"I know no Daniel, Dan or Jeng or something...fuck!"

"Stop lying," the first voice said.

"We saw you yesterday with Jeng and his girlfriend," the female voice sounded and he was afraid the kick would come with it, but it didn't. *Ah!*

"Oh! I only know Paris. I don't know the b...the guy who was with him I swear. Her name is Paris and she works for Little Michael."

"Where does she live?"

"I don't know where she lives. I can give you Little's bar address. But you guys have to promise not to say you found the address from me."

"What's it? What we do with the address and who we tell is none of your goddamn business. Sit up."

Chris looked up. They had masks on.

"1996 Yiy street southeast. It's a big building with a statement, 'Hibiscus Square'."

The lady wrote the address down, looked at Chris sternly as the other two guys walked away.

"What's all these about?" Chris asked. No one answered him as they left. *How the hell did they know Judy's house?*

Still hurting from the kicks, he got up slowly, dragged his aching body to the bathroom. There was only a big lump on his forehead. It wasn't bleeding. A sharp pain on his ribs sent a needle-like stabbing sensation through his right side. The right side looked okay though. There wasn't any damage showing. For about ten minutes, he stood drunkenly looking into the mirror.

"I gotta go to hospital."

Chris took a quick shower, came to the living room to have his lunch. It was getting late in the afternoon. He walked to the kitchen and opened the fridge. Beer bottles were lying at the bottom of the fridge. There were also fried fish and oven-baked chicken ribs in the fridge. He served himself, put them into the microwave, took two beers, headed to the living room and turned the TV on. As the food warmed in the microwave, Chris enjoyed some afternoon programs on TV. The microwave timer and the doorbell then sounded simultaneously.

"What again?" he said knowing that Judy couldn't ring the doorbell.

He hesitated. Silence!

"Dude, I can't be kicked again!"

The doorbell sounded again. Chris walked slowly, but composedly toward the door. His heart almost stopped when he opened the door.

"What, for god's sake, are you doing here?" Chris said looking around, fearing sighting the tormenters who'd just left.

"I don't know. We're having fun I guess," Paris said, looking at Chris like a sadistic monster.

"You can't stay here. You have to go, now!"

Paris brushed him aside and walked briskly into the living room. The young African guy followed her closely; his then rude stare now relaxed and friendly, his African dress giving him a professional air. Chris stood confused as the young man sat down in the living room. Paris headed to the fridge.

"Nothing I like like Uncle Beer," she said, grabbed two, and threw one at the young man who caught it in the air athletically and skillfully. She stared at Chris, smiled and went back to the kitchen, grabbed another and threw it at him. *I'm not the African guy.* The beer bottle landed on the floor; grounding itself into fine fragments. They burst into hysterical laugher as he stood stupefied. Chris fattened with anger, his skin reddening. They continued to laugh though. Then his anger ebbed off immediately, their laugher off like a blackout as the doorbell sounded. Now Chris's heart-beat was getting out of control.

41

"I've become wary of making speeches these days," Osmani said as Isaac and P.D looked at him.

The men laughed.

"Careful what you wish for. Unless you want to tell me the ambassador's case wasn't a mistake," P.D said and sipped his Fanta.

They were having breakfast at Isaac's house. Isaac had invited them for the first time to his mansion. It was a superb get-together.

"Well...I mean...the media has become very shallow these days," Isaac said.

Jane came with a tea thermo-flask, a piece of paper and placed them on the table.

"So, when and where's your next speech?" P.D asked.

Osmani sighed confidently.

"It's next week in University of Khartoum."

"Whoa...Khartoum? That's strange!" P.D exclaimed and looked at Isaac. Isaac winked.

"I at first felt that way. It's kind of Pan-Arab, Pan-African thing."

"What's it on?"

"'*Effect of Poverty and Western contribution to its aggravation.*'"

Both P.D and Isaac stared at Osmani. It was as if he'd botched something seriously important.

"Wouldn't it have been better if you focused on why poverty is prevalent in Africa in general; giving every reason you know about why the continent is so rather than giving only western contribution."

"I think P.D is right," Isaac said; playing with the paper Jane had given him.

"I didn't choose the topic. They handed it to me as something they'd want to understand."

"They'd want to know this too: that corrupt African leaders are the malignant cancerous agents of African poverty. You have to give them an unbiased view of the world," P.D riposted.

Osmani was starting to get irritated, but he knew P.D was right.

"Well, he hasn't discussed that with them. It'd be better if he asked if they have any interest in other fundamental factors," Isaac said and looked impressed with himself.

Both P.D and Osmani nodded.

"I..."

P.D's phone rang, interrupting Osmani.

P.D raised his hand to excuse himself. To take the call, P.D got up and walked out to the backyard. He came back and sat down quietly as Osmani and Isaac conversed.

"There's this idea of philanthropy a student asked me about in class once," P.D said staring at his phone and continued.

"I don't want to sound inconsiderate but I'll say it. A student asked me the wisdom of naming charity organizations after the people who established them."

Osmani frowned and said: "Okay, Okay...that's a silly question!"

"It's not!" P.D countered.

"I think it is. It's really a silly question. The naming is an appreciation or gratitude; a sense of purpose no one should question," Isaac said.

"You're right to some extent but listen. This is what the kid told me," P.D smiled. "'The beauty of any help is to let people wonder who did that supererogatory act. Once people know the act and associate it with you instantly, it becomes about you and not the people you help or the help itself.'"

"Okay, Okay, now that's mean, out-worldly unrealistic and contemptible," Osmani said.

"I thought so at first."

Isaac stared at Osmani then at P.D. He opened the paper and frowned.

P.D continued with his student's assertion.

"The charities then become different: not about help of the innocent *per se*. They become about portraying oneself as a humane character. It's not that these wretched people are important, it's that you're the one who helped them."

"That doesn't make any sense!" Isaac said.

The orphanage doesn't carry my name!

"Yes, indeed it doesn't!" Osmani agreed.

"If one just wants to help, why does it matter what name it's under. It shouldn't be about you, but about the help and the people you help," P.D stood with his student.

"Does naming the charitable organizations or the foundations after the philanthropists make any difference to the help given to the people?" Osmani asked.

Isaac frown deepened. He traded his gaze from the paper to P.D and Osmani.

"It doesn't change anything, but renders the whole affair a vanity."

"That's preposterous, Mr. Michael. You possibly don't believe that!" Osmani said.

Isaac was now deeply studying the paper. His frown had changed to a saddened face.

"Why'd I want to let you know I'm helping the poor? Why can't I just help while no one knows I'm helping?"

Osmani saw the point, but looked unconvinced.

Half-convinced, Osmani looked at Isaac and saw the look on his face.

"Are you okay, Isaac?"

No, I'm not!

"Yes, I am. It's a friend of mine. He wants to meet me."

Isaac stared at Osmani and at the paper.

"Can you guys excuse me for a while? I gotta make a phone call," Isaac solemnly said.

The two African gentlemen nodded.

Isaac left and came back. He sat down and looked at Osmani.

I don't get this darn fellow!

"I'm sorry I forgot. Jane is always fascinated by your speeches. She'd like to take you out and chat with you," Isaac said with pain, hidden but difficult.

Osmani looked confused as P.D frowned.

"Are you serious?" P.D asked, surprised.

Isaac nodded with an insincere smile.

"Are...?"

Jane appeared at the door, dressed up, perfumed and ready.

"See you guys later," Osmani reluctantly said.

P.D and Isaac sat silently for a while. Isaac still looked depressed and rattled.

"I hope I'm not being presumptuous, but you don't look okay, Isaac."

He sighed, looked at the paper and handed it to P.D.

P.D hesitated and then looked at the paper.

We kindly invite you to Osmani Osmani speech. Whatever you do, we're watching you. We know your every move.

The Pipers

"Who're the Pipers?" P.D asked.

Isaac sighed, looked at the ceiling, the pictures on the wall then looked at P.D again.

"You remember our first meeting?"

P.D nodded with unnerving curiosity.

"Well, Osmani said he was able to come because I called the ambassador."

P.D frowned.

"You see, I didn't call the ambassador. This was a personal meeting and I'd no reason to call the ambassador to postpone a state's issue for my personal gain. I don't know why he lied to me."

P.D sat back on his chair, looking thoughtful.

"Or maybe he's not lying. Maybe someone else is doing the lying."

"You mean *The Pipers*?"

"Could be!"

"I don't want to sound presumptuous but I think Osmani might be one of The Pipers. But who're The Pipers? During our last meeting he sounded very dismissive of what I said."

"I've never heard of them before. But don't jump to absurd conclusions. If something like this happens again then we'll have to talk to him. Or even warn him against possible misuse of his political positions by opportunists and radical groups."

Isaac blankly stared at P.D then said: "I too find my own rationalization of this situation hard to believe but the facts point his way."

P.D read the paper again and then looked up.

"The note looks rather unprofessional."

"You see, that's what makes it dangerous. These guys don't want to be perceived as powerful or dangerous."

"You're right. I see your point. However, let's be very careful with this. You have resources to commission a study to find out who these guys actually are. Talk to Pandian intelligence community. We could rush to conclusion to our own detrimental end."

Isaac took a long pause looking absent-mindedly at the tea cup on the table and said: "I'll open up a report and also start my own enquiries."

"As for Osmani, let's wait."

"He's..."

"That was a great promenade," Jane remarked as she opened the door.

42

Chris stared at Paris and Jeng like a tired boxer in a boxing ring. The doorbell kept on chiming.

"That's Judy," Paris said and took a rude, excited gulf of beer.

"What in the name of Jesus is happening here?" he asked, angry yet dead with anxiety.

"In the name of Mary what's happening is the doorbell that's ringing but no one is answering it," Paris said and they laughed again.

Chris looked at them one by one, but all they could afford him were mere winks. The doorbell kept rudely ding-donging away.

With no any other word left to say, Chris uncertainly and reluctantly dashed to the door. The sight of the creatures at the door almost made him faint. They were back. What was he to say? He was a dead man.

They were gravely intimidating: ghetto-rude.

"We lost the address, can we get it again?"

The lady said and tried to push the door, but Chris resisted.

"Are they here or something?" the lady asked.

"What do you mean *they*?"

"Paris and Jeng."

"No, it's some girl and we're having fun, okay? The address is 1996 Yiy Street, Hibiscus Square."

God don't let Paris's big mouth open!

Chris's internal organs were ablaze. He was sweating. *What if they push the door open and come in? God help me! God don't let those fools inside say a word.*

There was no doubt, Chris was done. His throat was parched, his joints achy and his palm oily with sweat.

"Who's it, Chris? What took you so long?"

Paris called and Chris's sweat started dripping onto the ground. He was dehydrating. The girl pushed again but Chris put his hand across her chest, nearly touching her breasts.

"You like them, eh?" she said smiling wickedly. The girl had a bit of Lil' Kim's attitude.

"He's freaking out, let's go. Let him have his time," the deep-voiced fellow said and Chris's soul started to enliven. The girl pushed the door again and, still, he resisted; standing like an immovable structure, a mountain. She looked at him, smiled and said: "I wish I could devour you. You're hot. Pray that Judy doesn't find out," she said and stared at Chris sensually.

"Who's that by the way?" Paris yelled.

Chris and the girl stared at one another like cocks after a long fight. That Lil' Kim had some stupid audacity.

"Let's go girl!" the deep-voiced fellow said.

She pushed Chris in the stomach, licked her lips and left.

Chris managed to breathe, sigh. He swiftly closed the door and headed back in quickly in case they came back. Chris's sole felt like he was walking on a hot metal floor. Every atom in his body was engaged. When he emerged, into the living room, the two bullies burst into hysteria.

"What happened to you? You're sweating like a pig, eh? What happened?" Paris asked.

What happened...you're what happened to me! These stupid kids don't know shit!

Furious and hurting, Chris remained silent, walked to the wash-room and wobbled back immediately; worried and confused.

"You guys are in danger, I think," he said as they looked at him with sheer blankness. It was as if he'd grown multiple horns like the beast in the apocalypse.

"You mean from Little?" Paris asked wearing a comical stare, a potential laugher.

Chris was in no mood to laugh.

"You guys have to leave now or you'll be dead. They're looking for you," he said pointing at Jeng.

"Who're these people you're talking about?" Paris asked.

"You don't even know my name," he said, speaking for the first time since Chris met him. He had a clear, groomed and carefully articulated American accent. Chris thought he was African because of the African clothing. He was skinny, light-skinned with pronounced jaw bones.

"I don't know whether your name is Dan, Daniel or Jeng, but they're looking for you. I don't know why they're looking for you. They're two African guys and one African-Pandian lady. They came before you came and then came back having lost Little's address."

"I don't know what you're talking about. No one knows me here in Panda. Do you even know who I am?"

Like it's my business to know! All I'm saying is your butt is in danger! That's what I know.

"It's not important whether or not I know who you are. All I need to tell you is that you're in danger. These guys kicked me like a dog."

"Paris, did you tell him my name so that he could make up stories to scare us away? He obviously doesn't need us here. By the way, my name is Jeng."

Chris became disillusioned.

Are they retarded or something?

It was becoming Chris's safety more than it was theirs. *Are they stupid or something?*

"I'm a student at Columbia University if you know where it is," he said looking at Chris then turned to Paris and said: "We have this

African philosophy professor who almost killed me when I said no one enjoys killing other people out of pleasure. He talked of ancient times when executions were done publicly and the king or queen presided over the killings. He said the audience was always reflected as enjoying the killing and the king or the queen also enjoyed the scene. But I said that..."

Before Jeng could finish the story, the doorbell chimed. Chris was a dead man then. His stomach rumbled. He thought he was developing cholera. *What do they want again?*

With no choice, Chris tiredly walked to the door knowing how he felt couldn't change anything. Whatever was to happen would happen anyway. At the door, he sighed, took a deep breathe, closed his eyes and opened the door.

Viola!

"Is that a new way to welcome visitors?"

Chris felt stupid. It was Isaac.

"Dude, how did you know I was here?"

"Your car? And by the way, you're not picking up your phone."

"Come in, please!"

"No, I just need to let you know that the flight has been rescheduled for tomorrow morning. You can sleep at my place. Prepare yourself and I'll pick you up at 12.00 a.m. tonight."

Chris managed to smile for the first time since Jeng and Paris walked into Judy's house.

43

Little looked curiously at the envelope Grace had given him and placed it on the passenger seat. He drove for a while then pulled up by the road side and stared at the envelope. Looking strangely at the envelope, Little felt goose pimples on his arms. He held the letter strongly and manly, however.

He curled his lips up. "What's in it?"

He picked it up, tore the flap slowly. It was a brown envelope with white and brown stripes on the edges. Little wondered what it contained. He then slowly budged his gaze down the paper to the first sentence. He stopped.

"What the heck?"

Dear Mr. Michael,

He moved his gaze up and looked at the date. It indicated Monday, January 12th. Still bothered by the content of the letter, Little quickly looked at his watch and it read: January 20th.

"Okay?"

He then quickly moved his gaze nervously down the paper.

I am writing to invite you to our meeting. It will be in the Methodist Church downtown. It's on First and Second Street, just across from Barclays Bank...

Feeling nauseous, Little frantically moved his gaze to the bottom of the paper. Realizing the problem, Little felt like his brain had jumped out of his skull; his heart speeding away loudly. Confused and flustered, he sprang up hitting the roof of the car.

That can't be!

He scanned the paper again; moving his eyes up the paper.

We'd like you to meet us on January 15ᵗʰ.

"Shoot! Shoot!"

Little looked around, across the street but there was no one around. His hand started shaking, his heart-rate increased and his vision started to get blurry. He moved his eyes further up the paper.

It would cost you a lot if you miss this meeting. Your life depends on it. If we don't hear from you by the end of the first day, things will happen. Remember you agreed to a favor.

Sincerely,

Your brothers and sisters in creation!

"You fooled me, damn you. What've I done to you? I thought you were dead. Today is...oh shit!"

Little turned the engine on and made a swift U-turn, nearly hitting the car nearby. The lady in the car screamed and horned simultaneously.

"Downtown!" Little breathed and gunned off.

His phone rang but he had no heart to answer it.

44

Isaac decided to keep an eye on Osmani. Osmani's actions were of great concern to him, but Osmani showed no physical signs to raise more suspicion. Isaac was no fool though. He did everything with caution, smartness and in a very personable manner. Perhaps Osmani was no fool too. Isaac discerned nothing, saw nothing, and heard nothing again. That made him even more confused and worried. But those two incidences needed no rationalization, but investigation.

Mr. Burns was torn between respecting P.D's advice and commissioning a private detective to follow Osmani's every move.

P.D was right. Caution! Caution! But Isaac's thoughts were getting out of control as he was losing intelligence ground against the illusive *The Pipers*.

Everyday, on his way home, Osmani invaded his head. He'd stare at the philosophical nothingness, helpless but determined. The due diligence The Pipers portrayed characterized Osmani. But one night was different. Isaac had not thought much about Osmani that night. He'd just left Judy's place after having enlightened Chris about the mission. He was to pick Chris up at his place and all his thoughts were wrapped around the mission. *Chris is fitting! Chris is suitable!*

The night was crispy and clearly romantic. A few clouds hid a few bright stars at the western horizon. Then a phone call interrupted his visual vacation; disturbing the quiet night. Isaac hesitated. The driver's eyes met Isaac's as he hesitantly picked up the phone.

"Burns!" he said.

The caller sighed.

"Christine?"

"Yes!"

"You sound depressed. I hope there's nothing wrong again."

She sighed again. Isaac always knew what that meant.

"We're against some Marxist and Pan-Africanist bullshit, Isaac. Pandian and Sivalsian security services have information about The Pipers."

"Good morning... not that yours is good. What do you mean, exactly?"

"I received a letter from someone in the Sivalsian security services that we're against a group that calls itself THE PIPERS. A hard drive obtained by Pandian intelligence office is shedding light on the nature of The Pipers. I don't know why the information is still being kept secret."

"The Pipers? That doesn't sound good."

There was a brief silence.

"Some of your offices in South Africa have been vandalized."

"What?"

"I also received a letter claiming that all your dealings will be detailed in an affidavit to be presented to the ministry of justice."

Isaac remained thoughtfully silent. He felt paralyzed. The hairs on his ears thickened and stood erect. He could feel and hear wind whistling through them. *Now what does that mean?*

"The guy in the security service didn't tell me who he is. The blackmailing letter was signed, *P. Brothers and Sisters.*"

Isaac remained silent for a while. *Dealings, what dealings?* He was lost for words. After a tormenting period of silence, he said: "Why does that worry you as if we're involved in some illegal enterprises? This is about Burns Investment. We'll fight them in court. They've chosen the way that'd favor us."

"Beat it, sir. This is Africa, Mr. Burns. When dealing with people who don't always follow the law, you don't always follow the law."

"What're you saying?"

She sighed. "You know what I'm saying, Isaac!"

"So...I mean...you mean such a move is going to be a concern to me?"

"Don't play dumb, Isaac, so beat it."

Christine voice was irritated. She chaffed at Isaac's assumed ignorance of the Africa's ways.

"Christine! What's going on?"

"We're fucked, Isaac!"

"What...I mean...what's Vincent saying about this?"

"He'll tell you himself."

"I don't believe this! I have to go to Hayiroh and Johannesburg."

"No!"

"What do you mean *no*?"

Christine sighed.

"They said they want to see Chris in Hayiroh on the 22nd."

"Wh...what...how did they know...?"

"We're being watched Isaac, being watched in real time very closely. I just don't know how they're doing that!"

"Let me call you back."

Isaac hanged up and called Chris.

Satan doesn't sleep. God does, lest his followers wouldn't be this wretched, demanding, ever-prayerful yet still poor and downtrodden.

Chris's cellular phone was switched off. Yes, turned off: the power button pressed.

"Not this time, Chris!"

Isaac called Chris's place.

Chris, please leave me a message.

"This is not the time, Chris! Damn it! Let's go back to Judy's."

"Yes sir," the driver said and took a swift U-turn.

Isaac arrived at Judy's and jumped down before the driver could even open the door. Standing outside, Isaac tried Chris's cell phone for the second time.

Chris, please leave me a message.

"No, No!"

Isaac ran toward the building only to come back running: worry-drunk, scared, confused, mad and screwed! The driver stared at Isaac as he acted frantic; fretting over something the driving didn't know. From the look of things, the driver instantly knew something was wrong.

"Head downtown please!" Isaac roared at the confused driver. The driver had already started driving toward the street, not knowing where they were going.

45

L ittle parked the car by the roadside and literally ran into the church. There was no one inside. He walked toward the altar but the church was as silent as a cemetery.

Little's lips curled up. "Anyone here? Please, anyone?"

Rude silence echoed his voice. Little's chest was thumbing like it'd never been before. His forehead glistened in neon light, sweat streamed undisturbed on his cheeks, his temple and his neck.

"I don't know what this means!"

Little stood for a while then turned. He took two rude steps then a voice called from behind. The voice was low but endearing.

"How can I help you my son?" a white pastor said, walking slowly toward Little.

"I..."

"They were here five days ago."

"Did..."

"They do their Bible study and leave. They left me a note saying that if a man comes looking for them, I should let him know that he'll get the message at his place."

Little stood for a while, frightened and confused.

Little grimaced and said: "This is a kinda weird question, pastor. I actually don't know who these people are. Do you know anyone among them?"

"Not really, but I know one fine young lady who sometimes attend our mass services. I don't know her name though. She's a white, brown haired, beautiful quick-talker. They were about six ladies: four Blacks and two whites."

"They were ladies?"

The pastor slowly nodded.

"Thanks, pastor!"

Little turned and ran out of the church only to find out his car wasn't there. He blinked, opened his eyes but it was all the same: his car was not there. On the other side of the street everything looked the same: nothing. He looked to his left. Nothing!

"You gotta be kidding me!"

Then a thought hit him and he looked at the sign.

NO PARKING. UNATTENDED VEHICLES WILL BE TOWED AT OWNER'S COST

"No fuckin' way. Oh great! Sweet! No car, intimidated, screwed up."

Little stood for a while then ran toward a nearby subway station. *No. Waiting time!* He turned, crossed the street and yelled.

"Taxi!"

The blue and white taxi took a swift, dangerous U-turn. Little jumped into the taxi and they were off.

"Are you okay, sir? You don't look alright...where are we going?" the driver asked.

"You know Hibiscus Square?"

"I wouldn't be a cab driver if I didn't know it. Actually, everyone knows HS. I hear the owner is a fine young man. No nonsense kind of a guy."

"Can you just drive?"

The driver nodded.

Little was mired in his own troubles and didn't want any silly gossips. The driver looked into the rare-view mirror and realized that the man was staring at him yet not listening to him.

The driver was a chubby, short Arab man with a finely-trimmed urban beard and moustache. His complexion was rather Caucasian.

"Sir, is everything alright?"

"Yes!" Little said in a raw, cowardly voice.

"The best way to deal with problems is to mentally uproot them instead of dealing with them as if they don't have any effect on you," the driver said.

Little frowned and said: "this ain't a movie sir, but I appreciate your oriental abstract."

"Just helping! I feel the pain of my clients."

"And I appreciate that. Would you just drive and shut up, please?"

The driver kept quiet for a while but then started talking again.

"My son was born here," the driver said with smugness. "He told me once that if you talk to a man who seemingly has a heavy heart and face; and that man responds to your questions with a humble, calm and irritated voice, then know that the gravity of his problems require an hour at a dinner table with you, himself and your wives."

Little frowned and looked at the driver as the car approached a junction. There were police cars, ambulances and fire trucks speeding toward the left of them, ahead.

"Why do you drive a cab?"

"And don't teach philosophy at the University?"

Little smiled for the first time and shook his head.

"I have a bachelor's in Philosophy and a master's degree in sociology from Lebanon. They're useless here, it's supposed."

Little's lips curled up excitedly. "You're a smart ass, you know that?"

"I...there's fire over there!" the driver said as he turned to the left.

Little heart sank.

"No, you can't do that! No, no...!" Little voice trailed off.

"What...?"

The driver looked into the rear-view mirror but couldn't see Little. He swerved to the roadside and jumped down to open the door. Little was shocked out of breath. The driver closed the door, jumped onto the driver's seat and drove to the scene.

The place was swarmed with fire trucks, ambulances, police and media cars. The cab driver jumped down and shouted: "Please help!"

"What happened?" two paramedics said, running toward the taxi.

Grace stood confused as fire-fighters struggled to contain the fire. She saw Little being hurled onto the stretcher and screamed: "Little, Little! Oh no, baby!"

She fiendishly looked at the driver and yelled: "What did you do to him?"

"I didn't do anything ma'am. He passed out when he saw the building ablaze."

Grace looked at the paramedics, at the struggling firemen and at the taxi driver then walked away.

46

C hris was waiting for Isaac to pick him up as he'd promised. He didn't know his phone was still off. The phone was out of power so he'd put it on the charger.

It was a fine day and his hopes had sky-rocketed, really running high. The sky was dark. A few miserable clouds feathered the horizon. Chris had heard of fine African foods: *Nyama choma* in Kenya and Sivals and *matoke* in Uganda. Chris hoped to visit these places as he settled down. They'd be memories of his African safari!

Despite his enthusiasm and hope of a new beginning, Judy's stance still confused him. What appalled Chris the most was Judy's seeming indifference about his going to Africa. She showed little if any emotions about his leaving for Africa. That kind of made Chris worried. Why couldn't she object to his going away, to Africa for heaven's sake? Couldn't she let him defend himself as a loved soul?

However, Judy seemed understanding. She wanted to see him on his feet again. Perhaps that was the reason. He couldn't tell. Perhaps she'd understood him well enough to have any worries. Those were mere speculations. But Chris saw a favorable fire in her blue eyes and thought better to exploit it for his delight.

"I'm going to my mum's. I'll meet you at Isaac's. Tell him I'm coming so that those rude guards don't make me wait at the door," she'd said, laughed heartily and left.

Judy, however, decided to come back after Chris's departure date was moved.

Chris waited. There was no sign of Isaac. After thirty minutes, he removed his cellular phone and realized it was off. He frantically turned it on.

No service!

You're fuckin' kidding me, right?

He dashed to the home phone. The phone wasn't at its charging spot and the holder was blinking. That meant there was a message. Still wondering where the phone was, he dashed to his bedroom and realized Isaac had been calling him and the ringer was off. Heavy-headed and dazed, he pushed the button but got no dial tone. He ran drunkenly back to the living room to check the charger. It wasn't blinking anymore.

"Okay, something is going on! I paid the darn bills."

Damn phone companies!

He had to call the phone company so he ran out of the house. A shopping center was five minutes from the house. Within minutes Chris was by a public pay phone. Angry and out of breath, he frantically poured the coins into the coin slot. *Damn whoever picks it up!* He hurriedly dialed the number before all the coins got into the slot. Extremely furious, Chris was panting heavily and sweating profusely.

This is Judy's phone. You know what to do: leave me a message. If this is my love, Chris, you know where I am, baby.

Strangely enough, Chris didn't want to get angry after having wrongly dialed Judy's phone yet he was furious. He hanged up, dialed the phone company's number but then changed his mind and dialed Judy's cell phone number. It was the same. He didn't know her mum's number though. For a moment, Chris stared at the souls passing by but nothing made any sense at all. Confused, he frantically poured some coins into the coin box slot again and dialed a 1-800 number.

You've reached Garacom customer service efficient phone service. Please listen to the following instructions carefully if we're to help you effectively for our menu options have changed. For inquiries concerning billing, press 1; for changes to your account, press 2; for technical help, press 3; for our seasonal promotions, press 4, for general inquiries, press 5 or stay on the online and a free agent will be able to help you.

Chris waited.

All our agents are currently busy. Please stay on the line and a free agent will be with you shortly. Our calls are answered in the order they're received. Please stay on the line to maintain your priority.

"You guys...!"

"Garacom, Brown speaking, how can I help you?"

Fuckin' Brown?

"Hello, Brown, both my cellular phone and my home phone are not working..."

"What's your name sir?"

"Chris, Christopher Fox."

The agent asked his date of birth, his social security reference number (SSRN), his address and many other security checks.

"Please give me a few seconds as I check what the problem could be."

"Sure, dude!"

Again, he waited impatiently. Then the young man cleared his throat as if he was about to give a very long, imperative speech.

"What happened?" Chris hastily enquired.

"If you forgot sir, you've disconnected your phone services with us."

I hope this guy didn't just come from the bar and braved his work with his dodo boss.

"Dude, what's that supposed to mean?"

The young man sighed with a tint of disappointment in the sigh.

"Sir, when you call us and tell us that you no longer want to have our services due to our inefficiency and unfairness, what happens is your wish is granted."

Chris felt stupid rather than angry.

"I didn't..."

"Sir, you called us about an hour and a half ago..."

Chris couldn't take all the nonsense happening so he hanged up.

What's this? Apocalypse? What the hell just happened?

There was no point calling anyone. How could he if he had no any slight idea who disconnected his phones. As he turned to go, two men, who he assumed wanted to use the phone, stared at him with their arms folded on their massive chests. Ghetto-rude!

"Hello Chris! My name is Dengiya. We're Judy's friends. We're going camping, do you mind coming with us?"

Chris smiled. "I appreciate that dude, but look...someone disconnected my phones: cellular phone and home phone. The phone company tells me I was the one who called and told them I was dissatisfied with their services. I didn't disconnect the service and I'm not dissatisfied with the service. I was supposed to leave for Africa today but the guy who made the arrangement hasn't showed up. I'd like to call him now because he couldn't reach me as my phones are disconnected."

"Do you know why you're being sent to Africa?" Dengiya said with his croaky voice.

"No! Why...but hey...this is none of your business?"

"Do you think you have a life?"

"What kind of question is that?"

"Judy loves you, but she's afraid of losing you. She told us the way Isaac is treating you."

"Judy talked to you about me?"

"She cares, Chris. Why'd someone who pretends to care about you send you on a mission you know nothing about?"

That made sense not that Chris didn't think about it. Chris just needed a period of respite.

"I have to see a friend of mine. Tell Judy to call me later...she's actually meeting me at Isaac's."

As Dengiya and company stood looking at Chris both Chris's and Dengiya's phones rang simultaneously.

"You were lying to us about your phones getting disconnected," Dengiya croaked, shaking his head, moving toward Chris.

Chris felt both stupid and furious. The phone was disconnected and now it was working. *Perfect, fuckin' perfect!* He was, presumably, just a stupid liar. *Can you believe something that just happened to you but you can't prove it to be right!*

"No, I swear..."

"Save your breath, Chris. We look stupid, don't we? We always are, don't you agree?"

Chris stared at the four men. They had disgusting muscles that browbeat one into subservience. Two of them were quiet and two were talking nonstop. Among the ones talking was one with a wild, nondescript face, with zits and creases on the fore-head. He could be a Pandian borne African; tall and slightly leaning forward. This man was perhaps a river Nilote of South Sudan, Uganda or Sivals. Chris couldn't tell. He was the one who called himself Dengiya.

The other one was chubby, short but kind-faced. He might have been South African for he had features that made him look like Mandela and N!xau of the movie *The Gods Must Be Crazy*. He had a pronounced, confusing accent.

"Do you mind coming with us?" the short one said.

"If I knew who you guys were, I wouldn't mind," Chris said as he tried to pass by them.

A big, long muscle straddled Chris's chest. Dengiya stood in front of him.

"We need you to come with us!" Dengiya said. His voice was croaky, soft and soothing. His face wasn't so soothing.

"Would you guys mind telling me who you are?"

"We mean no harm, but we don't fancy resistance," the short one said again.

Chris realized he was in no position to bargain with the guys. He tried to scan the place for where he could escape. They were professionals. One of the quiet ones approached, patted Chris on the back and placed a short-gun on his stomach.

"Do you mind?" he said.

Cornered, Chris couldn't run anymore, he couldn't shout. He didn't have to mind anything. The pistol said it all: just go with the flow.

"Can I call my girlfriend?"

47

Isaac was simply fried, thunderstruck, betrayed and scared. Whatever happened to Chris, it was only the gods who would tell. Chris had disappeared into thin air. After many trials with Chris's phone, Isaac didn't bother calling him again. The stupid message left on his answering machine or voicemail was irritating. Isaac couldn't lift his hand to call Christine and Vincent. He was utterly sapped of mental energy.

What if things went wrong? What if Chris knew what Isaac and company were up to? What if someone killed Chris? Isaac would be in a whole lot of nasty excrement.

Judy wasn't answering her phone either. Isaac had to drive to either Judy's or Chris's house; the only option he was left with. This time Isaac didn't think it was wise to use a chauffeur. He drove; his head blank.

There was no one at Judy's place. The doorbell echoed to the last sound of its life. He turned and drove to Chris's.

It was the greatest mistake Isaac had ever done.

Isaac had gone to the wrong place at the wrong time even though it was for the right reason. He was a walking stalk; not a human being. There were funny-looking guys at Chris's door. They were standing like body-guards. Both wore black, tight-fitting t-shirts with khaki jeans and black sunglasses. As Isaac approached, they stood still.

"Hello gentlemen, is Chris home?"

They slowly moved toward Isaac. Isaac moved back as they approached silently. With great futility, Isaac tried to run but someone stopped him from behind. Fright filled his stomach. He couldn't feel his breath, his feet and legs. Without a word, he stood looking at the three giant, black figures.

Isaac experienced a brief painful sensation in his stomach then everything else was history. The next thing Isaac heard was this: "They dropped you off and left. Are you okay?"

The doctor said the following morning as Isaac opened his eyes. Jane was sitting gloomily; dozing to be fair. *They dropped me off and left?* Whoever they were, Isaac didn't know.

Jane got up slowly and sat by Isaac's bedside. Isaac had bruises on his forehead, shoulders and right leg. No bones were broken, luckily.

"Who were they, doctor?" Isaac feverishly asked, pain and anger in his throat.

"I could ask you the same question myself, Mr. Burns."

"The doctors have done a great job to keep the media away from this," Jane said.

Isaac looked at Jane, who angrily added: "Why did you leave your bodyguards and the driver? Is there something I should know?"

There was nothing to discuss. He kept quiet and banged his head on the bed.

"You can go home, Mr. Burns. Jane can take it from there. These were minor bruises."

Minor bruises? Why did I pass out?

The doctor turned and looked at Isaac.

"I'm sorry. They drugged you but decided to neither kill you nor make your wounds severe. Why, you couldn't ask me that," he said and left shaking his head.

Jane drove Isaac home only for Isaac to find fifteen messages; all worrying. He called Hayiroh. Vincent was out of town. He was in Khartoum on a regional economic meeting. Christine had gone to South Africa with the Pandian ambassador. It was like everyone planned to avoid Isaac. After days of crippling anxiety, Isaac's eyes were blood-red with sleeplessness.

Isaac still didn't know the actual source of his woes. Chris had disappeared like a ghost. But Isaac was able to get hold of Judy a few days later.

"I've been looking for Chris myself," she'd said to his dismay.

For some reasons, Christine and Vincent weren't returning Isaac's calls. He was frying with anxiety and emotionally breaking down. It was useless trying to sleep. He could not sleep, could not eat; his world was crashing down on him.

Jane would look at Isaac and kindly and innocently advised: "It's a matter of time and you'll find them. It happens. You know they're very busy people."

And I'm not? Busy my soul?

Three days passed and Isaac was still waiting. Having run out of patience reserves, Isaac planned to fly to Hayiroh. It'd better end, he told himself. With his new resolves, Isaac found himself energized. However, Christine had a strong, begrudging sense of humor. In all honesty, Isaac didn't think it'd work on him if she called. When she called however, she talked with the same annoying humor without regretting it.

"Beat it Isaac! What's with the man? It's been three days already."

Just imagine that. No apologies, no explanations! Well, Isaac knew, supposedly, where she'd gone to but she owed him an apology. There she was acting innocent and blameless. Perhaps she was breaking some ice out of smart expectations; to calm him down. But cracking jokes was an uncalled for annoyance. *These...these...these...these people!* Isaac fought to utter *the word*, but couldn't. He was perhaps acting in a gentlemanly manner.

"I'm coming to Hayiroh," he said after a long, bitter pause.

"Great!" she said lightly not knowing that Isaac was internally a volcanic lava...deep down. If only she could see his face. He was a dragon; so much worse than caricatures of any demon.

48

Little slowly opened his eyes. Grace was dozing away on a chair next to the ward's door.

"Mum!" he slowly and sickly said. She was deeply asleep so he slowly sat up not to startle her.

"Mum?"

Grace sprang up despite his attempt to gently wake her up. Little was staring at her as she opened her eyes. With smile on her face, she slowly got up and sat by his bed.

"You're okay, baby!"

Little smiled and lay down.

"What happened to me mum?"

Grace struggled to fight tears.

"You were shocked when you saw the building ablaze. I'm sorry baby; I'm so sorry, I..."

Grace's voice trailed off. She looked at the swinging blue curtain at the window, then back at Little.

"Mum, don't be. We'll be okay. You know everything is covered."

Grace shot up and walked to the window.

"We have insurance mum and I'm fine, really fine!" Little beamed with incredible yet innocent enthusiasm.

"I don't know why they did that to us. I thought they understood us. They didn't."

"Mum, don't worry. They thought they'd blackmail us and break us down. They can't."

Grace scoffed. "We'll not be okay, Little."

Little twitched his right cheek confidently.

"Yes…"

"Nooo!" Grace said, raising her voice.

Little frowned. "Mum, are you okay?"

"No, I'm not okay and neither will you be!"

She scoffed again, shook her head vigorously, left the window and looked at Little.

"They finished us, Little…"

"Mum…"

"We vainly sing our being Africans; our being proud of our roots; the motherland. I've always believed in that. I just don't know what to think now, Little."

"What're you talking about ma?"

"We won't get the insurance money for the business, Little."

Little curled his lips up smugly. "Yes, we will. It wasn't our fault."

Grace smiled awkwardly, sardonically.

"They'd planned everything, Little. It's something that's been in the making for decades. I was just used."

Little frowned and slowly got up.

"What're you saying *ma*?"

She sighed ruefully.

"I knew these guys, Little. I was somehow part of them. How do you think Dengdit's letters came to you without any address or without you knowing the deliverer?"

"Wait, wait…what're you talking about *ma*?"

"They talked like they cared about all *black* folks. They talked of Pan-Africanism and *shit*. I felt for it, Little. I've never been a fool in my life."

"So you knew they'd burn down our business, *ma*?"

"No, no, it wasn't in the plan. I just don't know why they did that!" Grace talked as if she was about to burst into angry conniption.

"Why didn't you tell me *ma*?"

"They told me they didn't want you to jeopardize your business. They also have strict protocols and one can know only so much. You know what others don't know but you don't know what they don't know or what they know. You only know what you know. You're told a message and told how to convey the message to another person. The message is gathered in bits. It's hard to know everything about them. "

"What does it mean now, *ma*?"

"I don't know baby," Grace said very much dejected and re-signed.

"But we still can get insurance money for the business, right?"

"They've made sure we don't. They planned it in a brilliant way to make it appear like we did it ourselves to collect the insurance money."

Little frantically and angrily jumped out of bed.

"Why did they do that? What have I done to them...what have we done? They've been following me, they've been telling me to do stuff. They know how I feel about Africa."

"I'm sorry, I..."

"What's that?"

Grace looked at a yellow envelope on the table by the window.

"I don't know. Maybe somebody brought it when I was asleep."

Little looked at Grace then picked up the envelope.

49

Isaac was in Hayiroh in the morning and Christine was there waiting; standing tall, beautiful and strong. A few other friends were there too. Her brown face and black wick made her look like an actress. She was tall, slightly lean and upright. Her eyes were big, white and beckoning. She wore an orange dress that shone brightly in the heavenly sunrays of an African morning. *What's my point?*

There was no way Isaac liked that. She smiled and waved as Isaac emerged from the custom with a lady and two body guards.

Yes, Hayiroh was great; a holidaying spot. It was bustling, the sun bright and soothing; the people warm and welcoming. You could call it the typical tropic. But that wasn't the time. Isaac was fretted by everything he saw, unfortunately. Most annoying of all, was the sight of Christine; smiling, enthusiastic and cunning. He didn't want that.

"What brings you here?" she asked after they'd left the airport. They were on the way to the hotel.

"So things work out well, I guess." Isaac cunningly said. He didn't want to betray his black, inner man. That man, the man that kept saying: 'Christine, you're so screwed.'

She remained silent for a while.

"You're not the usual, vibrant Isaac I know, anything wrong?"

Like she doesn't know why!

"Well, journey of course!"

Christine drove skillfully. The driving was precarious as motorists wove through carelessly like their heads were chopped off. They were impetuous, thoughtless and brusque. The flow of traffic unnerved Isaac's already worked-up mind. The traffic was indeed disorderly.

On their left was a white ferrying van (locally known as *Adish)* with large writings on the side.

AFRICA'S SWEETNESS DRAINS INTO HYPOCRISY!

Angry and tired, Isaac stared at the writings. *Sweetness! Hypocrisy! Bullshit! I said bullshit*!

Isaac dismissed it. There were more pertinent and pressing issues to think about not some tired and impoverished philosophies.

The van was drifting slowly as if it was tracking them. It wasn't overtaking them nor was it remaining behind. The two vehicles remained perfectly lined up for about five minutes. Again, Isaac brushed away the occupant's curiosity. *My sleepless nights might have worked some magic into me.*

He looked at the writings again and the writings persisted; clear and taunting. They were in blue, in italic.

It was becoming hot; searing hot. He'd rolled down the side windshield for breezy air.

A young, dark-skinned and sturdy African sat up in the van, rolled the side windshield down. His action made Isaac snappish. He was poised as if he was about to grab a craved snapshot from a celebrity who'd just experienced a high-profile scandal. The man then swiftly threw something toward Isaac. It was rolled up in an artistically folded, brown paper. Isaac ducked, dodged it; accidentally pushing Christine's hands off the steering wheel. Christine screamed as the car skidded off the road, onto the sidewalk pavement and into a bus stop cabin—sending the crowd waiting for the ferry buses screaming and scared in all directions. Luckily, no one was seriously injured. It was only an old Asian woman who'd had a shock. Both Isaac and Christine didn't get the time to check what was in the note.

Isaac had to take Christine and the old lady to hospital. Christine had a dislocation on the left wrist. Isaac was fine. Well, not really fine. He wasn't hurt, but far from fine. All the rest in the car were unhurt.

Christine and Isaac left the hospital shortly after Christine was attended to. It was Africa of course. Names and status mattered more than anything else; that is, needs. Isaac felt embarrassed as Christine was led in; making the waiting patients groan painfully. What could they do? Refuse? Nothing!

Isaac was to spend the night in Hilton hotel at the outskirt of downtown Hayiroh. Christine was to come to the hotel after work to drive him to a dinner party. The Pandian ambassador wanted Christine in the office until two the following day. He'd had a party organized for Isaac. So Isaac had the whole day to spend before the party.

The following morning was a fine African morning. After breakfast Isaac took a short promenade then soon got bored and scared of the unknown. It was already 1.00 pm. He walked back to the hotel for lunch. Immediately Isaac arrived at the hotel, Vincent called about what could be done. Things didn't look so good. They'd no clue at all about who was responsible for both the blackmail and the South African offices' vandalism. They resolved to meet for further deliberations.

After lunch, the temperatures soared. It became relatively hot and humid. Isaac decided against taking a walk and went back to the hotel. As he walked to his hotel room, he heard a phone ring. Christine, Isaac thought. The time for his welcome party was nearing. He was elated as he picked up the phone playfully and childishly.

"Already done?"

Silence!

"Hello...this is Isaac...who's this?"

Silence!

There were voices in the background. The line was open but no one was talking. Then Isaac heard a car honk and someone cleared his throat.

"Listen Isaac, this is Michael..."

"Good god P.D! You scared the living hell out of me. What the hell was that for?"

Silence!

"Hello!" Isaac heard a beep and the phone line toned off. Looking at the phone, Isaac said to himself: "That wasn't good at all."

As Isaac put down the receiver, the phone rang again. He hesitated, took a deep breath and slowly picked it up.

"Isaac."

"You better come back to Day-Town in the next two days."

"What?"

That was it! He heard a click and the line was dead. Isaac waited for hours as if someone would call back but nothing happened. It was too much to shoulder in too long a time. Isaac was feeling like someone in an oven. He was sweating like a fat pig.

What does it mean for a man you commissioned for an assignment to disappear into thin air? You arrive in Africa only to nearly die in an accident. Then you get calls that were funnier than they meant! They got P.D?

50

"I told you we're Judy's friends," Dengiya said.

Judy's friends! Just imagine that. A gun against one's loin wasn't a sign of friendship, Chris thought.

"Guys, I know I'm in no position to bargain, but pointing a gun at me is no sign of friendship at all."

Chris was now being pushed toward a car parked on the roadside.

"Why're you guys quick in judging people?" the short one asked. His tone was offended and offending, his face changed to ferocious.

"Dude, I'm not judging! I'm just saying what I *feel* and what I *think* is right."

The man smiled sarcastically.

"When did masters of *reason* start to talk of *feelings*; and why's what you say always the most sensible?" Dengiya, the dark, large-muscled one, said.

"Whoa! What do you mean *you guys* and who am I to qualify as a *master* of reason?"

"Look at us, Chris! Just look!" Dengiya said. He was friendlier than the other guys. But Chris's last statement seemed to have infuriated him. He came closer to Chris as the short one opened the door. They stood looking at Chris.

"I don't know what you mean. What am I supposed to see? Nothing! That's what I think."

"Think!"

"Dude, this is ridiculous. Think? In reference to what?"

"Whatever you want to think about!"

"Nothing."

Dengiya glanced begrudgingly at the night sky and croaked. "Let me help you. What comes to your mind when you look or think of Germans?"

"Holocaust."

"And?"

"Intellectual development, superb technology."

"Good."

"Jews?"

"Anti-Semitism."

"And?"

Chris hesitated. Dengiya frowned questioningly.

"Brilliance."

"Arabs?"

"Mathematics."

"Chinese?"

"Strong tradition. Brilliant scripts."

Chris realized Dengiya's intention.

"I know where you're going with this," Chris said and looked at them one by one, their eyes barely visible in the dark.

"That's what you always think. You always know everything about everybody," the short guy said with a contorted face.

"No, man. You're wrong!"

"Typical! Can you ever say I'm right about anything?"

That guy used words in a very frustrating way. Chris hated him more than he hated their tired and seemingly pointless game.

"Man, I'm not who you think I am."

"And who's that you think I think you are, sir? The prejudicial judgmental judge?"

Chris realized he was getting furious. The guy was getting on his last nerves. Dengiya nodded to the other guys and they got into the car.

51

Little bitterly looked at the letter and frowned. He glanced at Grace and looked at the writings again. His face remained expressionless.

"What does it say, Little?"

Extremely upset, he looked at his mum, got up and walked to a cabinet by the window.

"What're you doing, Little, and what does the letter say?"

Without saying a word, he removed his jacket, slipped it on, grabbed the envelope on the table and threw it at his mum. He then walked furiously to the washroom.

"Read it for yourself *ma*. Since they're bent on destroying me, I'll let them finish the remaining part of me."

Grace's eyes opened wide. She got up, frantically grabbed the envelope on the floor, removed the paper and read it slowly. Her face changed as she continued to read.

Little came back from the washroom after having changed into civilian clothes. Grace had finished reading and was helplessly staring at him.

"What do you make of these, Little? Why do they treat us like we're some idiots?"

"We've been idiots, *ma*. We deserve to be treated so!"

Grace found herself sitting down on the bed. She looked at her son, stunned than angry.

"We don't deserve this, my son! We sure don't!"

Little's lips curled up angrily. "Yes, we do!"

"And don't tell me you believe any bit of what they wrote in that paper."

"Does it matter *ma*? What difference does it make whether I believe it or not. I lost everything."

"No you haven't."

"What do I have *ma*?"

"You have yourself, your brain."

"That's an incredible consolation *ma* but it ain't gonna to work."

"But..."

Little left the ward with long rude strides. He paced out of the hospital and onto the street. A taxi approached and he raised his hand. The taxi swerved and screeched to a stop in front of him.

The world outside whisked by but nothing made any sense at all to Little. From the day he was born, poverty, crime and disdain characterized his childhood. He'd sworn to leave such state of affairs behind him. No! They were laughing at him. He'd not run away from them. They bewitched him, they beckoned him. He'd been fixed. He couldn't escape.

Little remembered the prison and its indoctrinations. Now, such a vanity: how could he be so stupid as to fall for those stupid niceties? They then appealed, however. Why couldn't it be an alien party? Why's it always your own that destroys you? Solidarity, solidarity! Shit! They're just stupid idealisms, childish dreams. What one has is oneself and oneself. The most abstract and shallow of human constructs is solidarity based on color, historical and non-contemporary bonds.

The taxi kept going and going as Little's mind went from one alternative to another.

"Will that be here, sir?" the taxi driver said as Little raised his head to look at the meter.

"That'll be twenty-five dollars sir."

Little opened the door and jumped out. The front of the hotel looked nothing African or African-Pandian. It was a temple, a Buddhists' temple. Little looked left, right, ahead and behind him but all he could see were funny writings. He reached for his pants' pocket but remembered he'd left the letter with Grace. Confused, he stood staring disdainfully and angrily at the building.

Sometimes we think we've lost everything, when it's in fact the beginning of our life. He remembered a piece in that letter. The words seemed to be making sense as he looked at the temple. But the words were too idealistic and impractical to make any real sense to him. He was being taunted. His face contorted with fury. A car approached and he stared at the car. The car didn't stop. As he approached the nearest door, a man emerged from behind the temple.

"Over here, Little!" Wani said and left.

"Wani?"

What's this...a joke?

"Wani, wait!"

Wani disappeared behind the temple as Little followed him. Little ran after Wani only to see him enter another building. Having lost Wani, Little approached the door and hesitated. Fear started to melt him down as he approached the door of a very strange room. Inside the room, there were many jubilant voices. There seemed to be some celebratory ambience inside. Little rudely knocked but no one answered the door.

"Hello!"

No one answered.

52

Sister K knew her phone conversation with Sister J and her coffee meeting with Uncle D were positive only that she wasn't so sure. However, she was becoming increasingly concerned with how rogue groups and individuals were using their cause to enrich themselves. Journalists with informants inside intelligence organizations leaked some information about The Pipers. Shirts and pamphlets were flying around. Uncle D had given a fitting counsel that famous causes have always been misused in history. Theirs wasn't immune from such.

Uncle D had called Sister K up for a coffee meeting in Day-Town. They were seated inside an Italian café in *Little Italy*.

Uncle nodded. "We can't control what people think. We can't control the ills they undertake in our name, but we know one thing for sure: The nobility of the cause," Uncle D had said.

"I do understand that but I can't get this out of my system. The idea of rogues benefiting from a noble cause makes my skin crawl. I'm not so much worried about the hard drive. Dengdit and The maid were careful not to have anything sensitive on it. They'll know who we are and how we operate, but not the specifics," Sister K said.

"Don't let that unnerve you much. Focus on the task you can afford now."

"I know."

"What unnerves me is the death of innocent civilians in Congo and Sudan in the hands of opportunists. I talked to Mama and Grandma. We'll have to come up with methods that can control warlords and leaders in war-torn countries. This has to be done before the end of this phase."

"That'd be hard. It'd involve understanding the nature of the causes involved. Our success is aided by technology. These guys have primitive technologies if at all they have any."

He shook his head slowly. "Not hard if well thought out."

"Guess who I'm talking to? I don't know if there's anything Uncle D and Mama can't do."

He shook his head. "That's too much praise."

"But fitting."

Sister K stared at the coffee cup, then looked at Uncle D.

"The Maid had some concerns about the actual purpose of the treatment unleashed on Little Michael and Christopher Fox. They're suffering in a game that appears meaningless. She does know the end game though."

"Don't worry. We're approaching the end of the First Phase. They'll soon live a normal life."

"Uncle D, this cause has given me meaning and joy. I can't imagine my life without it."

Uncle D sipped his mountain dew slowly, looked at Sister K and said.

"It shouldn't be about what you do, but how what you do impacts others and how it makes you feel."

Sister K smiled.

"Which means?"

Uncle D shook his head slowly and said: "You know what it means. After the First Phase, you'll continue to help people. You'll have money to build orphanages or low cost housing in Kampala, or Nairobi, or Juba or Hayiroh."

"Life's such a funny thing. When I was young, I always wanted to be a lawyer, a doctor or a well-to-do business woman. I didn't imagine being enamored by the desire to help people without taking credit for it. If you and I exit First Phase, I'll make sure your statue is in every major city in the world."

"Is everything fine sir?" a waiter asked, looking at Uncle D and dropped a paper at Sister K's feet.

Uncle D nodded with a smile and said to Sister K. "I'd be very much offended. Remember we shouldn't take credit for our deeds."

Sister K laughed hysterically, bent and picked up the paper.

"What?" Uncle D said, very much curious.

"You know those who exit First Phase will be celebrated."

Uncle D smiled and nodded slowly. "You got me there!"

"Will all the current soldiers exit in First Phase?"

"Let's see what happens in Sivals. I guess we'll not meet here again except in Sivals; that's, if things go well."

Uncle D said as he got up. Sister K grabbed her jacket as they walked away.

53

Isaac was technically frying in anxiety. Internally, he was molten lava. Two o'clock whisked by and Christine was only a dream. Numerous thoughts played with Isaac's mind. *Am I being set up? Should I be patient and wait? Have The Pipers got Christine too?*

Isaac didn't have many favourable choices so he called the embassy. Some lady kindly told him that Christine left at 1.30 p.m. for the hotel.

My hotel? Indeed? My hotel? Now this is getting really, really worrying!

If hell is hot, then it's only one's situation that makes up hell. Sighting Christine was becoming so precious that every other concern just didn't exist for Isaac. Isaac's mind, soul and heart, were all wrapped around seeing Christine. *Just seeing her!* By 4.00 p.m. Isaac needed Jesus. Yes, you heard; the agnostic Mr. Burns needed our saviour lord Jesus Christ. Because of his situational poverty, he really needed the Jewish fellow for some ridiculous miracle. *Why was I ever created? Why did I in the first place connect with these bloody African issues?*

"Mr. Burns, you need to take this one easy. She'll be here," Isaac's assistant said.

He just stared at her.

"I'm sure everything will be fine," she added.

Isaac smiled and said: "Go with the boys and explore the city. I'll be fine. Enjoy the African night. You always dreamed of coming here. This is your chance. I have a lot to do."

"Are you sure, sir?"

"Damn sure! I'll be fine."

By five, Isaac had to do something. In spite of the heat engendered by anxiety and Hayiroh's weather, Isaac started to feel cold, his head spinning. His body started to ache. He was actually hot physiologically.

After the situation had drained Isaac of available energy, the phone rang. *I can't believe what Christine has done.* Isaac knew trouble was brewing. He craved only one thing though: to know what was happening.

I can't wait to at least speak to Christine.

Isaac just wanted to let out the filth in his heart...to let out the anger to be free of decency and discretion. *Decency and discretion hold people in servitude called civility.*

"I'm sorry Isaac. We'd organized something for you. You could have enjoyed it. But if you get better, we can always organize something. We don't get rich and humble people like you often here in Africa so it's a blessing that you're here," Edgar Morgan said.

Edgar was the Pandian ambassador to Hayiroh. He was a short, pink Jewish fellow with a good heart few can afford to have. Without question, Edgar was a human being with a beautiful heart, and a mind with keen eyes for success. Everything he suggested to the Sivalsian officials always worked out beautifully. But here Edgar was saying something that'd take Isaac a century to understand. Isaac felt his behind thick and hardened on the bed.

Silence!

"Isaac, are you okay? Is it becoming too bad? I can send someone to take you to hospital. I hear your bodyguards and the assistant are exploring the city. You know this is Africa and such things happen to new people. You know we're used to these things; almost becoming black."

Something was either amiss or the ambassador was drunk, Isaac thought.

"No, thanks I'm fine; it was just some headache," Isaac lied.

"Well, you have our number; call me if you need anything...anything at all."

Edgar hanged up. *Anything? I need Christine in the name of Jesus!* That was the *anything* Isaac needed. The situation wasn't supposed to be funny, yet it was. Isaac had no energetic heart to laugh though. Insane calm settled slowly. He composed himself.

Isaac didn't go to the party because Christine didn't show up. Not because he was sick. *What was Christine up to?* He was getting insane.

There was nothing else to do. Staying in the hotel was depressing. He then got out for a fresh air of an African evening. Whatever happened to Christine, Isaac had no control over it, but he had some control over making himself okay. As he got out of the hotel to the front stairs, two black Mercedes Benz drove by the court house toward the hotel. Isaac admired that luxury. However, he wasn't in the mood. He needed to hear from either Christine or Vincent.

Alas! There came out the giant, pot-bellied minister. Was Isaac to be excited? Perhaps, but he was not there. The real Isaac had left the body. It was this bloody, innocent white man in the sea of blackness. The minister and his body guards walked toward the hotel. They walked directly toward Isaac. He stood where he was. On reflection though, Isaac decided to go toward them.

Eh...what the hell?

"Isa-ac!" the minister said with a broad sarcastic smile, a red-orange gum giving comedy to his smile. His belly filled his frame. Was the minister concerned about anything: diabetes, blood pressure, heart attack? God knew that!

"How're you doing Mr...sir...?"

"C'mon, just call me Vincent. I won't take it badly," he said and laughed loudly. It wasn't a welcome laugh. They made their way upstairs, flanked on all sides by sturdy young men dressed in black suits and dark sunglasses. One young man dashed past Isaac, quickened his steps and turned to Isaac.

"Floor sir?"

He asked before the elevator opened.

"Seventeen," Isaac said.

"Where's Christine?" Vincent asked as they got into the elevator.

"They had a party organized for me at the embassy according to what she told me yesterday. She was to pick me up or send someone to pick me up. She's not shown up since yesterday. I could've hired a limo and go there with my group, but I just wanted to be polite."

"I heard you've caught fever...African weather, mm?" Vincent said and smiled irresponsibly then added. "Mm, I didn't take that as the reason you didn't go. I thought you were with her."

He served another demonic, but now conspicuously sarcastic smile.

"No," Isaac said with resignation.

The elevator opened. Isaac dashed to open the room but the same young man signalled him to stop. As advised, Isaac stopped, amazed at the unnecessary suspicion. He slowly and hesitantly gave the young man the key card. They stood by the door as the young man opened the door and entered. After a few seconds, the man came back. "There's a problem honorable Miochariya," he said frowning at Isaac.

"What do you mean there's a problem when I left here fifteen minutes ago?"

"That's enough a time for a chemical weapon to kill a population equivalent to fifteen worlds," Vincent said. Like he knew any chemistry, Isaac thought to himself.

"What kind of a problem?" Isaac asked the gentleman.

"Everything has been turned upside down and the bed sheets have been burnt."

"That can't be!" Isaac fearlessly said and dashed past the young man. The guards respectfully gave Isaac the way. *Oh, he's right.* It was a bloody fifteen-minute operation. Did the guards arrange it themselves? Was it in that devilish laugh?

The guards made their way in, surveying the room with overt suspicious glances at Isaac's corner. What could he do? Nothing! He stood fixed and frozen. Vincent walked up to Isaac, patted him on the back and said: "You have to trust these young men. They know things. Besides, this is Hayiroh not Day-Town or New York City, mm? There's been a lot of fishiness since you arrived."

Vincent slowly walked to the TV, picked up the remote and turned the TV on. It was the only thing in the room that was intact. They all stood with their mouths wide open as the announcer babbled incomprehensibly on *Sivals Television* (STV) news station.

...we are still waiting for the minister's body

to be brought out of the hotel.

"What...I mean...?!" Isaac exclaimed.
"Wait!" Vincent raised his hand to stop Isaac.

...the minister was said to have gone to the hotel to visit his sick friend. The said friend is a Pandian tycoon whose purpose of coming to the country is not known. It is unfortunate that the minister died before his connection to this secret visit is known. May god rest his soul in eternal...peace!

"Eternal hell," Vincent said as he turned off the TV. He looked at Isaac seemingly furious and disdainful.

"I've nothing to do with it!" Isaac timidly said.

Vincent stared at Isaac, looked at his men and said: "I didn't say you did."

Confused and angered, Vincent looked down for a while; angry but composed.

"Let's go," he said looking at Isaac.

"Go where?" Isaac asked looking stupid rather than confused.

Having stood thoughtfully for a while, the minister hurriedly left the room and the body guards ran after him. Isaac remained standing.

"The minister expects you to come with us," one of the security guys, who seemed to be the busiest and the smartest, informed Isaac.

"But to where?"

"You wouldn't ask me that question if you knew this is Sivals."

There and then, Isaac was informed.

Damn Sivals and damn Africa!

As the ministerial entourage and Isaac neared the elevator, Isaac saw the minister and the rest of his men coming back.

"What's happening?" Isaac confusedly asked.

"Let's go back in!"

The minister said, passing Isaac without any other word. Everyone obediently followed Vincent. The minister removed his phone and made two cabalistic calls. Isaac had no idea what was being done then. He stared like a mischievous child whose tricks have been discovered. There was one thing he could do though: wait. He had to wait and see how he might vanish.

There was still no sign of Christine.

Inside Isaac's hotel room, everybody remained standing.

"But no one told you the president would be in the restaurant!" one of the guards said.

"Okob, just let things roll the way they've been perceived," Vincent replied. Okob was the busy young man.

Isaac knew something else was connected with the day's dramas. What was with the president? Why were they back in the hotel room? Isaac's head was almost bursting. He had many questions than anyone could answer. To console himself, Isaac assumed everything and the talks were about the minister. Perhaps the contrivance had failed. There was some truth to the reports, however.

Then one bodyguard came in, nodded and a light-skinned, skinny young man entered. He looked scared as he was sweating, his hand shaking.

"H-e-l-l-o s-s-sir, my name is Jacob," he said stammering.

Vincent smiled and looked at him with interest.

"I'm not dead, take it easy young man. All we need is a new room.

"Right away s-sir!"

The young man flew off only to come back with two beautiful young ladies: a white girl whom Isaac thought he'd seen before and a native Sivalsian girl.

The white girl looked at Isaac and smiled. *She's familiar, really familiar?* She wore a red, yellow and black African dress. Her face was like that of a pretty-faced, innocent western girl who'd become enamoured by Africa and its innocence. She was so costumed that Isaac couldn't recollect where he'd met her. Her hair was blonde, her neck slender. She was skinny with straight, short and sparklingly white teeth.

"Ready sir," Jacob said.

The minister nodded admiringly.

"Thanks Jacob," he said in a more American-like matter-of-fact.

The entourage streamed into the new room, furnished like it had never been done before. The light yellow curtain smiled of purple decorations, the multi-colored bed sheets dazzled in green and red.

Vincent and Isaac sat down on the couches. Everyone else remained standing.

Okob turned on the TV.

54

Little stood outside the door for two minutes.

Wani is so fired.

"Hellooooo!"

The celebratory voices inside suddenly died down and a deepening silence set in.

"I'm gone. This is some stupid game I ain't prepared for at this time."

As Little turned to go, the door opened and the voices inside started laughing, all at once. At the door, Wallace and another young man stared at Little.

"I..."

"Don't worry, you're not too late."

"What...Wall..."

"This is a friend of mine, Dengiya. He works at the factory near HS."

"Wall..."

"You'll be fine..."

"It's a pleasure having you here sir," Dengiya said with a smile.

"Man, I'm really getting out of my mind right now. Can you tell me what the ff...ff...hell is going on here?"

"Someone will fill you in," Dengiya said.

Little was getting frustrated. He followed Dengiya like a bull heading to the butcher's knife.

Buddhist monks were moving inside the building from place to place. There was nothing inside suggestive of other religious symbols. They walked through the corridor as monks stared at Little. It was more of a hotel than a temple. As they continued to walk around, the place turned into some voodoo worshipping arena. On the doors were drawings of voodoo priests with funny yet informative writings.

Little stared curiously at the first three doors.

Number #3: *I was spoilt by abundance of nature.*

Number #4: *Will you always tell me who I am.*

Number #5: *All has been said, but not by me.*

Dengiya and Little continued through the corridors. After about ten doors and a boggled mind later, Dengiya stopped. He looked at the door on his right.

Number #9: *You have lost everything sir. You have lost nothing son.*

Little looked toward his left and saw a white cross. It was door number 1. Little remembered doors started at 3. There was still no door number #2. Number #10 said:

The sword tore you open and sewed you back neat.

The sword put you down but saved you.

The sword is ready...tell me what it is for now.

Little's anger was turning into confusion.
"What do all these mean?"
Dengiya looked at Little, smiled and said: "You'll only know what they mean if you pass the test."
"Test?"
Dengiya nodded. Little was getting unsettled yet curious.
Hell! Little are you dead?
Little's lips curled up. "What test do you mean? I've been tested long enough gruesomely and wickedly."
"Which means?"
"It means I lost everything I worked hard for to achieve."
"And?"

"What the ff...hell do you mean *and*?"

Little was getting furious. The man seemed insensitively stupid. He was brawny, soot black with a seemingly friendly and not-so-serious face.

"What I mean is people lose stuffs then get them back."

Little started to heave angrily. There was some movement inside door number #10.

"We thought Wallace and Wani died in the fire. You should talk to them and they'll probably explain to you what I mean," Little said.

Dengiya laughed.

"I know one thing. You own a business and Wallace works for you; and you haven't lost any shit."

"Wha-at?" Little yelled with a distorted face.

"Yeah, you heard me. It's now time to be quiet, you dig?"

"No, I don't dig nothing...and stop this oriental bullshit."

"I said it's time."

"Time for..."

The door opened. A huge, bearded man stood, staring at Little.

"Come on in...college boy."

You gotta be kidding me!

Little's heart jumped. He looked back at Dengiya but he was nowhere to be seen. Startled, he looked at the man in front of him.

No, that's not possible!

55

The atmosphere inside the hotel was tense. Isaac could hear sirens outside. The minister's entourage and Isaac sat dead silent as they listened to the confusion on TV.

...We are here to inform members of the Sivalsian public that the earlier reports about honorable Vincent Miochari-ya are not true. There has been a break in but he is safe and sound. We apologize for the inconvenience caused by such false information. The minister's friend is also safe and sound. We're waiting for details. We hope to get in touch with the minister for a public address...

"Turn it off," Vincent grumbled.

Isaac drunkenly walked to the window and looked down. The media was being restrained by the police; jostling, pushing and shouting. Three motor bikes made their way toward the hotel: one in front and two behind the first, perfectly lined up. The three bikes made a triangular shape. The presidential motorcade then appeared. All cars stopped along the way, cameras flashing everywhere.

"Isaac!" the minister called.

Isaac turned and saw the minister staring at him.

"Go with him," Vincent said pointing at Okob and paused. "They'll take you for questioning, bring you back to the hotel and we'll meet tomorrow. I've told Jacob to make arrangements for your room."

"Do you have any idea who *The Pipers* are?" Isaac asked.

Vincent smiled and said: "Isaac, I'm a government official and we don't dwell on baseless rumors. The security will take care of that and if there is such a thing as *The Pipers*, then we'll let you know."

Isaac then changed the topic.

"I need to inform the embassy."

"That has already been done."

"I also need to call my lawyers regarding the questioning."

"I've already informed them. You'll talk to them at the security services center. There's a video service in case they want to be present."

Isaac had to obey. Okob and Isaac faithfully made their way down with three other young men. The police waved their truncheons threateningly at the crowd as Isaac and company briskly walked to a parked Limousine. The sea of journalists started asking questions.

Is honorable Vincent really alive?

Were you here to topple the government with honorable Vincent?

What's the purpose of your visit?

Why was your visit secretive?

Why was your hotel room vandalized?

Can you comment about the incident?

Is that what the West does in Africa?

It was too much. Isaac couldn't believe his ears. They were all shades of journalists; hurling questions at him with no decency. He couldn't answer any for he had no answers to any of them. The questions and the ideas behind them were unsettling, annoying and baseless. Another worrying issue was that Isaac had no idea where he was being taken to. He then lost interest in trying to know what was wrong. He didn't want to know what was to happen to him either. He just followed like a cow being led to the butcher's cruelty.

The atmosphere became ironically serene as the Limo slid over that unprecedented headwall's smoothness. *I never felt like here.* At that moment, Isaac didn't hate himself for coming nor did he think it was good to come to Sivals. He just sat there indifferently, taking few unintentional glances at the man next to him. He didn't know his name, but he looked friendlier than Isaac would admit. Isaac knew one thing though: Hayiroh wouldn't risk diplomatic show-down with Day-Town. It was unthinkable. *Soon front pages in the west will be adorned by his pictures.*

What if their operations, tarnished by Vincent and Christine, were detected? That would be the upset. He scraped the premonition off his head. How would thinking about it help? Whatever Isaac thought about in that Limo, whatever he feared or braved, was all useless. He had no control over them, but he still had to stand his ground and say what he was required to say. It was the only important thing then.

Powerful emotions are hard to control. Isaac was not pretending to have some power over them. But he felt the overwhelming effect of his nerves mystifying his presence to calmness. He still wanted to know one thing: was the calm a result of complete destruction of his reasoning ability by emotions, or was it his reigning on his emotions? Sometimes we get numbed by emotions into passivity. This is true if bereft. At times emotions stir us into destructive tempestuousness. This is the case with religious protection of gods by different religious sects on different doctrinal bases.

As if gods are weak!

Isaac was just there; a log just waiting to be placed on fire. What wasn't clear was the use of the fire that'd be made out of him.

"We're here sir," the young man said.

Isaac looked out, and there, there, was the Sivalsian National Security and Intelligence Service (SNSIS); scripted intelligently in full and initials.

Sivalsian National Security and Intelligence Services

† SNSIS †

Security, Honest and integrity

The center was pronounced pejoratively by locals as *sin-cys'* because of its notorious history of torture. The new director is said to have reformed it into a respectable security organization though.

Coming out of the car, Isaac realized they were out of town. Lush with admirable greenness, the surrounding was breath-taking. It was statuesque. As he looked at the entrance of that massive structure, he felt his spine flexing cold and brittle, his vision growing blurry. For the first time in more than twenty-four hours, Isaac managed to land his eyes on the illusive Christine. He didn't know what to make of the sight of Christine. However, Christine burst out of the complex looking dejected, seemingly angry and disinterested. She looked at Isaac and he knew she'd been through the inferno of African purgatory. Her face looked wrinkly and hopeless.

Isaac didn't know if the fury was meant for him, or it was some acquirement from the interrogation. For the sake of his mental health, Isaac assumed he knew what brought Christine to SNSIS. *Questioning or plot, I needn't know...and for now, I don't care.*

56

I t wasn't something imaginable to a person of his kind but it so happened. There used to be years when a white man—and not in this case a rich man like Isaac—was revered in a soothing manner. But things have changed in a way one could paradoxically fancy.

Still, Isaac was treated well. However, the psychology of the whole affair left him surmising and, to some extent, belittled.

The interrogation room was professionally set up. The questioning was slow, seemingly acted and loaded with self-incriminating attachments.

"Don't mind about the co-incidence today at the hotel!" the interrogator said. He introduced himself as John Dono; his partner was something like Dickson. The other African name was too wordy for dear Isaac to remember. Isaac used to blame the Europeans missionaries who gave Africans European names as a sign of imperialism and determined destruction of the natives' cultural ways. *Now I see the point.*

However, cynics still maintain that it wasn't a question of convenience. It's believed the names were intended as part of Europeanization. During colonialism, Europeans didn't care what non-Europeans lamented. Non-Europeans were subjugated savages to be civilized; human-like social debtors to be meaningfully humanized. Now, to Europeans' chagrin, political correctness is a ruthless master, an indiscriminate ruler, a dictatorial straightener.

Dear Isaac took his time to answer the question. A host of arcane presentiment filled up Isaac's mind. Why was Christine looking dejected? Did she confess? Why's Panda sleeping on the problem? Why isn't Jane contacting him? Why's western intelligentsia quiet about The Pipers? Is there some puerile conspiracy? Are Christine and Vincent involved? Isaac knew the whole confusion could be a staged set-up to garner money from him. Well, Isaac had enough money to bring them the best Day-Town law brains. Anyone contemplating blackmail was beckoning woes to herself.

On hearing the news, Isaac's lawyers wanted to come to Hayiroh. Sivalsians intelligence officials assured them that Isaac wasn't in custody, but at his hotel room as the issue was a misunderstanding. The only thing Isaac had to do therefore was to trust his heart and say what he believed was right.

"I don't know what you're talking about sir?" Isaac said after a long pause. The men were truly professionals. They allowed Isaac to take his time. The interrogation was a complete opposite of what he'd expected: bloody nose, black eye, broken bones and things like that. *They're wary of Day-Town of course.*

"We learnt that your hotel room was vandalized fifteen minutes after you left and it so happened also that honourable Miochariya was going to visit you..."

"And we've learnt that the president was also going to the hotel."

Dickson, whose accent was heavy, completed Dono's statement. Dickson's words were pronounced carefully, his gaze soft but firm. Inside the interrogation room the atmosphere was very friendly and air comfortably warm.

"I'd no idea the president would be there..."

"Don't worry about it. It was the coincident issue that we were trying to make clear. I'd put it irresponsibility at the beginning," Dono said quietly and walked up to the window.

Dono then got a call and the two interrogators left the room. After about fifteen minutes of sitting forlorn and confused, Isaac looked up as Dono opened the door.

"We have to take you to the hotel, but I've one personal question for you. If you feel you can't or don't want to answer it, you can choose not to," Dono said. Isaac nodded awkwardly. He rightly took Isaac's response to be a *yes.*

"I'm sorry if that will be unbecoming of me. I am just curious. If I had a thousand dollars, hypothetically speaking, then my friend told me that if I went to South Sudan where people are dying, I can make five thousand dollars by building a school and a hospital using five hundred. Now, I tell my friend that however much the benefit would be to the people, I'd not be regarded as doing the right thing. My friend then laughed in my face and said 'all that matters is that you're benefiting the people'."

Isaac looked at him, down then at the ceiling. He thought the question was unintelligible if not conveyed out of arrogance, or rather, a bait to lure him into something intentional. Dono then suddenly left without saying whether he'd finished what he was saying or not. Isaac was shown out by a young officer, who took him to the waiting Limo.

Okob and Christine were waiting impatiently for him.

"Hi!" Isaac said to Okob and Christine.

"Good evening sir," Okob said and got into the car.

This time Okob didn't open the door for Isaac.

"How come you let this happen to you? Don't they know who you are?" Okob said with diffused sarcasm.

"What?" Isaac asked, rather surprised.

As the Limo entered the road, two police cars followed the Limo. Isaac had feared the worst. It later turned out he was being given security.

Okob dropped Christine and Isaac off at Christine's downtown office. The time Isaac craved for hours arrived when he no longer needed it. After a tormenting period of silence, both Christine and Isaac sat down simultaneously.

Christine's office was spacious and luxuriously executive. The filing cabinets behind the executive black leather chair were conservatively brown. Orange leather couches occupied the left side of the office by the window. The window made the office well lit. Multicolored Antique Tabriz rugs covered the whole office floor. African sculptures graced her massive table; engendering an ambience of authentic humanity.

"We can sit in the balcony," Christine gloomily suggested.

Isaac and Christine slowly walked to the balcony. Christine sauntered back to the office to fetch some wine. Their minds were tied with viscid intensity on the issues that none of them thought of going for dinner. She legged back to the balcony, sat down, poured wine into the two glasses she'd placed on the table.

"What did you tell them?" Christine asked with an effort.

"Well, I mean, they didn't ask me anything important?" Isaac said staring at the cars park down, below them.

"Beat it Isaac! What do you mean *they never asked me anything*?"

"They only told me not to worry about the coincidence at the hotel. The only thing one interrogator left me is some story whose relevance I couldn't know–perhaps only guess."

"They intimidated me. There's someone feeding these guys with information. They know everything about you and your business operations?"

Isaac lackadaisically shook his head and absent-mindedly said: "Perhaps it's Chris but I didn't tell him anything specific."

"That's weird, really weird!"

"Why didn't they ask me? Maybe they don't know we have a business connection?"

"Come on! Why do you think they took me in for interrogation? I think Hayiroh is getting some heat from Day-Town. They know everything about you—even your girlfriend, a girl named Paris!"

"Wait, wait. No, no, they can't do that. I know the girl, but...oh, no. I can't believe this is happening! She's Jane's estranged sister."

"What?"

"Yes, Jane's sister and I didn't have anything with her."

Christine shot up, walked to her office and came back with a large, brown envelope. Isaac impertinently stared. She pulled out another envelope inside the large one. The second one was yellow and smaller than the first. With one mechanical look at Isaac she completely tore open the yellow envelope, pulled out some pictures and handed them to Isaac. Isaac stared spellbound. They were pictures of Paris, Isaac and Jeng. Confused, Isaac just peered through the pictures as if something beyond the two dimensional papers on his hand would console him.

"They said you came here to kill the boy because he was messing with your girlfriend. They said you plan to leave Jane for her."

Isaac stared at the photos with a bottled anger. Such stupidity didn't deserve any reply, but it was damaging. It wasn't so much about it being stupid, it was about the scandal. Agitation welled up in Isaac. The veins on his face started to pink up. He became agitated and nervous. Lost in thought and rattled, Isaac paced the balcony as Christine stared, scared than surprised. To Isaac, one corner of the balcony was the same as the other. Christine never uttered a word as Isaac moved from place to place thinking; his right hand on his forehead; his complexion paling and his confidence waning. He was, as always during stress, dead. But this death was more worrying.

Christine stared at him with eyes that told him one thing: 'I feel sorry for you.'

What Isaac didn't understand was why he wasn't told all those things in the security office. They were cognizant of the facts and had told Christine about them, but they intentionally opted not to tell him.

Something is amiss. Christine tell me, please tell me!

There was something wrong, but how was Isaac to go about it in that hostile environment.

"I'm sorry, but there's more to the issue," Christine said and brought out another paper from her pink satchel and handed it to

Isaac, her eyes getting redder and sleepy. Isaac opened the paper, his hands trembling.

Mr. Isaac Burns,

You could play innocent. You could play dumb, but deep in you Mr. Burns, you know who you are. You know how much you love money and how every bit of any corrupt activity always had your account smile. You might be a casualty of war and we apologise for that, but I do believe the will is the key here, not who did what. The photos are destined for the media if you don't co-operate with us. We'll keep in touch.

The Pipers: we are closer than you think!

Isaac gasped, wiggled and hit the wall with his right fist.

"What can I do? What can I do, Christine?"

"It's 'what can we do'. We're all squeezed and crammed into the same tininess of that cup."

"I always wanted to be clean, Christine. I always cautioned you about corruption in Africa. They'll just think that I'm just another hypocritical Westerner."

57

Chris was taken to a Buddhist temple where he spent time in solitary confinement. There was neither sign of Judy nor the guys who'd brought him in. All he could do was read the oriental abstracts on the walls written in beautiful graffiti. It was kind of hard to read some of the writings.

The room was well furnished. A queen-size bed with embroidered, brown sheets covered the bed. The bed was placed opposite the door. There was a computer desk with an office chair on the left hand side of the door below the window. There was no computer on the desk. A small bookshelf was on the right side of the door. There were a couple of books on it. Chris was too upset to be in any mood for reading.

In the morning, to Chris's surprise, Little's body guard, Wani, and Dengiya came into the room with his breakfast. Even more surprising was how friendly they were.

Chris's dinner, the night before, was brought by an insolent white girl. Having put the food down, she fixed him with a complete, estranging disdain. Chris asked why he was being kept there and whether Judy would come and see him. She left without saying a word only to come back five minutes later chewing gum irresponsibility.

"You're a lucky son of a bitch. Why can't you enjoy this vacation before they change their minds?" she'd said, left and loudly slammed the door shut.

Chris curiously stared at Wani. Wani was surprisingly different. Seeing Wani was, at first, a psychological torture knowing who

Wani was. What took Chris by surprise was their amiable tone, their unexpected bonniness and carefully articulated words.

"Did you have a nice night sleep, Mr. Fox?" Dengiya said.

Chris looked at Wani and Wani smiled affirmatively.

Dengiya winked to assure Chris of the changed attitude.

"If only I knew what was happening, I could say I had a good night. Yes, the food was great and the accommodation excellent...but no, I didn't have a good night."

Dengiya sat on the bed as Wani sat on the office chair by the desk.

"I apologise for that," Wani said.

Chris couldn't believe his ears. An apology was the last thing he expected from *that* man. However, Chris assumed they were acting it all out of instruction, or out of mockery.

"I don't need any apology. The best apology would be sending me home. Do you also have Judy kept here?"

Dengiya looked at the window and said, ignoring Chris's plea: "I come from a region in South Sudan, called Jonglei. Its administrative headquarter is traditionally called Mading, but politically called Bor. I actually come from the northern part of Twi district or county. The payam headquarter is called *Wernyol*. My clan is called Adhiok. What the name means is mythical..."

"I don't want to know where you come from and what all that means. I just need to go home."

Again, Dengiya ignored Chris.

"I herded cattle and goats when I was young and played on treeless savannah plains, barefoot and naked. On that plain, one could see the other end of the world from one spot. It's a flat land..."

"What do I have to do with your childhood? I've never herded cattle, I've never walked naked, and I never caused any of those things to you."

They just looked at Chris with indifferent faces. But they were so calm that Chris felt sorry for himself. He realized the guys knew exactly what they were saying. *I'm about to be killed.*

"A very beautiful land," Dengiya continued. "During rainy season, we'd head toward our villages and take the cattle toward the east. We call that *Loh* in *Thoŋ ë Jiëëŋ*. During the dry season, we took the cattle either offshore or on shore where we had cattle camps. And you can guess the river..."

"It's the magnificent and the legendry River Nile," Wani said for the first time since apologizing to Chris.

"They'd," Wani continued. "Eat fish and drink fresh milk. They brushed using cow dung ashes. They had it all. They had few diseases and needed less as they were contended with what they had and who they were. They were known as brave but the abundance of food and the uncomplicated nature of their land didn't make them innovative in terms of inventing new things to go through life."

"I've come to realize that being content isn't good. It makes you complacent and timeless," Dengiya said.

"So someone had to make them have the need to be innovative," Wani said.

Chris's attention was now drawn and he started to feel sorry for them rather than angry. *Is there any point to this?*

"Sometimes you just have to be wasted and oppressed to see things clearly," Dengiya continued. "You then come to understand why some people become so innovative and successful."

They got up at the same time.

Wani opened the door.

"My name is Dengiya," he said and headed to the door. Chris already knew his name from previous night. Saying his name again meant they assumed Chris was indifferent to whatever they were saying, or Dengiya was just being arrogant.

"What do I have to do with you people? Is it just because I'm white?"

"White? No! *White* is only in your head, Chris. What we see in you is what makes us common: needs. Whiteness was only invented to make your position of power sublime. Put that thought aside for a moment and think about this. A few days ago you were about to go to Africa on a mission you knew and still know nothing about. Then you find yourself with people you don't know. You spend the night alone and in the morning you're told stories that seem to have absolutely nothing to do with you. How do you feel?"

Chris gathered himself to respond but they were gone. His mind was in disarray as he could hardly think.

Judy, please help me!

58

J eng left Panda for Washington DC after meeting Isaac with Paris. A week later he was in Hayiroh. It was midsummer: time to relax. But young Jeng had started to feel the best and the worst of his political ignorance. He hated it, but he'd come to realize that it would crawl if not walk to him in ways he'd never imagined. His life was seemingly a fancy fairy tale. Reality was jumping at him though.

This short tempered young man was part of a group who thought they could clean Africa. Fools educated in the west they are. They saw themselves as part of the newly made brooms, but they made one big, foolish and unintelligible assumption. Idealism courted them and they enjoyed more than they needed. But they still thought they knew what it was like to be born African. They had the best the world had; they enjoyed all freshness of every technological 'newness'. Whatever happens back here–in Africa and for Africans–was not something they understood. But who they were, and what it meant to be African was something they only understood in sweet mockeries of westerns kids.

"You have everything just as you say, but do you think god sent them. You have to think, coerce yourself and that's how you see all these flickering, flashing, rumbling, excitement, life and shit."

Jeng would wink angrily, but he had to eat that humble pie. It was the truth. He had to bear it the way delivered if decency was to be strapped around him.

Being a minister's son was good until he went to the US for studies. It started with the bustle, glamour, fun and show off, but things started to change as teenage ignorant playfulness gave way to young adulthood. Playful questions became questionable, every skit was screened before acceptance, conscious awareness of one's societal place started to grow. Young Jeng started to see things differently. He started to ask why he was lucky among the sea of destitute African children; what he did to deserve his fortune. Then it started to turn insufferable.

He wanted to know everything from his dad. A day after coming from Washington DC, he tried to inquire from his mum. His mum played down everything.

"You'd be better a man if you asked the owner of the business," his mum had mocked. It was an intelligible skip, but it was to the point. Why skirt at the periphery of the cake as if he was alien to the party. It was his father and he had to tackle things head on.

"I tried the same thing, but it ended with my being ignorant, so I dropped it," she'd added with unreserved motherliness; her son gazing with interesting awe.

Aatieŋ'oh was a typical African princess. She was humble, quiet, but intellectually a nonpareil character. The most amazing thing about her was that she had a long temper and a short tongue. At fifty five, she commanded respect from her kids and her husband. Vincent not only respected her, he revered her. She was avid, innovative, but annoyingly conservative. Her daughter, Mary, always mocked her about why she went to Oxford.

"You should have stayed home than go to Oxford," she always said. "It never changed you."

Unlike her sister Esther, Mary didn't consult her mum in intellectual matters as she thought her mother was a diamond in the name of a nut.

"She just wants you to think," Esther would tell her sister. Mary was 20, Jeng 26 and Esther was 32. Esther was their step sister. Her mum left Vincent when she was only ten.

Aatieŋ'oh was a typical Luo. She was traditional and unrelenting in any talk that implicated her people, but she was realistic. In most of her talks, she knew what she had to say to give the young a chance. Being a western educated African, everyone expected her to be a

European in African skin. She wasn't. Her friends were stunned at the choice she made in life. She married a half-baked man who many detested for his wealth and political involvements.

Her actions were traditional when she was expected to embrace intellectual liberalism; something she regarded as a misused myth. This gave Mary a feeling that her mum was psychologically unbalanced. An unrecognizable brain is the profitable strain, Aatieŋ'oh would think to herself.

"Being weird is part of a typical genius," Esther would always stand by her mum.

"A PhD is a studied scale not an inbuilt trait, remember?" Mary would retort back.

The May of 2007 made Vincent realize that his house had had a new man. He'd had an obedient, smart and promising heir to his business, but Jeng's summer holiday in Hayiroh that month had Vincent startled. Jeng grilled his father two nights after he arrived from D.C.

The Americans and their self-righteous ways spoilt my son, Vincent had thought. Whatever he had would be his son's. Vincent could not understand why Jeng wanted to know more about him.

"When did you start your business dad?" Jeng asked an hour after arriving from Washington. He wanted to work with the poor kids in Kibera, Kenya, just like his sister Mary was doing during her holidays in South Africa's Soweto.

Jeng saw himself as having no purpose in life except that soulless banking and rude management of his father's car companies.

"Dan…"

"Dad, why do you call me Dan?" he said and left for his room.

Jeng's objection to the name was not that strong in the past. Vincent realized that Jeng's questions and objections were loaded. Though Jeng didn't like being called by his *Christian* name, Daniel, Dan in short, Vincent realized the tone of the objections and the questions, were new and seemingly intended for a purpose.

Aatieŋ'oh had watched the drama silently as if she was not allowed to utter a word. She was reading Achebe's polemical bashing of Nigeria's political pretensions: *The Trouble with Nigeria*. She'd read it more than a dozen times, but she never stopped reading it.

When Jeng came back, Okob was already in the living room standing as stiff as his muscles could allow.

"Sit down, Okob," Jeng said and pointed at a seat nearby.

"No," Vincent said.

"Where're you going? You've not explained to me what I wanted to know," Jeng said and sat back on the couch. Okob didn't sit down. Vincent looked at Okob but he was like a sixth century philosopher's statue. Embittered and confused, Vincent looked at his son and realized he had some order to restore. *America and its ways!*

"I thought you wanted to talk so I called Okob to drive us to town."

Vincent tried to be as pretentiously calm as possible.

"I'll drive."

"No, sir I…"

"I said I'll drive. And please stop calling me sir!" Jeng said not letting Okob finish his worry.

With anger taking the best of him, Jeng realized the rude order in his voice and apologized.

"I'm sorry, Okob."

"Sorry about what sir?" Okob asked; a little alarmed.

Am I being fired?

"I shouldn't be yelling at you!"

"I like that, Jeng," Aatieŋ'oh said and resumed her seemingly perennial reading.

Vincent was getting embarrassed if not angry. His son's behavior was infuriating, but his decency had to be kept on a safe and blanched safety box.

Okob on the other hand knew the minister as someone who could not be talked back to. Someone was doing a superb job.

Allahu Akbar!

When Vincent nodded at Okob, he vanished with a smile.

59

Father and son drove in silence.

Okob was pleased with the person he was for the first time since he was employed by the minister. Aatieŋ'oh had intervened for Jeng wanted to be alone with his father. She'd reminded him of the person his dad was.

Okob mellowed out in the minister's position as the son and father sat in front. Despite having spent a lot of time driving on the right in Washingon DC, Jeng had no problem driving on the left. With uncontrolled traffic and careless Adish drivers, Okob thought Jeng would have a hard time driving.

The kid was good!

Okob looked back and saw a black Mitsubishi Pajero following them at a distance. He busied himself on his phone and assumed nothing.

Their black Mercedes slid smoothly in the soothing breeze of sweet and comforting Hayiroh evening. It was nine, a comparatively late time in Hayiroh.

The Pajero sped up, overtaking them with a whistle.

"The issue of traffic is something we have to look into," the minister said smugly. No one commented. Fortuitous comment, Okob thought.

"There's something I want you to know, dad. I've nothing to say. It's you to tell me if I've something to say or something to know. And if you think I'm talking to you this way because of my being in the states, then you better think of something else," the son said glancing occasionally at his father as they turn toward an Italian restaurant. He wheeled toward the parking lot.

Okob looked around and saw the same Pajero parked a clear distance from where they'd stopped.

Two security guys rushed to service them.

"Wait please!" Okob said pushing the minister and his son behind him.

"No, Okob, just relax for once."

Okob felt Vincent's gaze, remonstrative and insouciant eyes on him and gave in. The Pajero that'd come with them and the two guards whispering to themselves a few meters from them concerned Okob. However, he had to obey the boss and his confusedly behaved son.

"I'll meet you guys in there. Let me deal with these guys."

"I think Okob should do that for now. We should be getting in." The father said with a ministerial rather than fatherly concern.

"I'll be fine, dad," the determined son stressed.

Jeng said and headed toward the seemingly respectful parking lot attendants. Okob remained uneasy. Vincent and Okob started walking briskly away, toward the restaurant. Jeng walked toward the guards and stood humbly in front of them.

"It'd have been better if your dad had come too," one of the attendants said.

"What? What's his coming to you guys got to do with parking the car? A bigger tip?" Jeng replied with reproachful defiance.

"Honorable Miochariya!" the second attendant called the minister.

Vincent stopped and looked back as Jeng became infuriated. Okob immediately realized something was wrong. The seemingly calm condescension from the attendants was suspect and wanting.

"This is what I knew," Okob said dashing back.

"What...?"

Okob interrupted Vincent with a hand across Vincent's chest. Vincent was closely behind him. As Okob tried to remove his cell phone, one of the attendants warned: "If I were you, I wouldn't do that."

Vincent stood behind Okob as the two men stood behind Jeng; a pistol on his back.

"Who are you guys and what do you want?" Vincent cautiously asked.

"The *honorable* will tell us!" the men said in a perfect unison. They were hooded so recognizing their faces was hard. Darkness and a Blackman's face!

Vincent tried to move toward them, but Okob pushed him back. These were some of the occasions on which Okob's *being* and *services* were exhorted and exalted to renounced comfort. It'd become part of his life and whether it made him more human or not, wasn't a tingle on his intuition. Yet, he put his safety on the forefront—endangering it like jungle animals whose lives in the hands of carnivores are a mere chance.

"What do you mean young man?" the minister said with pride and courage of a coward who shouts threateningly knowing people around will give him the protection he needs.

"Oh, Uncle Vincent doesn't know what we young men are talking about."

"Dad, what...?"

"Shut up young man! Did I tell you to open your naive American mouth? In Panda, you vacation and lie on your back, on the softest of all softness and open your mouth wide with white girls giving you delight; and everything falls into your boyish mouth without you lifting a finger. And here you want to talk when those who know what life means want to talk. If you know what life means, then I'll let you talk bu..."

"But if you'll shout: oh daddy, when I... when I vacationed in Day-Town, me and my girlfriend had this desert...it...it looked awesome...you know daddy...and I love Pandian girls."

The first man spoke, followed by the second one, who interrupted the first one by mimicking what he thought was Jeng's way of talking. They then laughed loudly.

"Tell us what you want!" Okob said after a period of silence.

"Tell us what you want?" one of the men asked with a contemptuous and contemptible mimicry of Okob's voice.

"Gentlemen, is this going to end or is it a joke?" Vincent asked.

"You'll tell us why you wanted to kill the president!"

"Mm...What...?"

"Wait...wait...wait. I'm done," one of them interrupted Vincent, who'd started to fume.

"Let my son go now and deal with me you bastards!" Vincent said pushing Okob behind him. He metamorphosed from a minister to a father, leaving Okob as nothing but just another body.

"Move one step and your pretty boy will be fifty three hells away."

Vincent stopped moving.

"Okay! That's perfect Uncle Vincent. Now, to go back to our story; your rich white Pandian tycoon is here. What's the purpose of his visit?"

"Do you guys know who you're dealing with?"

"Shut up pretty boy! We know your pathetic minister of natural resources of naturalized impoverishment."

"Just say what you guys want. Money? Anything?"

"The 'bastards' don't need anything sir. All we need is the truth. You know what this boy means to you and what Christine and Isaac mean to you. If you care about this boy, then tell us what your connection is with these two Pandians."

"Dad, what's going on here? Do you know who these bloody guys are? They seem to know a lot about you. Since this Pandian friend of yours came here, things have never been good. Do they have anything to do with him?"

"I don't know what or who these guys are and what they are talking about."

Jeng hissed. "Dad, don't you know Isaac?"

"I know Isaac but I don't know what these guys are talking about."

"You don't know? Fine!" one of the guys said.

They pushed Jeng toward their car.

"Wait! Vincent yelled as he started to sweat profusely. He started heaving as if he'd been hiking.

"Whatever you guys want, I'll give or tell you, but my connection with the guys you said is very much business-like and confidential."

"I thought the word *whatever* said it all. There'd be no secrecy left if you wanted to tell us or give us 'whatever'. In that *whatever*, what we need is in there, and besides, it's not whatever that we want, it's your connection with those bloody Pandians. F-u-l-l-s-t-o-p!"

One of the men said as Vincent stood confused and rattled.

Okob was left out of the drama so he found time to alert the president. Well, someone alerted the media. In no time, the place was surrounded, siren everywhere. The gunmen watched as the place swarmed with people armed with guns, cameras, curiosity and seriousness.

One of the kidnappers pulled Jeng and laughed demonically.

"Whoever did this will be sorry for the rest of his life. If you young man did it, then you have lost your job, and if you Uncle Vincent did it, then your marriage is over. As for the young man with us, he couldn't have done it, but if he used his American sophistication, or has some wires on him, then he'll blame no one for he's dying soon."

Vincent looked around.

"Mm, did you do it?" Vincent asked staring sternly at Okob. He was protecting his boss's family. What wrong did he do?

"I said did you?"

As Okob tried to open his mouth, a sniper hit one of the gunmen on the right shoulder. He fell down with a loud thud as the other man firmly grabbed Jeng by the arm.

"Are you okay?" he asked his partner as he took firmer grip of Jeng.

"I'm fine," he said groaning.

"I'm sorry guys, please don't hurt my son. I'll make sure all these people leave."

The wounded man crawled onto the vehicle. The second one, still standing, pointing the gun at Jeng, looked at the minister and said: "You've spoiled everything, but there's still room to make things right. However, if you're thinking of going home with your son, then think of it as impossible as seeing your grandmother at Esther's Wedding."

"Mm mm...Please..."

"Wait sir. I need one favor."

"Any favor if you will not hurt my son."

"Hurting or not hurting your son is not the question now, the question is our way out of here."

"Let my son go and I will call everything off."

The man laughed derisively.

"Sir, your son is going with us. If you'll waste any more time, then I'll shoot your son and shoot myself, got that? Now, call everything off now before I get drunk with fury."

"You can't take him."

"Okay..."

Before Vincent could respond, his phone rang.

Aatieŋ'oh was on the phone.

"Are you guys okay?" she asked, strangeness rather than sadness in her voice.

"I will call you back please honey."

"Vincent...Vincent!"

He hanged up.

Before he could address the offending fellows, the president called. Vincent was busy and disinterested.

"Sir, my patience reserves are drying up fast—this is Africa!" the man said.

"What's going on? I sent a very powerful contingent; why isn't something happening? I heard one of them has been shot."

"Sir, they threatened to kill Jeng unless I let them go."

"No, they can't because…"

Vincent got concerned and hanged up. He was concerned more about his son than anything else, not even what the president would think.

"Can I send my body guard?" Vincent asked looking directly at the remaining gunman. The suit and the tie were suffocating Vincent. He was sweating away his anxiety so he loosened the tie and removed his suit.

"Yeah, you can let him go. I don't need him by the way."

The scene was surrounded by police and sharp shooters. Mischievous onlookers and annoying media curiosity hummed noisily.

Okob looked around nervously. To assure him, Vincent nodded and Okob dashed toward the busiest, lanky gentleman who looked like the commanding officer. The police had circled the place, some hiding behind their cars.

Okob walked over to the officer in charged and conveyed the minister's message. Okob came back with obvious fury.

"He said they have strict orders from the President to secure your safety."

"What?" the minister yelled.

"He refused!" Okob said with conspicuous shyness.

Vincent twisted, turned and walked around angrily.

"Sir, do you know what the point of my comfort is?" the gunman asked leaning on the car. "You're sacrificing your son unknowingly."

Okob ran back again, played a minor scuffle with the officer heading the contingent, grabbed the microphone and ran back.

The place was now swarmed with more curious onlookers as the incident was already on the evening news, live. Noise reigned as the word of stand-off gripped the nation. The news was on TV, on the Radio, on the internet and in people's living rooms.

"Don't shoot, let them go! Don't shoot, let them go! They have my son," Vincent said immediately he took the microphone from Okob. Without saying any other word, the gunman pulled Jeng into the car and gunned off.

Aatieŋ'oh rushed to the scene only to see her son go away with supposedly unknown people for seemingly unknown reason. Having seen the kidnapers go away, the officers stared helplessly.

Vincent kept shouting at the police: "Don't shoot! Don't shoot!"

Aatieŋ'oh jumped down from the car and rushed toward Vincent.

"They took him for your life? You're old yet you think you have a life sweeter than your own young blood," Aatieŋ'oh yelled as Vincent stared speechless and stupefied.

"Ma..."

Okob tried to defend the minister, but Vincent raised his hand and Okob closed his serving mouth. Aatieŋ'oh took one angry look at Vincent and stormed off without saying another word. Two body guards with her followed faithfully. Hurt, confused, belittled and worried, Vincent stared at his angry wife then got into his car.

60

"Dengdit?"

Dengdit nodded approvingly as he patted Little on the back. His gracious smile still had Little confused and in shock. Dengdit's face flashed beneath his deep black beard.

"I thought you were dead!" Little calmly and uncertainly asked. Amused, Dengdit shook his head twice horizontally, peered deeply into Little's eyes and said: "It depends on your definition of death. If death means being buried in the cemetery, then no, I'm not dead. But if death means having no significance as per other people's recognition then yes, I'm dead. If death means transmogrification, then yes, I'm dead. Now you can say whether I'm dead or not."

Little looked at Dengdit and the guys around him but found his mind blank. With exhilarating calm descending on him, Little's lips curled up excitedly. "But I received a letter from your friends in prison saying that the 'forces of evil have won.'"

Relaxed, Dengdit laughed and showed Little a chair. They sat down but Little's face was still scouring the walls and the faces around him. *I'm damned if I say I understand what's going on!*

He laughed in a deep dignified manner. "It was all staged."

"But how and why?"

"Everyone needs money, right? The purpose of working is to earn a living, right?"

Little nodded reluctantly.

"There you have the answer."

"I don't understand!" Little said with a frown.

He was feeling stupid. However, some sort of calm was settling on Little.

"Just say anyone who helped us made sense of his life."

"What have I done to you? I thought you liked me."

"What have we done to you?" Dengdit calmly said.

Little felt irritated. Even with enormous pain, he tried to remain calm. His thoughts were in distemper.

Dengdit just stared at him.

"Look, I had a good life after I left prison. Now it's all gone. Why did you do that?"

To little's annoying surprise, Dengdit started laughing and looked around, staring at the faces around him. Some were standing, others seated on the couches, the beds and the wooden chairs.

"It's my life we're talking about here, sir. You can't vent your anger and societal indictment on a fellow African trying to get out of the circle of societal you-smell-stay-there."

Having seen Little's pain and serious face, Dengdit stopped laughing and looked at Little in a way he'd never done before; his playfulness in words' profligacy giving way to a serious tone.

"Do you count your loss in terms of what was burnt or in terms of money?"

"Everything is valued in terms of money."

"Are we malicious and stupid?"

Little frowned. *I don't care anymore who you are because you are just stupid villains.*

Little crooked his lips. "What's that supposed to mean?"

"What I just said?"

"I don't...look... make me understand everything and I'll..."

Little suddenly stopped.

"What?"

"I now get it. You're fighting for your friend who went to college."

"Sounds like an epiphany from a dunce."

"What?"

"That story didn't happen. I coined it to enlighten you."

Little shook his head. "That was a hateful, misleading enlightenment."

"It isn't now."

"What's this, some Pan-African bullshit?"

Dengdit got up, removed an envelope from a drawer and handed it to Little.

"What's this?"

"Open it!"

Little slowly opened the envelope.

"Plane ticket? To Africa? Is this a joke?"

"I'm afraid not...and it isn't negotiable."

Little looked at another piece of paper in the envelope and read it.

You'll find the total amount of everything you lost in your account immediately you come back from Africa. We know every cent you lost. Please, carry out the mission very well.

"What...?"

"You've been a nice host to Wani, Wallace and Paris. They're our good warriors."

"What're you talking about? You mean?"

"They were placed there to protect their identities."

Little sneered. "No, wait, wait! So the success of my business was staged too?"

"Well, the success of the business is solely from your ideas. Grace didn't get the money from the bank though. We gave her the money. She had an idea but she didn't quiet trust everything she was told. She's hard-headed you know."

"But..."

Dengdit placed crossed fingers on his own mouth to hush Little and left the room. He came back, looked straight at Little and said: "We're running out of time. Things are going to happen."

Completely dumbstruck, Little stared at Dengdit, at the floor, but remained quiet. The reality of the whole drama was starting to sink in.

Africa? Shit!

61

For a day, everything was quiet. Isaac was able to get a clean and comfortable African breath. The comfort came when Jane phoned him at his hotel. Business was okay. There was neither sign of Michael nor Osmani though. There was too, no word from Jeng's kidnappers.

Okob picked Isaac and Christine up as instructed by Vincent. It was a smooth drive. Okob was always on time. They'd arrived an hour before the gathering as Vincent wanted to talk to both Isaac and Christine to skin some issues clean.

During the few days he'd known him, Isaac considered Okob as a naturally quiet person. Perhaps so! But that day was different. Okob stunned them for the first time with out-of-character wit. Christine sat sleepily in the passenger's seat, Okob gloomily turning the wheel. Isaac was behind them.

"I haven't come to terms with why Africans didn't develop a long-lasting craft of writing. Don't count Ethiopians."

Okob said and looked as if he'd said nothing.

Neither Christine nor Isaac seemed to like the statement. Isaac didn't actually know the answer. Silence reigned for sometimes then Okob said again.

"What if someone gave in to what others call the stereotypical view of things; that we're just not able to do it? Perhaps someone among us is thinking of lost Egyptian writings, or the Ethiopian Ge'ez, or Nigerian Nsibidi...you count the list. Well, that might be an appreciable consolation, but how for god's sake do we have to rely on archaeological histories whose truth is subjectively interpreted."

He kept quiet and the message seemed to have hit Christine like a hot, ember-red welding rod. She sat up, looked at Isaac interestingly. Isaac's look was a mechanistic one. She looked at Okob and at Isaac again. Okob was just driving; not seemingly concerned about the predicament he'd left his passengers.

"Wha...?"

"It's good to be put in a situation where you feel someone wants you to be there, there, where you're so important; where history cannot follow you and reminds you that you've so much to be thankful for; that you're fond of raising fingers when you can't even say after pointing the fingers where you'd actually pointed them to."

Now silence.

Christine was interrupted. Both Christine and Isaac were thunderstruck, yet sitting reflectively.

Isaac looked out of the window. He transiently envied the sight of the kids – dust-footed in red soil — playing football with jubilation he craved. For a moment, he wanted to be like them for once, just once. To be happy! But what would they say if he told them he envied them? What if they came to know that he was a rich white man from the richest nation on the planet?

First, he was of a privileged race and a privileged nation. What would they think? He'd just be thought of as someone mocking the African kids. Poor Sivalsians! Rationalized, Isaac's craving could go down well with others as simplicity, but historical differences cannot make that happen. Happiness was something Isaac needed, but couldn't get.

Okob drove smoothly, whistling excitedly. Isaac searched Christine's face to deduce what she was thinking about, but she just gave him some this-is-only-what-I-can-afford smile.

After a while, she came back after having gone to some seemingly alien mental universe.

"What book have you been reading; I'd love to read it. You make us seem stupid."

"A wise person doesn't make a wise person stupid. A stupid person with stupid ideas makes the wise *appear* stupid, not actually stupid."

There was Okob again. Isaac heartily, though silently agreed with Christine that the words were not of Okob's calibre. *You're right, Christine*. Perhaps Isaac's and Christine's thoughts confirmed Okob's message: the stereotype. However, the person Okob was known to be could uphold Isaac's thoughts as true. Perhaps Okob had been a smart guy trapped in a difficult situation, but the facts made what Isaac had in mind true. One had to know Okob to judge Isaac.

"This is not it Okob. It's just...oh God!"

Christine found herself stuck and lost for words. The first comment about Africans was good for her. It might have been aimed at Isaac or the west as a whole. Okob's second input trapped Christine unconsciously and getting out of it wasn't as easy.

"You know what? There're people you feel comfortable with to empty your head out in their presence. I never aimed it at you guys, but I wanted to see that my mind doesn't dry out before it gets used meaningfully," Okob said, turned the engine off as his passengers stared stupidly at him. They'd never even realized they were already in the minister's compound.

Okob opened the door for Christine. When he came to open Isaac's door, Isaac had already opened it.

The arrangements were topnotch. You couldn't sight any African-ness in sight though. From the food, the furniture, the pictures on the wall, everything looked sophisticatedly foreign. The required African-ness was missing in the room's décor.

Okob showed Christine and Isaac to the house.

Aatieŋ'oh was in the living room reading. That was what she mostly did. She was a quiet lady of few words. Everyone in her house even the 'government' respected her opinion. A seasoned professor in her own right, Aatieŋ'oh had made herself a name. She taught African philosophy, sociology and Mathematics at a local university. Unlike many educated African women, she never made a big deal of her brains.

Isaac was amazed at Aatieŋ'oh's excessive show of simplicity and humility. Christine was used to it. It was a big welcome one couldn't expect from a lady of her calibre.

The maid had prepared tea for the visitors. Instead of bringing the tea, the maid came to the living room and said: "the tea is ready to serve Mama Esther."

The voice was so sweet and humbling that Isaac fought back tears.

This is how we should always live; this is how humbling life should always make us feel.

"Come and say hi," Aatieŋ'oh said getting up as the maid came over to greet the visitors.

The maid was a short lady with oval, brown and almost orange face.

"Hello," she said quietly and softly adjusting her black dress and a red apron.

Isaac was ecstatic. The simplicity and humility was stupefying but beautiful. He'd never experienced something like it anywhere.

The house looked affluent; members of the house seemingly sophisticated and arrogant. But for Aatieŋ'oh, the most feared in the house, with the brain one could only envy, to serve tea when the maid was present, couldn't be anything but humbling.

"Vincent is inside. He's traumatized by Jeng's kidnap. He feels like everything is his fault," Aatieŋ'oh said on her way to the kitchen. She crouched and looked at Isaac after coming back with the tea.

"How many spoons do you take, Mr. Burns?"

"Well, I don't usually use sugar, but for record you can put one."

"Me too!" Christine added when Aatieŋ'oh looked at her questioningly.

After stirring the cups of tea, Aatieŋ'oh sat down.

"What about you?" Isaac asked.

Aatieŋ'oh had sat down having not served herself. She smiled graciously then said: "I drink neither tea nor coffee."

No one was surprised. She was *a surprise* herself.

"I'm so sorry about Jeng. I've no idea what these guys are looking for," Isaac said.

"A minister's son? It could be anything," Aatieŋ'oh said and sighed looking at the ceiling.

"You don't look as worried as you should be."

Christine looked disapprovingly at Isaac. He immediately realized what he'd just said was irresponsible. Nothing showed concern or anxiety on Aatieŋ'oh's face though. She picked her brown book up and looked at her visitors.

62

O n the night of his arrival at the temple, Chris had seen Dengiya quarrel with one of the monks. The debate was so heated that he'd stopped to listen. The monk saw Dengiya and started calling out. Dengiya tried to ignore him but the monk won't let go. After the exchange of words, Chris was led to a room.

That was then.

After Dengiya and Wani left the room, Chris started to reflect on the events. Nothing made any sense at all. Most of the events bordered on silly. The books on the shelf were all revolutionary books though. *I still don't understand why.*

Chris got up and stared at the books one by one. They all looked the same. As he sat on the chair, the door suddenly opened.

"We gotta go," Dengiya said and stared unsettlingly at Chris.

"Where're we going?" Chris asked, fear in his eyes.

"Just follow me."

Without uttering any other word, Chris followed Dengiya through a maze of corridors. They were half walking half running. Dengiya was tall and black, really soot black. The only parts of his body that were lighter were his teeth and eyes. To be honest, he was your typical African, or literally, a black man. His long legs did great injustice to Chris's shorter ones.

"You know what dude...I'm not going anywhere this time," Chris said, sat down and leaned on the wall in one of the corridors."

'What're you doing?" Dengiya asked with his croaky voice.

"That's exactly what I'm supposed to ask you."

"Look, we don't have time. We've got a problem and we should go."

"No!"

"Please!"

"You'll have to shoot me."

Dengiya kept on looking around from place to place; looking unsettled. Agitated and frustrated, he looked at Chris then looked away.

"Can we go please?"

"Dude, I hope you've heard what I just said. You'll have to shoot me."

Dengiya furiously sat down next to him and said: "You were a part-time, contract accountant and a respected police officer before you were sent to UK to retrieve *that* tribal artefact."

"I know you read that in a newspaper."

He ignored Chris and continued to talk.

"When you came back from the UK you were offered a position as the chief accountant in one of Burns' Investment companies."

Now you're getting somewhere.

"What're you doing?"

He ignored Chris still.

"They offered you part-time hours for a full-time pay. They also gave you the choice to remain a detective if you wanted."

"How...?"

"We know stuffs, Chris!"

"But..."

"You chose to honor them by committing to them full-time. You left the detective work."

He stopped, got up and looked at Chris.

"How did you know all these?"

"I can go on and on. You're a nice man Mr. Fox and we'd want you to remain this way."

"What's that supposed to mean?"

"We have a way of knowing people Mr. Fox. Your going with me is..."

Dengiya couldn't finish that sentence.

63

Aatieŋ'oh's visitors drank their *shai*; all lost in their respective mental worlds. The well-aromatized *shai* transiently relieved them of their nightmares. Then Aatieŋ'oh decided to break the silence.

"People assume many things. Well, it's natural for a mum to stress over ill-feelings or something bad happening ...or what has happened to her kids. Should I be concerned now? All I can do now is wait for them to call so that I give them whatever they want. Worrying about it can impair one's judgment into complete stupidity."

Aatieŋ'oh's remarks were a little harsh for they indirectly referenced her husband. She was right though. Getting worked up could drive Vincent into doing something drastic.

Okob then walked downstairs with Vincent in tow. Vincent looked pale and weak. He had a big wooden stick for support. The visitors tried to stand up but he waved and they remained seated.

"I'm sorry, Vincent," Isaac said as Vincent took his seat.

Vincent made himself a cup of tea. Isaac stared completely surprised. *Why isn't Aatieŋ'oh making his tea?* As Vincent was about to take his first sip, a phone rang, disturbing the then unwanted peace. It was as if everyone knew the call was about Jeng. Rude silence settled as the phone continued to ring. The maid peeped but Aatieŋ'oh nodded in some codified signal and she was gone. Okob peeped and one look by Vincent sent him off.

"Is someone going to answer the phone?" Isaac asked, curious about what was happening.

Christine was surprised too.

Aatieŋ'oh seemed disinterested and engrossed in her reading. Isaac looked around the house and realized the house had many gadgets hooked to the ceiling and the windows of the living room.

Detectives investigating the kidnap had set up recording equipment in the house to trace the call should the kidnappers call. Aatieŋ'oh objected and the officers left without removing the gadgets.

"There's a rightful owner of the call," she said looking at the window.

Vincent got up without any expression on his face. Aatieŋ'oh continued to talk freely as if nothing was happening.

The living room atmosphere was still and annoyingly unnerving. They all sat quietly as if each and everyone was engaged in some devilish contrivance.

Aatieŋ'oh's behavior was becoming apparently mischievous and insolent.

"When I was in England, I heard of this police officer. He was dutiful and patriotic. On one fine day he walked into a store owned by a Zimbabwean to buy drinking water and a pack of cigarettes. When he entered the store he saw Mugabe's picture on the wall with writings: *'Being faithful to a bad cause is better than being disloyal to a holy one. When 'good men' maliciously set up a helpless 'bad man'; the latter kills part of himself.'* First, he didn't like Mugabe's picture and secondly, the statement was immoral, he thought. He bought his items, stared at the picture silently and left the store to the owner's surprise. On the following day, he came back but the picture wasn't there. He looked everywhere but Mugabe's defiant portrait wasn't there. Instead, Mandela's portrait was installed perfectly in position—the writings now: 'Spirit of reconciliation, but only if all the spirits truly reconcile.'

"There..."

"Excuse me..."

Aatieŋ'oh momentarily looked at Vincent and looked away. Vincent was about to say something. She ignored him and continued with her story.

"Three days later, the shopkeeper was shot dead by a gang of rowdy kids as he came out of his shop after closing for the day. A year passed and no suspects were found. Five years after the shopkeeper was killed and the shopkeeper's wife continued with the business as an honor to her late husband, the police officer wrote a note and committed suicide outside the shop. The note read: 'I had pleasure killing him for what I assumed I knew and wanted. I had assumed control over my conscience. But now, as I write this nice note, my life has become a struggle every time I see the sun. I have come to realize that however much one hates; one's hatred cannot transcend one's nature-given sub-consciousness. I hope he'll forgive me when he sees me'."

Satisfied with the extent of her story, she stopped and looked at Vincent.

Isaac stared at her.

Is she the one who taught Okob?

Vincent was still standing patiently.

"It's someone from *The Pipers*. He says he's fine."

"Who's fine?" Aatieŋ'oh hastily asked.

"Jeng."

"Good god!" Christine exclaimed.

"What next did he say?" Aatieŋ'oh asked.

"They've not demanded any ransom amount," Vincent said.

Vincent sat down as everyone stared blankly at him.

"They don't want any ransom. There's some classified information they said they want."

"I hope it'll have to be declassified!" Aatieŋ'oh said with overt cynicism.

"I wished it was that easy," Vincent said and kept quiet.

"It's my son. The president has to declassify that information."

"We'll have to negotiate something else. That information can be dangerous to the whole country."

"Ugh! I see! I know you care about this country so much but this time I'll have to care about my son. You don't have to do anything; I'll talk to the president myself."

"You don't understand. It's..."

"The President will make me understand."

"Mm, I wished it was that simple."

"It's not simple and that's why we're talking about the president of Sivals. Besides, there's nothing impossible for a mother who's about to lose her son."

The room then turned dead silent. Outside, the wind gently passed through beautiful and green tropical leaves. They slowly swayed from side to side. That beautiful ambience contrasted with the pending doom inside.

Was there any classified information? Vincent knew there wasn't any. Isaac too knew there wasn't any. It was a predicament. But how were they to convince Aatieŋ'oh there wasn't anything to be declassified?

Vincent started to sweat, Isaac became feverish and Christine just stared blankly.

"When did they say they'd call back again?" Christine broke the unnerving silence.

"They didn't tell me," Vincent said.

Aatieŋ'oh got up, grabbed her keys and called Okob. Everyone soullessly stared as Aatieŋ'oh and Okob left. Not a word! The tension brought in some mysterious gloom: bleak and stupefying.

Christine was starting to feel the pinch of her own negligence. She'd tried to play the system, but the system was stretched beyond its elasticity. Perhaps there was a mole in their system; inside Burns' Investment. There was no time. They could have used their resources to locate the cancerous element among them. Christine had stared at Aatieŋ'oh as she left.

Perhaps the foil is among the three of us.

Every soul was lost in thought after Aatieŋ'oh insolently left. Another phone call tore through the silence. The maid answered it and looked at the visitors, completely confused. Vincent dragged his feet toward the phone.

"It's for you, Isaac!" Vincent said.

Isaac first looked at Christine. Unless it was Aatieŋ'oh, no one else knew he was at Vincent's. He got up slowly and timidly.

"Hello!" Isaac said in a cowardly voice and sat down on the couch next to the phone.

The caller remained silent.

"Hello, this is...this is Isaac Burns."

"Hello Isaac," a female voice thrilled.

"Who's this?"

"This is not Jane, ugh! Don't worry she's fine. Please wait for The Pipers' rep. He wants to talk to you."

"Who're you and who're The Pipers?" Isaac asked raising his voice to the surprise of Vincent and Christine. One look behind and Isaac realized everyone was looking at him.

"Hi Mr. Isaac Burns! Africa is tormenting you, eh? Don't worry about who we are because that's neither going to help you nor us. We know you're a good man inside, but you're a gullible capitalist because of money and that makes you immoral by association. How does it feel to feel useless...that your money can't make you feel good? The uselessness you feel now is an everyday occurrence to the thousands of hands you employ as tools, not people. They know you exist but you just don't know their existence. Their existence is manifested only in your profits. You're like a god to them, a god they know but who doesn't know them. What they do for you isn't appreciated because you supposedly give them life: that's money. What you do for them; that is, the pay, is appreciated by them every single day and you know that."

"What do you guys want?"

"I know you have lots of money, but we don't want any money. You know what I hate from people who pretend to know what they lord over other people? Self-righteousness!"

"What the hell is that?"

"I sent you a note and I was happy you heeded our advice, but one thing wasn't done. Remember a call you got in the hotel before Vincent went to your hotel room, and before Jeng was kidnapped, it was Michael who was kidnapped."

"Wha...?"

"Wait...Wait...Wait sir. What doesn't matter to you or anyone of your likes is that what we say doesn't matter; whether in history or now. All that's given to us as credit for our existential views are all honorary. Don't venture into patronizing Africa about its primordial and atavistic greatness and stuff. The simple thing I'm telling you is to give us the information by this evening and if you fail to give it to us, both Jeng and Michael will die and we'll have your scandalizing photos sent to the media. I hope that sounds pretty Pandian, not African isn't it? And mind you me, we know how to use Paris's photos. We know she's Jane's sister."

You can guess how Isaac was feeling then. He tried to talk, but he could only wheeze, he tried to move but his legs were five-thousand pounds heavier.

"I know you now feel like Kilimanjaro is on your head. I'll make it simple for you. Bring the information; all the *stripping* information and details of the Khartoum's operation. I don't mind whether you come with the most sophisticated military unit. Come to the Church in Wernom next to the Sivalsview market tonight at 20:31 sharp. You'll find a black paper on the entrance. In it, you'll find a laptop computer. Open it and you'll see a program called *raped, bereft and deranged* at the top right corner. Open it and follow the instructions. You'll have someone guiding you in case you don't understand something in the software. If you finish the information successfully, the computer will open a window telling you how to get your guys."

"But…"

The caller hanged up.

Isaac looked at Christine and Vincent. What was registered on their miserable faces was 'what did she say?'

"If we give them the information, both Jeng and Michael will be alive."

"No, No, No, No…you don't tell me Michael is also kidnapped," Christine said.

Before Isaac could know why Christine vomited those nos, her cell phone rang. She answered it briefly then gave the phone to Isaac. It was the ambassador.

"You're required in Day-Town in the next two days. There's credible intelligence that your life is in danger."

"Sir, I'd want to believe whoever said that, but I doubt anyone would want to harm me here in Africa," Isaac said pretentiously to the Pandian senior diplomat.

"We all have our jobs, Mr. Burns. We trust the people the government gives certain tasks to protect our citizens wherever they might be on this planet. They know exactly what they do and why they do it. I'd advise you not as a government servant, but as a friend; it's serious. Furthermore, they don't want to understand what we have to say. So, prepare to go."

That was the striking part about Isaac's going to Africa: surprise and psychological torment. Isaac tried to convince the government he wasn't in danger. He was in no position to bargain. Stakes were high. Risks involved in his leaving Hayiroh were even more unnerving. Isaac still had two days to sort things out. Two days was enough time to help rescue Jeng and Michael.

64

Chris heard a loud bang then there was complete silence. Rattled, he turned and saw Dengiya lying on the floor, bleeding.

"De..."

"Go!"

"No!"

"Dengdit and the guys are outside waiting in three identical trucks."

"I can't leave you here. Besides, I was kidnapped."

"Go! No one reported that you were kidnapped. You'll be considered part of us."

"What?"

Dengiya quickly handed Chris a paper containing the compound lay-out.

"Just go!" Dengiya yelled.

Chris ran away as uniformed officers ran toward Dengiya. As the officers neared, Dengiya pulled out a pistol, placed it inside his mouth and daringly pulled the trigger. Obviously, Chris didn't want to see the ghastly aftermath. He ran, really sprinted away.

The passage was complicated. After several turns in that maze of corridors and passages, he found a way out. As he arrived outside, gunshots were raining down on them. He tried to get back in, frightened to death. A black van approached. Someone inside the van yelled.

"Get in!"

Without knowing who was calling him to get in, Chris jumped on and the truck speed off as bullets rained on them.

Chris realized Wani was hit on the left shoulder. He tried to help him but Wani brushed him off.

"Dengiya's dead?"

Wani said nothing.

"I said Dengiya is dead!"

Everyone in the truck stared at Chris as he yelled. Wani looked at Chris, at the other guys and said: "He shot himself when he was injured."

"How did you know that?"

"I thought you were smart, Chris."

Chris looked back. Three police cars raced after them. As they approached a junction, the three vehicles split. One drove straight ahead, the other two drove left and right."

"Who're those guys?"

"Pandian Security Service (PSS) and the FBI," Wani said.

The shooting stopped but the car after them was unyielding. They were turning and turning but the police car wasn't giving up.

"How does it feel to be used?" Wani asked. He was driving like a professional Formula One driver. Chris was seated next to him.

"What do you mean?"

"You know Aretha Michael, right?"

"That stupid bitch! She set me up but I couldn't prove anything. Hey, how do you guys know all these?"

"We know things, Chris."

"You guys have insiders, I think."

"Ever heard of Freemasons?"

"Yeah, I read about them in history books. Are you guys part of them?"

"No, we aren't part of them. *The Pipers* use the same secrecy method. We now know that contemporary freemasons are more about keeping secrets than about the organization being secretive."

"So you've penetrated all governments. That's what I think."

"Not all governments but governments of interest."

The tail-gating car behind them neared.

There were some ladies behind. Chris heard some shootings then laugher. He looked back in the side mirror. The police car was ablaze. Then there was more laughter. Wani looked at him, put his hand behind the driver's seat and removed an envelope.

Chris took the envelope and opened it. In it was a passport, a plane ticket to Hayiroh and a pamphlet.

"Why do I have to go to Hayiroh?"

"Read that pamphlet when you're on the plane. It'll give you everything you need to know."

"I've never been to Africa."

"I'm African and I'm sending you to Hayiroh, doesn't that mean anything to you. The P siblings will take care of you."

"Can I call Judy?"

"You're asking too much, Chris."

"I need to talk to her. The police are looking for me now and she's dying of worry."

Wani ignored what Chris had said and suddenly pulled up by the roadside. He then pointed at a car parked next to a T-junction near a convenient store. Their truck was on the main street. Down the t-tail there was a kid drinking what looked like coffee.

"See that white kid on a bicycle?"

Chris nodded.

"He'll ride you to the taxi that'll eventually drive you to the airport."

Chris curiously looked at Wani and the white kid on the bicycle. Wani only winked at Chris.

Funny enough, the kid wasn't looking at them.

"Go! You have about two hours and thirty minutes. If you miss the flight, you'll miss on your life."

Still uncertain, Chris sat staring at the kid from inside the car. There was no sign the kid was aware of their presence. Not so sure of what was required; Chris jumped out of the truck and looked around. The kid looked like he had nothing to do with Chris.

Now I'm dead.

Chris braced himself and walked slowly ahead. The rude child remained in the same position in the same place.

"What the hell is wrong with these people?"

Scores of people walked by so Chris glanced back. The truck was gone. Still confused, he stared at the kid. The kid was like a stone statue.

Chris's mind was blank; he was shaken. He wobbled ahead, toward the boy. Then he heard a siren and his heart jumped. Luckily enough, the police car passed the T-junction.

As he neared, the kid threw the cup into a garbage bin nearby, wiped his mouth with the back of his hand and rode toward Chris. Chris had no luggage.

"Get on!" he said and looked straight, away from the T-junction. Still confused, Chris jumped on and the kid rode off. He passed two alleys then turned into the third one on the right.

"There's the taxi," he said and rode off.

"Who...?"

The kid didn't even look back.

The taxi was parked about fifty meters away. Chris hesitated, looked back, but there was no one in the alley. There was someone in the taxi, however. Everything was like a bad, silly dream that'd simply go away come morning. Extremely confused, Chris wanted to run.

These guys know a lot about me. These guys are like wind. They're everywhere. They're like spirits.

At that point, running away was pointless so he braved himself and walked to the taxi. After a slight hesitation, he opened the door without talking to the driver. As he was about to say something, the taxi took off.

"Hello Chris! Remember me?"

It was a voice he couldn't forget.

"You're kidding me, right? Get me out of this taxi right now!".

"Oh, baby Chris wants to get out. Just enjoy the ride, go to Africa and come back a changed man. Forget about me for a while. Just think of me as a taxi driver."

"You destroyed my life and you think I can take it just like that? Do you know what I've been through? Why do you guys take people's lives so lightly?"

"If I destroyed your life then I do know what you've been through. And if you're still the Chris I know, then you better know The Pipers will take good care of you."

Chris was so furious that he could hardly talk.

"Chris, do you know what it feels like to be put in a position where you feel you're important, but then you realize that the help being given to you is actually meant to make you feel really down and stupid in the eyes of others. The only problem is that you feel excited and the contrivance behind everything you're doing evades you. By the time you realize the game was meant to make you feel stupid and worthless, the damage has already been done.

"I was a beautiful young lady in Burns. Everyone wanted to sleep with me and I thought I was loved. I went out with the president of our branch and I rose in rank knowing that I was a good worker. When I realized many co-workers didn't regard me as much as they did when I came to the company, I started to check myself. I broke up with the president and hell broke loose.

"You can't have everything Chris. If you get one chance use it but don't always look for more than you can handle. How many aid agencies help poor kids in Africa? How much money goes into administration...?"

"Why do you guys vent your societal and racial grievances on me? Who am I?"

"We get involved with people with clean conscience. We wanted you to feel what's like to be the doormat of the society, to be poor, to be inconsequential...and then again, to be powerful and rich, because you'll be."

"I would've been rich in Burns."

"But with a soulless body."

"How's what you guys are doing 'ensoulling'?"

"You'll be rich when you've understood what's like to be a non-entity in the face of the society. You'll have the heart to respect that homeless man on the corner. You'll have the decency to know that that single mother with five kids isn't just a drain on government's money, but a human being whose reasons for being so should be studied to help the rest avoid the same situation. You'll also have the decency to know that you get sick, you get angry, you laugh, you cry, you get embarrassed, you achieve, you fail, you die, but you're just a human being with blood and flesh; a human being with hopes and dreams."

Aretha went on and on and Chris lost interest in what she was saying. He was furious but helpless. Everything about him was in their palms. They had a complicated organizational web and running away would be stupid. After a few minutes they arrived at the airport. Chris's brain was as blank as a new white board.

65

D engdit knew the bullet through his neck was fatal but he knew he would live through it. The bullets have destroyed the car. The lady next to him was long dead. Behind him, in the van, there was no sound of life. He figured they were all dead. Shook and angry, Dengdit looked into the rear view mirror and the police cars had increased in numbers; the chase ferocious. He kept on driving but his vision started to blur.

This is the end, Dengdit. You've done your job.

Weak and slowly getting unconscious, he took heart and kept on driving as police cars neared. He was now crossing from lane to lane as cars on the street rammed into one another.

"You'll be worth nothing, Dengdit. Whatever you do is wrong. Just stay in school."

He thought about his father. He'd always wanted Dengdit to be someone; a doctor, a lawyer, an engineer or even a professor. But Dengdit was stressed by life. His mum died of crystal meth (methamphetamine) addiction. His father became everything to him. But everything his father told him was contradicted by the realities of life. His father had ideals of the young. Ajak Agut-thiang was always hopeful despite having no cause for much hope. During the night, he worked as a machine operator: a dangerous and stressful job. During the day, Ajak worked as a janitor at a private clinic.

"How do you have so much hope in yourself when all you do can end you should you make a small mistake?" Dengdit would marvel at his father's resilient spirit.

"If you don't drive well on the street, you can end your life and that of others. If you take too many therapeutic drugs they can end your life. If you eat too much of anything it can disease your body. It's a question of degree son."

Dengdit's vision was wasting away. As his strength withered, he still kept his hands firmly on the steering wheel.

"You'll never amount to anything, Dengdit. Why can't you just become a comedian or an actor instead? You'll be better off doing that."

That was his high school teacher. He'd given Dengdit a revised edition of his maths class text. The text was elementary and could not actually prepare him for any tertiary standards.

"This is revised sir."

"It's revised not to kill your interest in education."

The teacher always called him in and talked to him.

Dengdit looked to his left and could see police cars blurring away. Someone seemed to be talking but he couldn't actually understand what he was saying.

He thought about his father again.

"Your mum gave in to the pressures of life. Everyone has his or her own problems. You just have to deal with your problems and curve yourself a comparatively comfortable enclave."

Ajak Agut-thiang was a man who'd defied life. His problems were his. Blaming others was inexcusable to him. Ajak worked in a factory because he didn't go to school. Even if a great deal of external forces led to him dropping out of school, he saw no reason why weak-heartedness should be ignored or excused. He blamed himself for any failure.

"I just don't understand you, father. We're so conspicuous to the police. We're so feared anytime we seek employment."

"I can grant you that, but think about this. Many of our people seek employment not having any experience at all. When they're not successful in interviews, they run and sing race songs."

Dengdit wanted to be like his father. He failed. The outside world was oppressive and hopeless that he found his father either stupid or defeated. But he admired him for his strong-heartedness.

One day Dengdit came back from school only to find his house full of gloomy faces. Many of them wore work clothes. He knew something had happened to his father.

Dad, dad...

Dengdit came back to the present. He looked out of the window, but he could hardly see anything. He felt and heard a bang and everything became quiet.

66

L ittle had never been to Africa before. He looked around and he liked what he saw. The weather was hot but soothing, people bonny. He saw a man waving a flyer with his name. The man was well dressed and friendly.

"Mr. Michael, pleasure to meet you."

"My name is John."

"Nice to meet you, John."

"This way please."

John led Little out of the airport and to the parking area.

"Do you know where I'm going?"

"I was advised to drive you to Sheraton hotel."

"And where's this Sheraton?"

"It's in the city center...well close to the city center... very nice," John said smiling.

The drive was short, rough but scenically pacifying.

John dropped Little off at Sheraton hotel and left. As Little approached the counter, a lady smiled at him at a distance. She was white and looked familiar. As Little approached, the lady busied herself with something on the computer.

"Excuse me!"

She looked up slowly and Little cringed.

"Your reservation has already been made."

She handed Little the key card. Little tried to talk but he couldn't. The lady assumed not to know Little and busied herself again.

"Are...?"

"Everything has been readied for you, sir," the lady said again.

Little stood looking at the lady.

"Is...?"

"Your transport to the airport early in the morning has been arranged by your friends."

Little stared at the lady, stupefied and petrified. She was blonde, lean and seemingly indifferent.

As a man next to the lady started to notice Little's curiosity, Little left.

He walked falteringly to the elevators. The room number was 1005. He punched the tenth button and up he was gone. Surprises had become part of his new life so he gave up getting worked-up by surprises. The elevator door opened.

1005.

Little scanned the rooms' doors then *voila*: 1005!

With some hesitation, he slid the card in and opened the door. As he sat down on the bed, there was a knock on the door. Through the peeping opening he could see a white lady standing. It was the same lady at the counter.

Little hesitated and then opened the door.

"Hello Little, remember me?"

"So you knew all along my business was a joke, a convenience for someone else."

"Looks can be deceiving, right? Some people think that's a cliché but it isn't."

"I thought this was a Pan-Africanist thing. How did you get involved with these Pipers thing?"

"So you thought all along I was some dumb white girl trying to get a rich black man's money. Oh, poor Paris!"

"You could make a good actress, Paris."

Paris, my innocent Paris is part of The Pipers!

"Can you tell me the point of all these drama? People are dying!"

"I don't know. In every war people die."

Little's lips curled up. "What war?"

"Do you know Isaac Burns?"

"Yeah...that wealthy bastard?"

"Do you know his girlfriend?"

"No!"

"Her name is Jane. She's my sister."

"What?"

"I wanted to be a lawyer after watching and reading civil rights stories. They inspired me more than anything. As I took race relations history course in the US, Panda, Canada, the Caribbean and South America, I became someone else. I decided to major in History and Anthropology. That infuriated Jane. She told me she wasn't going to pay my school fees. She wanted me to study political theory to prepare me for Law School. I didn't see the difference between the two majors anyways."

Paris walked past Little and stood by the window, looking outside.

"What has...?"

"Just wait!" she said and continued. "After months without talking to me, she got worried and called me. She'd rented an apartment for me in downtown Day-Town. As we talked about my future, I saw a story on TV about Pandian and American banks that deal with oppressive regimes. You know what these banks do? They don't put the details of the parties they send the money to. They call that *stripping*. I started to study that. I came to learn that some of the money sent through stripping is used to fund war crimes against innocent civilians without anyone taking responsibility or anyone being held accountable. In South Sudan, civil population is being displaced to make way for oil operations. They're not compensated. I started to befriend Jane closely; going to her house without her knowing. Then out of curiosity I befriended the door lady so I could understand her take on such things and suffering in Africa and American ghettos. Little did I know she wasn't just a guard but a spy incognito. I became enamored by everything she said. There I became fulfilled. I finished my BA and instead of going to law school

I joined them. The problem with The Pipers is that you just know a little. You just know what you're supposed to know. That protects the organization."

"You haven't answered my question. What's the point if people are dying?"

"We've been taking money from banks and sending the money to villages...to ghettos."

"You blackmail them and force them into..."

"They had to either lie to their shareholders or face us. Little, look at what the US and Panda did in Guatemala and Columbia; the death of innocent civilians. We can complain all we want but at the end of the day power rules. What we, the west, do isn't considered immoral but what others do is immoral. We can kill people in the name of national security but when others kill in the name of their national security, they become terrorists. How many women and children have we killed in Iraq and Afghanistan?"

"How do you feel after having done such things?"

"You'll understand tomorrow. Okay, then I realized that Burns Investment was involved in *stripping*. They were involved with the Chinese and Malaysian mining companies in Sudan: Sinopec and PETRONAS respectively. They prolonged the war in the South and everywhere in Sudan. That put the stamp onto my complete dedication to his cause."

"It's illegal. It's wrong however much the benefit is. You can plan some lawful ways."

"Don't be naïve, Little. Anyone who seemingly cares about Africa is after making his or her name. Who cared about Rwanda in 1994, South African during apartheid, the messed Somali, the ghettos in the US and Panda? Why aren't USA and Panda part of ICC? Why's Nelson Mandela still considered a terrorist now...in 2007?"

"But Africa is still poor."

"We're doing our part. Enjoy your night and flight tomorrow. Make sure you take mosquito repellent and net. It gets nasty down there in South Sudan."

Paris left and Little didn't know what to think. He remained seated like a log. After a period of boredom, he turned the TV on.

Breaking News!

It's been days since honorable Vincent Miochariya's son was kidnapped. We've received words that his wife, Aatieŋ'oh and his body guard Okob, haven't been seen following the night of their son's kidnap. There has been no request for ransom. Unconfirmed reports claim that the group responsible needs some classified information declassified.

Then the pictures of Aatieŋ'oh and Okob appeared on TV.
"John? What the hell?"
The man shown on TV as Okob was the same John, who picked Little up from the airport. *Okay, maybe they just look the same.*

Little tried to think but felt agitated. He picked up the phone but then put it down. *Now what?*

The view from his window was magnificent, beautiful city skyline. He lazily walked to the window but came back to the phone.

I can't be in this shit man.

As he was about to open the door, Paris was already there.
"Don't be surprised. Just do your job and shut your mouth."
She said and left.
"What...?"

67

C hris got out of the taxi and realized that Wani was gloomily staring at him.

"What's wrong?"

Wani sighed, looked up, fighting tears then said: "They've finally killed Dengdit."

"How?"

"You'll know everything when you come back. Just follow the instructions as laid down in the pamphlet."

Chris looked at Wani and knew he was deeply stressed. Wani was up only because he had something to do. After talking to Wani, Chris made his way toward the counter. He had no bags to check in so he took his boarding pass from the ticket booth. As Chris made his way toward the gates, Judy came to his mind.

Where the hell is Judy? Why isn't anyone looking for me? Am I this useless, non-existent?

Having gone through security, Chris dreamily walked to the information board to check the gate number. Gate three, it said. His connection was through Heathrow Airport to Hayiroh.

Chris arrived at the gate as boarding started.

"Get ready with your boarding passes please," a lady at the counter announced. They lined up faithfully. Chris's seat was 21 in the economy class. To his left was a beautiful white lady. To his right was an old African man. Chris smiled and the girl smiled back.

"Long flight, ugh?" he said.

The old man just stared so Chris assumed the man didn't speak English.

"Going to London?" the girl asked.

"Hayiroh actually."

"Wow, Africa! I've never been to Africa. I always want to go to Africa but my dad keeps on spoiling my plans."

"Maybe he has a point."

She frowned. "A point?"

Chris smiled, looking at her. She sardonically frowned again and Chris's smile disappeared.

"I'm sorry. I was just trying to rationalize his position."

"Okay, I'm young and stupid, but why can't you rationalize my position?"

"I didn't..."

Furious, the girl brought out a novel and started to read. Chris tried conversing but she wouldn't talk.

The pamphlet Wani had given him was on his lap so he grabbed it and virtually scanned it.

"You can now switch off all electrical devices: cell phones, laptops, radios...during takeoff. Also make sure your seat belts are securely fastened," the flight attendant said. They were ready for takeoff so Chris opened the pamphlet.

Dear Chris,

Why do you think you've never met my family?

Judy? It never crossed my mind!

The drama was becoming too close for comfort.

Why was I with you even when you were down, hopeless and disowned? I'm sorry to say that you were used. But I'm happy to tell you that you'll be happy for the rest of your life. By the time you receive this message, I might be alive or I might not be alive. If you get furious at me for having put you through this, you'll have a choice not to see me again if I'm alive and in jail. However, if I'm dead then your anger is taken care of.

Chris looked around as his head was spinning. The lady next to him was still engrossed in her reading. Chris was getting furious at Judy. *I thought you loved me, Judy.*

I don't know my biological parents. I was adopted by a catholic priest who raised me. He was a missionary in the Sudanese Capital, Khartoum. I was raised in Khartoum until I was twelve when my father was killed. He died there trying to make life better for millions of South Sudanese displaced by Africa's bloodiest civil war.

The Sudanese government accused him of being an agent of the West and Zionist movements. He was consequently ordered to leave.

However, he told the government that the only disowned people in the world are the South Sudanese people. No one in the world had any interest in them. The only time they were considered significant was during the slave raids by other Africans, Middle Eastern people and Egyptians. They were strong and were used as labor force.

As Chris read on, he became emotionally perturbed. His sweat pores were getting worked-up as he began to sweat; his hands shaking.

My father taught me that people are the same. The only difference among people is the natural disposition to work. But little encouragement can change that. The smartest are the audacious. The stupidest are the weak-hearted. Everything from slavery, to racism, to claim of supremacy is just a question of survival. Nothing else!

Judy, I didn't know you were this miserable. Chris started to feel privileged over Judy. *At least I knew my parents.*

Dengiya is/was a great man. I met him in one of the facto-ries I'd visited. I worked as a safety officer with Retain Your Life (RYL) employment agency. He was a student at a local university. He was working to support his mother and sib-lings.

His mum almost died of starvation in South Sudan. His fa-ther was killed during the war. His two sisters and four brothers were and are still his responsibility.

Dengiya told me he at times slept for two hours only. His story made me hate myself. I tried to seek meaning in my life.

How I became part of The Pipers is a long story. We are not what the media has made us out to be. Our cause is noble, but there are elements among us, who're trying to turn it into something of self-aggrandizement.

"What do you want to drink sir?"

"I'm fine," Chris said to the flight attendant without even look-ing at her.

"That's impolite!" the girl next to him said whispering into Chris's ear.

Embarrassed, Chris looked at the rude girl and at the attendant.

"Excuse me ma'am!" he called the flight attendant.

She came back with the same enamoring smile.

"I'm sorry! That was rude of me. I was really drawn in by the book."

"I know. Sometimes a good book is better than wine and din-ing," she said with an angelic smile. Chris felt relieved so he re-sumed his reading.

This is a fulfilling campaign. You'll not actually join us, but you'll be a changed man once you fly back to Day-Town. You were put into this situation in order to feel how it is like to be taken for granted and disenfranchised; to live in hopelessness by design. Your life for the last few years was modeled after an African man's life.

With love, from Judy

Chris turned the page. On top of the following page was a heading in block letters.

FOLLOW THE INSTRUCTIONS CAREFULLY!

68

On the day *The Pipers* called Vincent's house, Isaac took the call very seriously. The instructions the caller gave Isaac were explicit. Isaac stressed that they be followed as exactly stipulated.

These guys have insiders' information.

As Christine, Isaac and Vincent drove out of Vincent's house, a white Toyota corolla showed up at the entrance.

It was exactly eight o'clock and Isaac knew they were running out of time. A different young man was driving as Okob had gone with Aatieŋ'oh to god-knows-where. Media reports called her disappearance a kidnap while Vincent ignored them completely.

Isaac and company left the compound in three cars and split three ways to confuse the media.

Vincent lied to the president that some ransom was requested. The president put politics aside and gave in to the family's position.

There were some discreet forces sent to guard the church, however. To the public, the security forces, if anything happened, would be reflected as acting on leads.

Before she disappeared, Aatieŋ'oh showed no typical emotions of a mother whose only son has been kidnapped. However, her meanness toward Vincent always confused everyone so her mental and emotive states were hard to read.

As Isaac and company drove away, Vincent's gate man phoned. The man in the Corolla wanted to talk to Isaac.

"We can't go back. They'll kill them," Christine complained.

"What if it's one of the same guys?" Isaac said.

"Then we're in danger!"

"Let's go back!" Vincent ordered.

"Remember your son's life," Isaac said.

"Worry about your friend, Michael. As for my son, follow my instructions."

They all kept quiet as Isaac stared at Vincent for a moment.

Is Vincent involved in a staged kidnap?

"Turn back!" Vincent told the driver authoritatively.

"Wait sir. Are you sure you want to do this?" Isaac asked with an unpretentious seriousness.

"He'd be a good asset if he knows something about The Pipers," Vincent said again and the truth in his word became too apparent to contemplate.

"Let me talk to him first," Isaac said and grabbed the phone.

The driver duly stopped the car and pulled up by the roadside.

"Who're you and what do you want to say?"

"I can't say who I am and what I want to say to you. Look, my presence here has not been detected and if detected, you either don't find me alive and you don't get the information you need or one of you dies."

That doesn't sound good.

Isaac hesitated as Vincent and Christine stared at him, expecting a word.

"Why should I believe you? Look, you saw the news about the tip off. We're on our way."

"*The Pipers* aren't what you think. They're just playing with you. Do you think...Look, the more I talk to you the more it'll be reall..."

"We can't go back!"

"Vincent is involved in a plot to oust the president and the money comes from you."

Every hair on Isaac's body stood erect. *That's something.* The vandalism in his hotel room, the president in the restaurant: they were all calculated.

Who's actually the bad guy? Are there really The Pipers or is everything a hoax?

A moment passed as Isaac fought the urge to look at Vincent.

"Drive back!" Vincent ordered the driver.

Isaac looked at Vincent and realized he was serious.

"We're coming now," Isaac said and hanged up.

"No, please," Christine said. "Your son!"

"These are all chances and risks. We can't ascertain the authenticity of the calls nor can we be sure of what the man is saying. But this looks more immediate than this blackmail."

"Please!"

Christine pleaded, almost to tears but Vincent was recalcitrant.

"But why'd...okay forget about it."

Vincent was about to say something but dismissed it. It was a tough choice.

What was what and who was who then became insignificant. They had to go where emotional appeals and impulses drove them. But that wasn't so much an emotional appeal. The odds were juggled and the best alternative was the one that urged them to drive back. However, they were simply humans and that defied their own reasoning.

Christine had told Isaac once that decisions can be based on reason or emotion; and both species of decision making could be wrong or right. However, decisions based on emotions depend on the strength of emotions. Their being right is a matter of luck. Even if a reasoned choice can turn out to be wrong, its being wrong appeals for the simple fact that we are humans.

Did their impulses appeal or was it their rationalizing the situation? Who cares!

For Isaac and the minister, it was nonsense to think too much about their driving back. Christine didn't like the whole idea so she sat there, dull and desensitized.

They arrived home and the guard opened the gate. Isaac jumped down first. As he was about to shake the man's hand, Isaac recognized him as one of the agents who interviewed him at SNSIS. Before Isaac could meaningfully position the man's image, a loud bang hit and the young man was on the floor lying lifeless. The echo tore through the stillness of the summer-like heavenliness of an African night. Everything momentarily stood still, timeless.

Vincent and Christine had taken cover under the car. Isaac, however, stood helpless, frightened and confused; staring blankly at the lifeless man in front of him.

"Dono!" he said absentmindedly then everything blackened.

Minutes later as Isaac tried to get up, two strong hands pressed him down. He slowly gained his bearing and realized that Vincent was on the phone. The two steely hands were two hard-faced paramedics putting him onto an ambulance.

I wasn't in shock, was I?

"We're fine Your Excellency."

Those were the last words Isaac heard as Vincent hanged up. Isaac gave one last look back as the scene started to teem with the media, the police and the onlookers.

Vincent waved at Isaac as the ambulance roared away. Its size dwindled and melted into the blackness of the street.

69

Everyone in the village gathered as two big black men explained to them the content of Uncle D's letter. Uncle D maintained everything as usual. He'd sent a video message asking the village elders that his friends be received well. In the video Uncle D answered the question kids had always asked him: "Why don't you build concrete houses and schools for us?" Of which he'd always politely answered: "That time is coming soon, my friends!"

"I know I've been a little selfish, but receiving my friends will be the most important thing of all the things you'll do for me. Concrete houses will soon mushroom in your village. The world will know Werpionkor. You'll be walking and working in the middle of the night as if it's midday. Your children will go and study in the land of the ghost-looking lady, who went there with The Mama. What a beautiful time they had? Anyone I sent, you received with good heart and you treated him/her well. Your gods and ancestors will be known the world over as you'll worship and sacrifice to them anytime of the night and day. I can't go into detail of what's going to happen within the next few weeks of my friends being there, but you'll reap a lot of beautiful fruits you sow in your godly and prince-ly garden. I know you'll trust what I'm saying because not a single word I told you disappointed you. I'm your son. Thank you a lot. "

BG2 got up with a smile and waved at the elders. He removed the DVD and looked at Nyanbenypieth.

"We're greatly indebted to you. We're very mysterious people but you've helped us a great deal. The mystery will come to an end in a few weeks. As Uncle D said in the video, the coming days will herald in an age in which Werpionkor will be on the lips of everyone in the world," BG2 said with sobering humility.

"Being mysterious is the nature of the gods. And if mystery is around us, we accept it as a word from the gods and time will come when the mystery will deliver whatever it was pregnant of. As our wise people of yester years say, anything pregnant will eventually let go that bulge whether that thing likes it or not. No man or woman complains about why a woman is not giving birth when she has been pregnant for only three moons turns. We listen to our gods and ancestors and that is what we are doing. The gods will give us the answer through you," Nyanbenypieth said with spiritual edge.

BG1 then got up as the elderly lady extended her hand for a welcome handshake.

70

J eng didn't know where he was. He was getting stumped though. On the first day of his kidnap, he was hurled into a dark room, a really Cimmerian room. Then a call from his mum salved his pestered spirit.

"Obey everything they say and you'll be fine. I'll pay them and get you back, honey."

"They treat me well, mum. I don't understand."

"They wouldn't get any money if they hurt you."

The captors treated Jeng with a colorful regality. It'd been three days since he was kidnapped. The captors took him to a hotel somewhere in Westland immediately Aatieŋ'oh called.

There was always a brazen lady at the door. Any time he picked up the phone in his room, another lady answered it. He couldn't call the police. Then on the third morning the brazen lady at the door walked in with the room service lady. The room service lady put down Jeng's breakfast and left the room. The contumelious guard walked intrepidly straight to the window and curiously stared outside. Jeng boldly got up, disdainfully stared at the lady then sat down, got up again and paced to the window.

"Is this the best way to make money? Do you guys think you can get away with this?"

"We got away with so many things, Jeng."

Jeng jaunted back to the dining table and started to take his breakfast.

"Not this one this time. My father is a powerful man in the government. He's the president's..."

"Most trusted man. You just don't know shit son."

"I go to one of the best universities in the world."

"Columbia University!"

"So you did your research! Yeah Mama!"

She slowly walked back, sat on a brown couch by the window and placed both legs on the couch.

"Let me ask you a question," she said.

"I'm not going anywhere ...I'm here," Jeng said with a huge load of muffin in his mouth.

She cleared her throat as if she was about to deliver a lengthy speech. Then there was a churlish knock on the door.

"Before I ask you a question, let me introduce you to my friend; the beautiful and the charming..."

The door brusquely opened.

Jeng dropped a fork in consternation.

"Paris?"

"What's this...some girl's game?"

"Hello Love!"

"Like I was saying, I have a question for you."

Jeng gawked intensely at Paris then at the girl but couldn't think of what to say. The girl continued. "Who do you blame about Africa's problems: the West or the corrupt African leaders?"

"Paris please tell me what all these mean."

"You'll know in a matter of minutes," the lady answered.

"And who're you?"

"She's Judy. Remember the funny white dude, Chris?"

"I remember, but tell me this is just a joke."

"Everything in life is a joke, love," Judy said.

"The only thing that's no joke is death," Paris said.

"Everything from birth to all forms of unconsciousness is a joke. Everything in your life is a joke. The only true thing that brings you back to you is death. Death is the ultimate truth and truth-engenderer in human existence. It equalizes everyone into involuntary egalitarianism," Judy continued.

Paris sat on the chair next to the dining table as Judy sat on the bed.

"What's with this philosophy nonsense?"

"Who do you blame: the West or the corrupt African leaders?"

"I don't care! Guys, I'm freaking out here! Do you expect me to answer you in this harrowing and torturous state? I was kidnapped by guys who never appeared again and I'm being guarded by women and treated like royalty. Please tell me something before I go insane."

"We have Mathare hospital in the neighboring Kenya; just like UK's Hanwell Asylum."

"Do you girls think I'm joking?"

Jeng jumped to his feet, angrily grabbed the breakfast table and violently turned it upside down, fuming at Judy.

"I'm fed up with all this nonsense. You either kill me or let me out of here!"

The girls remained seated as if nothing happened. They neither cringed nor did they respond.

Jeng felt stupid so he slowly sat down. *They're hardened criminals!*

"You're used to this, ugh? Yeah Mama!"

"That probably helped. The Mama will be here soon," Judy said.

The girls then laughed hysterically until a knock on the door surprised them.

"There's The Mama," Paris said.

The door slowly opened.

Jeng girlishly rushed to Aatieŋ'oh.

"Thanks mum. Please give these people their money and get me out of here. They treated me well but they're torturing me mentally."

Jeng said shivering.

"Sit down!" Aatieŋ'oh said and sat on the bed.

"Please do it quickly before I go insane."

"Be strong son. You'll hear more telling tales than your seemingly excruciating condition."

"What?"

71

L ittle knew he had to keep quiet. Everything he saw made no sense at all. The same man; John or Okob–whatever his real name was–drove him to the airport.

The single-engine plane he was traveling in made loud noise and Little almost developed headache. After hours of head-splitting rumbling, they arrived at the town of Yei.

Yei is a small town with many mud-walled and grass-thatched huts. It was a rainy season and the airstrip was flooded and muddy. Without doubt, it was some god-forsaken hell. However, the lush greenness impressed Little. It was the most beautiful thing he'd ever seen. Its frondescence was heavenly. The roads weren't tarmacked, but they were lined beautifully by trees. Two military men approached Little as he alighted from the plane.

"Mr. Michael, welcome to New Sudan."

New Sudan?

"Your next plane *leaving* in 2 two *hour*. We can take you to *beny's* place *to relaxing*," one young man said in a broken, accented English.

They all entered a tiger-looking military jeep colored in black and yellow. As they entered the town Little could see a few iron-roofed buildings. The surrounding was simple but breath-taking. Little was starting to relax in spite of rude uncertainties ahead of him. The atmosphere was relaxing and soothing. There wasn't the bustling and noise of Day-Town. He loved it; cherishing every minute of his existence. It was simply serene.

I now know what serenity means. This is Africa. This is where I was taken.

Little felt important for the first time in his life. *I was being served by my brothers in my motherland.* He fought tears back. After a few minutes' drive they arrived at a huge, grass-fenced compound. There were two mango trees in the middle of the compound, and three along the circumference of the compound. Four iron-sheet-roofed and brick-walled buildings graced the compound. A group of men was playing cards and dominos on the floor under the middle mango trees. There was a group of women laughing and cooking next to one dirty building. The car was parked next to the spot where the men were seated.

"That is Commander Michael Garang," one of the men, who brought Little, introduced the commander. The commander was a short, pot-bellied fellow with humorous import.

"Welcome to New Sudan," the commander said.

"Thank you sir."

"You are home. Feel free. I will get ready and we will be in the airport in about an hour."

Despite his accent, the commander's English was superb.

Little didn't ask where they were going. A feeling of significance was overwhelming him. Even if he was going to die, he knew he was home, he was free.

After that brief introduction, Little was led to a tin-roofed hut. The accommodation had a double bed, a chair and a table. It wasn't fancy but it surprised him more than he'd thought. He then was shown a grass-fenced structure, about two meters in diameter, in a name of shower. After shower he was served an incredibly humbling lunch.

"What's New Sudan?"

Little asked a lady who brought him food. The lady shook her head, smiled and left. Little conjectured that she either wasn't allowed to talk about it or she didn't speak English.

72

Chris left the airport by taxi to intercontinental hotel.

Everything was prepared to no single fault. He was impressed. The services were excellent and the city was beautiful. What concerned him though was the traffic. The driving was precarious and the ferrying drivers reckless. The Adishes were a complete disaster.

It was evening and he had many things to do. By the window, the city stared at him with amicable mockery. The Hilton hotel, the inter-continental, Best Western...Holiday inn...all smiled familiarly at him. *Didn't know such views existed here!*

After shower, Chris called room service. Anxiety was stuffing his stomach. He couldn't eat so he picked up the phone.

"Who's this?"

"I was told to call this number," Chris said with uncertainty.

"Told by who?"

"I can't tell you that."

"Well, my name is Isaac Burns of Burns Investment."

Rattled, Chris suddenly hanged up. Still confused, he got up, but sat back down. He walked to the window and the Sivalsview Conference Center stared at him.

What the hell was that? Isaac?

Now composed, Chris picked up the phone again and dialed the number.

"Who the hell is this?"

"Come to InterContinental Hotel, room 300," Chris said. "Please come and come alone."

"Do I sound stupid to you?"

"Do you know something called *stripping* by some western banks?"

"I don't know."

"The honest you are with me, the better things would be for you."

"Why do I sound stupid to you?"

"Because *The Pipers* have a lengthy affidavit of *stripping* that implicates you."

Isaac sighed painfully.

"My every move is being watched. What time did you say?"

"I didn't say any time, but you can come in about an hour."

73

J eng sat on the bed, confused.

"Mum what's happening?"

Aatien'oh motioned at the girls and they faithfully left the room.

"Mum, please!"

Aatien'oh walked to the window, stared out for a while then said: "I had a wonderful family back in Western Sivals just like you have: a wonderful father and mother, and loving and supportive siblings."

Aatien'oh then turned and looked at Jeng. Jeng sat still; quiet and staring. Aatien'oh then continued.

"A ruthless tribal war broke out two years after I was born."

"Why're you telling me this now mum? You've always told me that. What have I done?"

"Just listen, would you?"

Aatien'oh said and sat down on the chair.

"My parents and all my siblings died during those clashes."

"You were then adopted by an Irish missionary, who took you to London. You attended Oxford then you disagreed with your father when you decided not to attend school. You then met my father when he was invited to speak to Sivalsian students and community in London. Mum what's new in that story? You're my mum and I know everything about you."

Aatien'oh stared lovingly at her son, got up and walked to the window again.

"Sometimes people resort to drastic measures just to feel okay."

"Did you stage this fake kidnap mum just to tell me that?"

"This was only a distraction."

"From what mum?"

"During those tribal clashes, there was one enthusiastic young politician who wanted to make it really big on the political front."

"So that's the man who fathered me, great. I'm not angry. Can we please go?"

"This young man was so ambitious that he didn't know that pitting one community against another was wrong. He thought that democracy could be brought about by letting people sacrifice themselves when he sits with his opponents and drink beer in Hayiroh hotels."

"Are you telling me that the clashes were engineered by a politician for interest?"

"Maybe it wasn't his interest but his stance was misunderstood ...perhaps."

"Then why do you blame him?"

Aatieŋ'oh stared at her son.

"I'm sorry mum. I didn't..."

"Not until a few years ago did I know the truth as to who killed my parents. My father talked against hatred among different tribes in Sivals. That wasn't in the interest of many politicians. When the clashes started, politicians saw that as an opportunity to get rid of him and blame it on tribal hatred."

"What has that got to do with me?"

74

fter an hour of beautiful afternoon nap, commander Garang sent for Little. South Sudanese society was strange. Women stayed in their own quarters away from men. They cooked, washed dishes and conversed away. Man only sat and played cards and dominos, waited for food to be brought and ate. Well, that was during the wartime. During better times, men herded cattle, farmed and did other chores that were seen as hard for women. At times men's and women's roles overlapped.

Children had their own quarters but one didn't see them much unless when playing mini-soccer or children games. That was Little's little assessment.

A young man, who Little assumed was a body guard, came to fetch him.

"It's time to fly, Mr. Michael."

Little and the man walked out of the hut, and to the car.

"If I'm not being imprudent, where're we going, exactly?" Little asked the commander.

"We'll talk on the plane."

Little and the commander entered a new Mitsubishi Pajero. Three other soldiers entered the same car with them. Two other vehicles followed them including an artillery mounted jeep. That was the first time Little ever got a chance to see those guns in real life. He'd only seen them on TV and movies.

I love Africa.

The commander looked at Little and said: "You'll have to call your mum and tell her you're home...and that you're okay."

"Am I allowed to do that?"

The commander smiled and handed Little a fancy looking phone. Little stared at the commander then dialed the number. It rang for a while then Grace picked it up.

"Little Michael. Just as I thought I was stupid, my god told me I've never been stupid."

"How did you know it was me?"

"I've been told everything, Little. It's beautiful. I've never been this proud in my entire life."

"Mum, I was just calling you to let you know that I'm doing great."

There was silence.

"Mum, are you okay?"

"I know you're home son. You're home."

She hanged up.

The commander looked at Little and smiled.

"I heard you asked my younger wife something about *New Sudan*."

Younger wife? Man, I love Africa.

Little smiled.

"Yeah, I did. People keep saying welcome to *New Sudan*."

"Let's go!" the commander yelled and off they were gone.

The entourage followed the same route to the airstrip. They called it airport. It was nothing closer to a port.

"New Sudan is a political idea of our leader. Ever heard of Sudan People's Liberation Movement?"

"I heard it from someone I knew."

Little was starting to feel at home. The guns and mean faces didn't concern him anymore.

"What comes to your mind when you hear New Sudan is: where is Old Sudan? North Sudan is inhabited by mostly Muslims and the South is inhabited by Christians and animists as your people in the West would say. During the colonial era, the Europeans kept the South as a protectorate. They only allowed missionaries to go to the

South and not Muslims. Our brothers in the north, a few who were Arabs spread Islam in the north. Africans in the north who weren't protected from Islam by Europeans became Muslims. Islamized Africans were cheated into believing the supposed inferiority of African cultures and traditional religions. They started to see themselves as Arabs and Muslims in spite of their skin color."

Little's company was now passing the beautiful area of mango-trees-lined roads. With no doubt, Little was engrossed in Commander Michael's narration.

"During the protectorate era, South Sudan didn't undergo any development while the north enjoyed a relative period of development. When Sudan gained independence, Southerners were given a choice of independence. But having no credible knowledge of the northerners' beguiling attitude, some southerners decided that unity was the best option. A good number of the southern leaders wanted independence, but they were not successful in making their voices heard. Their failure was a big mistake. Northerners knew that the soul of the country was South Sudan."

"So they started to marginalize South Sudanese through introduction of Islamic laws."

The commander nodded and continued.

"Even before independence in 1955, smart and informed South Sudanese knew marginalization would happen as religious, cultural and social differences were enormous. These Southerners started a mutiny in Torit in 1955. This war ended in 1972, but soon after, the agreement paper was placed in the latrines. This let our late leader, then a young man in 1972, to lead the current rebellion."

"Wha...?"

"Now the question of New Sudan! Our leader didn't think separation is the best solution for the Sudanese problem. He wanted Sudanese to see their differences as incentives rather than liabilities. He wanted a country in which people of different races and religions come together while respecting their differences as blessings."

"Just like United States, Panda, Canada, Australia and others."

"A Sudan where everyone's dignity is recognized and people of all races and religions are treated equal and given same opportunities to prosper as per their natural abilities."

"That's the New Sudan? Very impressive!"

They arrived at the airstrip, jolly and fired up. There was a United Nations aircraft together with an American made chopper. They boarded the United Nations aircraft. Little looked out through the window and looked at the commander. His lips curled up happily. "I haven't seen anything like this in my life, not life like this."

"This is the land our brothers in the north want to take away from us."

Little smiled. "I could die defending this."

"You have a point."

Little looked at the mountains, the dense forest and he fought tears back. He was feeling childish but he knew it was worth it even if he would to be termed a sissy.

"We are going to Bentiu in Unity state (formerly Western Upper Nile). It is one of the places where you will see the mercilessness of not only the Sudanese government, but also, the masters of morality."

Little couldn't get his eyes off the window.

"Is it possible to live here...I mean, can I change my citizenship?"

The commander laughed.

75

Isaac stood outside InterContinental Hotel. He looked back but the taxi was gone. The building stared back at him. In front of the hotel tourists of all sorts, but mostly westerners, mingled and meandered around. He walked in and to the counter.

"How can I help you today sir?" a lady at the counter asked politely.

"I'm coming to see someone in room 300."

"Does he know you're coming?"

"Yes, he does."

"And what's his or her name sir?"

"I think you can find that out."

"It's our policy not to give our guests' names out."

"I didn't say you give me the name. You asked me and I said you can find that out."

"I'm sorry about that. What's your name sir?"

"Isaac Burns."

"It wouldn't be long."

Isaac thought the man's voice had sounded familiar over the phone despite an attempt to hide it. The lady at the counter made a call as Isaac stood reflectively.

"You can go now sir."

Isaac uncertainly made his way to the elevator. He'd mastered the art of disguising himself. The blue jeans, yellow shirt and grey suit made him look sort of western. The cowboy hat and brown sunglasses made the incognito trick superb.

Who's the man and what does he want?

Isaac jumped out of the elevator and scanned the doors for number 300. He paced along for few more steps and 300 appeared on his left. Not knowing what to expect, Isaac took a relaxing sigh and lightly and slowly knocked on the door. There was shuffling of papers inside, thumping of feet then the door opened.

"You gotta be kidding me! What're you doing here? Where've you been?"

"Just get inside. I know you're part of this. You know every god-damn detail."

"What're you talking about, Chris."

"What's Vincent up to?"

"Well, I mean, his son has been kidnapped. That's what he's up to."

"No, that's not what I'm talking about!"

"That's what I know. Who told you about *stripping*?"

Chris slowly walked to the window.

"You wanted to send me here to be involved in a coup and get killed? God what the Africans claim is true! We impoverish them, give them impossible conditions they can't meet then hold them hostage...then blame them of incompetence and backwardness."

"Wait, wait, what coup are you talking about? Don't listen to hearsay. You aren't that naïve, are you?"

"Don't play dumb with me, Isaac. You know everything! You planned everything!"

"Look, whoever these ...the...The Pipers are, they're lying. They kidnapped Vincent's son to blackmail people. I know some of my associates did some illegal operations but they were necessary."

"What makes you so sure Vincent's son was kidnapped by The Pipers? Why couldn't it be that he staged it to divert public attention... to play victim."

"Do you even hear what you're saying, Chris?"

"Tell me about *stripping*."

"We saw an opportunity in the oil industry in Sudan. We tried to exploit it through the Chinese and the Malaysians. Business is about taking risks."

"Do you know what the money you send does?"

"Well, tell me."

Chris walked back to the seat and sat down as Isaac slowly walked to the window.

"I'll tell you. The money is used to destroy the livelihoods of hundreds of thousands of civilians in South Sudan. People are displaced without compensation. The place is cleared of trees so that Southern rebel attack is repulsed from a distance."

"How do you know all these?"

Chris angrily dashed to the drawer, pulled out a pamphlet and threw it at Isaac.

"I'm naïve, am I not? Read that and you'll tell me if you have any conscience at all."

Isaac walked back and sat down.

"Did you call me to come and tell me that I'm an unscrupulous, immoral son of a bitch?"

"That pamphlet makes you appear like one, or even worse than that, but no, I didn't call you here to tell you that."

"Then what?"

"That was my personal input."

Isaac angrily grabbed the pamphlet from the floor and walked to the window.

"There's a lecture today in the University of Hayiroh. We have to attend that," Chris said.

"Who's lecturing?"

"I don't know and I don't care."

"Then why do you want us to go."

"I want to know what he says and not who he is."

76

"This has everything to do with you, my son. I'm sorry it's not going to be easy."

Jeng shot up.

"What's not going to be easy?"

"When I disagreed with my father, I was financially desperate but I wanted to be independent. I had a boyfriend who was a PhD student at Oxford. We dated for quite some times. He was from South Sudan, however, he was a student and penniless. I loved him nonetheless. When I met Vincent, he was a gift from the gods. I'd asked him a question during one of the meetings with Sivalsians in London and he kind of felt uneasy. He later sent someone for me after the meeting and we had dinner that night. He lectured to me about Sivals and how it was relatively better compared to other African countries. He talked of the cohesiveness and maturity of tribal connections in Sivals unlike countries such as Sudan, Kenya or Nigeria. He sounded intellectual and moral in his political take. Anytime he came to London, he'd call me up and we met. Soon the relationship turned romantic, one thing led to another. When I realized what was happening…"

"You found out you were pregnant. I still don't understand mum!"

"I was still seeing my boyfriend."

"Oh crap!"

"Yeah! My…"

"What was your boyfriend's name?"

"I can't tell you now."

"You what?"

"Let me finish the story!" Aatieŋ'oh said raising her voice.

Vexed and impatient, Jeng suddenly sat down.

"Story? People's lives are about to be destroyed and you call this a story?"

"I see. So you assume you're the only one being hurt. I lived over thirty years of lie. I had to make some painful decisions just to feel okay. Do you think I'm enjoying this? I've thought this over for years but I couldn't get any better solution for it."

Jeng looked down, furious.

"I didn't tell Vincent I had a boyfriend but I'd told my boyfriend that Vincent could help us now and in the future. Vincent was so close to the president that some Western journalists had called him Sivals's vice president. He had money and we needed it. I was young and stupid. When I realized I was pregnant and Vincent was nice to me, I made the worst decision any young person can ever make. I told my boyfriend the child was Vincent's. He left me without even saying anything to me. Vincent advised me to remain in school. I finished my BA and he told me to go back for my masters then D.Phil. There was nothing like Vincent then: he represented to me the father I didn't have. You enjoyed and still enjoy what I never had. I kept you like a glass. I met my ex-boyfriend during my Doctoral graduation ceremony. He was working as a financial consultant in a bank. He didn't get any job as a lecturer until a few years later after he moved to the US. Vincent had to leave that night for Hayiroh. I was to spend a week in London then join Vincent in Sivals. I loved my boyfriend and he loved me. He was the one who left me."

"God mum...no!"

"Ten years after we settled in Hayiroh, I got rumors that Vincent was involved in the tribal clashes that killed my parents. Knowing the remarkable person Vincent was I'd no reason to believe such claims."

"No, mum, that's not true!" Jeng said fighting tears.

"That's true."

"It was Vincent Jacob Miochariya."

Jeng tried to get up but his feet were glued to the ground by sadness. He tried to talk but his mouth was glued shut by the scope of consternation.

"Tell me my son. What was I supposed to do?"

77

Little was having the time of his life. As the plane flew over the forests, the mountains and the plains of South Sudan, Little saw a white thread meandering north-south.

"Is that what I think it is?"

"Yes, that's the great Nile. Envied for complete control by everyone; most notorious of all is Egypt. Egyptians signed a pact in 1910 with the British. That agreement gave them more than fifty percent of the Nile waters. Most part of the Nile lies within the Sudan. Countries such as Uganda, Tanzania, Sivals and Ethiopia whose lakes contribute and so are the sources of the Nile waters, aren't allowed to use the waters. Egypt threatens anyone else using the Nile waters for developmental projects whatsoever, except Sudan in dismal terms."

"That's absurd!"

"That's the absurdity killing us in Sudan. Things that just don't make any sense are blindly pushed ahead. Egypt was the only country that was independent when the pact was signed and is the only one bound by that agreement. It just doesn't make any sense to let countries that need the Nile waters for their developmental goals to be bound by what they weren't party to."

Little enjoyed the Nile as it raced toward Egypt. He felt dreamy but jovial. In his elementary school history lessons, Little read stories of the Nile, the African safaris and thought they were fairy tales. They weren't. They were as real as reality itself and death.

The plane started to descent and Little started to see the realities of the Dark Continent. There were several black dots beneath them.

As the plane descended farther, Little realized the small black dots were burnt huts. The plane hovered over the villages and he could see several large, white tents and people clamoring for what he couldn't make out.

"What're those huge tents for?"

"This is where World Food program (WFP) stores relief food before it distributes it."

"And what're those people doing on the ground?" Little said with a frown.

"They are picking up the spilled maize."

"Spilled maize?"

"Oh, you call it corn in Panda and US."

"Why'd they do that?"

"What WFP brings is not enough."

"That isn't healthy."

"Health is a luxury here, Mr. Michael. People barely have anything to eat; their houses are destroyed by government forces assisted by the Chinese and other western business people and governments."

Little's lips curled up as usual. "What?"

The plane touched down as one Toyota Land Cruiser and two pick-up Toyotas drove to the airstrip. One of the Toyotas was mounted with artillery. The cars were painted green to blend in with the forest. Little, the commander and two other soldiers entered the Land Cruiser. Other soldiers precariously climbed onto the pick-up trucks. Their legs dangled dangerously, almost touching the ground.

"This is a very dangerous place," the commander warned.

Little frowned, twisted his neck and looked at the commander. "Dangerous?"

"We have various militia groups allied with the government here."

"You mean Arab militia?" Little said with a frown.

"No, Southerners."

"What for?"

"You have seen the way those people were picking up maize grains on that dirty ground."

"You mean the militia allies with the government not because they want to but because they want to survive? But how do they benefit?"

"We are freedom fighters: we don't get paid."

"I see the point," Little lips curled up with a nod in agreement.

The roads were really dusty and rough. However, Little was so enthusiastic that he felt no fear, no effect of the impassable roads. Along the road Little could see carcasses and bodies of dead people lying on the ground, not buried."

"Why aren't those people buried?"

"You'll know soon."

They drove on. A few kilometers drive away they came across a pile of rubble. There were several dead bodies lying beside the rubble.

"What happened here?"

The convoy stopped. Commander Garang got down as Little followed him with his camera. The commander walked toward one of the rubbles, looked up then at Little and said: "The tribe that lives here is called Nuer. This is the oil rich region. A few months ago, this was a nice village full of cows, goats and planted vegetables. Now see what became of this village and think about the people you saw picking up the grains of maize."

"You mean to tell me these...?"

"This was their village. I will show you a picture I took with one of the local girls a few months ago. My youngest wife is from here. I'm not actually from here. I'm from Jiëëŋ (Dinka tribe). They call us Dinka Bhar El Gazhal. It is an Arabic term meaning the Gazelle River."

The commander dejectedly walked to the car as Little followed. They drove from one bulldozed village to another. The sites of rubble mixed with human bodies were debilitating and disheartening. In one village they found four people burnt, charred inside one hut. It was horrible. It became too much for Little that he had to puke.

78

Outside the hall, Chris and Isaac could see people standing by all entrances.

"I don't think we'll get a spot," Isaac remarked.

"We have a spot. That's what I've been told."

"You reserved our seats?"

"I didn't?"

"Then how do you expect us to get seats."

"I thought by now nothing should be a surprise to you. *The Pipers* are ghosts, real ghosts."

Isaac looked at Chris curiously then said: "I think I know who's lecturing in there."

Chris looked accusingly at Isaac and stopped walking.

"You know him? You sure do know a lot of things."

"I said *I think* I know. I didn't say I know him. One of my advisors on African issues is a Sivalsian lawyer and diplomat. He said things I didn't say and acted really comfortably with them. I told P.D about Osmani's actions but he played them down. I've been calling him but he's not been answering my calls until yesterday. He called me and told me he's been tied up. I just didn't have something to say. P.D argued that it could be The Pipers setting him up. He's a well-respected lecturer and public speaker. I don't know why he still works at a consulate in Heritage."

Chris and Isaac entered the lecture hall. It was even worse inside. The lecture hall was full to the brim. It was asphyxiating. From the front row to the last seat at the back, all were occupied. The two gentlemen stood at the back, confused. Isaac looked at Chris and said: "So where're our seats?"

"In the front row," a young man next to them bewilderingly said with an indifferent edge.

They stared curiously at the young man. He didn't look like an usher, and didn't appear interested in them either. A big tribal scare on his left cheek frowned at them. Hesitant and confused, they braved their way to the front as that mass of blackness rained snowy orbs on them. Chris could feel rays of admonishing, judging photons drilling holes on his body. Two white people making their way to the front in a hall packed with black people wasn't comfortable at all.

Whoever arranged that knew the stakes and the embarrassing consequences. It was a set-up: history remade to embarrass them. They felt thousands of eyes boring through their souls: judging, lamenting, cursing etc.

This is not good...not good at all.

It wasn't right. Even in the most innocent of terms, it isn't right, Chris thought. They couldn't afford even the most clandestine of glances. Everyone was staring at them, silent, and perhaps, judging. Isaac was emotionally paralyzed. *Osmani is now coming to finish me.*

They made their way to their seats: 3D and 4D. Isaac was internally fretting about everything around. Chris was just curious.

"I don't think this is such a good idea," Isaac whispered.

"I hope you're not telling me that because I don't know why we're here," Chris said.

As the two gentlemen made themselves comfortable, someone walked to the podium.

"That's not Osmani!" Isaac said.

"Someone introducing him, I think!"

"Thank you ladies and gentlemen. Today's lecture is from one of the most accomplished scholars Africa has ever produced. Some of us have read his books and papers. A few among us have had the privilege of hearing him speak. We've waited for a long time and if I start chronicling the content of his resume, we will have to stay here for the next three days."

There was laughter and applause.

"Ladies and gentlemen, it's my pleasure to introduce to you Dr. Michael Pelebaidien Dhuengdakah."

"What...this is some sh...sh...?"

Isaac almost jumped to his feet.

"So P.D wasn't kidnapped?" Chris asked with a sarcastic smile.

"I don't understand. Is...?"

"Maybe they kidnapped him and conditioned him to give this lecture."

"Well, we'll see from his mood."

"He's perhaps been coached during kidnaping."

"I have to call Vincent. The whole thing might be a sick joke."

"That'd be a bad idea!"

"Excuse me?"

"You're excused, but that'd be a bad idea."

Isaac frowned. "Who the hell are you?"

"How many surprises have you had Isaac to still ask that question?" the man was speaking without even looking at Isaac.

Confused, Isaac looked at Chris but Chris only winked absentmindedly.

79

"I'm sorry son!"

"I've always been happy in my life. I had everything. I had it all. I guess no one can get away with ultimate happiness in life. One has to get a small pinch of life's bitterness."

"Vincent and Christine have become some ruthless people. Southern rebel in Sudan are our brothers and sisters, but Vincent decided to collaborate with the north. The president trusted him and he chose to give secret intelligence to the Sudanese government in Khartoum. That cost the lives of civilians and dashed any hope of success for the African cause in Sudan. He intimidates tribal leaders in South Sudan so as to turn against their own sons and daughters. They then collaborate with the government. He gets funds from the government of Khartoum to lure rebel commanders into defecting. I couldn't take it anymore."

"What happens now?"

"There's someone I'd want you to meet."

80

"I'm sorry about that commander. I'm just not used to this," Little said after having vomited.

"I understand."

"We..."

The commander couldn't finish the statement. There was a huge explosion in front. The land cruiser stopped as the vehicle ahead was engulfed in a ball fire. Little was about to run as bullets rained down on them. He was scared out of his brain. *Real life!* Luckily, the commander caught his arm and said: "Stay with me."

The soldiers in the other vehicle behind started shooting. Little and the commander got down and took cover on one side of the car. The commander kept on shooting in intervals. The shooting continued continuously then sporadically.

One of the soldiers came running toward Little and the commander and said in Thoŋ ë Jiëëŋ.

"Let's go!"

The commander swiftly got up. As they were about to get into the car, a bullet tore through commander's right shoulder and they bowed down. It was getting too *real* for Little; extremely and deadly close.

I was wondering why a Blackman's journey could be this smooth!

"The commander is hit..." the soldier shouted.

"Don't say that, it'll weaken their morale," Little bravely said, invoking his movie and video game militancy. Completely engaged and fearless, Little ran to the commander, removed his own shirt and placed it on the gun-wound. Little was now sweating profusely. The shooting then died down as Little hurled the commander onto the passenger seat.

"You'll be fine commander," he said.

Little told one of the soldiers to hold the shirt onto the wound to keep the pressure on. He was driving fast toward the displaced camp. His fear had disappeared, his resolves magnificent. The other car was behind them, but hardly keeping pace with Little.

"Please stay with us!" Little kept saying as he drove through those rough, impassible roads. The bumps, the turns and twists didn't concern him. He was a *son*.

Stay with us, please stay with us.

The soldiers had already radioed the clinic. As they arrived at the camp, a local ambulance rushed to them. One of the doctors, a white lady, ran to the car. She entered the car as Little stopped the car.

"How's he doing? My name is Dr. Anne Cunningham."

"Really bad! He's lost a lot of blood," Little said.

"Let me have a look."

Dr. Cunningham looked at the bullet wound and nodded at Little.

"Drive us to the airstrip. We just don't have the facility to help him here. We'll fly him to Yei hospital for an operation."

Little drove wildly to the airstrip.

"Do you think he'll make it?"

"I think so."

"You think so doc?"

"He'll be fine, god! What brings you here anyways? America, Panda and the west had had enough to make these people miserable. You Americans just don't get it."

"First of all I'm not an American. And aren't you part of the west. What're you, Swiss or French?"

"I'm a British-Norwegian and when I say the west you know what I mean."

His lips curled up. "I don't. We're all part of the west."

"Yeah Mama! What're you here for; trying to befriend the commander so that you get a chance in oil money if they succeed in defeating the government? Let me tell you one thing Mister. They'll never win. And you know why? The west is in business. You can't destroy a business interest of someone you know will be your business partner tomorrow. What do you think the Pandian government does if it knows Russians are arming the Sudanese government and the same Russians have agreed to lessen restrictions and conditions on imports and exports to Panda? Do you think they'd condemn the Russians? If the French saw the South winning, supported by Panda, the US and possibly Israel, they'd think they'd miss out...and you know what they'd do?"

Dr. Cunningham was talking angrily while she kept on checking commander's blood pressure and the liquid dripping into his arm.

"They'd support the Sudanese government."

There was complete silence as they arrived at the airstrip.

Dr. Cunningham was making several calls. The plane was ready and they quickly boarded. Little lifted the stretcher onto the plane by himself. It wasn't so much a stretcher. It was a piece of blanket sewn to two long, wooden logs.

Dr. Cunningham was really furious, seemingly at the west and Little.

The commander was placed onto the stretcher as Dr. Cunningham checked his condition.

"What do you want here? If you hadn't come he'd perhaps be okay. I bet he was shot protecting you. He's a commander you know. He looks wretched and ruthless but he's protecting his people, his own."

"My name is Little Michael. You might not wanna know or you might not believe this, but you make me happy and you make me proud of being an African-Pandian."

Dr. Cunningham frowned, looked at Little and smiled sardonically.

"So I'm supposed to believe that all of a sudden you've become enamored by Pan-African spirit. How gentlemanly of you? Do I look stupid to you?"

"When I was young I was a child delinquent. My mum was a very strong lady and she wanted me to be in school. However, the realities of the outside life didn't match what the teachers taught us. I sold drugs and abused drugs until I was arrested. I was careful and smart. I wasn't caught selling drugs. But one day the police were chasing a boy through our neighborhood. The boy passed us and disappeared into our neighborhood. When the police arrived, they thought I was that boy. They thought I was just playing smart to be assumed I wasn't the one. I had drugs in my bag. You can guess the rest."

"What's your point? That you're a victim of social injustice?"

Little ignored her.

"I met many guys in jail. Some were stupid, others were smart and promising. They told me that the shortest way is not always the safest."

"Good lesson."

"When I came out of the hospital, I decided to be on the best side of the law."

"Hospital or jail?"

"I'm sorry...jail."

"You learned a lesson...good boy!"

"Would you stop being stubborn and be humble for once?" Little said getting frustrated.

"Ok, ok...now you're starting to understand the Pan-Africanists."

Little was getting upset. He knew she was being unreasonable but real and truthfully angry.

They were now crossing the Nile. The span of the savannah cried beckoningly below them.

"Mum told me she got me some loan from the bank. I thought she had trust in me. I started a bar and a mini-restaurant. The bar became an overnight success. I was happy and proud."

"You then decided to invest in oil in an impoverished African country were you could easily blend in and fake an accent whenever you could."

Little's lips curled up angrily. "What's your problem?"

"My problem is you coming here to fuel the war and fake annoying empathy. Now you want me to feel sorry for you. I don't feel shit for you and I wished you were the one shot. I'm sick of callous opportunists like you. I see them everyday."

"I'll ignore that. But listen to me because you aren't listening to me. How many Pandians like me come to South Sudan to exploit the innocent?"

"Thousands if I might tell you. Some are arm dealers, some use Africa as a middle ground for drug trafficking, some try to show that they're better than the wretched Africans. I was born in a family of seven (six girls and one boy) in east London to a British mother and a Norwegian father. I grew up poor. When I went to university, I met many rich African, African-Pandian and Caribbean students, who bragged about their wealth. They gave little interest to the death, wretchedness and poverty in Africa and their countries. They disgusted me...and so do you!"

Little was getting frustrated but he knew Dr. Cunningham had a point although directed at the wrong party.

81

D r. P.D Michael majestically made his way to the podium. His gait was slow but firm; smile not wide enough but reassuring. The crowd rapturously welcomed him with affirming standing ovation. With a humble smile, he scanned the audience then cleared his throat.

"I'm sorry I'll not be able to pay for your lunch if you missed it for this lecture," he said and laughed. The whole arena ruptured into applause.

Isaac, boiling in fear, perplexity and anxiety, didn't know what to do. With P.D confidently and mockingly on the podium, Isaac was starting to lose his breath.

Chris was having the time of his life, becoming a windsock if you like. Surprises were numerous so he decided not to waste time getting worked up in expectations.

"But I can guarantee you one thing though."

"What's that...a date with your daughter?"

Someone yelled in front as P.D smiled girlishly.

"I can guarantee one thing though...and that's, by the time you leave here, you'll not even think of food to eat because whatever you'd eat would stink."

There was dead silence. Then the hall burst into laughter causing Isaac to jump in fright.

"I've always wanted to give this lecture but my friends always said: 'It ain't safe there'. I waited for so long and I realized it wasn't ever going to be safe. But I told myself one thing. Are there people living in that unsafe environment? Do they have bullet-proof pants, shirts and dresses? Well, I can get me one."

There was thunderous applause, so loud that Isaac covered his ears. *They played me. They played me.*

"For those who came out of curiosity, the topic today is*: The Fundamentals and Realities of African economies: the inside and the outside effects.* For the rest, I apologize for boring you."

"The late, great Mwalimu Julius Nyerere realized in 1980s that structural adjustment program was meant to supposedly change the Tanzanian economy for the better regardless of what it would do to the average poor Tanzanian. The answer to the question: 'Do we have to starve our children to pay our debts?' is *Yes*, sadly! And Mwalimu was shocked to learn that fact.

"But let's talk about what most of us are familiar with: Corruption. One of the easiest ways to get rich in Africa is to have an influential position in the government, or being associated with any influential politician. Being a businessman with independence or independent-mindedness is a risk. You can only succeed as a businessman if you have political muscles holding you up."

He took a sip of the bottled water and continued.

"We get donor money for development. It all then goes into the pockets of the powerful few. The leadership or even the president knows that and he knows exactly who is benefiting. But his political life is in the hands of those embezzlers. Who among us is naïve enough to think that he can stand up and cut away the very two feet he's standing on?

"The corrupt politicians are forced either by personal desires to be rich or by the need to have financial strength to stand against threats to one's survival in African political scenes. The weak-hearted presidents give in to those bullies and the pandemic contagion invades. But a few who stand up to these few bullies get isolated. The fabric lies with a few Western partners. The president is either conditioned to shut up or lose the support of tribes the bullies come from, or he is overthrown. To this point, he has to comply or *the jig is up.*"

P.D paused as the hall remained as silent as a church's graveyard. Then it burst into raucous laughter.

Isaac felt like he was going to faint. He looked at the man who'd warned him against making any call. There were two vacant seats to the left of the man. Isaac hadn't noticed the seats when they arrived. *Someone else was missing. Osmani! They fuck'd me up!*

The man who introduced P.D came up to the podium and whispered something into P.D's ear. P.D cleared his throat and smiled with a superior smug of a scholar.

"I'm told the government's agents are here. They want the lecture stopped immediately. I bet they think we're designing a revolution here."

"No! No! No!"

Part of the audience shouted angrily and another part laughed.

"I'll tell you a story because we'll not be able to finish the lecture. There was a nation..."

The hind door suddenly opened and the hall became dead silent.

Two people walked in through the hind door. They were a middle-age woman and a young man in his mid-twenties. The hall remained silent as the two strangers walked silently through the aisle.

P.D recognized them, smiled girlishly and said: "I guess our late-comers decided to take their lunch after all."

The hall burst into laughter.

The young man with the woman looked around uncomfortably while the woman just walked on comfortably.

"What they didn't know was that the speech would be short; shortened by the fearful hand of the government."

There was further laughter.

The man and the woman walked bravely to the front and sat down.

"Now, I'll not name that country."

Someone again walked to the podium. There was increased movement outside.

"A multinational corporation approached the president of that country. They wanted to invest in banking and also channel some money into mining exploration. The president was excited about the generosity of the company as the owners first proposed investing in the community. They proposed building two clinics as a pilot project. They wanted to build them in the president's home village. The president was noble enough and saw that as irresponsible. They changed the plan. They decided to build one in the president's home village and one in the neighboring village. That was done. The president saw them as exceptional in every sense. They also proposed to build two schools in the president's home town and another in the capital city. They promised to fund the schools for five years before handing them to the government or any interested private party. The president was in the cloud. He told the nation that similar projects will be supported by the government in other parts of the country."

The movement outside increased. There were sounds of boots and cars honking outside.

P.D continued as the audience was intrigued, silent and attentive.

This time, Isaac was growing past his fears. He was wary though; fearing his name being mentioned anytime.

"The project started in earnest as the president's status and popularity grew from the grassroots to the highest level of the government. The company then started the exploration. First, they started by bringing in what they called the *minds of the operations*. The president was offended but he saw some sense in what they were doing. The project continued. When the brain of the workforce making the exploration was comprised of 60% foreigners, who were paid six times the pay of the local workers, the president became discontent. He summoned the company's Chief Operation Officer (COO). The COO good-naturedly promised to look into the situation.

"For the president, the deluxe attitude of the caring explorers remained intact as the amicable atmosphere remained."

82

The plane hovered around Yei as it prepared to land. With the magical hands of Dr. Cunningham, the commander was getting stable. Dr. Cunningham did a superb job with meager to nonexistent medical resources.

Little looked at her and said. "I told you I thought my business success was a result of my genius."

Dr. Cunningham suddenly turned and looked curiously at Little.

"Ever heard of *P Siblings* or *The Pipers*?"

"Not until yesterday."

"The callousness of people like you almost forced me to be part of them. I was put off by their violent methods, however. You can't end violence with violence. I also didn't know how to get to them. They're very secretive."

"I learnt yesterday that they were the ones who gave mum the money."

"Don't tell me you're part of them else I'd kiss you now."

"God, I couldn't have kissed you!" Little said sarcastically.

Dr. Cunningham felt embarrassed.

"I'm sorry."

"It's okay. I know why you said all those nasty things to me."

"I'm just pissed off...at the west and the Arab world."

"One of them was a friend of mine in prison. He used to mock me and when I got out, he started writing to me very philosophical questions. He was the one who staged my business. I guess he'd seen some potential in me. I don't know what potential I had. When my store was burnt down, I thought I'd loss everything."

"They burnt it down?"

"Yeah!"

"What for?"

"To divert secret service eyes."

"Smart, aren't they? But why did you come here?"

"You can't let it go, can you?"

Dr. Cunningham smiled.

"They gave me instructions to come to Africa. I didn't know where I was to sleep and who I was to meet and what I was to do. They planned everything and I've never been very proud of being black."

There was silence.

"I'm sorry. I didn't mean..."

"Hey, I'm black in everything except this covering."

"I still don't know why I...well, they chose to give me the bar to be a sanctuary for their people, but I don't know why I was sent here."

"How do you feel now?"

"Great, well, not after the commander was shot. Actually, I feel mixed. There's a sense of exhilaration about how I've been treated by *The Pipers*. But I feel really saddened by what I saw today: callousness, poverty, destitution...abject misery...it's bad!"

"He'll be fine. So there you have your answer, I guess!"

"I thought you're supposed to be a doctor and not..."

"I took philosophy and psychology classes at the University. I still read Emanuel Kant now."

"I love that dude. His Ethics is remarkable though impractical."

The plane touched down and the ambulance was already in the airstrip. Commander Garang was rushed to the ambulance as Dr. Cunningham jumped in.

A gentleman walked toward Dr. Cunningham and handed her an envelope.

Dear Dr. Anne Cunningham,

*Open it with love and present it with dignity to Mr. Little
Michael, the unofficial sibling.*

Dr. Cunningham smiled, jumped down from the ambulance and
walked majestically toward Little.

Little was getting into another vehicle to follow the commander.

"Take this and go back aboard that plane. It'll take you to Arua
in Uganda, where you'll fly to Kampala then Hayiroh."

"No, I have to see that Commander Garang is okay first."

"I'm sorry I misjudged you. Look, your job isn't finished. The
commander will be okay, don't worry."

With extreme excitement swallowing him, Little smiled flirta-
tiously at Dr. Cunningham and joked: "Can I get my kiss now?"

She smiled, walked off, looked back and said: "Don't push your
luck, Mr. Michael."

Little slowly admired the envelope Dr. Cunningham had given
him, kissed it without opening it then got out of the car. He walked
back to the plane like someone being pulled back by something he
can't part with. Dr. Anne Cunningham turned and saw Commander
Garang waving at Little.

"Spread the message," Dr. Cunningham said to Little as she ran
back to the ambulance.

"I will," Little said fighting tears.

*What a difference a day can make in a person's life? Why do I
have to leave? This is home! These're the people I should be with.*

83

Werpionkor was bustling with Uncle D's friends. They'd invited the villagers to what they called a tradition. They also wanted the villagers to show them what their tradition was like. The young and the old danced the night away as excitement coiled heavenwards. Teenage boys and girls danced in the inner most circle. Women and girls danced in the middle circle and men in the outer circle.

Traditionally, elderly women sat on the northern side and elderly men on the southern side. With Uncle D's influence, both the northern and the southern sides became mixed gender-wise.

Men wore only shorts; their faces and bodies decorated in white and red chalk mixed with oil extracted from a wild plant. Married women covered their breasts with strips of clothing; their lower trunks graced by mini-skirt looking traditional clothing. Girls wore only traditional clothing tied as knots on the left or right shoulders. Some girls danced with their breasts fully exposed.

Uncle D's friends enjoyed the night with a company of beautiful girls of the village.

84

Honorable Vincent Jacob Miochariya couldn't believe his eyes and ears. With P.D at the podium giving a childish and mocking lecture, Vincent felt restless.

President Johnson Eekedu was seated with his entire cabinet and all security officials in People House.

"We have to storm the hall and take them your Excellency," honorable Miochariya said.

"We have been over this for days, Honorable Miochariya. The intelligence we have so far is that they are working with the army. I'm not sure the lecture has anything to do with the so called *The Pipers*. Well, I sent Ezekiel abroad and put John Tielroorich as the acting army chief to give us time to act if some elements in the army are involved," the president said and sat back.

"Sir, Mr. Michael was supposed to be in Jamaica as we were told by the Jamaican government. What is he doing lecturing in Hayiroh? These people have my wife and son."

The president curiously and intensely stared at the screen. The lecture was live on TV. The camera moved through the audience and the president slowly sat up; still staring fixedly at the screen.

"I think I saw something!" the president said.

"I think I saw something too," another minister added.

"What something, sir?" honorable Miochariya asked.

Rattled by the president's comments, Vincent swiftly looked at the screen but the focus soon shifted back to P.D. The president looked at Vincent then at the screen again.

"Please sir, let's just take them!"

"Honorable Miochariya, the hall is besieged. They can't go any-where."

85

"**A** week after the president approached the COO; two ministers approached the president and informed him that those employed by the company are being intimidated by the police and the ruling party supporters. As the president was about to act, an article appeared in The Mail and Guardian, reprinted in New York times, Washington Post, Globe and Mail and the Day-Town Governor. The article alleged that development activities are being impeded by the ruling party so that the money the multi-national corporation wanted to generously use to benefit the people can go into the pockets of few.

"Encouraged by the letter and the western leaders' responses to it, the opposition rallied against the president. The government tried to give speeches to pacify the wronged and correct the misunderstanding but they weren't effective. The construction of the clinics and the schools was stopped amidst claim of insecurity from ruling party supporters. The government became unpopular and the opposition had an upper hand. The embattled president dissolved the parliament and called early elections. He lost. The new government didn't make it its priority for construction to resume; claiming the projects were only built in the former President's home village and town: an emblem of tribalism and corruption, they'd argued."

P.D walked away from the podium, off the stage and down to the front row.

Aatieŋ'oh got up, scanned the audience slowly and walked majestically up the stage and to the podium.

"I don't have to introduce myself. I was supposed to be the one introducing P.D, but hey, things happen."

Everyone stared speechless.

"Oh, the media...yeah, I wasn't kidnapped. My son was but he's here. And by the way, we didn't take lunch."

There was gasping, sighing and giggling.

"I have my own story. Because we have some hardworking fellows outside, I'll give you an economically superficial but eye-opening scenario. Ethiopia produces coffee. Sivals produces coffee. They can build their factories, process the beans and then export the processed products. They don't largely. African countries can build factories to process agricultural produce or build factories to manufacture cars and other machinery, they don't. Why? Is it corruption? Is it political instability? Or is it lack of technological know-how? I'll tell you."

§

As Aatieŋ'oh stood at the Podium, Chris squinted and slowly sat up.

"What? Did you just see a ghost?" Isaac said looking at Chris.

"I think I've seen this woman somewhere."

"Somewhere? You saw her picture in the news...that's the *somewhere* from where you saw here. Don't tell me you dreamed about her. I've seen people who rationalize their dreams after they've seen an incident that resembles their dreams."

Chris stared blankly at Isaac and looked at Aatieŋ'oh. The exhilaration he felt flexed his memory back in time; so swift that Chris was almost jolted off his seat. The impression of the lady shone in Chris's intuition so vividly like it was yesterday. Years had gone by but the lady's form was imprinted indelibly on his mind. Her African dress; her African gait, her classy look, all remained the same in spite of her age. It was no surprise her words calmed Chris down, her figure enamored him, and her charisma unmistakably exuberant. It was Oxford with no mistake; an African lady with flamboyant grace.

Chris's sweet memories were now answered, the lingering question, rested. The ghost of Liverpool mission was laid to rest.

86

The ministers stared confused and speechless. Vincent had his mouth for eyes.

On screen, Jeng, Isaac and Aatieŋ'oh kept appearing.

Aatieŋ'oh kept rumbling on.

"I'll tell you the answers," she said again after a pause and continued. "What can you do with a processed coffee if you get charged about 40 – 50 percent import duty but beans are taxed 15-35 percent? The choice is clear here. You can't build a processing plant that'd cost you money instead of making you money. We know such plants could employ hundreds of people. But no, the factories are built by the buyers of our coffees so that they build their factories, their people get jobs then they sell us the processed beans. If they don't have people working in their factories, they help our people immigrate to go and work in those plants where they pay taxes. They invite 'skilled immigrants'; professionals in their own countries, who become manual laborers in the coffee-buyers' factories. If you're adamant enough and build factories, you'll have to tell me where you'd export it to. Do you think it'd be made easy for you?

"Do you think someone who knows you would, in the future, compete with her can give you reasons to defeat her? No, absolutely not!"

She paused for a while.

The People House was as quiet as Golgotha.

She soldiered on.

"Now, do I think our leaders are blameless? No! Then what the hell am I talking about? This is what I'm talking about. Those who make it hard for others to prosper shouldn't point culpable fingers. I know, however, that some of our politicians engineer dirty tactics and you know who suffers: the hard-working men and women of this nation! But that's a fraction of what makes us destitute. We are perceived in a given light, and that given light is reinforced by our leaders."

"Sir, *The Pipers* are smart. Don't be shocked if they announce on TV you've been over-thrown. That Isaac you see on TV is behind all the drama. He's my friend and I know him. I know what he's capable of doing."

"I think honorable Miochariya has a point Your Excellency," another minister concurred.

The president looked at his cabinet.

"Call the security to take them..."

"They have security outside," Aatieŋ'oh was not letting go. "They want to arrest us claiming P.D, Mr. Isaac Burns and I here are plotting to over-throw the government."

"What?" the president jumped to his feet.

"See, Your Excellency?" Vincent exclaimed smugly.

"Is your wife part of this?"

"No sir. They are using her. They want you to think she is part of them, can't you see how angry she is."

"They're now meeting in People House as we speak."

"I can't believe this. How do they know these?" the president fumed.

"We don't know Your Excellency!" the terrified security chief said.

"What's happening? Why is she still talking? Where is the secu...?"

Vincent couldn't finish the statement. On screen, two uninformed men approached the podium where Aatieŋ'oh was standing as two others approached the front row. The screen suddenly turned green then grainy white.

The president and his men held their breaths.

"We'll have to go live and straighten everything out. These *P* nonsense think they can hold all of us hostage," the president said; standing, furious and determined.

"Look Your Excellency!" Vincent said; his mouth wide open.

They all looked at the screen and Aatieŋ'oh was standing majestically.

"Wha-at?"

"Can you doubt again that the army is behind them?"

The president grabbed the telephone and yelled.

"Why are my orders being defied? I want them dead or alive!"

President Eekedu was furious and restless. He was pacing from place to place as his cabinet members stared, speechless and clueless.

"I'll now leave the floor for questions. The army and the security men have given us about fifteen minutes before they take us."

P.D walked up to the Podium. There were several hands raised.

"Yes, the lady in the brown dress in the third row," Aatieŋ'oh said.

"Dr. Michael, don't you think that blaming the west is naïve. If we make sure that whatever is African's contribution to the problem is got rid of first, then we can rightfully blame the West."

"I feel you. It'd be hypocritical to do otherwise. Was that what I just did? No! The *scale* of corruption in Africa is a result of scarcity of resources not the willfulness of Africans to be corrupt. African contribution now is a small percentage of what's keeping Africa behind. The corrupt African leaders are supported by the west. What if the superior intelligence in the west identifies those corrupt leaders and isolates them, refusing them entry into their countries and making sure their investments are denied expansion or frozen, then Africa can prosper. Yes, corruption is bad, yes; our leaders shouldn't think I'm praising them. But we have to get to the root causes of the problem. The only people the west scales away from their borders are those who stand up to the west on principle. Those who are known to be corrupt but are seen as no political threat to the west are allowed free reign and an opportunity to save the looted money from Africa. How many corrupt dictators have Panda, USA, Canada, UK and other western countries supported? Wasn't Mussolini admired one time in the west? Wasn't Panama's Noriega first an America's favorite? Why's Museveni's brutality tolerated by Panda and USA? And why was it the threat from Wall Street that forced Canada's Talisman out of Sudan? Kid, read!"

"Mine is a follow-up to that question. Starting by blaming someone else sounds escapist and childish. Why can't you start blaming yourself? You're in New York teaching and only writing papers."

P.D smiled broadly and looked at Aatieŋ'oh.

"I've blamed myself more than enough. Let me ask you one thing: how many leaders have stood up to the west and survived either physically or politically? None...unless the west fears them."

"First, get the media out of there and fish them out!" the president yelled again to the officer in charge of the arresting squad.

The security forces and the army men grabbed P.D and Isaac. One soldier looked at Aatieŋ'oh.

"You'll follow us."

"You're not arresting me?"

"We know they coerced you into this."

Aatieŋ'oh smiled at her son, shook her head and said: "Let's follow them."

As they got out of the building, a huge explosion rocked the place. Everyone inside scrambled for a space to get out, causing monstrous stampeding.

Inside People House, the screen went black.

We will know who the president is!

P.D and Isaac walked toward an armored truck in handcuffs. Three soldiers were standing by the truck and three were behind them. Aatieŋ'oh and Jeng were a little behind. P.D looked toward his right. A soldier was crawling beneath another truck parked behind the truck they were walking toward. P.D stopped.

"Let's move!" a soldier behind him yelled.

P.D smiled, looked at Aatieŋ'oh and shook his head. In a blink of an eye, P.D grabbed Isaac's and Chris's hands as Aatieŋ'oh grabbed Jeng's hand. They simultaneously threw themselves onto the ground as a plain-clothed, huge black man threw gas masks at them. Bullets rained on the soldiers. Within a few seconds all the six soldiers lay down wounded as tear gas filled the air. Then two army vehicles burst into flames.

The audience was running helter-skelter. After about a minute, two other civilian-clothed men ran toward the truck. A truck sandwiched between the blown-up trucks was intact.

"Let's go," P.D said as Aatieŋ'oh got up. Jeng, Chris and Isaac ran toward the truck, all with their masks on.

87

President Eekedu held his breath.

I have to exert a lot of pressure, I have to be strong, and I have to be the president.

He looked at Vincent, at another minister and at the security chief and said with a raised voice. "I need an update; I need an update, now!"

Everyone stared, helpless and anxious. The head of security, the acting chief of staff, the police commissioner and the defense minister, all looked lost and nervous.

"You did the right thing, Your Excellency," Vincent said.

President Eekedu looked at the head of security with vivid sauciness.

"We need an update. We need to know what happened for us to address the Sivalsian people."

As the head of security prepared himself to confirm the arrest, a call came in. Shock and fear was written on everyone's face.

"People House...we are listening."

"I am sorry sir..."

"Sorry about what...?" the president jumped up to his feet, bending over the phone in the center of the table. The officials looked frightened than angry.

"I am sorry Your Excellency. The contingent we sent to the scene has been wounded and incapacitated and we have no idea where P.D, Aatien'oh, Isaac and the rest have gone."

The president furiously looked at the acting chief of staff, the defense minister and the head of security.

"Explain that to me. It seems honorable Miochariya was right."

"Your Excellency, I have no idea else I wouldn't be here. Please understand me. Besides, our soldiers were shot," the chief of staff pleaded.

The president made a quick phone call and two civilian-clothed men worked up to the chief of general staff and the defense minister.

"Take them in for interrogation."

The head of security, chief of staff and the defense minister all looked astonished.

"Honorable Miochariya, you will coordinate intelligence with the security chief, and you will also be acting as the defense minister. I will form a committee to look into this problem. I need a nationwide search. I need them alive."

President Eekedu was rightfully furious. From the time he became president, Eekedu considered himself a very liberal-minded person. Coming from a poor background and making himself out to be a significant voice in Sivalsian political scene was something no one doubted. The cabinet had only a single man from his tribe. The government had all the elements of almost every single tribe. That was claimed to be his point of weakness. He had no any right-hand man from his tribe as many African leaders always do. But he'd not lost the backing of his tribe. As a sound political figure with suave eloquence, Eekedu assured his constituency that all they needed was development not cabinet positions. In all his political rallies, he reiterated that sons and daughters of the land with resources should make sure their grassroots areas are well serviced. To make sure his tribe didn't complain he made sure help was available to his constituency.

Eekedu was of military background and security training.

At first, Eekedu ignored the reports about *The Pipers* as naïve subversive contemplations. However, as *The Pipers* started to intensify their savvy political moves, the president realized the group had to be given a weighty political muscle. He'd also been briefed by Panda and western intelligentsia about *The Pipers*. Now, he knew the problem was up his neck as the ministers sat as if they were hypnotized. But the president was internally burning. Vincent's ego on the other hand was inflating with pride and anticipation

I'm getting along just right.

88

Little stared at the city's skyline as the airplane prepared to land.

I'm home.

He looked outside and the environment was lush and green. Unlike South Sudan, Sivals was modern, vibrant and bustling. Heavenly tropical climate, friendly frondescence impressed on Little the similarity between South Sudan and Sivals.

This is Captain Andrew Miorialiya. Welcome to the beautiful Hayiroh. It's now 3.21 pm local time. The temperature is about 25 degrees Celsius. Thanks for flying with Serpo Air. Hope to see you again.

The plane touched down and skidded to a stop. Modeer' airport was about 30 kilometers southeast of Hayiroh. It was used mostly by aid agencies working in Sudan, South Sudan, Somalia and other war-affected countries in the region.

As Little emerged from the plane, he saw a man waving at him. Little waved and the man walked toward him. It was the same man. *Okob or John?*

"Hello, again, Mr. Little Michael. My name is Okob Beyeiya."

"Nice to meet you, Okob," Little said, smiled and shook his head.

"Pleasure to meet you, again, Mr. Michael."

Okob tried to take Little's bag but Little looked at him and said: "I'm home man, let me carry my bag. Just relax and do the driving."

Okob smiled and shook his head delightfully. A black Mercedes was parked a few meters away. As they approached, Okob remotely opened the trunk.

"Nice weather out here," Little remarked.

"It sometimes gets really hot."

Both men got into the car. Little looked at Okob.

"I heard some people talking on the plane that there was a coup plot here."

Okob laughed as Little stared at him.

"Was that funny?" Little sounded offended.

"Indeed it was. You know, some people will say anything to make sure their agendas (or hopes in their terms) are fulfilled."

Little's lips curled up. "What's that supposed to mean?"

"Most of us, Africans, blame the Europeans for our messes. There's a point in that, I mean; they're to some extent right. However, what remains confusing is the fact that we haven't cleaned ourselves but we blame others. If we don't make sure we clean our acts, blaming the Europeans becomes escapist and stupid."

"I don't follow," Little said with a frown.

"We have a group of people in the government who want to oust the government and set others up."

"How do you know...?"

"I know I'm just a driver, Mr. Michael."

"That's..."

"That's what you meant...I take no offense however."

Little was lost for words as Okob gave an assuring glance at him. *Who the hell is this driver?*

"Where are we going?"

"Good question...home...we're going home."

"Home? What do you mean home?"

"Home is home."

"Man, you're freaking me out."

"I'm sorry."

Little remained quiet for a while as the car sailed smoothly. They passed avenues and streets lined with trees, perfectly aligned. The Adishes' drivers were doing the usual: honking and driving recklessly. As the world around them slid by, Little relaxed his muscles and breathed in the beautiful scenery.

It was mother Africa, literally. The parks were beautiful, the gatherings were religious and assuring, and the people were busy, seemingly determined, but bonny.

"How is your mother?"

"She's doing great. I talked to her today."

"I'm sorry you had to go through that. The commander thought the area was secure but he obviously had bad intelligence. Dr. Cunningham said he's doing fine."

There's no point asking how he knows all that.

Okob looked at Little through the rare view mirror and said: "There's a phone over there. Call the number on the paper next to it."

"And say what?"

"Don't worry. Whoever answers knows who's calling."

Little, stop being surprised.

Little reluctantly picked up the phone, stared at the number, stole one glance at Okob and dialed the number.

"Little, where're you?" someone asked.

"Tell him we're about five minutes to the house," Okob said.

"We're about five minutes to the house."

Little covered the receiver with his hand and said, looking at Okob: "Do I have to ask who that is?"

"It's either Wallace, Wani or P.D."

"Bye Little!"

Little slowly put down the receiver.

Okob turned into a massive, white compound. At the gate, Okob honked. A short, brown-faced guard peeped through the hole on the gate then swiftly opened it. As Okob drove into the compound, two BMWs and a military truck drove in after them. Okob looked at Little and said: "You are home."

Little got down and scanned the compound. The house was yellow with brick-red tiles covering the roof. A circumference of a fence guarded the compound. There were flower gardens lining the footpaths. It looked more of a hotel than a house.

The occupants of the truck got out first. They were wielding guns professionally. Little cringed and frowned. They waved having seen uneasiness on Little's face. Okob walked toward the house as Little followed.

Then the occupants of the BMWs got out so Little stopped and stared at them.

First it was Chris and Wallace who got out followed by Aatieŋ'oh and Jeng. In the second car, P.D and Isaac with two other men Little didn't know emerged.

"Hello Mr. Michael! I've heard a lot about you. My name is Michael Pelebaidien Dhuengdakah."

Little absent-mindedly handed P.D his hand. Then everyone followed with introduction.

My name is:

Jeng

Chris

Aatieŋ'oh

Isaac...

With perfect military precision, everyone walked into the house. After a while Wallace emerged from the house, jumped into the military truck and drove out of the compound.

89

President Eekedu was simply worked-up. The turn of events wasn't working in his favor or anyone's for that matter. The People House was unnervingly quiet as no one had any better suggestions. Unlike many African leaders, the president chaired the meeting with one other minister, sitting on two lonely chairs in front. The cabinet, members of the intelligence community, the police and the army chiefs, were all seated in two columns; making a shape of a rectangular figure with one missing width. The constant update from the police and the intelligence head wasn't promising.

"It seems like we've been out-smarted by *The Pipers*. I need them captured...do you hear me?"

The president said pointing at the security officials.

Vincent cleared his throat, looking at the president.

"Your Excellency, we have every route leading out of the city manned by both the police and the army."

"Honorable Miochariya, we don't know the elements in the army that are helping these people. This makes it likely that if the army is working with them then they would let them go."

"Your Excellency, you have already talked to all the neighboring countries. They have assured us of their extradition should they be captured."

"Honorable Miochariya, you talk as if you don't know diplomatic games. Extradition involves a long process and it would overshadow the truth we are trying to find out: Who are *The Pipers* and what do they want from us? We have to make sure they are apprehended within our borders. In that case, if human right watchdogs voice their concerns like always, we'd have to assure them of the independence of our judiciary."

"We'll also have to be careful about diplomatic conflicts with Day-Town. You all know Isaac Burns is a wealthy Pandian. They can fabricate issues to make us look bad. They've every power and resources to affect us," the foreign minister, Steve DiDengo, said.

DiDengo was a tall, lanky man with a smooth voice of an egalitarian professor. He played his role like it was supposed to be. It was no wonder he was one of the cautionary voices in the cabinet. His partitioned hair made him look classy and worthy of attention. The smoothness of his voice gave credibility to the African wisdom he exuded.

"Honorable DiDengo, let us apprehend them after which we'd worry about Day-Town."

"Let's not indict the army before we know the actual truth," the chief of staff said looking at the president. He'd just come back to the room with the minister of defense after the president changed his mind.

"I agree. I just need an answer that is all," the president said remorsefully, knowing he'd over-reacted.

"And we are trying sir," the chief of staff said.

"Sir, the top leaders in the intelligence community are here. Besides, if the army was involved it could have declared its intentions by now. We know the chief of staff is here and we are in constant contact with all the zonal commanders. Ezekiel has been very instrumental in giving us valuable information. What I suggest we do is to continue to find avenues to capture them and let us hold a press conference to straighten things out with the Sivalsian people. They need answers and they need to know you are not only still in charge, but comprehensively and commandingly in charge." the security chief said and looked at the president.

The president got up, walked back and forth behind the officials as they stared, speechless and confused.

"Maybe P.D's speech is a code."

"The speech was plain and silly sir. There was nothing like a code in it," Vincent said.

"P.D talked about foreign companies and the president becoming unpopular...and the opposition winning the election."

"I don't see any relevance to our situation."

"It's to reflect the corruption in many African countries. We've seen how opposition parties, or even people within the government, gang up to belittle the president and his government. The speech could or couldn't have any connection with Sivals," DiDengo said.

"Our only indictment against the army is the wounding of the contingent and the disappearance of the pair. Let's focus our energy on capturing P.D and Isaac," President Eekedu said and sat down, looked at the police chief and asked: "How are we doing so far?"

"We have set up check points all over the city. We have also sent a message to all police forces in the country to make sure the same method is used."

"Have we got any word from the Pandians and the Americans yet?" the president asked looking at the security chief.

"My office is working hard now as we speak. I just received a message that the Americans have released some valuable information although they have refused to talk to us about others. Pandian security chief is still deliberating on what to release. They have the best intel about *The Pipers*. Because of Isaac, we don't know when they'll release the intelligence. I heard that there's a burnt hard-drive discovered yesterday when a certain location of interest was attacked. They're trying to see if they can retrieve some information from it. They're not sure if the hard -drive has anything to do with The Pipers. All those killed in the operation had no IDs and no one has come out to identify them."

"I'll call Quincy Deliberative to ask the president for their cooperation. You can read to us what we got from the Americans."

"Right sir. The message was coded so it had to be decoded by our security personnel with the help of the Americans."

Central Intelligence Agency

Washington DC

Top Secret #20010911

'The Pipers' is a group of Pan-Africanist minded individuals who have taken it upon themselves to 'rid' the world of capitalism. Their central tenet is to build a socialist and pacifist society where we have no poverty or war. Knowing that such utopia is impractical and impracticable should be a consolation to everyone affected by the illusiveness of The Pipers. However, The Pipers use methods that are hard to detect. One of their dangerous methods is the undetectable infiltration of various governments.

They have people working within the governments and companies they target to give them insight and secret information. Some of the people have worked for years to gather information. The most deadly tactic they employ is that they are not of the same race. They are not only Africans. They have all kinds of people from Singapore to Nhom Penh, From Ottawa to Sao Paolo, from Glasgow to Cape Town. This confuses the intelligence.

You have people within your government who work for The Pipers. They could be cabinet ministers, they could be secretaries, they could be ambassadors...anyone. Some could be government liaisons or affiliates working for various companies both foreign and local. Simply put, we cannot describe a P Brother or Sister.

The chief put the letter down and looked at the president.

"So that's all we've got?" the president asked.

"That's not much of a help," honorable Miochariya added.

"I think that information is valuable," DiDengo said.

"Mm...how so honorable DiDengo?"

"It tells us first of all that a *P Sibling* could be anywhere even in this room. It also tells us that we shouldn't narrow our search for the truth of what happened."

90

Everyone sat gloomily in the living room. Little didn't quite understand why everyone was sad as if they'd just come back from a burial. However, having been inundated with crippling and mind-blogging surprises for quite sometimes now, Little decided to just watch and let things slide as they happened.

They were all seated in the living room except Aatieŋ'oh, who'd gone to the kitchen to help the maid prepare drinks for the visitors. The maids looked really rattled by both the sight of Aatieŋ'oh and the strange faces they'd only seen on TV. But one thing assured them: their mistress was home, safe and sound. She'd been a respectful boss for all they knew.

"We've been through a lot in the last 72 hours so I think some of us deserve an explanation," Isaac said, breaking the crippling silence.

P.D looked at Isaac, moved to the edge of his chair and said: "We're all victims of lack of numerous explanations. But what we have to focus on now is safety first then explanations later."

"Well, aren't we safe here? And who're we running away from?"

"That's the very question we need answered, Mr. Burns. All I know is that we aren't safe...having seen how we were snatched at the lectures."

"And who are *The Pipers*, professor? Are you or Osmani part of them? What a fool I've been? And my friendship with you guys was too good to be true...not a cliché, not a cliché!"

"It's irresponsible to say that, Mr. Burns, don't you think? But listen; let's figure out these issues when we're all ready. What I can only tell you is people take a lot of *shit* sometimes just because they need something so badly. They endure a lot of nonsense just to arrive at their destination."

"I don't follow."

"I'd..."

P.D couldn't finish the sentence as Aatieŋ'oh and the two maids flocked into the living room with soft drinks in two trays, a thermo-flask and tea cups in another.

"This will perhaps calm down our nerves," Aatieŋ'oh said.

P.D got up and picked up a can of iced tea. The maid tried to help the guests with drinks but Little objected.

"We'll do that ourselves ma'am."

Aatieŋ'oh looked at Little delightfully and smiled: "That makes me hopeful, Mr. Michael...really hopeful."

Little smiled satisfactorily at Aatieŋ'oh, got up and picked up a can of Coca Cola.

"Some, if not most of you, are wondering about what's happening. You've probably been surprised more than a dozen times so you've stopped asking yourself why and how."

"That surprise makes you special somewhat. There'll be a press conference in a few hours from the president," P.D said.

"And something tragic is going to happen if we don't act."

"I think it'd have been better if you let us in on some details because I'm not getting anything," Chris said, speaking for the first time since they arrived at the house.

Aatieŋ'oh looked at P.D then at Chris and said.

"We're wary of tapping...that's all. We came here because Vincent isn't coming home until we're apprehended. That's why we came home. It's the last place they'd want to check. Besides, the city is manned now by government snakes so we don't have much of a choice."

"What we need to do is to find a way to contact the president," P.D said.

"And say what?" Isaac said, raising his voice.

"For us to help, we need to at least understand something," Chris said.

"You're talking to *The Pipers* so don't hold back guys. They know better than you might think. What they like to do is to play dumb, a weapon they've used for years. What's comforting though is they aren't after killing anyone. And more comforting to me though is my father is not a douchebag at least," Jeng said and drained up his glass of tea.

Aatieŋ'oh looked disapprovingly at Jeng and said: "That wasn't necessary, Jeng."

"What's necessary, mum? That some people have to re-adjust their lives and identities because someone wanted to hit back at someone?"

"That's enough, Jeng!" P.D interrupted.

"That's too soon, don't you think?"

"I think that's enough...and I'd ask you to leave right now," Aatieŋ'oh ordered Jeng.

Furious like never before, Aatieŋ'oh got up, pointed at Jeng then toward Jeng's room.

"Your mum deserves some respect here, don't you think?" Okob said, grabbed a can of Coca Cola, walked to the door and added: "I'd want to catch up with Wallace."

"Man...!" Jeng said shaking his head.

"I thought you were old enough to understand. Part of the delay was intentional because we expected such a reaction from an early age," Okob said.

"I'm sorry, ok? I'm just mixed up you know...mixed up!"

"And we do understand. All we know is your life will never be the same again...and not in the way you think," Wani said and walked to the door.

"Some people sacrifice their lives for good causes but they're never paid anything. We count this as part of the sacrifices you've made and are still to make. At least your life will never be shoddy from now on," Okob added.

Aatien'oh sat back contended. She stared at Jeng, Wani and Okob and nodded her approval.

"I'm sorry...I said!" Jeng said again after realizing his mother was staring at him.

Aatien'oh cleared her throat then looked at everyone one by one and said: "None of us can say exactly who a *P* Sister or Brother *is*. If you read any documented intelligence with any government in the world, they'll never tell you who a *P* person is and how they look like."

"Being a *P* person is a matter of conscience not a matter of racial or linguistic reductionism," P.D said.

"We do know that the content of people's consciences can be different, however, when a group of people become like-minded because their consciences are tormented by ubiquitous ills around them, their differences disappear and they become a unity of conscience. We can see this phenomenon during the civil rights movements in the US and Panda," Aatien'oh said with a glow of satisfaction on her face."

"What we're simply saying is *The Pipers* is not an organization, it's a conscience content. That makes all of us here *P* something at least."

"It must have started with a single conscience before the *unity* of consciences was arrived at," Isaac sarcastically said.

"That's a task for historians. Our interest is what those united consciences are up to and up against," P.D rctorted back dismissively.

"They've achieved many things without those things being attributed to them. And they've saved many governments from being overthrown by malicious, rapacious government ministers or influenced military."

"Building of concrete homes in South Africa's Soweto is a result of both guilty and aroused conscience. The mission Mugabe politicized for his benefit was a result of aroused conscience. The destruction of caste system in India was brought about by aroused conscience. We can go on and on. Simply put, the *P* has done a lot of things for people all over the world and mostly in Africa. But they don't take credit for it until now perhaps."

"I know I'm not supposed to talk, but if *P* thing is a clean conscience, then how do we explain the death of all the soldiers at the lectures?" Jeng asked.

"Did anyone say the deaths, if there are any, had anything to do with *The Pipers*? The deaths might have been engineered by sympathizers of *The Pipers* and...you might not have read the papers, there has been an official apology. Remember however that the soldiers were only wounded, not killed," Aatieŋ'oh said.

"No one knows I'm in Hayiroh...well, not many people. I can pass the message to the president," Little offered.

"Getting to the president will be extremely difficult at this time," Wani said.

"Calling would be very dangerous too. The Pandians and the Americans have been alerted. Any signal will have us located within minutes. Little can probably use a public phone to convey the message," P.D said.

"They might dismiss it as *The Pipers'* ploy to divert attention," Aatieŋ'oh added.

"At this time, I doubt they'd ignore any information."

"I think I'll go with Mr. Michael. I don't think anyone knows of my presence here. Besides, it's good to have two people just in case."

91

For President Eekedu, the press conference would be one of the highlights of his presidency. Inside the People House, the make-up ladies were preparing the president's hair and face. A paper with the speech was on the table next to him. He picked up the paper, scanned it for a while, shook his head and called.

"I don't like these lines. You don't have to write exactly what is in the intelligence report. We can't appear vulnerable. We have to appear like people who know what they are doing."

"I understand Your Excellency," the speech writer said and rushed off.

Vincent, the chief of police and the chief of security walked to the president.

"How is everything?" the president asked.

"It's overwhelming Your Excellency. The media presence is too much. We tried to control their presence by giving out permits but it's too much," the security chief said.

"What we plan to do is to put something like the police tape and hold the press conference outside the House," Vincent said.

"That sounds like a good idea," the president said.

"I'm against the idea Your Excellency because we still don't have P.D and Isaac and we don't quite understand the nature and the intentions of *The Pipers*," the security chief said.

"You have a point, but we don't want to appear too scared, do we?"

"Sir, I'm not concerned now about our being called scared but I'm more concerned about your safety so as to hold this country together at these difficult times."

"We've gone through this over and over again. You even assured me that the 1 square mile of the People House is secured. I don't want our president to appear vulnerable. You know the media manipulates every given political situation," Vincent said.

"We know *The Pipers* have out-smarted every intelligence organization in the world not to mention our own. I just want to be sure."

"What do you think chief?" the president said looking at the police chief.

"I think we have a lot of police presence and we should be fine. I just don't want to be too cocky as to say we are hundred percent certain. We haven't found our fugitives and that raises a concern with me. I am therefore forced to side with the security chief. We can't leave anything to chance."

"Fair enough! We'll take that to the cabinet for further deliberations as we still have about an hour. Or what do you think honorable Miochariya?"

"What the two gentlemen are saying seems fair enough. They know their jobs better."

92

Little and Chris looked back at Aatieŋ'oh as they jumped into a parked, black BMW X5. The lady security guard at the gate faithfully opened it. Little looked at Chris with confidence, turned the engine on, stepped on the gas pedal and drove slowly to the gate.

"Are you ok?" Little asked Chris.

"Yeah, yeah...well, I don't quite understand what's happening exactly."

"I don't either but I know one thing."

Little said as he drove out of the compound.

"What?"

"They don't mean any bad."

"Dude, I know that but...what if we get killed."

"Sacrifice I guess. I still don't know why they picked me?"

Little and Chris sat silently in the car as they drove along. The past few days had been daunting and exhausting. The African night outside whistled by, the atmosphere quiet and comforting. Silence invaded as the two men sat wordless; lost in their own thoughts.

It was like they were back in high school again; in Chris's rusty truck playing on the beach with naughty girls. Good old times.

"What's that?" Chris said pointing ahead.

"What?"

"It looks like a police check point."

"Shoot! There's a curfew tonight. How did we miss that?"

Little slowed down.

"Don't do that or they'll be suspicious."

Little drove slowly as the check-point neared. At the check-point, there were two police cars and a military truck. The truck was parked almost in the middle of the road. Two police officers walked toward Little and Chris from the two police Land Cruiser pick-up trucks parked on the roadside. Still not sure of what to do, Little drove to the roadside and parked the car. The two officers approached; wielding their batons threateningly.

"Hello officers," Little said as the men approached.

"You guys know very well that you are breaching the curfew."

"We're sorry sir. We're new in town," Little said.

"Being new in town doesn't mean not being able to listen to the radio or watch TV."

"We're sorry sir."

"And where are you guys going? The city is on curfew. We'll give you a permit to make sure you don't get in trouble with other law enforcement officers. Are you Americans?"

"No, we're not Americans. We're Pandians," Little said.

"Today is not a good day to be a Pandian in Sivals."

"Why's that officer?"

"Long story."

The officer walked back toward the parked pick-up truck to grab a writing pad. The other police officer remained standing next to Chris and Little.

Little looked at Chris and whispered: "What do we do? Can we go back?"

"I don't know man. We're left with about thirty minutes to the press conference. We'll tell them we're going to a hotel; to go and book one."

The officer, who'd gone to the pick-up truck, came back with two military personnel. As the police officer tried to write the note, the soldier squinted then shone a flash light at Little and Chris.

"Wait!" the soldier said to the officer writing the note.

"What is it?" the police officer said looking up.

"I think I know the white man. I saw him walk into the lecture hall with P.D Michael."

"No, sir, I think you saw a different man. These white people look the same," Little said lamely.

"Can you gentlemen get out of the car?"

"Sir, you saw a different man."

"I hate when they do this. I heard you said you are Pandians. You're bent on destroying this country but we'll not let you. *The Pipers* have been really slick, but I think we are slick too. So you drive in the middle of the night to go and do what...kill the president?"

"Sir..."

"Shut up! You are going to the press conference I take it."

"No, sir, we're going to book ourselves a hotel," Chris said for the first time since the soldier accosted them.

"Take them in and show them that this is Sivals."

"Bu..."

93

President Eekedu emerged from his office followed by his chief of staff, his vice president and Vincent. He looked relaxed and confident. What appeared on the faces of his senior officials was depressing if not premonitory. President Eekedu was tall but stocky. His hair was completely shaved off; making his scalp appear shiny. That was his style. He walked with short strides but his long legs made them appear longer to short people. He had some exotic gait not characteristic of military people. His large, wide eyes moved from one face to another as he gathered their thoughts. Most of them looked either hesitant or uncertain. His age was between forty-five and fifty.

"I gather you have deliberated enough about the venue of the press conference. We have just over thirty minutes."

"I was for the view that we hold the conference in the press room of the People House. However, as I thought of it, I realized that we have to exert our presence and reassure the Sivalsian people that we're in charge and that they're safe," Mr. DiDengo said.

"That sounds rational, but we have to first guarantee the safety of the president. The Sivalsian people will find comfort and assurance in the president's message and the details he will outline in the speech," the vice president said.

"I'm actually ambivalent. I was first for the view that the press conference be held in front of the house in the lawn as usual with important announcements. But as I listened to the chief of police and the security chief, I realized much is still not known about the fugitives and *The Pipers*. So whatever you decide, I am for it," Vincent said and sat back.

"We have given you enough information to act on Your Excellency," the security chief said.

The president stared at his desk, looked at his cabinet members and said: "Let's show the *P* nonsense and the Sivalsian people that we can't be cowed."

Like all pretentious world leaders, the president didn't want to admit that they'd been out-smarted by *The Pipers*. The group was illusive even to the world's most sophisticated intelligence organizations, in the west.

By all accounts, however, Eekedu was one of the well celebrated and successful African presidents. While the gap between the rich and the poor in Sivals was still staggeringly unnerving, it'd significantly improved since president Eekedu assumed the presidency.

94

Little and Chris sat in that dark cabin at the back of the truck. They couldn't see anything as it was pitch black inside. Their hands we cuffed to a metal post in the middle of the truck. The whole situation appeared silly but real, ominously and satanically real. Their tribulations even during childhood were always puzzling. Little unwillingly remembered one time when Chris had to give him a black eye to save him from a mob of racist, emotionless white kids.

Chris had left Little in his worn-out truck to go and buy some drinks in a nearby convenient store. When he came back, he saw with startling shock a mob of white kids circling around Little. Little was arranged in the middle as the mob threateningly brandished their baseball bats in a celebratory Jim Crow or apartheid mood. They were teenagers drank with malicious and ignorant indoctrination. Nothing could stand in their way. They mowed down any obstructive figure or object on the way.

Little was squatting in the middle as they shouted. *'Beat the nigger! The world hasn't changed! Beat the nigger!'*

Little was completely sullen, staring with an expressionless face. When Chris pushed his way to the front of the group, the group fixed him with vengeful, disapproving eyes. Chris had to pretend he'd finally secured an opportunity to avenge his anger on Little, the Nigger. He punched Little in the face and grabbed a baseball bat from one of the mobsters. They were impressed by the supposedly courageous action. He assured them that he'd beat the hell out of him. The mobsters patted Chris on the back and moved on in their marauding, racist adventures.

Little shook his head and whispered: "That's the end of the president."

Chris groaned his disapproval. "Dude, you're talking about the president? This is the end of us!"

"P.D is always meticulous...I just don't know how the curfew evaded him."

"Or maybe he just handed us to the sharks knowing exactly what his plans are. Remember he was vague about everything he was saying."

"I don't think P.D would do that!"

"I just thought of something. What if they ask us about P.D's and Aatieŋ'oh's whereabouts?"

"And I guess they'll make sure we say it. It never crossed my mind for a minute. Why did you have to think about this?"

"You'd still think about it eventually. Someone is controlling them and I believe that's why they aren't asking us. That's what I think."

"Things would be fine if they take us to the press conference."

"As long as they think we're a threat to the president, they wouldn't allow us near the president."

"Man..."

The door opened and the military fellow shone the flashlight again at Little and Chris.

"That light is not good for the eye especially when someone has been in the dark for a while."

The man sneered. "I don't care that much. Get out of the truck."

"What exactly have we done? We're being held because I look like someone you saw somewhere?"

"I know we are a lower form of humanity, but just listen to me for once because you are in Africa. Give me some respect, would you?" the officer said and Chris cringed.

Chris hated such cynical attitudes so he stared at the man as he pulled them down the truck. They were still in handcuffs.

"Why do you have to make every statement dramatic?"

"Emotions mark us in everything we do. You are always self-controlled and showing of no emotions. Why should this surprise you? Self-control helps you commit historically unspeakable crimes without feeling anything: emotionlessness during slavery, colonization, Jim Crow, apartheid, police brutality etc. Emotions afford us the elastic capacity to forgive; something you can't afford."

"Man, I..."

Chris tried to talk as he was getting frustrated by the self-righteousness the man exuded.

"Save your breath for later."

"Why're we getting out of the truck? We need to know what you're planning to do with us. If we're being charged with something then let us know so we can call our lawyers."

The man smiled sarcastically, shook his head and said: "I am not a police officer. I am a soldier so don't talk to me about charges."

"Besides the curfew and your thinking my friend here is someone you saw at the lectures, is there anything else we're being held for?" Little asked.

The man showed Little and Chris a bench under a small tree and said: "Someone is coming to pick you up. Whatever they'll do to you after this, will be up to them."

"That doesn't sound promising," Chris said.

"Considering what Sivals is facing right now...nothing should be surprising to you," the officer factually said.

95

President Eekedu was confident the decision to hold the press conference in front of the house was the best idea possible. It also invigorated his resolves to put the issue to rest.

"We are ready your Excellency," the police chief said.

The president got up as the rest of the cabinet flanked him; all suited up. The police chief and the security chief led the way with secret service agents around them.

Outside the house, the media presence was enormous. There was murmuring, but as the president emerged from the house, the whole media presence burst into applause. The president and his entourage made their way toward the set-up microphone. As the president waved, the whole environment became as quiet as a graveyard. After a few glances at the crowd and back at his cabinet, he walked slowly but confidently to the microphone.

§

Hayiroh was awake but silent. Every household with a television set was watching live as the president walked to the microphone. President Eekedu was a trusted soul. He'd changed Sivals in a way many never thought possible. With no doubt, he was a true national leader with no tribal leaning whatsoever. This, many Sivalsians acknowledged. However, that night was a critical moment for both the president and the Sivalsian people. The past twenty-four hours saw many incomprehensible things transpire. Whatever he was going to say would have a huge impact on his life at the People House.

The Sivalsian people stared; watching as his strides seemed to have turned into a movie slow motion. He approached, adjusted the microphone to his height and looked straight into the camera.

"Good evening my fellow Sivalsians. The last twenty-four hours have seen us witness many mind-boggling occurrences. But I do believe the country we have come to love and cherish, the country we have spent our energies and our sweat building, will stand the same tonight, tomorrow morning, the next day, and to infinity."

There was applause starting from the president's men and then it rippled through the crowd.

"We are strong..."

96

It wasn't so much about success but impact, Uncle D would tell them. She knew her journey had been colorful and inspiring. Inspiring to who? No one. Who knew what she was doing? Who knew what she did for a living? Her parents thought she was working for an international humanitarian organization between Day-Town and Hayiroh. She was her own audience, her own inspirer, and her own admirer. Well, it colored her world in a manner she wanted. Self-inspired people are never swayed. They're never unnerved by silly prejudicial trifles.

Sister K had made her way to the outskirt of Hayiroh, however, she couldn't make it in time to the press conference. She knew too that the security presence would be overwhelmingly heavy. Rattled, she looked at the gas tank and it was half full.

That'll take me to the nearest petrol station at the outskirt of the city.

The 1992 Toyota Land Cruiser was the queen of the African roads.

Sister K was red with mud and dust; sweating profusely from the pangs of Africa's solar anger. Having realized that she couldn't reach her targets by phone safely; she pulled up by the roadside, fumbled through her purse, removed her phone, scanned it then started to type. She stopped briefly. *I have to do it or he dies.*

Get him out of there. Get the...

97

P.D looked apprehensive.

"I think we miscalculated issues a little bit," Aatieŋ'oh said.

"Something went wrong with Little and Chris. The president's talking for god's sake," P.D said.

"And maybe Sister K is arrested too. This doesn't look good."

"I doubt Sister K is arrested. That'd mean we've failed terribly if something happens to the president. The culmination of this phase would be terrible."

Aatieŋ'oh walked to the phone and grabbed it.

"What're you doing?"

"Calling Vincent."

"I don't think that's such a good idea."

"What other choice do we have? The president will die in the next minute or two if we don't do anything."

"And how do you think the phone call would help keep the president from being killed?"

"It'll buy us time."

"For what? Remember we don't know the fate of Chris and Little. And we don't even know where Sister K is. Even if we buy time, we don't have anything in progress."

Aatieŋ'oh stared at P.D. *He's right!*

"Now, what do we do? Do we just sit here and let them win?"

"I'll give myself in. This will disrupt the speech and force an emergency cabinet meeting."

"I'll assume I didn't hear that. Besides, you don't have time. Remember, if the conspirators catch you, they'll laugh. I have confidence in Sister K. There's no way she can fail."

"Being the co-chair of the cabinet, Vincent is going to do whatever he can to make sure he gets away with everything. I don't understand how this government works."

"This is actually a good thing for our democratic process. We don't talk of junior or senior ministers. This idea is actually one of the best in terms of not making sure other ministers see themselves as powerful."

§

Sister K cursed as a bird fluttered about and interrupted her. Looking at the time every now and then, she fingered the message into her phone, reviewed the message again, hesitated for a moment and hit send. Seemingly angry, she threw the phone onto the passenger's seat.

We've failed. We've failed.

After a minute, she quickly grabbed and frantically dialed a number. The phone rang for a while then stopped. *What a treacherous monster!*

She redialed the same number again.

"Who are you? I can't talk now, but how did you get my number?"

"Sir, don't do it. We've all the information of your conspiracy to kill the president and frame foreigners and the vice president."

"Hello...hello! Shit!"

The other person hanged up on Sister K.

I just screwed up. I just killed the president.

Sister K was born in Kingston, Jamaica, to a black mother and white father. When Sister K was two years old the family moved to Heritage, Panda, where she grew up. With her mother as a medical doctor and father as an accomplished and widely read political scientist and scholar, Sister K grew up in coveted neighborhoods. Like many well-off, pretentious black North-Americans, Sister K's parents didn't approve of her listening to Hip Hop, R & B and Reggae. Because of her wealthy upbringing, Sister K didn't realize the prejudice facing black Pandians until she went to Day-Town to attend university.

There, no one knew her wealthy background. Reality had it that she was just another black drop in a white sea. Her face wasn't typically African. It wasn't Caucasoid either. She was stereotyped for more than she could imagine. At first, black students didn't approve of her 'too English' pronunciations, her too European hair, her too judgemental view of black attitude toward progress and her lack of knowledge of black and African history. *You thought Tupac Shakur was an African novelist? Wole Soyinka wasn't a Japanese scientist, you...you—?* Yes, they couldn't say it but she knew the word.

Then the white world's face that'd been her childhood delight and source of inspiration turned dark.

What scholarship did you win? You're in a basketball team, right? You must be a good sister? What's life like in the ghetto? What do you think of Africans? Do you feel you have anything to do with Africa? Coming to this university must be an achievement to you I guess?

Sister K was lost, out of place and furious. She'd call her mother and cry her heart out. Growing up is a challenge, she'd advise. And soon Sister K would leave university with the same bright upbringing. But there was one problem. She was darkening by the day. Yes, the white substance in her skull was turning self-analytical and observant. The corporate world would snap the slim social thread that was holding Sister K to her childhood life.

Sister K came back to the present and smiled. She looked into the rear view mirror. The cloud of dust curled up and fanned sideways. She smiled again.

How beautiful? I'm no longer lost. I'm no longer out of place. I'm fulfilled. I'm African.

98

"We are strong and we are determined to keep our country strong and keep you safe. I would not let anyone take away our pride. We are a sovereign nation and that will remain so. We..."

Vincent walked up to the president and whispered something into his ear.

"Your Excellency, we have got some good news. We have caught two Pandians who were with P.D and Isaac at the lectures. They were making their way here armed and dangerous. Thank god we caught them in time. They are being interrogated about the whereabouts of P.D and Isaac."

The president nodded, smiled and looked into the camera. Vincent walked back to his position and his phone rang. He removed it, looked at the number then pressed the off button and looked at the president.

"I am sorry about the interruption but honorable Miochariya is not a man who interrupts people unless he has something of national importance to say. Before I continue, I just wanted to let you know that we have in custody two culprits. We cannot rest until we bring all of them to book. Now, let me continue.

"As I was..."

The president couldn't finish. A bullet tore through the president's left shoulder just above the heart. He felt back with a loud thud. Another bullet hit the Vice President in the chest. The crowd jumped into commotion as Vincent, the police chief and the security chief all ran toward the president. Commotion and tumultuous wails filled the fair.

"The president has been shot!" the police chief shouted mournfully.

"Can someone call the ambulance, please?" the security chief said with sadness-clogged voice.

"Please hurry!"

The crowd was confused; everyone running helter skelter.

"Please hurry!" Vincent urged.

"I..." the security chief couldn't finish the statement as his phone rang.

"Sir, don't answer that phone. Let's help the president and the vice president. Any phone call can wait."

The chief frowned. "Someone just shot the president and the vice president and we have no clue as to who that was. I have to answer this and I have to follow the direction of the shot. I know you will make sure the president and the vice president are taken to hospital. Sir, this is personal...it is my duty to have credible intelligence but I have failed. The least I can do is to find his shooter. I will personally interview the guys who have been caught."

The security chief looked at his phone, hesitated again then spoke into the phone. The female voice over the phone sounded confident yet irritating. Her authoritative voice surprised him; however, he wanted information not entertainment. Rattled and feeling guilty, the chief allowed the best part of him to reign on his impulses.

The country is in turmoil; this is not time for arrogance.

§

Sister K had been holding her phone for a minute.

"Sir?"

Not being answered, she kept on yelling into the phone.

"Sir I..."

"This is not a good time to call unless you have something valuable to tell me."

There was a slight pause as Sister K thought of good words to say.

"Listen to me very carefully sir."

"I am listening but don't waste my time because the president has been shot."

"You'll be shot too if you don't listen to me very carefully, dear."

The chief cringed.

"What did you just say?"

"I said listen very carefully."

Rattled by such a blunt utterance, the man kept quiet.

"Okay. Inside the People House is a cleaning lady. She'll give you an envelope. Take that envelope and listen to its content."

"Am I supposed to just believe what you just told me like that? What if you're framing me about the death of the president?"

"Do you know who I am?"

"No!"

"So how do I feature in the killing of the president? I can't frame you when you don't even know me...and I'm not about to be caught, am I?"

"What if people become suspicious and assume that I have something to do with the assassination attempt. I would look bad if I am spotted sneaking back to the house for a reason people will never understand."

"The president and vice president have been shot, possibly dead."

"Don't say that."

"It doesn't matter what I say. Anyway, it's all about taking risks. You might be taken for a culprit for a while but you'll be exonerated at the end."

"Who're you and why do you seem to know these...oh, you're one of *The Pipers!*"

"I didn't say that but just go. Be careful!"

"Give me something at least. I am checking the lion's mouth don't you think some assurance would be a great justice to me?"

Sister K remained silent for a while as she stared at the dusty road ahead of her.

"On August 27 last year when the president called you to his office, you were worried that things might be ending for you. You wrote a memo and saved it on your computer."

"But...how...?"

Sister K hanged up.

I just failed; she said to herself and turned on the engine. With bitterness and guilt surging inside her, she looked back into the rear-view mirror at the trail of dust she'd left. *It's dusty and cloudy but it'll settle down.*

99

I t was over. Chris sensed it and Little knew it. Mother Africa: enigmatic, always surprising, yet knowledge defying. Their miserable heads would soon add to the content of the Nile. They'd be chopped off or shot out with an RPG. It was only the night; black, wordless, speechless night that'd witness it. How can she tell anyone? She'd see everything; hear their pleading voices, their begging eyes, and groans helplessly. Premonition and gloom were the words. It was dark; pitch black. The darkness said it all: cruel, pregnant, inscrutable and whipping with cruel, uncertainty lashes.

As they sat under the tree still in handcuffs, a black Mitsubishi Pajero toddled toward them. The soldier who'd taken them to the bench loudly called out.

"They are here!"

A tall, dark and chubby fellow in civilian clothing jumped out of the car; two uniformed officers closely in tow. They slowly wobbled toward Chris and Little. Even in that darkness, Chris and Little could sense their dark, sweaty faces.

"Did they say anything?" the man said with a quick, squeaky voice.

"I didn't ask them anything."

"Good. They will tell us who shot the president."

"Wha-at?"

Chris, Little, the officer guarding them and the soldier all said in unison.

"The president was shot about ten minutes ago by an unknown sniper. And I guess these idiots know very well who that person is," the man squeaked.

"First, this gentleman said he saw me at the lecture and now this?"

"My name is Dickson by the way. I'm a special agent with SNSIS. We are heading to the headquarters so if you have anything to say, that will be the place to say it," the squeaky voice said with a disempowering poise.

A group of armed police officers walked toward Chris and Little. They brandished their batons so Chris and Little knew there was no room for rational discussions. With soldiery discipline and unsung precision, the two gentlemen got onto the truck as the uniformed officers sat around them, still brandishing their batons.

The captives knew that being charged with an attempt at the president's life in Africa needed no trial. Well, maybe something with semblance of a trial. The cases are always judged with self-righteous political mediocrity. No. They call it free and independent judiciary. Without vexing anyone, it was absoluteness; unquestionable, ideal absoluteness of the laughing gods.

Chris's and Little's fate was sealed. The darkness and the ominous trees hanging over them weren't lying. Their future was as dark as the silent night. However, they sat silently in the truck without anyone landing any rude hands on them. That was unexpected. But no, maybe some monstrous disciplinary metals awaited them. They might be the start of Sivals' arduous social and political screed.

"I heard that that place is terrible," Chris whispered into Little's ear. *He had to start it; the white boy had to start it again.*

"Don't even remind me of it," Little said and looked at the silhouette of the uniformed officers.

"It would be good for you if you remained quiet," one officer said with rude finality. That pretentious calm was frightening.

The officers were surprisingly quiet as the truck rumbled noisily along. Outside, it was pitch black. They couldn't see much so they had no idea where they were and what was happening in the city. Because of the curfew perhaps, the night was calm; graveyard silent.

That day reminded Chris of their days in high school. There was a sense of uncertainty inside that hot and humid truck. The officers' dark faces didn't tell Chris and Little much. They just assumed the "you're doomed tonight" conjecture.

Neither Little nor Chris knew exactly what he wanted to do after high school. They were good students though. Well, before Little lost hope in societal corrective advice.

In the summer, they'd drive to the beach in Chris's 1975 Chevy truck; sweaty and shirtless. The truck was so old that the original blue color was almost gone. While many guys in school made up mocking stories about Chris's truck, the girls liked their modesty. It wasn't good in winter though because of the sorry state of its heating system. So during the winter, they used Little's mum's car. They were just teenagers enjoying their time.

However, as they sat in that truck, besides the fact that they were by no means enjoying life, there was a deep sense of uncertainty as to what their fate was going to be. They could just disappear into thin air if the government so wished.

Chris's thoughts got interrupted as the door opened and the officers jumped down. They got down slowly and hesitantly after the officers had jumped down. With nothing else to do, they scanned the surrounding. The writings that stared at them in the face were scarier than they'd thought.

Sivalsian National Security and Intelligence Services

† SNSIS †

Security, Honest and integrity

Honesty, Integrity…my foot, Little sneered. They walked into the building through a large, sliding glass door. With the officers surrounding them, the two gentlemen walked through walls painted yellow. It was a long walk from the main door to the interrogation rooms. The officers were still silent as if they'd been specially instructed not to talk. After that long walk through the maze of corridors, the felons were shown the rooms.

100

The security chief looked scared more than he'd been before. While feared and hated at the same time by opposition parties, he was still just a simple man among men. Besides the fiery look on his face, he was a principled person. Because of the chaos during the shooting, the chief was able to find his way into the People House. However, he had little to say if he was found in the house when he should be in the SNSIS office interrogating the suspects or being in his office instructing his officers to make sure the assassin was apprehended. He was sweating as he made his way through the corridors of the People House. Given his state of mind, the chief found himself wondering in the hallway. Because of his status and the way he was feared, the security guys in the house never bothered to ask what he was doing in the house. He was their boss and asking him would mean loss of one's job or a severe disciplinary action.

"This is stupid!"

He walked past another two doors. As he passed the third, he saw a lady in the president's office, cleaning. Uncertain, he walked back slowly and the lady waved.

You gotta be kidding me. The president's office? Am I being killed?

The chief hesitated while staring at the lady. Having seen hesitation and fear in the chief's eyes, the lady walked toward him, slipped an envelope into his suit's pocket and walked past him whispering: "Go...don't say a single word!"

The chief swiftly turned and walked back the same way he'd come.

"How's the president sir?" the lady who'd just slipped the paper into his pocket asked.

The chief looked back surprised, hesitated then said: "He'll be fine!"

Completely rattled, the chief frantically made his way out of the People House, through the crowd of the house cleaners, who were making sure the lawn in front of the house was in order. He walked straight to his car. His two body guards were waiting by the car.

"We were worried sir. Honorable Miochariya and Dickson have been calling nonstop," one of the body guards said with concern on his face. Upon seeing the security chief the driver turned on the engine. He then drove onto the road as one police car followed them. With all the security concerns, extra security for all the top brass of the government was paramount.

"Where are we heading to sir?" the driver asked.

"SNSIS please!"

"Yes sir."

"Any news from the hospital?"

"We are told the president will be fine but we don't have any clear cut message from the doctors. What honorable Miochariya said when he called was that the doctors are hopeful that the president will be stabilized," the chief's assistant said.

The uneasiness on the chief's face was apparent. Never in all the years they'd worked for the chief had they seen the chief so distracted and unsettled. He was sweating despite the cool breeze outside and through the window. The assistant assumed it was the fate of the president that worried him. There was no much talk as they drove toward SNSIS.

The chief was wondering about many things. What would Vincent and company think he'd been doing since the president was shot? He'd not been answering his calls. Besides, the envelope in his pocket was another cause for concern. What was in it? Did the envelope hold the key to who shot the president? What if the envelope was incriminating him? The chief had no reason to relax.

Then his phone rang. The assistant stared at it then said: "It's honorable Miochariya."

The chief nodded.

"Hello sir."

"Hello Chief. We have been trying to reach you to no avail."

"I am trying all I can to make sure we get the shooter."

"I'm sorry to tell you this but the vice president has been declared dead. The doctors are positive about the president but they are not so sure."

"That's sad."

"You have to be careful. I got some information that you were in the House while we were calling all over for you."

"I'm a security person and some of the things I do remain clandestine until times for debriefing come."

Honorable Miochariya remained silent for a while then said.

"Mm, so you'll debrief the cabinet and the nation about your going back to the house and about the call that made you go there."

"I sense some interrogation in your voice Honorable Miochariya, am I right?"

"The V.P is dead and the president is in a critical condition. I do belief any change in my tone and voice would be understandable, would it not?"

"I understand sir. We are all rattled and I take this personally because I am the intelligence head. So if I do some things that are not understandable, I do believe people would understand because of the nature of the incidences of the last twenty-four hours. I am heading to SNSIS to see what Dickson has on those fellows so far."

"Dickson has already debriefed me on those guys."

The chief's body guards and the assistant were starting to sense some problems with the way the chief was answering the minister. Besides his previous calm, his sarcastic responses to honorable Miochariya were a cause for concern.

"What did you just say?"

"Mm, I said Dickson debriefed me."

"On what protocol?"

"We have a national crisis and we weren't able to get hold of you. I am heading to the press conference."

"And you will talk about this?"

"No chief! Continue to your office to be debriefed. And in the next press conference, you will explain what you have found out from the two fellows."

"This is a breach of security protocol."

"We called you sir...and this is a crisis!"

"Dickson didn't call me."

"I'm the one who called him."

"That doesn't mean he couldn't call me. I got your missed call but I didn't get his?"

"I told him it wasn't necessary."

"Because of?"

"He debriefed me to know not to go and do your job!"

"Dickson knows the protocols and he knows the circumstances under which this situation is allowed."

"With all due respect chief, the president has been shot and the vice president is dead. Is it time to talk of protocols? Just prepare yourself for the next press conference. The press and the nation are waiting for me. I have only five minutes to prepare. Let us know as soon as possible."

Vincent said and hanged up.

The chief looked at the phone, at his assistant and at the body guards.

"What was that about?" the assistant asked.

"Nothing."

"That wasn't nothing sir!"

"He's worked-up about my not picking up the phone. He said Dickson debriefed him."

"He what? That's a serious breach of protocol."

"He's buying into the idea that this is a national crisis."

"I don't like him at all."

The chief stared disapprovingly at his assistant. She lowered her gaze and said: "I'm sorry sir. I just don't like him. They might blame you as having not done enough."

The chief looked at his assistant and smiled.

"They are actually doing that already."

§

Despite the events of the last 24 hours, honorable Miochariya put on a very brave face. With the light blue and white color of the hospital wall behind him, he stared straight into the camera. His composure, his posture and the choice of his words had a substantive calming effect on the nation. Since the incidence at the lectures, there had been no official message from the government apart from the declaration of curfew. It was time the government told the nation it was still in charge. One of the unique features of the Sivalsian government was the fact that they had no prime minister; however, the president selected a minister to chair the cabinet anytime they met. It was neither the president nor the vice president who chaired the cabinet meeting all the time. Because of the problems of the day, the president and honorable Miochariya were the co-chairs of the cabinet meeting.

It was now incumbent upon honorable Miochariya to put things in order. And by all account, his face on TV showed that he could do it.

Honorable Miochariya cleared his throat, looked at his notes then at the camera and said:

"About an hour ago, we experienced the most horrible event this nation has ever faced. We had two of the faces of this nation fatally shot. I'm sorry to announce that our dear V.P has passed. We send our heartfelt condolences to his family, friends and relatives. He gave his heart and soul to this nation and he died in its service. While I don't have much on the condition of the president as we speak, the doctors are positive about his being stabilized. We will soon hear some good news."

He paused, picked up a glass of water next to him, looked at his notes and continued.

"As a government, we want to assure you that we have everything under control. Our nation is under threat from foreign powers. We have possible suspects in custody. Our able security officers will squeeze information out of these foreigners. Instead of leaving us to make sure we capitalize on our meagre resources and bring our economies to the 21st century level, they plot to destroy our countries then sing our proclivity to corruption and leadership incompetence.

"However, this is a nation of able men and women and we will show these foreigners and their collaborators that we will prevail. This short message is to assure you that we are doing everything we possibly can. In exactly two hours' time, we will update you on both the condition of the president and the security situation as far as the death of the VP and assassination attempt on the president are concerned. I will take a few questions.

"Honorable Miochariya, are *The Pipers* real or are they just political figment of imagination?" a lady asked

"We have intelligence that claims they are real but as a government, we can only talk of things that have been verified by our security experts. So far, we haven't verified any claim of their existence. That is all I can say."

"There're claims that had the government not played down the intelligence, things would have been resolved long time ago," a gentleman asked.

"We didn't play down any intelligence. All we did, like any other government, was to study the available intelligence before any decision is made."

"Would you now say you were wrong in the way you acted?" another lady asked.

"We took all the necessary precautions any government would take. So I wouldn't blame the government."

"You alluded to foreigners being behind the death of the VP and the assassination attempt on the president, what credible intelligence do you have to back that up...or are you just being inconsistent," another lady asked.

"While we are still to authenticate the information, we know the two gentlemen in custody, and I am not going to say who they are, were with P.D and Isaac at the lectures. They disappeared with them only to turn up on their way to the press conference. It is no brainer guessing there is a link."

"Is there a possibility that this could be an internal work?" another gentleman remarked.

"That is a silly claim. While this could be a conceptual possibility, there is absolutely no ground for such an assertion."

"We know the chief of staff is not in the country and we know the government had sent a very well-trained contingent to the lecture hall to apprehend Isaac and P.D...is there a possibility, as it's being claimed, that the army is behind this?" another gentleman asked.

"I don't know...we will check the facts."

"Your wife didn't appear like someone who was kidnapped and she didn't talk like someone who was forced to say all the things she said. What do you think is your wife's role in this?"

"Mm, she is a victim...that is her role? I think that will be..."

"One more question sir...the last one."

There was silence as a lady walked to the front. Two security men walked toward her so she stopped.

"Dono was killed in front of your house when he was going to say something. He wasn't armed and he obviously didn't have any ill intentions against either the government or you personally. He was well respected by all his colleagues so thinking that he had something against the government would be ridiculous. I have a copy of the letter Dono wrote to Dickson claiming that he's been contacted by Sister K and Uncle D of *The Pipers* that there are high profiled figures in the government who're plotting to assassinate the president. It was claimed, and you are aware of this, that Dono was killed by *The Pipers* because he had credible intelligence of how they could be identified and stopped. Were you aware of the letter? And if you were aware, why was the letter hidden?"

"I don't know where you got the letter and I wouldn't ask who gave it to you, but I'll tell you one thing young lady. We are a government and there are sensitive information we deal with every single day. We don't act on intelligence on a single instance. Decision making in the government requires due diligence and critical analysis to make sure the integrity of the information is established. We will update you in two hours."

Honorable Miochariya said and walked toward his car as the security officers followed him.

"Bu..."

Honorable Miochariya didn't look back. However, the minister seemed to have done well in the press conference. There was no doubt he felt good about himself. He looked back at the press members, waved and entered his car.

I will be ok!

101

To make sure Little and Chris didn't carry any information that'd give them away, P.D and Aatieŋ'oh were to send the information when the two gentlemen were at the press conference. As Little sat in his interrogation room, he felt calm and gratified. The uncertainty of the last twenty minutes was gone. Having grilled him for the last twenty minutes, the interrogation officer left. There was nothing suspicious found on Little and Chris. The information on their cell phones wasn't of any help intelligence-wise. As Little sat there trying to enjoy his new developing ambience, Dickson pushed the door open. Little stared at Dickson as he stared at Little at the door.

"So you don't want to admit your role so as to make life easy for some of us."

Little smiled with a superior edge and said: "Sir, have you ever been to South Sudan?"

Dickson first cringed, and then bent toward Little and said.

"Is that a trick question?"

Little served him a derisive smile. "I can't trick my way out of here, can I? No, sir, it's not!"

The agent wiped his forehead with his white handkerchief. "It's a warzone, so no; I have no reason to be there."

Little grinned with his usual curled lips.

"You know there's a civil war there, don't you?"

Dickson smiled.

"I'm an African. Do you have to ask me that?"

Amused, Little shook his huge head. "You're an African but you haven't been there so I should ask you that question, or shouldn't I."

Vexation sweated Dickson's face. Sweat stamped his wounded ego. He fixed Little with a monstrous stare. "Stop that stupid charade and think of how tough things could get for you if you don't confess or tell us who wanted to kill the president."

"I came from South Sudan yesterday and I've seen first-hand how innocent people are dying because of people's greed. Oh man, I've seen white people who put their lives on the line to help innocent African people in warzones and you tell me you've no reason to go to South Sudan? Man, and then you contradict yourself by saying I shouldn't ask you about civil war in South Sudan because you're an African?"

Dickson sneered. "Do you know who I am?"

"Man, I've seen people dying in my arms; people who're determined to help their people by all means. So if you're talking about torture, then go ahead and torture me."

"You're a piece of shit! Do you know this is not Panda?"

"I'm more African then you are. My skin is darker than yours. I've read more about Africa and Sivals in particular so don't think I'll get scared because I'm from Panda."

Dickson was getting really worked-up and angry. Little's words went deep through his heart.

"I'll show you who I am. So you guys think you can plot to kill our president and then start disrespecting our nation with vain arrogance?"

Dickson furiously said, his eyes getting red with anger as he walked to the door.

"You've already shown me who you are, man. And no, I can't disrespect Sivals. It's only people like you who I despise. Not the average Sivalsian but the likes of you."

Dickson looked back with devilishness at Little then angrily opened the door and slammed it shut.

"Gotcha!" Little said and laughed.

Fear had mysteriously left Little. The walls smiled at him with confidence and freedom. He was home. The claustrophobic enclosure was made roomy by the developing motherland ambience. Walls! These walls supported him, they urged him on. Fool him, annoy him, they whispered.

His childhood was characterized by similar walls. They were dreadful. Past walls! Their character had been fright production and belittlement. The walls closed tiny damning rooms. It was different. It was damning, it was disempowering and it was self-righteously contemptuous.

But here Little was empowered. His conscience glowed with pride and superior perplexity. Perplexing to his own self, his own mind, his own soul: he had no idea why. It had just descended on him from nowhere like a long, beautiful dream. He couldn't explain it but he felt it. He crossed his hands at the back of his neck and stared at the door. *I'm home.*

§

Chris's life had turned into a nightmare. The walls he'd been confined in and the ruthless officers in front of him with a pen knife were laughing death onto his face. On his forehead was a red lump caused by a hit from the officers' guns. His left cheek was pink with a palm print from the officer's blow. However, Chris managed to endure the excruciating pain without giving in to the officers' intimidation. A black camera on a tripod in front of him seemed to have been turned off. They didn't want any visual evidence of torture or any incriminating visual. There was a voice recorder in front of him. It seemed to be working.

Chris couldn't tell if they just forgot or they intentionally left it running. The only guy who'd told Little and Chris his name walked into the room. He appeared personable and professional; however, his entrance into the interrogation room seemed to have changed everything. He whispered something into the officers' ears and left.

The two gentlemen laughed and Chris knew hell was breaking loose. The thin, brown officer with a baritone voice walked toward him with his pen knife.

I don't think I can hold on any longer.

"We will ask you for the last time for confession...or tell us where P.D and your fellow countryman Isaac are," he said and pulled Chris's left hand. Chris immediately pulled his hand away knowing what he was about to do.

"I told you, I don't know."

Like a wicked ancient English witch, the offending officer motioned at the other officer. That officer was a short, coal black fellow with mild temperament. The short officer walked slowly toward Chris.

"He leaves us with no option. Hold his fingers down."

The short officer stared at Chris with passionate eyes as if to tell him: "I don't want to do this but I have to." He then pulled Chris's hand. Chris tried to resist but the man's grip was steely. With one swift swing, he laid the fingers onto the table next to the recorder.

"Dude, you aren't going to do this surely, are you?" Chris fearfully asked.

"I am going to ask you for the last time. Where are P.D and Isaac, and who is behind the president's assassination attempt?"

With fear written all over his face, sweat and tears rolled down his pink face. The officers looked at Chris and burst into raucous laughter. He stared at them and slowly and inaudibly said.

"I don't know."

The lean officer pushed down on Chris's left index finger and pressed the penknife onto the finger. The pain was unbearable yet the grip was monstrous. Blood started gushing out.

"You'll go places, son," his mum would say. "You're a special boy."

Like every human action made sense of after it has passed, Chris had, if temporarily, proved his mum right. His high-profile detective work and his keen eyes for numbers were too fitting not to prove his mum right. So it was true. He was special. However, with his downfall at Burns Investment, his mum's words lost meaning.

After her husband, Jack, died in mysterious circumstances in a factory he managed, Joyce Fox raised her son by herself. It was claimed that an African manual labourer, incensed by what he called Jack's racist management style, pushed Jack into a running machine. His head was instantly smashed into a flat, boneless meat as Jack was touring the plant. However, many Africans in that factory knew Jack as the fairest hand of capitalists they'd ever worked for and with. Whatever the case was, no truth was established. Investigation produced nothing and it was left inclusive.

Chris was four when Jack Fox died. Jack Fox was a tall, brown-haired, pink-faced, long-faced, clear-faced fellow, who loved to work. It was no wonder Chris was a workaholic. Joyce, on the other hand, didn't like work as much. However, she pushed Chris with unwavering vigour to make him successful. With poverty and the likes of Little as Chris's friends, one had to give Mrs. Fox godly credit.

When success called on Chris's door, he resolved to pay his mum in kind. Not disposed to hard-work, Joyce soon lost herself in alcohol and drugs. It was free money from a successful womb; her own son. She'd soon frequent rehab centers. With all her attempts to come clean, Joyce succumbed and lost her battle with drugs and alcohol and died when Chris was in jail. The fiery-faced fellow managing the prison refused to give Chris time to go and bury and mourn his mum.

Chris slowly opened his eyes. He'd fainted. There was no one in the room. His left fingers were bandaged but still soaked in blood.

102

The security chief stared at the world cruising along by his window.

I have failed. They are right.

He stared at the occupants of the car. They were laughing the night out despite having not slept a second in the past twenty-four hours.

What is exactly happening?

Then suddenly the car slowed down. Ahead of them was a police check-point with officers milling around.

"Why are we slowing down?" the chief asked.

"Check point maybe!" the assistant said.

The driver slowed the car down and came to a full stop at the check-point.

"This is the chief's entourage," the driver said.

"I know," the officer said and walked to the chief's window.

As the officer approached, the chief rolled down the window and angrily asked.

"What is this officer?"

"What sir?"

"What...?"

The chief got down but couldn't finish the sentence as the police vehicle behind his car made a swift U-turn and drove off.

"What's going on here officer? Aren't you putting your career and life in danger?"

The officer looked condescendingly at the sky then at the chief.

"No sir. We have been instructed to tell you to wait here..."

"Wait here...by who...what?"

The chief was losing his breath with anger. He pointed angrily at the officer as his body guards jumped out of the car. The rest of the officers at the check-point swarmed the area.

"We are just following orders sir."

"Orders from whom? The president is in the hospital and I don't want this unnecessary waste of my time."

"We have been instructed to detain you here and search your car."

§

"We are running out of time, Dickson. I need something!" Vincent anxiously said.

"We've cracked one of them. I'm sorry to say this now but P.D and Isaac are in your house."

"What did you just say?"

Dickson, out of respect, took a deep breath and said.

"Chris said P.D and Isaac are in your house, strangely."

"Mm mm...no, that can't be!"

"Who's in the house, sir?"

"The security guard and the maids. I called a few hours ago to tell them I wouldn't be coming home until things are clear. I told Esther and Mary not to come to Hayiroh until things are clear."

"The maids have probably been intimidated."

"And how could Isaac and P.D be that stupid?"

"That is actually smart sir. They knew your house is the last place we would expect them to be in."

"Isaac is such a son of a bitch. Make sure a capable force is sent there and make sure we control the intelligence this time. No messing up this. We don't have more time for messing up. I am counting on you."

"We have already sent a squad to the house. They are half-way."

"Is Aatieŋ'oh also there?"

"Yes sir. I'm sorry to ask this. Forgive me for asking but I am just curious about your wife."

"Don't be ridiculous. Aatieŋ'oh is passionate and she hates talking too much. She is just playing along for the sake of Jeng. How about the chief?"

"We found out from the surveillance cameras that he went back to the house to pick up something from the cleaning lady. We couldn't tell at first because his moves through the house seemed aimless until we realized that the cleaner slipped something into this pocket. We don't know what it is and what it contains. It might be something valuable. What do we do with him after the search?"

"Get me that information and let me know what it contains. If he cooperates or doesn't know much then take him into custody. If he knows a lot and not cooperating then deal with him. What happened to the girl?"

"We don't have any idea."

Vincent paused, looking tense and worried.

"What do you mean you have no idea?"

"We checked the room and it seems like the girl has disappeared into thin air. Our security checked all the workers, who work in the house but there's no one missing. The last record we have of her is her going to the cleaners' change room. The one who normally cleans the president's office wasn't cleaning at the time. Surveillance cameras and her co-workers corroborate that. She's under questioning in case she's an accomplice."

"That doesn't sound good. Someone inside the house might be working with them."

"Most likely so. We have to promptly get P.D and the information with the chief if we are to be safe."

"Get me the chief and let me know when P.D is in custody."

"Yes sir."

"And remember, we are running against time. I am monitoring the president's condition."

103

P.D knew things were not going as per the plan despite the fact that his plans were numerous. Failure was something he'd never contemplated. A look at the faces in the house told him that risks had to be taken. While he had confidence in his colleagues, his being confined to Vincent's house was a great obstacle.

"If what you're saying is true, then let me call the Pandian embassy. They can give us protection or afford us a chopper," Isaac said.

Aatieŋ'oh laughed and P.D just shook his head repeatedly.

Isaac frowned and shook his head angrily. "Why're you guys so dismissive?"

"They're monitoring all calls and comparing them with the voices in the system. Your voice is already in the system. It's a question of identifying that it is your voice and then track the call."

"But look guys, Little and Chris are in SNSIS now. Don't you think they know by now we're here?"

"We don't have any choice Isaac. Either way, they'll find us unless Sister K does something miraculous," P.D said.

"I'm tired of sister this or sister that. You guys have to do something."

"How about Sister J and The Minister...where are they?" Aatieŋ'oh asked.

P.D looked disapprovingly at Aatieŋ'oh.

"C'mon P.D! We've been through a lot together. Stop seeing me as this innocent, callous capitalist!" Isaac angrily said.

P.D looked at Isaac and said: "I don't see you in that better light."

Isaac cringed with a grave, distorted face. "You call what I just said 'better light?'"

"Yes..."

"Turn up the volume!" Aatieŋ'oh said, raising her voice authoritatively at Jeng.

"Slow down mum!" Jeng said with resignation.

"I said turn it up!"

Jeng raised his hands as if in surrender and turned up the volume. What the announcer said made the room turn freezing cold. Quiet. Silent. Doom stricken.

At the bottom of the screen were words one always wants to hear in a favourable situation, in a celebratory mood.

Breaking News

The anchor turned her head sideways and said with a cold, melancholic tone:

We've just received some breaking news that The Pipers have been holding honorable Miochariya's wife and his son in their own house. It's hard to believe such a claim, but it seems The Pipers are more daring, intelligent and smarter than anyone of us had ever thought. The army and the security forces are on their way to Honorable Miochariya's. The information was obtained from two of the suspects alleged to be behind the assassination attempt on the president. While the security and the army have warned us against airing this information, we took the risk for the sake of the nation. The government has been giving us little to no information on the state of issues and the current uncertainty in our nation's history.

We're ready to face the consequences if any. We're sorry to announce that the vice president, for those who haven't heard, has finally lost his life. Our hearts go to his family and friends and the whole nation. The president is still listed in critical condition. We'll keep you informed as we get more news. In a related...

"Turn it off!" P.D said.

"So it's over?" Jeng asked.

"The embassy could have helped us. You guys seemed to have forgotten who I am. If the Pandian government knew I was in this situation, they'd have conditioned the Sivalsian government to make sure I go into a secure place."

Aatien'oh looked curiously at Isaac. She removed a picture on a drawer behind her, scanned it slowly for a while then threw it at Isaac. Curious rather angered, Isaac looked at the picture then cringed and sat back on the couch.

"Why're you showing me a picture of starving and dead people?"

Aatien'oh hanged up her head and said: "That's what your money does, Isaac. That's why we're confined her. When western banks indulge in immoral and unspeakable *stripping*, the money sent can be used for any purpose; worst of all is what you see in those pictures."

"I don't understand what you're saying."

"I see. Then I urge you to let us do our job. This is something beyond anything you can imagine. Do you think they care who you are. They have enough resources to frame people and they can rightfully do so. It's now drummed into everybody's mind that the death of V.P and the assassination attempt on the president were carried out by *The Pipers*. The Pandian government has it that you're vacationing in the Kenyan town of Malindi and that you've informed people not to be disturbed. The Sivalsian government is controlling the fact that you're involved in the assassination and the coup attempt. You're dispensable, Isaac, highly dispensable. You can get killed and they have many avenues to put you on the wrong or frame you and other people."

"This is hard to believe."

"Do you know where Christine is?"

"No."

"She tells the ambassador you're fine."

"But why?"

"Mum, does anyone care that we're about to get into custody?"

"You and I will remain in the house because we were kidnapped, remember? P.D and Isaac will be in the guest house and I'll make sure no one searches my house."

"Do you think they'll believe you if they know far more grave things to think about and do?"

"We'll..."

Then the phone rang interrupting P.D. Everyone kept quiet as the phone rang for the first time in three hours. P.D looked at Aatieŋ'oh, who looked rattled. She slowly moved toward the phone as it continued to ring.

"I don't recognize the phone number," she said.

"The security knows we are here so you might as well pick it up."

Still rattled and unsettled, Aatieŋ'oh slowly lifted up the receiver.

"Don't say a word and don't move out of the house. I know the security forces are on the way. I've someone on his way with a strong hand. I'm sorry we've been slow. The government has kept a firm control on everything. Everyone working inside the government is being spied on by his or her colleagues so getting insider's information has become really risky. We've tried the chief to make sure the information goes out but the chief seemed to have been cornered. Sister J is trying to get to the hospital but Vincent is staying by the president's side. However, our voices in the army are still strong. We didn't want to put them on the spotlight but someone is on his way."

Aatieŋ'oh slowly motioned at P.D. Uncertain of what she was saying, P.D frowned questioningly. She motioned again then extended her hand to give P.D the phone.

"It doesn't matter anymore Sister K. They know we're here and it'll be a matter of minutes before we're in custody or killed."

"I know they're on their way. We'll beat them."

"I doubt that."

"Trust me. I'll make sure someone in the security gets the tape. The tape with the security chief will be destroyed if Vincent is behind this. It sometimes appears to me that someone is framing Vincent."

"Let's stick with the plan Sister K."

P.D hanged up and looked at Aatieŋ'oh.

"It's no use. But why did you give me the phone."

"I wanted to remain kidnapped. This is what we'll do. There's a space between my fence and the next one. You'll wait there until I'm done with them. I'll call Vincent with my own complaints about his lack of initiative to find us. We'll have one of our cars outside the gate with Jeng and one of the maids in it. Once you see them, try to drive away and I'll let them know that they've taken you with them. They'll chase after you. Drive as far as you can then stop and wait for them. Then give them an impression that you're angry at the officers that the kidnappers have disappeared into the neighbourhood and that you're too tired and confused to either run or do anything."

"Wow!"

"We've no time to get surprised, let's go," P.D said.

"I didn't know you were this good mum."

Aatieŋ'oh looked disapprovingly at Jeng. Surprised at his mum's ingenuity, Jeng grabbed the keys and headed to the door. Aatieŋ'oh nodded at the maid and she followed Jeng like a sheep heading to a slaughter house.

"What if they shoot at them?" Isaac asked.

"Until they know who's in the car, they wouldn't," Jeng said.

"Don't be so sure!"

"People are dying, so be it."

P.D stared at Jeng then nodded at Isaac. As they got out of the house, the sound of cars and siren tore through the atmosphere.

"It's over, P.D. Just give it up!" Isaac said.

"Quick, run to the backyard and climb the fence," Aatieŋ'oh said.

P.D looked at Aatieŋ'oh and smiled with surprised smugness.

"What now?" she angrily asked.

P.D smiled with defeated resolves. "Let's face it. It's over. There's no use running away."

"I didn't just hear you say that, did I?" Isaac asked.

"Please go...!" Aatieŋ'oh said. "Maybe that's Sister K's plan."

P.D frowned. "With sirens? I doubt that."

"It could be a perfect disguise," Isaac said.

"You're right."

Jeng pulled out the car from the garage. He jumped out of the car and frantically opened the gate. With surprising athleticism, he jumped back onto the driver's seat but as he drove through the gate, two police cars blocked him. He suddenly braked.

"Oh great...SNSIS!" Aatieŋ'oh said.

104

A dark cloud of ominous uncertainty hangs over Sivals. The night slept quietly, the hours long and the morning refusing to come. It was a dreadful silence of an impending gloom. Not a single soul walked about. It was so dead silent in Hayiroh that snoring disturbed the still air. Police and army conversations annoyed the annoying night. Even the insane seemed to have gained their sanity. The homeless seemed to have suddenly found homes. No one offended the deserted night streets as the city slept; haunted by the ghosts of *The Pipers*.

The chief felt belittled. For all the thirty years he'd been in the security services, no one had ever dared to confront him; no one: no pot-bellied businessmen, no foul-mouthed, rapacious politicians, or self-righteous Europe proselytized Africans(Christians that is).

Fools had tried before and suffered their fates. All the ministers feared him. However, the chief knew with the events of the last 48 hours, strange things could happen. What he didn't expect however was the magnitude of the officer's insolence. Rude, callous and insensitive, the officer's action was something the chief couldn't wrap his head around. He didn't want to understand it either.

Born and raised by a single mother in a nation that doesn't always see such family structure, Kerac Kin knew he was to show his mum the love she'd shown him. With a clear mind and sharp brain, Kerac went through high school and university without paying a single dime. He won scholarship after scholarship.

When he decided to join the security service after his first degree, his mother became upset. Like every parent, she wanted her son to join respectable professions like medicine or law or engineering. After five years of strained relationship with his mother, Kerac had to convince his mother that the choice he made might have been bad for his mother but good for his mental health. It wasn't long before the old lady's house became the first concrete and tile-roofed building in the entire village. *I've come along way.*

As he furiously stared at the commanding officer, and other officers with their guns pointed at him, he looked at his bodyguards, who also had their guns ready.

"What's the charge here officer? Am I the one who shot the president, or are you with the ones who shot the president?"

"I can't answer that sir. Just let me do my job."

"You'll have to give a better explanation than that, officer."

"You have nothing to hide Chief Kin, do you?"

"What're you talking about?" Chief Kin's assistant asked.

"Let us just do our job."

"You'll only search the chief's car over our dead bodies," Chief Kin's body guards said in unison.

The commanding officer waved and the arresting officers moved back, their guns still pointed at Chief Kin.

"Sir, this is an issue of national security. We'll have to do everything possible to make sure we find the president's shooters."

"And what makes you think you should look my way?"

"Immediately the president was shot, you moved back into the house and took something from one of the cleaners. The security forces checked the house and found no trace of the cleaner, who gave you whatever that thing is."

"And who authorized that when I'm the security chief. I'm investigating the assassination attempt on the president and the death of the V.P. As the security chief, I'm not at liberty to tell you fools anything."

The commanding officer moved back and frantically dialled a phone number. He finished talking but as he walked toward Chief

Kin, one of the arresting officers shouted: "The chief is getting out his gun to shoot."

There was complete silence as the chief tried to remove his phone from the holster.

"Don't do it sir!" the commanding officer said.

"Do what?" Chief Kin said, looking bewildered.

As Chief Kin tried to remove his phone, the commanding officer shot him twice in the chest. The gunfire then tore through the air. Chief Kin fell down on his face as his assistant fell on him.

105

P.D walked toward the gate as the officers pointed their guns at him.

"What do you think you're doing?" Aatieŋ'oh asked completely taken aback.

"I'd like to talk to my son."

"Sir, I would ask you to raise your hands and stay where you are!" one of the arresting officers warned.

"What do you think he's doing?" Isaac asked Aatieŋ'oh.

"I don't know what he's doing but whatever it is, it's not promising."

Jeng stared, in the rare-view mirror, as P.D walked toward the car. He tried to open the door but the officers warned him.

"Stay in the car son."

Jeng managed to get out of the car though.

"Sir, we have orders to shoot to kill so get down on your knees and raise your hands."

"Don't do it *Pï*...Dengiya and Dengdit are all gone... please don't!" Aatieŋ'oh implored him.

"Don't do what?" the commanding officer asked, curious and confused.

"I'd like to talk to the boy," P.D said.

"We can't let you do that sir. He's a victim of kidnap."

P.D stopped walking and said: "He's my son."

"What?" the officers and Isaac said with their eyes almost popping out. They looked at Jeng, at P.D then at Aatieŋ'oh.

"What the hell was that?" Isaac asked.

Jeng stood looking passionately at P.D for the first time. His hostility seemed to have given way to a man who'd realized something he'd been ignoring.

"Jeng, there's nothing as stupid as a man who lives for no cause. It doesn't matter how stupid what you believe in is. As long as you believe it fervently and explain to people why you believe it, then your name is worth the man you are."

"What're you talking about *Pï*?" Aatieŋ'oh wondered.

"Be your own man and find out what your purpose in life is. Remember, it's your integrity first through deeds, your people second through deeds, then everything else after."

"Mum, why's he talking like that?" Jeng asked staring at his mum.

"Officers, I'd like to make some calls. Can you bear with me?"

"We can't let you do that sir."

"For god's sake officers... can't you stop being robots for once and realize that..."

"Don't, honey, please don't!" P.D said interrupting Aatieŋ'oh with an ominous gesture.

P.D then dialled a number and said. "Sister K, it's time."

He hanged up and dialled another number.

"Sister J, make sure they pay for it."

He hanged up and dialled another number.

"Dengkor, we've achieved a lot. Leave Sivals tonight. A cause is not blessed without a great sacrifice. Be a good soldier and obey orders! Go into hiatus for a year from the moment I sleep in approximately twenty seconds."

"Mum, don't let him do that...please mum!" Jeng said, tears rolling down his cheeks.

"I'm sorry, honey, I can't!" she said, tears streaming down her temple. Jeng stared at P.D as P.D stared at the officers. It was the first time Jeng had ever seen his mum shed tears in public.

"There're men, but there're men who make the very existence of *a* man required. I love you P.D and will always love you."

"No, mum, no...!"

Jeng tried to run toward P.D, but P.D removed a short-gun as the officers started to tear him up with bullets. Jeng stood back horrified as he watched P.D slowly fall down; first on his right knee, then his left knee, left on his side then down on his stomach. Having seen P.D go down, Jeng looked at his mum. She was still standing in the same place, quiet; tears still streaming down her cheeks. Isaac was on the ground. He'd fainted.

"The indispensable vanity and naivety of those who seek the *truth* is the very meaninglessness of life," Aatieŋ'oh said walking toward her house as the officers ran toward P.D and Isaac.

"We will have to take you to the hospital," one officer shouted running unsuccessfully after Aatieŋ'oh.

With tears still streaming down her cheeks, she slowly glanced back once with fiery, damning eyes and continued to trudge to the door. Jeng, rattled and not sure what to do, ran after his mother.

She didn't look back at her son.

The old, love collegiality surged in Aatieŋ'oh's mind and heart. *P.D is gone.* Even as a young man, his resolves were always fixed with stupidly unwavering idealism. He despised the self-righteous and liked the humble wise. She was his courteous voice, the warning nudge, the guiding echo. Her playful and cautionary winks seemed to have emboldened the man. To be done even by blood, he'd say.

Their dreams then, were just like typical ideal niceties of the young to be lost in the walls of Oxford, to be dreamed about and left on the ceilings of university hostels.

Even with slave blood and sweat on the walls of Oxford halls and libraries, P.D still laughed about his university. The past has passed...it's the lesson for the deeds of today not the hostage or captive of the current, he'd say.

They'd go onto the hills in Oxfordshire and admire the breath-taking architecture of Oxford, the genius of the time. How beautiful! The green hills of Oxford and Oxfordshire brought closer the natural beauty in South Sudan and Sivals. It was home in a different form. Go, my friend, go, she murmured as she entered her house.

The atmosphere tensed; wind stood still as if mourning. Uncertainty whipped the air like angry, violent hurricane. Trees swayed minimally, birds perched as if scared. It was a day like no any other day.

Jeng was shocked out of his breath as he stopped at the door. His mum had entered the house, swimming silently in tears. The officers at the gate swayed from side to side as P.D's body lay on the ground. It was grim. It was silent. It was excruciatingly disheartening.

He scornfully looked at the officers. His anger was more precious than their lives combined. *They're not worth it.* He swiftly turned and looked at the door. Everything stared at him with angry finality. The unfair atmosphere seemed to be compressing his lungs. He couldn't breathe.

However, Jeng knew whatever he felt and whatever he intended to do wasn't wise. He'd started to admire the man and what he stood for only to be taken away from him so quickly, so unfairly and so heartlessly.

He remembered the mocking words of his American schoolmates. Yes, Africa was poor. And yes, America was created by people; people just like Sivalsians. But what was the problem? Why was Africa mired in perpetual innovation drought? No credible invention, no remarkable and appreciable influence on the world. Something was wrong. Perhaps his classmates were right. Something is wrong with Africans, something terrible evolutionary-wise. He was afraid to say it but he knew it. Every data and thought that came to his mind proved it. Yes, it is —. He couldn't bring himself to say it. But the kids were right. He'd started to despise his father. No, maybe not his father! Maybe the man who raised him! Jeng was mixed up.

However, the thought of P.D made his heart glow with pride. He knew his brain would soon devour every article, every book written by P.D. At least P.D had left him something: words, real African words for his Columbia colleagues.

I'm here.

I'm coming.

I'm me.

I'm me that shouldn't be defended.

I'm home.

'Be your own man and find out what your life purpose is. Remember, it's your integrity first through deeds, your people second through deeds, then everything else after.'

106

The phone rang once as the nurse disapprovingly stared at Vincent. There was massive security presence in the hospital and also in the president's ward. Vincent had been staying next to the president since he was admitted. The last briefing by the doctors indicated the president was responding well to treatment.

Vincent pressed the answer button and walked out of the ward. He nodded at his security officer and he realized the minister didn't want to be followed.

"Hello Dickson. What happened to Chief Kin and P.D?"

Dickson sighed, hesitated for a while then said: "They all pulled guns on our officers. Chief Kin refused the orders and pulled out his gun to shoot at the officers. P.D begged the officers for time to make some calls. He was given time to make all his calls, but instead of complying with the officers in the same manner he was treated; he brought out his pistol and shot at the officers. The officers had no choice but to respond in self-protection. P.D said things that are hard to understand."

"We need you to compile the intelligence for the press conference in a few hours' time. We will have a short cabinet meeting in the hospital board room. We need you to debrief us together with the deputy chief of SNSIS, the chief of general staff, the defence minister and the police chief. You've brought the situation under control. I need to thank you. This is the spirit of professionalism we need. I talked to the deputy chief and he agrees with me in the same manner. You have served your nation in a markedly brave and efficient manner and you'll be rewarded for it."

"I appreciate your words sir."

Vincent turned off the phone, sighed, looked at the officers guarding the ward and walked back into the ward. The nurse looked at Vincent and said.

"The president moved his head."

"That's good news," Vincent said and turned on the TV.

"Put the volume down Honorable Miochariya. The volume isn't good for the president's recovery efforts."

Vincent laughed looking at the nurse and said: "Call me Vincent. I am very modest. Addressing me Honorable Miochariya makes me feel distant and old."

The nurse laughed, checked all the gadgets strapped around the president and walked out of the ward.

"I'll be back soon, Vincent," the nurse said with a bright, insincere smile.

The minister stared at the nurse as she walked out of the ward. He then smiled, turned and looked at the TV. The two body guards were staring out through the window. The lady anchor on TV announced:

With all the events of the last 48 hours, we have finally received good news. We have just received information from SNSIS that the government has managed to contain the situation. We received news that P.D, the one who is thought to be the brain behind all the chaos Sivals has faced has been killed in a gun fight. Our security officers were trying to arrest him when he opened fire on the officers. The officers responded by opening fire to protect themselves and subsequently ended up killing P.D.

We have also received information that Chief Kerac Kin of SNSIS has also been killed in a gun fight. The circumstances behind his death aren't clear. We expect the government and the deputy security chief to give us more information.

The government will soon update us on the condition of the president and the arrest of the coup plotters. We have a number of foreigners involved in the coup attempt and the assassination attempt on the president and the death of V.P.

Our correspondents are outside the hospital where the cabinet will be meeting soon. We expect an official response after the meeting.

Vincent then turned off the TV, looked at the body guards and said: "They thought they could get away with it."

§

It wasn't characteristic of St. John's General Hospital to be swarmed with the media. However, nothing else could describe the hospital better than to say it was swarmed with the media and the curious, average citizen. Vincent, together with the entire cabinet, emerged from the hospital main entrance into the sun-rayed front of the hospital where the media was waiting impatiently.

SNSIS deputy chief, Dickson (who was the director of special security operations), the minister of defense and the chief of general staff walked to the microphone.

As usual, Vincent hesitated, looked back at the cabinet then at the media and the crowd gathered in front of him. The crowd was understandably quiet, but unnervingly motionless. The silence stirred the minister's heart as it espoused the crowd's emotions. The look on the faces around him made him realize that his words had to be carefully articulated. Any slip of tongue would be disastrous to the country that was already unnerved and rattled.

"Fellow citizens, I greet you in the name of our great nation, and in the name of our president who is still in a coma. We also as a government, and as a nation, extend our heart-felt condolences to the family of our beloved Vice President, who lost his life in the full service of this great nation. I said in our first press conference that this country is resilient. I knew that whatever monstrosity our country faced, we would manage to get through it. I would like us to take a few moments to remember our V.P."

There was brief silence as everyone remained quiet and still, motionless.

"Last night, we witnessed a sad and an unspeakable tragedy. As a government that cares about its citizens and the integrity of our country, we didn't want to feed our citizens with information that was incomplete. It is with great honor as a cabinet that we tell you we have managed to get the required information to adequately inform each and everyone in the country.

"The criminal master-mind of all the tribulations our country faced for the last 72 hours, Dr. Michael Pelebaidien Dhuengdakah, was killed in a gun fight when our able security forces acted on intelligence. We also have Pandian tycoon Mr. Isaac Burns in custody. Together with Isaac is Mr. Little Michael, also a businessman from Day-Town, Panda, and Mr. Christopher Fox of Day-Town, a former police officer. The information we obtained from the latter two gentlemen has been very instrumental in bringing this nightmare to an end."

The crowd raptured into applause and ululations. Vincent waved his right hand and the crowd was quiet.

"Without compromising an ongoing investigation, I'll let the deputy chief of SNSIS and the director of special operations take your questions as they are the heroes of the night."

Vincent waved at the crowd as it gave him a standing ovation. The arena became so loud that the hospital staff had to come out in force to remind the cabinet that they were standing in front of the hospital with hundreds of sick people inside.

The deputy chief of SNSIS nodded at Dickson and Dickson moved to the microphone. As the crowd became silent again, Dickson looked back at Vincent and said:

"Let's keep the applause to a minimum. We are in front of the hospital with sick people inside including our dear president."

He sighed, looked back at the ministers and continued: "This morning I stand here as a proud Sivalsian not because of what I did as a person, but because of what brave men and women, who are willing to protect this nation by all means, did. I have to remember Chief

Kerac Kin, who had served this great nation with all his heart. He died in circumstances I can't address now. Until we fully investigate, I can't answer any questions in that regard. However, we have to remember him in our prayers.

"Last night, after the president and the vice president were shot, we made sure every inch of the city was manned after the curfew was declared. This ensured that every car that went out last night was searched. Assuming that Sivals has no sophisticated intelligence network, two of the Pandian coup plotters tried to drive toward the press conference venue. We managed to intercept them; however, they had already sent a sniper to the scene. As we readied ourselves to drive them to SNSIS office, the news of the president's assasination attempt reached us. However, we didn't sleep until we got the answers. We managed to squeeze confession out of them. I can't go into the specifics of what they said, however, I can tell you that we are left with no doubt that this is a high level state of aggression by some elements in the Pandian government and the capitalists tsars toward Sivals. We are coordinating a joint investigative unit with Panda to leave no questions unanswered. So far, I can tell you from the intelligence standpoint that the worst is over and I will let Honorable Miochariya brief us on our president's condition."

Vincent patted Dickson on the back, walked to the microphone and adjusted it.

"As the director of special operations has said, the worst is over. That is good news for us all. I don't want to do the doctor's job. The doctors have arranged for a press conference this afternoon to address the president's health condition. All I can say is the president is responding well to medication. I am glad to say that he opened his eyes once so that should be a cause for celebration."

The crowd burst into cheers as Vincent waved it quiet. He looked at the cabinet behind him, at Dickson then walked away still waving at the crowed. *We've done it, we've done it!*

107

Tears slowly rolled down Sister J's eyes as she drove along. She knew their plan had gone awry, however, she knew P.D death wasn't an accident. Sister K had called the night before that she'd gone back to Werpionkor, their meeting point. They all knew the village very well. Dengkor had refused to get out of the country until the issue was brought to its logical conclusion.

It was surprising that Wallace and Wani were already in Werpionkor making the arrangements for their meeting. While not used to driving on such roads, Sister J was humbled by the dusty and rough routes. Because of the impassable nature of the tracks, the journey took about ten hours. The enthusiasm in her heart made every concern a nonentity. She put on Bob Marley's CD into the player and sped up. The few trees marking the open savannah rolled by as she drove along. Only one car passed by in more than three hours.

It was clearly a middle of nowhere. However, Sister J knew a cause a person fervently believes in can take a person to strange places. She started to sing along like a teenage girl expecting a beautiful first date and a possible first kiss from a boy she loves dearly. Tears were flowing even as she sang: *One Love.*

However, she remembered her childhood. The dust and heat of Khartoum were unmistakable and ominously fiendish. It was ages ago. However, the death of her father impressed bad memories onto her head with unmistakable clarity. The place was hell-hot and as merciless as the people who ruled it. The laws were devised and divinized for unquestionable imposition. The majestic Nile snaked along haunted by the iron hands of mean, sanguineous generals. The innocent black souls inhabiting the city professed the dark, pious righteousness of the generals. It was miserable. And the desert heat agreed; the dust corroborated the draconian generals' social and religious reorganization. Their pious fervor was remarkable. In the mix, their opportunistic stomachs growled with the aid of foreign arsenals.

As the sandy world sailed by, the desert Khartoum with its ghostly characters cruised through her head. Death marked the flanks of the Nile. Poverty smiled as she perched with the birds on the trees along the Nile banks, flew northwards with the current and swam with the souled destitute fishing for their meals. She hated the thought.

How did she get here? In the middle of Africa! A white woman alone! In the middle of a place not even on the map yet! Justice! She smiled with familiar joy trickling down her spine. Ignorant fools masquerading as knowledgeable claques. She shook her head.

Interspersed, hopeless tress counted themselves as she cruised along. Strength, resolves, determination and wait...self-sacrifice, propelled her. She smiled. Sweet tears still rolled down her cheeks as she thought of P.D.

Never will I ever know another man like you.

P. D. Michael was born in 1935 to a successful South Sudanese family in London, UK, the first of the three siblings. P.D's mother was a medical doctor and his father was a renowned businessman in London. His sister Nyanluel, who follows P.D, died of car accident in Washington DC after attending a conference. She was in her final year of her doctoral program in marine biology. P.D's brother, Johnnie, lived and worked in London as a certified accountant and a civil rights lawyer. Johnnie didn't like P.D's political ideals and rarely talked to his older brother.

While his life wasn't that of poverty, P.D was unnerved by everything he saw around London especially the poverty-stricken parts of London. He internalized his rage and minimized his contact with the family so as to make sure they didn't know what he was doing. While the family knew P.D had radical ideas, no one suspected he could form a powerful organization with the average people.

He made the average person feel significant with few words.

Sister J met P.D when he worked undercover as a factory worker. Sister J had recruited him through Retain Your Life (RYL) employment agency. It was an experience Sister J couldn't forget and would never forget.

108

Sunny days should always bring good news and good fortune. However, the president didn't know what to expect. Many questions remained unanswered and more continued to crop up.

President Eekedu knew getting out of hospital was unexpected. Given the explanation the doctors gave him, it was sheer miracle he was able to get out of the hospital. Those three grueling weeks in the hospital changed the country forever. With the interest of the country still at heart, the president defied the doctors' advice; to rest for at least six months before he got back to work.

However, the message the president received from the state-owned television station, Sivals National News (SNNews), had him on his toes.

The message was vague and incomprehensible. An old lady from a village he'd never heard, requesting to talk to him live was a cause for concern. There was nothing to fear though. Still, it wasn't everyday that the president got such requests. He didn't even know such a place existed in Sivals. With the events of the last few weeks and the weird nature of *The Pipers*, the president knew something monstrous was coming his way. He just didn't know what it was.

"I don't feel good about this Your Excellency?" Vincent said. He was acting as the V.P before the government was restructured.

"We still need answers. A conference with an old lady wouldn't hurt I guess!"

"Mm mm...we can just send our security officers to that village and bring her here."

The president looked at a nurse who'd just brought his medicine.

"Thanks dear," the president said, looking at the nurse and then looked back at Vincent.

"We don't even know where that village is. We don't know the name of the village and she'd explicitly said she doesn't want to come to the city."

Vincent looked unsettled.

"With due respect sir, *The Pipers* are capable of anything. I am still afraid for your life."

The president took his medicine, smiled at Vincent and said: "You've done your patriotic part by being there for me and for this nation. If I died through any foul play from this, I know we would have a capable leader. Let's go through with this."

Vincent looked back as Aatieŋ'oh and Jeng walked to the president's office.

"Hello Aatieŋ'oh... hello Jeng. I am sorry you had to go through all that. We failed you as a government. I heard P.D tried to make up stories to soil your good name."

Aatieŋ'oh smiled and nodded.

The president smiled as Dickson and the deputy chief of SNSIS entered the office.

"Have the two fellows been brought in yet?" the president asked.

"They're outside Your Excellency," Dickson answered.

The president was still on a wheelchair. A nurse was by his side, the other two nurses dropped in and out of the office in turns.

The office felt tense as various government officials entered the office conference room. A lady walked toward the president and said: "We have about fifteen minutes to go live, Honorable Miochariya."

"Okay," he said.

Little and Chris were pushed into the room in handcuffs and the president looked up. The two men were all dressed in brown overall mostly used for political prisoners in Sivals. Chris looked at the front only to see Jeng and Aatieŋ'oh seated comfortably in front next to the president.

"Dude, what's this, a joke?" Chris asked with a frown.

"More than you'll ever understand, Chris," Jeng said.

"The president himself is presiding over the court on a wheel-chair? You gotta love Africa!" Little said and laughed with curled lips.

No one uttered a word.

The police officer, who brought Little and Chris in, pushed them ahead and showed them two chairs.

A big flat screen TV faced the audience. There were three big cameras facing the president behind the TV. All the senior govern-ment officials were seated. The big conference room tables were removed to make the place roomy for more chairs. While the rest of the ministers were seated, Vincent remained standing. There was complete silence as the lady on the screen call out.

> *Your Excellency and the Sivalsian people, I greet you all. We are about to go live to a place none if only a few among us, have ever heard of. However, I was told not to say the name of the place or the name of the person. We wish this brings us all the answers we need. We as a station would want to apologize to anyone who would be inconvenienced by this broadcast.*

The screen transitioned to a dry, desert-like place with a lonely mud-walled hut. Its roof was made of grass. Everyone gasped. Under a mango tree was an old lady possibly eighty or ninety years of age. The old lady was seated on a plastic chair with a row of old ladies and old men. Behind the old lady were two women and a man all in military uniforms. Behind the old woman and the elders was a ring of young people and children standing solemnly.

In her hand was something that looked like a framed picture. In front of the old lady were two cameras. A big black man appeared in front of TV and everyone in the room gasped.

"Okob?" Vincent marveled.

"What is this?" the president said looking at Vincent.

"I have no idea Your Excellency!" Vincent said, fear written on his face.

"Don't look at me, sir?" Aatieŋ'oh said looking at the president.

"Is this some game or what? Were you actually kidnapped? Vincent, what is this?" the president said as he was starting to get vexed. Vincent shook his head and said: "You'll have to ask them Your Excellency!"

"This better be good Dr. Miochariya because I am not going to be pleased."

"You..."

The lady on the screen coughed and everyone was quiet.

"I say hi to our president. I also say hi to our people of Sivals. Receive our greetings in the name of our elders, our young men and women, our children, our cattle, goats, sheep, chicken and everything that breathes here. We also bless you in the name of our ancestors and our gods. It's not customary for a woman to address strangers on behalf of our village but one man changed everything."

She laughed when a white lady next to her whispered into her ears.

"I have been told not to call you strangers."

Some people in the room giggled.

"Don't feel bad because we are a very hospitable village. Let me go back to my topic because I am old and will forget what I was saying. What was it again...?"

Everyone laughed both on screen and in the room. Even the angry president managed to grin.

"And you have to persevere because old people are slow. And pray that my bladder holds well else you would be waiting for another thirsty minutes as I go to pee. And it would be rude for you to leave, wouldn't it? One man showed us that anything can change as long as why it has to change is well understood. We felt really saddened when we heard of his death. We are seated in front of his house. I hope his son comes and develops it to a national museum. Oh, my old age is coming back again."

Some people giggled in the room.

"Stop laughing at the old lady. Yes, I remember what I was saying. We didn't even know his real name until yesterday. We didn't know what to do and how to approach the topic. The young people who informed us of his death told us they couldn't pass the message they wanted conveyed to the president because someone there wanted to kill them. He showed us that even when you are highly educated in the language of people you don't even know, you can still have a meaningful conversation with people who are poor and uneducated. Let me not bore you. This man's name is Michael Pelebaidien Dhuengdakah."

"What the hell is this? This old lady is wasting our time. So *The Pipers* want to claim P.D is some sort of poor people hero?" the president yelled.

He looked at Vincent and added: "Make sure we locate that village and bring that old lady here!"

"I'd prefer we listened to what the old lady is saying first," Aatieŋ'oh said.

"And what makes you think this old lady will tell us something valuable," the president angrily riposted.

"Be calm our leader. I hear that you are upset. Don't be. I'm an old rag but I know what you don't know. I know the dead man with that long name I can't pronounce. You were shot while he was trying all he could to help you not to get shot. I don't know the name of his organization..."

"The Pipers!"

Someone shouted off-screen.

"Whatever that means! The people who wanted to kill you and take over the government are not the good man's people. Those people are within your government. You are too nice to see what could have cost you your life and put our country onto the hands of fat men who don't care about us. Well, you have not done anything for our village, but that is not important now because the good man's son and his mother will build our village. I'm done. There are good people next to you, who will tell you the rest."

"What?" the president yelled.

Aatieŋ'oh tried to get up only for two big security officers to grab her by hand.

"I have something to say," she said.

The president angrily stared at Aatieŋ'oh and said: "You and P.D wanted to put a stunt against me and use that old lady to clean P.D's subversive acts and the assassination attempt?"

"I'll take care of the situation sir. This is personal because I have been treated like a fool by my own wife and son?"

"My Jeng has nothing to do with it. Yes, you're a fool...and you sit down!"

"You're not yet the president, Dr. Miochariya...and don't you talk to my government officials that way," the president commanded.

Vincent stared with his eyes and mouth all open wide.

"Would you let me talk for a minute, Mr. President?"

"Talk quickly because I am sick of all the nonsense of *The Pipers!*"

"The good man's son the old lady was talking about is my very own Jeng."

Everybody started to look around, at one another.

"I'm not going to narrate to you how I met Vincent because all of you will have ample time to talk to me and get the answers. P.D and *The Pipers* are people who stand for principles and are bent on helping the poor at all cost. I was part of *The Pipers*. My name was The Mama. And whatever dirty politics my dear Vincent told me went to *The Pipers*."

"You are a disgrace to marriage and civility," a voice yelled angrily from behind.

"She's civil and more caring than anyone of us in this room," Honorable DiDengo said.

"I have to go to the washroom because this is too much for me Your Excellency," Vincent begged.

"Don't worry, Mr. President, what I'll say is going to help strength your leadership and resolves. So no, Vincent, there's no running away. And I want the security to guard him well."

"Who are you to talk to a government official that way?" another minister shouted.

"She's the best!" DiDengo said smiling.

"And what's your deal, Honorable DiDengo?" the president asked, turning curiously to DiDengo.

"Mr. DiDengo was *The Pipers'* honorary member."

"What?" Vincent yelled.

"Let this woman shut up!" another minister shouted angrily.

"Let her speak!" the president ordered.

"Thank you Mr. President. My family was killed in my village in western Sivals when I was a little girl because of tribal clashes. When I was adopted by a missionary and moved to London, I always believed my parents were killed by pure accident. Only many years later did I learn that my parents were murdered because of a young man who had high political aspirations. It was only ten years ago that I learnt of the man who let me run to the bush to survive. The worst part of it is not that my family was murdered; it is that I married the very man who engineered the death of my family. What consoles me though is that none of my biological children is his."

"She is crazy Your Excellency. She doesn't know what she is talking about," Vincent shouted.

"Sit down Vincent!"

"I know she doesn't know what she is talking about but let her talk. We will arrest her later," the president said.

"The man who fathered Jeng is the very same P.D, who's supposedly the coup plotter and the criminal mastermind behind the death of our dear V.P and the assassination attempt on the president. I actively joined *The Pipers* when I heard that Vincent engineered the political violence that caused the death of my family..."

"This is outrageous. Would you let this madness continue Your Excellency? This woman is obviously insane. She needs medical attention. Jeng, please say something. Did they drug your mum?"

"No Sir. She's as sane as any sane person can be," Jeng said playfully with a sarcastic smile.

"Mr. President, let anyone, who cares about this government and nation, shut up and listen to this woman," DiDengo said.

"I cannot continue to listen to this preposterous nonsense!" Vincent said and tried to get out of the room.

"Your Excellency, don't let him get out. He's the one behind everything you and everyone else went through."

Vincent scoffed. "Can you believe this? Can anyone possibly believe this crazy woman?"

"Don't forget that this crazy woman has been your wife for more than twenty years and she's got a Ph.D from one of the best universities in the world so sit your butts down."

"Watch your language Dr. Miochariya," the president cautioned.

"I'll take care of the situation," Dickson said trying to get up.

"Dickson, Dickson my friend. You don't think the death of Dono went without anyone knowing what happened. Sit your ass down, Dickson!"

Dickson remained standing. The deputy chief of SNSIS got up, and walked toward Dickson.

"As the acting head of the security, I do believe we need to listen to Dr. Miochariya's claim in its entirety then we can dismiss it and arrest her. So I urge all of us to be quiet and let her brief the president."

The deputy chief then moved toward Dickson.

"Mrs. Miochariya, you know damn well that these are grave allegations," the president said.

Aatieŋ'oh nodded at the president and motioned at Jeng, who got up slowly.

"You can't proof anything you're saying," Dickson said.

"On the contrary sir, there's so much proof *The Pipers* have. Honorable DiDengo can tell you more," Jeng said.

President Eekedu looked at DiDengo then at Vincent.

"Don't tell me you believe this nonsense Your Excellency," Vincent said.

"Before we see the video, is there something you two have to say?" the president asked.

"You see, we could have saved the V.P but Dickson and his group made it hard for any information to reach the president. Most of the intelligence was hidden from late Chief Kin and his deputy. Every single inch of the People House was in Dickson's hand. Every single ministerial office was bugged. Dickson knew all ins and outs of your lives. Dono died because he wanted to disclose an internal working that was preparing to oust the president. Chief Kin was killed because he had a tape of some of Dickson's and Vincent's meetings. You were shot to frame Isaac, P.D and Chris. Chris was specifically sent to be framed but we had Chris's girlfriend as an important member of *The Pipers*: Sister J, or Judy Morning Grant. Okob wasn't just a driver. He has master's degrees in sociology and chemistry, but he had access to information *The Pipers* needed. *The Pipers* make sure schools, hospitals and affordable housings are built in remote villages. We changed lives. Even if I lived a lie, I managed to find a cause through the man I loved but let down. When Vincent requested that Dickson went with him to Khartoum, it wasn't because of the seriousness of the situation and the intelligence cooperation, it was because they wanted a secure place to deliberate, and also, because of the support the Sudanese government had promised them. Vincent wanted to smoother the president in the hospital, were it not for the fact that one of the nurses received a text from Sister J not to leave the president's side. The lady who gave Chief Kin the tape is *The Maid* or Paris Baker. Isaac didn't know that his girlfriend's sister is a sophisticated member of *The Pipers*. She was deadly because she looked like an innocent, blonde white trailer trash from a small down in Alabama, USA."

Chris and Little couldn't utter a word. They were completely lost for words; staring in an exciting awe.

"These two gentlemen here should be freed. They were arrested on their way to warn the president about the sniper. We couldn't call because all the calls going to the president were either bugged or answered by someone Dickson had commissioned to screen the calls. We couldn't go through to the president and we didn't want our internal officers to be exposed. Dickson made sure each officer spied on the other to make sure no information escaped them. Our officers therefore were therefore outsmarted by Dickson and his boss, Vincent."

"Did you do this to set me up, Dickson? Did you think you could come from that far to be the president?" Vincent said coming toward Dickson.

"I will ask you to stay back Honorable Miochariya," the deputy chief of SNSIS said moving toward Vincent.

"No sir, you can't do...!"

Dickson couldn't finish the sentence. Vincent suddenly sprayed Dickson with bullets as everyone ducked for cover. The deputy chief promptly jumped toward Miochariya as other officers ran to help him. The minister was pinned down and handcuffed.

"I lost two fathers in a month!" Jeng said as he stared at the black screen.

"So I have been a fool all along!" the president said as people came back from their hiding places.

"No, you haven't been a fool. This is a price you pay for being too accommodating," Aatieŋ'oh said.

"They only called me, *The Minister*! And sometimes you have good people working for you even when they don't do much to help. I met P.D in one of the symposia we had in Day-Town about fifteen years ago. He invited me for dinner with his wife, Angela or simply the *Grandma*. What we talked about that night changed my life. I couldn't sleep because my life felt empty. P.D or Uncle D had a way with words. He always made you feel empty and wanting to do more supererogatory things for others. By then I was a junior officer in our embassy in Day-Town. When he realized my genuine concerns, after having tested me enough, he introduced me to the idea. He didn't want me to join them for my role was well defined. He fed me with information and I made sure every government official was checked. I have a list of the things I've done. There's something you should know about *The Pipers*. Once a member or an affiliate is known by others, he or she ceases to have any connection with the organization and all his links to the organization are severed. I'll resign from my position with immediate effect to go into teaching and private business. That's how I'll continue *The Pipers'* missions," Honorable DiDengo said.

109

The president threw a feast no one could forget. Judy, also referred to as Sister J, knew P.D didn't die in vain or by accident. She was the chair of the committee tasked by President Eekedu to organize the party.

Aretha, also called Sister K, sat next to Chris and Little. Paris, who was called simply as 'The Maid,' wanted to play the role she'd played all along. She was serving food and drinks.

The president wanted the luncheon to be both stately and intimidate. Hilton hotel in downtown Hayiroh was a fitting and welcoming place.

"Listen up everyone!" Judy said. "As one of the principle pillars of *The Pipers*, I can tell you that anyone whose identity has been revealed ceases to be a member of *The Pipers*. We're no longer members of The Pipers. We'll not know the leadership and what *The Pipers* are doing for a number of years. However, they'll still protect the poor and expose the malicious, callous and the rapacious, because these pernicious people will always exist. President Eekedu, even with some of the errors he's made, remained a respectable figure in *The Pipers'* circle because of his dislike of tribalism. And baby Chris, I'm sorry I had to treat you the way I did but you now know what it was for. I'm white but we have one doctrine among *The Pipers*. It says..."

"Oppressed or aroused conscience has no color. After all the things I've seen, I'd be a fool if I have something else for you. Respect and love that's what I'll say," Chris said.

"And Little, despite the fact that people were scared of you and wondered why I was close to you, you'll be a fool if you don't marry me," Paris said as she poured water onto Little's glass.

"I'll be the chief moral officer in my company. We profess moral superiority but it's high time someone did what he preaches. I'll create a foundation for the construction of affordable houses in some of the world's poorest slums, anonymously of course. I've been changed and if I talked too much about how I've been changed, I'd be doing a disservice to my conscience. I'll go back home a changed man. Thank you all and thanks to *The Pipers,* whoever they are now," Isaac said.

"All I can say is that people of good conscience still exist even in our competitive capitalist world where profit and status override civility and morality. I thank you all...and above all, *The Pipers,*" the president said tearfully.

"I'm a changed man," Chris said, getting up to greet the president.

"And I'm a man who's found home and a sense of self. My business is moving to Hayiroh," Little said extending his hand to greet the president.

Thök de Ka

14436829R10236

Made in the USA
Charleston, SC
11 September 2012